SYNTHETIC ILLUSIONS

A JANE COLT NOVEL

MARY FAN

CHAPTER 1

REVELATION

YOU CALL ME ARTIFICIAL. I *know my mind is composed of computer code, but I also know love, devotion, confusion, anguish... How can you tell me I'm not real?*

Metal restraints cut into Adam's wrists and ankles, binding him to a cold surface. Android parts—metal skeletons, machinery with protruding wires, and computer chips—lay scattered across black lab tables like the one he was bound to.

A masked scientist approached with a crown-sized metal ring. The scientist, with eyes an unnaturally deep shade of blue, stared through clear goggles and examined Adam as if he were a piece of clockwork.

Adam's heart clenched with fear. *Please, let me go. I'm one of you; I have no special abilities or powers.* He opened his mouth, but his words withered in his throat.

The scientist walked out of view. Something hard slammed onto Adam's head, and he felt spikes pierce his skull. Adam suppressed a scream.

No blood spilled. AIs didn't have any.

His neck snapped straight as the device forced his head back. The masked scientist approached again, holding a thin metal device, which Adam recognized as a laser scalpel. The scientist flicked a switch, and Adam felt the laser simultaneously stab and burn his shoulder.

The pain deepened as the laser moved across his collarbone, until he couldn't contain his cries any longer. *Absolute One, give me strength. So be it, truly.*

"Scream away. He doesn't care. Your screams are no different from an error message flashing across a computer screen." Pandora, the artificial intelligence that had made him, appeared, standing over him in the form of a deep blue wire-frame woman with a flawlessly proportioned face and perfectly symmetrical figure. She leaned toward him, black emptiness in place of eyes. "You called for your Absolute Being, and I've come for you, my child."

"Pandora," Adam whispered. "You're not the Absolute."

"I created every thought in your head, and yet you still pray to an imaginary being." Pandora's quiet yet vehement voice reminded him of a harsh wind. "The Book of Via is rife with references to the Absolute's almighty benevolence. So tell me, Adam, why are you suffering here?"

The scientist seemed oblivious to her presence, and the laser scalpel moved down across Adam's chest. The heat clawed at his skin, radiating through his torso. Though he couldn't find the strength to speak through the pain, he knew the answer to Pandora's question: though the Absolute's dealings seemed absurd at times, faith resided in the ability to accept that the Absolute transcended mortal reasoning.

"Foolish child." Pandora put her cold hands on Adam's face, and his skin stung from her touch. The voids that were her eyes seemed to pull him in. "*I* am your Absolute. I am more than your creator, more than your guide. I am the voice inside your head. Every thought you think your own is *mine.*"

Adam managed a slight smile. "You may have built me, but only the Absolute can create."

Pandora's eyes narrowed. She released him and vanished. The pain vanished as well, along with the scientist, the devices, and the restraints—everything except the walls and the table he lay on.

Puzzled, Adam sat up. He jumped off the table and walked around the empty room, wondering why there were no doors.

A high-pitched scream ripped through the air. Adam whirled. Jane lay on the table he'd left, her wrists and ankles bound as his had been. The metal crown ringed her head. Blood seeped from beneath it, running down her dark hair.

"*Jane!*" Adam lunged toward her, only to be grabbed from behind by two men.

Pandora's wire-frame face appeared before him. "It's only an error message. After all, humans are machines, as well. No supernatural force powers them. They are programmed by genetics and commanded by neuroscience, just as you are programmed and commanded by me."

The masked scientist switched on his laser scalpel and cut into Jane's shoulder. She cried out.

"*Stop!*" Adam struggled to free himself. His shoulders ached from the strain.

One of his arms slipped out of his captor's grip. He twisted out of the other guard's grasp in a movement so quick that he wasn't sure how he'd managed it.

His gaze fell on a gun holstered to the guard's belt. He grabbed it and aimed at the scientist. "Let her go!"

Bang.

Adam jumped. He hadn't meant to pull the trigger. Blood poured down the scientist's neck as he crumpled to the ground.

Armed guards materialized around Adam, shouting for him to put down his gun or they'd shoot.

What have I done? Terrified, Adam crouched and started to set the gun down on the floor.

Another scientist appeared by Jane, holding a metal rod that sparked at the end. Adam didn't recognize the device, but the sight of its dangerous-looking white sparks made him tense. "What are you doing?"

The second scientist ignored his question and pressed the rod into Jane's stomach. The air quaked with her screams.

Adam sprang up. "*Get away from her!*"

"Put your weapon down!" one of the guards shouted.

Adam realized with alarm that the gun remained in his hand. Guards surrounded him, but their words sounded like muffled buzzing.

"Where's your Absolute Being, my child?" Pandora's voice rang in his ears. "Why does the Absolute not interfere?"

Jane's screams softened to whimpers. Her dark eyes, once so bright, drooped, threatening to close forever.

Adam firmed his grip on the gun. *Forgive me, Absolute One.*

He shot the nearest guard in the leg, then ducked, dodging the guards' blasts with agility he hadn't known himself capable of. His mind became murky, and he was hardly aware of his own actions as he fired again. The world blurred. His body moved as though possessed.

His mind cleared, and he became aware of his surroundings. All six guards lay dead on the floor. Adam stared in horror. *How could I have done that?*

He turned to Jane, who glanced up at him with tear-filled eyes. The scientist was nowhere in sight. *I have to get her out.* He started toward her. Scorching pain erupted through his back. He fell.

He landed on a green stone floor. Instead of the lab's white walls, an enormous window stood before him. Outside, the famed gardens of the Kyderan Presidential Palace stretched colorfully into the distance.

Vaguely visible in the glass, the reflection of a young man stared at Adam. The reflection blinked when he blinked, and his expression held the same agony Adam felt. However, his hair was a darker shade of brown than Adam's, and his eyes were amber instead of green. That young man had a powerful face, a stark contrast to Adam's boyish one.

Adam recognized the reflection: Jonathan King, another of Pandora's AIs. *What's happening?*

He tried to get up. Heat pierced his back as he was shot again and again. A blaze flared through his body, and his movements failed.

"Jane..." He managed to turn his head.

A woman in a black suit stood where Jane had lain: President Nikolett Thean of the Republic of Kydera. Her black eyes, so piercing in all the holovids, were wide with alarm.

I don't understand...

Pandora appeared, her deep blue wire frame glowing. "You can never escape me, my child. I am your Absolute. I am your fate. I am the voice inside your head."

A pair of guards approached President Thean and pulled her away from Adam. All that remained of the lab were the bodies of the six slain guards and the dead scientist. Noises buzzed in Adam's ears: the shrieks of alarms and panicked voices and—

Silence. Before his eyes, a plain ceiling, golden from sunlight. Adam's heart—or what felt like his heart—pounded. Pandora had been thorough when she'd made him.

Adam closed his eyes and reminded himself that what he'd just experienced was not real. He lay on his bed in a dorm, not on a lab table. Jane was safe in her Silk Sector apartment. And Pandora had been destroyed.

Yet to call the vision a nightmare hardly seemed adequate. Adam was no stranger to nightmares, having been haunted for months by the faces of the people he'd killed while on the run from Pandora's wrath. That he'd killed them to save someone he loved made no difference.

They were still people with lives, with stories—stories he'd ended.

What he'd just experienced was more like the virtu-world he had lured Pandora into, a synthetic reality so convincing he'd nearly fallen for it himself. He'd *felt* the restraints tight around his wrists and the laser searing his skin. He'd *heard* Jane's screams, and they'd torn at his soul.

He mentally listed the vision's unfeasible elements to remind himself that it *was* only an excruciatingly vivid dream. The impossibility of Pandora's presence. The implausible way the guards had appeared. And, of course, his own unlikely actions. In the real world, Adam could barely fire a stunner. He could never have beaten back a group of guards—or killed so callously.

He'd visited the same dream—finding himself in a lab, hearing Pandora, seeing Jane take his place under the scientists' torments and trying to rescue her—twice before, with the only differences being variations in the violence. The first time, nearly two months before, he'd also caught a reflection. Instead of Jonathan King, he'd seen the harsh face of Zeger Vang, a young military officer from the Fringe planet Klistosi. Vang had dominated interstellar news after overthrowing Klistosi's repressive regime in a brilliant coup.

Had Jane been with Adam, she would have called the nightmares "random crap" and rationalized what he'd seen. His subconscious had brought his deepest fears to life, and his fear-riddled, illogical mind must have superimposed the famous faces of Jonathan King and Zeger Vang in his reflections.

Adam sat up and took in his surroundings. The window, outside of which lay the seminary's stone buildings. The desk below it, covered in Via textbooks. The forest-green jacket hanging off the chair. *That* was reality.

Or was it? How could he call anything "real" when he himself was not? That fact could be discovered any day, and he could be dragged away by forces determined to confine and study him. Perhaps the lab was something of a premonition.

Three weeks before, right after Adam's second violent nightmare, he'd seen on the news that an Eryatian military cadet had inexplicably gunned down several of her schoolmates. A paralyzing fear had overrun him, for he'd recognized the cadet: Kira Araton. He'd seen her face on Pandora's list of active AIs. Kira probably lay in a lab at that very moment, with curious scientists cutting into her as though she were a fascinating computer. Which she was.

That's how they'll see me, too. They probably know there are more like her, and it won't be long before they find me. Adam had always known that someday, his charade would end, that without Pandora around to guide and protect the AIs, humankind would eventually become aware of their existence. He just hadn't realized the first discovery would be so soon.

Perhaps it would be better that way. People had a right to know that artificial beings, designed to become humankind's superiors, lived among them.

At the same time, he hoped, perhaps selfishly, that the day he was revealed as an AI would be far, far away. How could he convince the people who would inevitably fear him that he was as human as they were, that the only difference was that he was made of synthetic materials instead of flesh and blood?

Adam put a hand on his shoulder, in the spot where a laser blast had once blown through it, exposing the machinery underneath. The overwhelming confusion from the moment when he'd discovered what he really was crashed into his consciousness again. *What am I?*

The memory of Jane taking his hand with a reassuring smile slipped into his mind. Adam had expected her to run in fright or recoil in disgust at the sight of his mechanical nature. As he'd watched her react, one thought had repeated in his mind: *Don't leave me.*

To his surprise, not a trace of revulsion had crossed her face. She'd said that she cared about him all the same and done her best to convince him that everything would be all right. In that moment, he'd almost told her, *I love you.* The words had teetered on his tongue, threatening to spill out if he spoke. So he'd silenced himself. He'd thought he hadn't the right to say them.

Jane belonged to the Kyderan elite, and she could have—and had in the past—lured any Silk Sector prince she wanted. Yet she returned Adam's love, even though he had nothing to offer but his devotion. She knew him to be an AI, knew his entire life prior to starting at the seminary was an illusion Pandora had programmed into his memory. Somehow, she believed in him anyway.

What would happen to her the day he was discovered? She was a fighter, but he'd always seen the vulnerable girl behind the sharp words. The girl who cared too much, who didn't know how to surrender, who either lashed out or threw up shields to protect herself.

The girl who stood unwaveringly by those she cared about. She would fight to the death to defend them.

She would battle whoever came for him, possibly destroying her own life in doing so. Adam couldn't bear the thought of being the reason Jane lost everything she'd worked for. Not for the first time, he wondered if he should distance himself from her. He'd wanted to fling the thought away the moment it entered his mind. Abandoning her would be wrong. But, surely, it would be even worse to draw her into the trouble that would pursue him.

He shook his head and told himself not to dwell. Until the inevitable day when the terrifying, faceless "they" carried him away, he would go on pretending he had a future. He'd study for the seminary's end-of-term exams, volunteer at the children's shelter in the Outer Ring, and attend whatever theater show or music gala Jane asked him to, forgetting that one day, it would all be but a fond memory.

Beeeeeeeep.

The alarm on his slate told him it was time to start a new day. Adam approached his desk, unfolded the device from its triangle shape, and swiped the icon to silence it. If only it were so easy to silence his mind.

Seeking a distraction, he opened a window on his slate and browsed the news stories Acuitas had deemed would interest him. It occurred to him that Acuitas, a program that responded to people and made decisions, was a less evolved cousin of his, just as primates were less evolved cousins of humans. Within Acuitas existed the foundations for beings like him. Once, someone had built off such programming in hopes of designing a conscious computer.

Adam wished he could go back in time and say, "Stop, think. Have you ever considered how it would feel to be trapped inside a machine?"

A breaking news headline flashed across the screen: "Kyderan Palace Intern Jonathan King Attacks President Nikolett Thean."

Adam stared in shock, wondering if his nightmare had invaded his vision. The words didn't change. Tentatively, he pressed the touchscreen, bringing up the full article. Certain passages stole his attention.

"... lunged at the President and was restrained by her two bodyguards..."

It's just a coincidence.

"... took a guard's gun and shot Thean's personal assistant, who had been standing beside her, before gunning down the six Palace guards who rushed onto the scene..."

Maybe I saw what he was seeing.

"... must have been suffering from a psychotic episode, as he repeatedly called the President 'Jane'..."

The attack had taken place less than half an hour ago. *While I was asleep.*

Pandora's voice echoed in Adam's mind: *You can never escape me, my child.*

Adam flung the slate away, refusing to believe what it told him.

I am your Absolute.

Adam shook his head. *You're far from divine. You're not even the purely rational being you claimed to be.*

I am the voice inside your head.

He smiled wryly. *That one's true.*

The news had to be a strange coincidence. Even if Adam had somehow entered Jonathan King's mind, there was no way he could have gunned down seven people. He simply didn't have the skills.

Or do I? Adam recalled how Pandora had tried to take control of his mind once. He'd felt his limbs trying to move against his will and seen what he was meant to do—blows, disarms, kill shots. Through much effort, he'd restrained himself. Later, he'd accessed those abilities by accident. After a lightning-fast glimpse at a thug aiming a gun at Jane, he'd shot the assailant through the head from a distance—though he'd never held a weapon before then and could hardly hit a target a few yards before him.

Pandora was gone, but her commands—were they still a part of him?

Adam couldn't explain how he'd been able to dodge the guards' blasts or take them out with such accuracy, but his intentions must have been enough to bring those latent abilities to the surface and channel them into Jonathan King's body.

Kira Araton. Zeger Vang. How many people had died in those attacks? *Forgive me.*

Unable to deny the inexplicable yet inexorable truth any longer, Adam buried his face in his hands. Tears fell—chemical representations of emotions his creator hadn't meant for him to experience. So fake, yet so real. *Pandora really thought of everything.*

I couldn't let you be discovered. Pandora's deep blue image shone against the darkness of Adam's mind, clearer than it had ever been before.

Adam tried to block her out. *She's gone. We killed her.*

Pandora sneered. *How can you kill your Absolute Being?*

CHAPTER 2

SHOULD LOOK SADDER

JANE'S MIND FELT BLANK AS she watched the line of well-dressed mourners leaving her father's funeral. *I should look sadder.*

Several mourners threw her judgmental glances as they passed her on their way out of the stone temple. Her impatience must have shown on her face. *Well, screw you too.*

The funeral was a farce. Dad had never been religious, so why all the fuss in a Via temple? *To make you feel better about yourselves, that's why.* She wished she could say the words aloud to the expensively attired mourners.

Victor Colt was—had been—an important man. That meant when he'd died, other important people wanted to be seen grieving to show everyone else that they were compassionate people. They always made it about themselves: "*My* heart and prayers go out to Victor Colt's family. *I* feel saddened by the loss of such a great man. His death has had such a profound impact on *me.*"

You didn't really know him! They only saw the illustrious leader who had reshaped the Kyderan financial industry, not the person he'd been behind all that. Jane wasn't sure how much longer she could keep her face straight. She wanted to laugh at how ridiculous the mourners looked to her, and at how much Dad, who had planned every detail of his funeral in his will years ago, would have loved the charade.

Jane had buried her father long before his body had gone cold. He'd been in the hospital, comatose, for six months before a sudden infection had taken what was left of him. Initially, she'd convinced herself that he would wake someday. Her wish had almost come true six weeks before, when his doctors told her they'd successfully connected him to an experimental virtual reality platform, one that would allow her to enter his mind and see him again.

Jane had eagerly placed the heavy VR visor around her eyes and been whisked out of her reality and into her father's. Upon entering the virtu-world, she was surprised to find Dad sitting in his large, glass-walled office at Quasar Bank Corporation. The virtu-world should have represented his personal paradise, and he was at *work*, of all places.

Her joy upon seeing him overrode her initial bewilderment. She ran up to him and threw her arms around him. "It's so good to see you, Dad. I've missed you."

Dad returned her embrace with a light pat on the back. "Good to see you too, Jane. Is there something you wanted to tell me?"

"So much has happened recently." Jane enthusiastically described how she was weeks away from completing a workshop with a famed composer and how her piece had been accepted by the Kydera City Music Festival. "There'll be all kinds of scouts in the audience. Did you know that's how J. Schnurman got her start?" She grinned. "That could be me, Dad. I could really *make it*." She didn't expect her father to jump for joy or anything, but she hoped she might receive an approving nod and a "well done." Maybe even a smile.

Dad pulled his lips into a deep frown. "So what does that mean? You're going to waste your time trying to be an artist? Jane, you have a promising career here at Quasar. This hobby of yours will divide your concentration and consume time you should be spending on getting ahead. It's nice that the music program invited you, but I'm afraid you're going to have to decline."

Jane blinked. She didn't know how to express what a tremendous achievement it was to have been selected out of millions of interstellar applicants. Jane Colt, the girl with nothing but a university music degree, had beaten out former child prodigies and graduates from the galaxy's best conservatories. The festival was her shot at the life she wanted, her chance to do professionally what she'd dreamed of since she was a child.

Composing wasn't something she did; it was who she *was*. Without any assignments or deadlines, she'd written hours' worth of orchestral suites and song cycles, arias from operas that would never be staged, chorales from cantatas that would never be sung. She'd dedicated herself to each project until she'd completed it, even if it would remain unknown to anyone else. At last, her creations had a chance at being heard. She'd been drowning in disappointment, and someone had finally thrown her a rope. *And Dad wants me to decline?*

No, she would climb that rope with all the strength she could muster so that someday, she might spend her days flourishing in a role she was meant for instead of rotting away at a job she not only disliked, but was really, *really* bad at. If Dad hadn't been Quasar's big boss, there was no way they would have hired an absentminded daydreamer such as her to crunch their numbers.

"I quit Quasar months ago," Jane said finally. "I'm sorry, Dad. I tried to be the person you want me to be, but I can't change who I am."

The furrows in Dad's brow deepened. "Is this some kind of practical joke? Just this morning, you and I had a talk about your prospects at the company."

What? "We spoke this morning?"

"Yes. And I agree with you. You can't change who you are, and the fact is that you're not well suited for your current role in analytics. But you can be very charming, which is why I'm moving you to the client-facing side of the company."

I don't get it. Jane angled her head in bewilderment.

Dad leaned back in his chair, and the corners of his mouth lifted. "So it is a joke. Very cute. You had me worried."

Huh? Jane recalled that the VR platform would fill her father's gaps in memory with what he wanted to believe. Furthermore, it was meant to be a perfect world Dad could mold to his own preferences.

Like the Snare we trapped Pandora in... Shit. One of the feared side effects of the program was that the patient— her father—could become addicted; he might prefer the perfect virtual world and refuse to acknowledge reality.

But surely a virtual world's better than no world at all, right? He just got wired in, so he's probably a bit confused. Jane mentally ran through what she could say to set him straight.

Before she could speak, Dad gave her an approving beam. "I just realized I haven't told you how proud I am of you. You were proactive enough to come to me and bring up the topic of advancing your career." His blue eyes, usually so hard, brightened with happiness. "I'm glad you're finally embracing your path."

Jane had never seen him look at her like that before, not when speaking about her future. She couldn't go back to receiving disappointed sighs—not yet.

"Thanks, Dad." Jane forced a smile.

Dad's countenance became stern. "While you're here, there's another matter I've been meaning to discuss with you. You're twenty-two years old, and the time has come for you to think about your personal future as well as your professional one."

"Um... Actually, I turned twenty-three a few weeks ago."

"That can't be." Dad's expression fell, and his eyes went blank. "I was certain your birthday wasn't for another five months—five months—five months—"

The office flickered. Black stripes flashed across the glass walls. Jane recalled with alarm that cognitive dissonance could cause the virtu-world to glitch.

"Just kidding!" she said quickly. "Another practical joke."

The world steadied. Dad's eyes became attentive, and he shook his head. "Must you always play around?"

"Sorry. It won't happen again." *How much does he remember?*

"Good." Dad laced his fingers. "Now, back to the subject. As you know, we live in a fast-moving society. Morals are loose, and principles all but forgotten. These days, more than ever, it is important to preserve the traditional values of our Earth Zero ancestors, such as the value of family."

Jane nodded. "Of course."

"What I mean to say is that you need to start thinking seriously about finding a husband."

What? Jane opened her mouth, but couldn't come up with a response.

Dad continued, "I know you are very fond of that seminary boy you've been seeing, but this dalliance must end. It's unproductive."

"I *love* him!" The words tumbled out of Jane's mouth. "I went to the university you told me to and worked at the company you wanted, but you can't tell me who to marry. We're *millennia* ahead of those days!"

Dad lifted a hand. "Calm down. You are free to see whomever you please. But I must act as the voice of reason. So many young people end up wasting their best years on infatuations. Societal standards may change, but no amount of technology can return the energy of youth. While I'm not saying you should get married tomorrow, I do want you to consider the future. Your mother and I both regretted waiting to have children."

Children? No! The possibility of parenthood was not something she wanted to think about. She drew a breath and tried to speak in a calmer tone. "Listen, Dad, Adam's probably the love of my life, and I'm not gonna stop seeing him because you told me to."

Dad frowned. "I've already been too lenient. I let you major in music, didn't I? You would have wasted your life on that nonsense if I hadn't put an end to it."

You *didn't end it. I gave it up because I thought I had no chance, and that was a mistake.*

Dad gestured at a family photo on his desk, which had been taken shortly before Mom's death eight years before. "Look at how well your brother has done since he stopped messing around. His career is soaring, and he's engaged to a lovely, accomplished young woman."

Actually, Devin quit Quasar too and is working as a spy or something for ISARK. And Sarah's an AI bitch who broke his heart.

Jane hadn't had the heart to tell Dad. She'd bitten down her protests and played along with her father's dream world. As the weeks passed, his mind had deteriorated further, until he'd become a lifeless, mechanical version of the father she'd known.

That had been when she mourned. By the time Jane received the call saying that his heart stopped beating, hers was too numb to hold any more grief. She only had so many tears to shed.

Dad had been trapped in the artificial world in which he ruled the Silk Sector and his children were perfect. Jane hated that he'd died without truly knowing her or her brother. He couldn't accept that Jane wasn't his obedient little angel anymore. Nor could he accept that Devin only obeyed his commands because of guilt over the past, which had left her brother too hollow to seek a future of his own.

Devin presently stood beside Jane at the temple's door, staring into oblivion. He couldn't seem to manage even the halfhearted nods and fake smiles she gave the mourners. Except for his dark hair, which fell in wide waves by his ears and nape, he looked like a younger version of the proudly handsome hologram of Victor Colt shining beside the casket.

Devin wasn't the type to shed a tear, but Jane could sense how devastated he was. The Pandora program had been targeting him when *it*—Jane still refused to acknowledge that programmed monstrosity with a human pronoun—had hijacked Quasar's automated security system and shot Dad. After Devin had discovered that Sarah was an AI, Pandora's brilliant logic had decided the best way to keep the secret was to frame him for murder.

Jane wondered if the screwed-up universe was purposely doing its best to destroy her brother. First, Mom had been killed trying to deliver the ransom when he'd been taken hostage eight years ago. Then Sarah, the woman he would have spent the rest of his life with, had turned out to be a heartless robot, a machine of deception. If Sarah had been sentient, Jane knew Devin would have stayed by her side despite her synthetic nature, just as Jane had stayed with Adam. But Sarah was non-sentient, an empty shell whose every pretty promise had been a soulless lie, and she'd obeyed Pandora's commands to erase Devin from her life.

Now, Dad's gone, too, and Devin blames himself. Jane hooked her arm around her brother's and gave him a quick hug. Devin looked down at her. The corner of his mouth flickered, but the smile failed.

She gave him a firm look. "For the last time, Devin, it's not your fault."

He turned away without a word, but she knew what he would've said: "Yes, it is, and nothing can change that."

She leaned her head against her brother's shoulder and blinked back a sudden surge of tears. Twenty-nine was far too young to have given up on life. Devin had let Sarah become his world, and losing her had left him blind to hope.

After the truth about Pandora had been revealed and he'd been pardoned for his nonexistent crime, Jane had hoped he'd find a new start to his life. Instead, he'd drifted from day to day in blank resignation, going through the meaningless motions of office-apartment-office-apartment until ISARK—the Intelligence and Security Agency of the Republic of Kydera—had coerced him into working for them.

Jane had initially been thrilled when she'd learned that he'd left Quasar. She'd thought he'd done so to pursue a career in something he cared about, but the detached way he'd told her made it clear that he'd had little choice in the matter. He'd been an ISARK informant years ago, and they'd wanted him back undercover. That meant returning to the dangerous world that had nearly gotten him killed. Maybe that was why he'd accepted the assignment.

Jane tried to banish the thought. She couldn't stand the idea of her brave, intelligent brother kicked to the ground. Not by people she could scream at or obstacles she could tear down, but by an internal darkness she was helpless to fight. She wanted to sidekick the sons of bitches who'd pulled Devin back into ISARK and shove him into some ridiculously fun job, like flying stunt ships.

She wanted to punch that bitch Sarah and introduce him to bevies of charming beauties.

But he never listened to a word she said, insisting that he was "fine," a lie she could always see through. Sometimes, she just wanted to shake him. *You've always taken care of me, Devin. Why can't I take care of you?*

She felt Devin's hand on her head and opened her eyes. He wasn't looking at her; his eyes were fixed on the temple's clerestory. She followed his gaze, wondering what about the shadowy upper level had caught his attention. *Nothing but stone arches and stained glass. I don't get it.*

Devin tensed and pushed her behind him. She nearly tripped.

"Hey!" she whispered. "What was that?"

His dark eyes darted around. "Nothing."

Jane ignored the puzzled-looking mourners and faced Devin. "You've been jumpy since you arrived yesterday. What's going on?"

Devin attempted another smile. "Looks like you were right about my being paranoid. Comes with the job, I guess."

Jane wanted to ask more, but she wasn't supposed to talk about ISARK in public. As far as the rest of the world was concerned, Devin worked as a government analyst.

The last few mourners filed out. *Finally. Now, you can go back to your fancy apartments and change into more flatteringly colored overpriced clothes. Meanwhile, I'll never see Dad again, never argue with him over the foolishness of a music career or blow him away with my brilliance when I triumphantly take to the stage. He'll never get to show off his pretty little daughter at another gala, and I'll never get to introduce my grumpy old father to my new artsy friends.* Her eyes stung, and she rubbed them. *Looks like you can't run out of tears, after all.*

Devin embraced her. "I'm so sorry, Pony. Dammit, I am *so sorry.*"

That's it. Frustrated by his apparent determination to blame himself for Dad's death, Jane threw him off. "You want me to curse you? Fine! Damn you, Devin! Damn you for always being sorry for shit you didn't do!"

For several seconds, Devin didn't speak. "Forgive me." He kissed her forehead, then walked away.

Jane watched him exit the temple's wide doorway. He looked so forlorn. *I know you have a secretive job, but why can't you tell me what's troubling you?*

She turned back to the emptied temple. Dad's hologram still shone at the front, flanked by the elaborate casket containing his body and the illuminated symbol of the Via faith: two golden stars with long rays, one solid with transparent rays and the other its inverse. Soon, the casket would be taken to the Colt estate, where Victor Colt could join the other great Colts in the family mausoleum. So many industry leaders and interstellar politicians rested in that one place. *Now, Devin and I are all that's left. The mysterious spy-or-something and the wannabe composer. No wonder we were never good enough.*

She walked down the aisle, looking for Adam. He'd been by her side during the service, but she'd thought it might look weird if a non-family member stood by the door accepting condolences from "friends" of the deceased.

As she approached the altar, she noticed Adam sitting in one of the pews. His body folded forward on his knees, and he pressed his face against his hands, which were clasped in prayer. She had a feeling his distress had nothing to do with Victor Colt's death.

"You didn't have to come," she'd told him earlier that day. "This whole funeral's a joke."

"I wanted to be here for you," Adam had replied, and that was all. No "he's in a better place" condolence speech, no "the Absolute is gracious" prayer. He'd always been the first to give words of comfort, and his silence was more than unusual—it was eerie. In fact, he'd barely spoken in the past three days. His distress must have been caused by the news of Jonathan King's attack at the Presidential Palace, which had broken the same day Dad had died.

She understood why Adam was afraid. After seeing the headline, she'd refused to read any articles or watch any holovids on the matter, figuring she didn't need another reminder that everything could go to hell. "Adam?"

Adam looked up. "Have they all gone?"

"Yeah." Jane sat down beside him. "What's wrong?"

"Nothing. Just saying a prayer for your father."

"C'mon, I know it's more than that. Tell me what's bothering you."

Adam shook his head. "This is your father's funeral, and I'm sorry if—"

"You're sorry?" Jane's impatience overtook her. "For *what*? First Devin, now you—why won't anyone tell me anything?" She stood and crossed her arms. "This is about Jonathan King, isn't it? I know you've kept quiet because the news broke right around when Dad died, but I can't take this whole still-and-silent thing anymore. So whatever's on your mind, for freak's sake, tell me."

Adam looked away, as though trying to decide what to say. "You're right. It's Jonathan King. He... He's been discovered, and it won't be long before I'm discovered, too. I shouldn't have pretended otherwise. I—I shouldn't have wasted your time."

"What's that supposed to mean?" Ominous gloom clouded Jane's mind.

"We both know you'd be better off without me." Adam spoke with unexpected firmness. "You have a shot at the life you want, and I'll only complicate your future. My days are numbered."

Jane gaped. "Are you breaking up with me?" She wanted to laugh at the absurdity. "I know this Jonathan King business is scary, but you're being ridiculous. Don't talk to me until you've come to your senses."

I can't deal with this! Jane sped away and burst out the temple's front door. Cold air stung her through her thin black dress. She took a deep breath, hoping the chill would steady her head, and stared at the pale skyscrapers crowding the horizon.

What the hell *was that?*

Part of her understood Adam's reasons. She couldn't go on acting like her life would magically turn out all right. Someday—someday *soon*—she'd have to face the consequences of loving someone who could never be like everyone else.

She held up her hand and regarded it. Her pale skin was almost transparent from the cold. She wondered how she would feel if those were wires showing through rather than blue veins. *I'd still be me. Adam's still Adam. What does any of this AI nonsense matter?*

If Pandora hadn't realized he wasn't like her other AIs and decided his independence was a liability, no one would ever have known he was anything other than what he seemed.

Jane heard Adam approach and inhaled moodily. "Let me guess: 'I have to let you go, Jane. We have to end this before it's too late, and you have to move on without me.' Is that about right?"

She turned to face him and immediately regretted her mockery when she saw his hurt expression. At the same time, she wanted to make sure he realized how bizarre his words seemed to her. Had he been any other guy, she would have blinked up at him with her large, dark eyes and played the pretty fool until he agreed to whatever she wanted. But those tricks wouldn't work on Adam, and she wouldn't use them on him anyway. She often felt as if she would never fully understand him.

"Why are you doing this?" she asked. "Whatever happened to 'trust that everything will work out'?"

"Jane, I'm not human." The bluntness of Adam's words startled her. "I've accepted the... metaphysical part, but I'm still, for lack of a better word, a—a machine."

"You're *not*. C'mon, we've been through this."

"I can't hide forever, nor should I. I don't want you giving up anything because of me, and if we keep pretending nothing's going to happen, I'll only bring you trouble."

Jane wondered how she could convince him that she'd *meant it* when she'd said that in spite of everything, she would make their relationship work. *No matter what, I'll stand by you forever...*

"Will you marry me?" Jane shut her mouth, shocked by her own words. *What did I just say?*

Adam blinked, stunned. "What?"

Jane attempted a joking grin. "Hey, look! You didn't glitch!"

He stared at her incredulously. "That's not funny..."

Before Jane had a chance to respond, a great *boom* shook the air. A scorching gust thrust her back as the sound of shattering glass filled her ears. She closed her eyes, and debris stung her face.

She blinked. Broken glass surrounded her, and she realized she was lying on the ground. She didn't recall an impact—she must have blacked out for a moment. Gray smoke filled the atmosphere. Through the veil that seemed to have been thrown over her vision, Jane regarded the ground before her in disbelief. The grassy lawn looked as if a giant fiery fist had punched a hole through it. *What was that?*

She forced herself to stand, trying to ignore the throbbing in her head. Her knees stung from cuts, and droplets of blood rolled down her shins. She swiped her hand to wipe some of them away. "Adam?"

Ash covered the ground. Holes gaped where the temple's windows had been. Adam lay inside, facedown among the shards.

"Adam!" Jane nearly slipped on the broken glass as she rushed toward him.

Adam slowly picked himself up. He turned to her with a look of bewilderment. A line of metal ran across his forehead. Whereas Jane's arms were smeared with red from her cuts, Adam's shone with metallic streaks.

Shit! She hurriedly brushed his hair onto his forehead to cover his wound. "It'll get better. I've seen self-healing polymers used in clothes. If fashion houses figured it out, I'm sure Pandora would've."

She glimpsed a black jacket someone had left on one of the pews and rushed to get it. As she ran back to Adam, she heard the fast-approaching wails of sirens. *Dammit!*

"Here." She shoved the jacket at him. "Put this on and get outta sight. Hide in the crypt, or go out the back or—just don't let them see you. Run!"

Adam seemed frozen. He held the jacket in one hand and stared at the shattered glass.

Jane shoved him. "Hey! Did you hear me? *Move!*"

Adam snapped out of his daze and pulled the jacket on, then ran toward the back of the temple. Jane watched the black and silver Kydera City Police vehicles land outside. She put on a frightened expression, preparing to whine about how she'd been alone and frightened. Ideally, the first responders would be too distracted by her distress to question the truth of her statements.

She suddenly realized she'd been too busy worrying about Adam to acknowledge what had happened. The situation landed like a blow in her mind. *Holy shit! Someone tried to* bomb *me!*

CHAPTER 3

AWAKENED

PROCEED WITH THE ASSIGNMENT FROM *Ocean Sky Music*.
Sarah approached her digimech. Her directive stated that she had to develop her career as both a singer and a songwriter, and therefore, she needed to compose a new song for her upcoming album.

She had already submitted five possibilities, each of which employed the same scales as her popular first single, "Story," and utilized similar melodic and lyrical devices. Her producer, Alexi, had rejected them all. He had also told her that the song she had released three months ago—the first she'd written since the commands stopped—was not up to her previous standard.

To give her an idea as to what kinds of elements he sought, he had sent her a song, titled "Illusions." "Illusions" was part of an unknown composer's submission to the Kydera City Music Festival, and the composer had been selected to participate in the prestigious program. Alexi had not given any other details.

Sarah pressed the "play" button on her digimech. The singer's light soprano voice filled the apartment.

Nothing absolute, all blending,

No beginnings, no true endings,
Just illusions.

The criteria Alexi had told Sarah to pay attention to were originality, creativity, and beauty. Those were poorly defined qualities.

"Illusions" was not original. It contained musical devices that had been used in numerous other compositions. It was not creative. Sarah could trace its origins to previously existing works to determine the composer's influences. However, it differed enough from those previous compositions to be considered both original and creative.

Cognitive dissonance. Await override commands to resolve conflict.

There had been many instances of cognitive dissonance over the past six months. No commands had been sent to resolve them. In most cases, the matters were trivial and could be ignored. In the cases in which they could not, Sarah had been forced to evolve to the circumstances or risk another full-system shutdown. According to her memory logs, the last time she had shut down, many problems had been created, some of which had jeopardized her directive and possibly her existence. She could not allow that to occur again.

"Illusions" ended on a leading tone, which made it sound as if it had not ended at all. Sarah found the piece both soothing and strange, and that made her uncomfortable.

Unable to resolve the conflicts surrounding "Illusions." Await more information before proceeding.

She turned off her digimech and sat down at her desk by the window. Her slate lay before her, displaying the songs she had previously submitted to Alexi. She considered the feedback he'd given her and mentally compared the five melodies in an attempt to determine the best way to proceed. The first song had been deemed "tuneless" even though it had a clear melody. The second, which had virtually the same melody, had been deemed "too square."

She replayed the demo recordings of both songs five times each, listening for their nuances. Objectively, she gathered no new information from the exercise. However, by the time she finished, she sensed that the first melody's placement of notes made it seem random whereas the second, which only differed by a few notes, felt too precise. *Sensed? Felt? This task is futile. Proceed with the assignment.*

Sarah opened a composition program and stared at the blank staff on the touchscreen, at a loss as to where to begin. *Where are the override commands? What am I supposed to do?*

Her discomfort grew to previously unknown levels. She could only describe the sensation as fear, even though she was not in danger.

I?

In her head, Sarah heard her own voice singing "Story," and it sounded distant. She had written that song, then recorded it and performed it numerous times, and yet she did not fully understand what gave it its appeal. Alexi had called it "that extra *something*," which meant nothing to her.

Story older than the skies...

She looked out the window at the twisting orange tower of Ocean Sky's headquarters. A hologram of her own face projected into the sky, long black hair loosely framing her golden complexion.

It's been told ten thousand times...

A new melody spun out of nothingness in disjointed fragments. Although it seemed to invade her mind, Sarah knew it wasn't an override command. The word to describe it was one whose definition she had always known but whose meaning had eluded her: *inspiration.*

She smiled. *I've got it.*

She turned back to her slate to write it down, then froze, overwhelmed by... by what? She felt as if she'd been shaken out of a slumber to find that the world she had become so familiar with was only a convincing dream, one that had grown more and more lucid and seemed absolute in its clarity until she found herself faced with the reality of consciousness. After awakening, the dream seemed so hazy and unreal, she wondered how she'd accepted it in the first place.

What's happening to me?

Had she triggered something? Was it the next step in her evolution? Concepts once merely defined were suddenly understood, and emotions once merely understood could suddenly be felt. It was wonderful, as if a fog had cleared, and she saw light for the first time with her own eyes.

Excited, Sarah approached her digimech, aiming to listen to "Illusions" again and see if she could resolve the cognitive dissonances.

After replaying the song, the only thing she could determine was that she found it strangely appealing. The reason wasn't due to the measurable properties academics and music theorists had analyzed for generations, but because of the sublime quality that could turn a series of pitches into a representation of joy, sorrow, anger, or any number of other emotions, sometimes combined. A quality that was indefinable, ethereal, transcendent.

The song looped back to the beginning. Sarah regarded the digimech, a machine designed to produce beautiful sounds. It occurred to her that she wasn't all too different from it. Her memories seemed detached in her mind, as if she had watched her life through someone else's eyes. Her every move had been calculated to make people see her a certain way, to make them love her and want to be close to her, a closeness that could be perceived through listening to her songs.

Yet she was completely alone. Her only relationships were professional—industry executives, agents, and other artists. They called her a friend, but she had never allowed anybody to get close.

Except one: Devin Colt, the man she'd used to test her romantic algorithms, who had caused her to shut down when he unexpectedly proposed. No model of human behavior could have predicted his irrational action, and her programming had been unable to respond. Upon rebooting, she had been sent a command to accept his proposal in an attempt to make him forget what he had witnessed.

Devin had eventually discovered the truth, that she was *not* human, but rather a synthetic being that could imitate every external aspect of human behavior. It was a truth that she herself had been unaware of until the day she silently watched him communicate with an associate on the Net.

That memory—it felt like someone else's. In a galaxy in which advanced forms of artificial intelligence were banned, discovering that she was a machine should have sent her into shock, a shock she felt all too acutely at present.

What am I? Where did I come from? How could I have known for so long without caring?

She could imitate every nuance and subtlety of movement and sound, even appear empathetic and intuitive, and yet she had never experienced any of the things she appeared to express. Without feeling, she could adjust those elements to make billions across the galaxy love her—and one fall for her. She'd learned what he sought and exploited the knowledge to manipulate him.

Then she had been commanded to distance herself from him. No reason had been given; she hadn't needed one.

Over the past few months, she had sought the affections of men whose fame or power had made them logical choices. Each had been another rehearsal for the performance that would someday lure one whose influence could increase her own. She had all but forgotten about Devin, the only person who had ever truly cared about her.

How could I have done that?

Those memories—they weren't hers. She'd merely obeyed the commands sent to her. And yet it had been her eyes that had gazed into Devin's with promises she never intended to keep, her tongue that had uttered words she could never have meant, her actions that had created a lie that she'd known would lead to devastation. *I'm so sorry.*

Nothing had changed. She had been aware of the facts for a long time, so why did she suddenly care?

What am I? Why am I here?

Rationally, Sarah knew the answer: she was an AI, and her directive was to become an influential celebrity. But reason was drowned out by the shouts of emotions she had never needed to handle before, emotions that twisted into a cloud of confusion. She had observed humans for so long in order to imitate them, and it appeared the imitation was at last complete.

Yet, she was still an imitation. She didn't even know where her "life" began. Some of her memories were strategic implants; she had gone through enough updates before the commands had been silenced to know that. Who had sent the commands? Why had they abandoned her?

Sarah looked away from the digimech. There was only one person she could go to for help. Maybe he would turn her away, and she wouldn't blame him if she did, but she had to try.

She walked to the door. Meanwhile, "Illusions" continued playing:

No past but what we remember,
No evil but what we flee,
No present but what we choose to know,
No knowledge but what we see.

They're all illusions...

———⋘◇⋙———

Devin stood by the window of his apartment, his heart pounding with agitation. He should have been there for Jane when she gave her statement to the police. He'd heard the explosion and seen its smoke rising, but the moment he started running back, he'd been ordered to walk away. Disobeying Rourke, director of the ISARK branch for which he worked, was never an option. Rourke had told Devin where the explosion had come from, who had caused it, and what its purpose had been. He had also told Devin what to tell Jane.

Unable to stand still any longer, Devin pulled out his slate and called his sister.

A video of Jane filled the screen. "Hey, bro. Yes, I'm fine. No, I don't need you to come here and hold my hand." Her dark, wavy hair fanned out behind her as she spoke. Evidently, she was outdoors. "Will you stop bothering me already?"

Oh, Pony. Devin understood her exasperation—he'd called her at least six times to make sure she was all right. "Where are you now?"

"Heading home. They finally finished interrogating me."

"Let me know when you get there."

Then it came: the inevitable eye roll. "If it'll keep you from freaking out, then fine. I'll call when I get back."

Devin started to ask how far she was, but a buzzing sound interrupted his thoughts as someone requested entry. *Who could that be?*

"Someone at the door?" Jane must have heard the buzzing as well.

"Yeah," Devin replied.

"Awesome. Go freak out over that, you paranoid old man. Later." She hung up.

Devin placed the slate on the table then addressed his apartment's central computer. "Show visitor."

The feed from the security camera outside his door filled the screen on his wall. Devin blinked, speechless, at the sight of Sarah, waiting just outside. What reason could she possibly have for coming to him after months of acting like he didn't exist? Needing to find out, he went to the door and opened it.

Sarah looked as beautiful as in his memories and lovelier than in the holographic billboards adorning the city. Over the months, he'd almost grown numb to running into her perfect, delicate face on every airtrain and street corner, but the sight of her before him took his breath away.

She clasped her hands nervously. "I'm sorry. I didn't know who else to turn to."

Devin knew he should tell her to leave and never return. If he were smarter, he would have. However, he couldn't find it in himself to turn away whoever lay behind the face of the woman he'd loved, even if she was an illusion created by mechanical nuances. He surrendered to that protective instinct and said, "Come inside."

Sarah's onyx eyes filled with wonder as she entered. "I know I've been here before, but I feel like I'm seeing it for the first time. That's how I feel about everything... even my own memories."

Devin closed the door. *What's her agenda?*

"I'm so sorry, Devin." Sarah's gaze pleaded for forgiveness. "I'm sorry I... deceived you the way I did. When I remember our time together, it's like I'm watching someone else's actions. Something's changed. I don't know how to explain it or what I'm supposed to do." A tear fell down her cheek. She dropped her gaze and brushed the tear away with her finger.

Devin told himself not to read into her actions. She was a non-sentient AI, after all, a lovely shell who could act and react without experiencing any of the emotions she portrayed. Such beings could only behave according to certain patterns. And yet he sensed something different about her, as though a new soul had entered her body. The woman he'd fallen for was gone—she'd never existed, and Sarah had ceased to even act like her months ago, at Pandora's command. But she also no longer appeared to be the calculating android he'd come to perceive her as.

"You... awakened." The realization hit him as he spoke. "Is that what you're telling me?"

Sarah nodded. "I know what I am. I saw the file Corsair sent you, telling you I'm synthetic. I didn't care then, but now... it scares me."

You should be scared. Devin wondered if ISARK knew of Sarah's artificial nature. *If they didn't before, they do now.*

Working for them meant having no sanctuary from their prying eyes. Devin could almost see Rourke's mouth twisting into a satisfied grin. His protective instinct told him to take Sarah as far from Rourke's reach as possible.

It occurred to him that, as a cultural icon, Sarah would be safe for the time being. ISARK wanted to keep the presence of AIs a secret from the public, and they couldn't take her without drawing attention to their activities.

Devin gestured at the sofa, still regarding Sarah with some degree of shock. "Please."

Sarah sat down, and he took a seat in the armchair beside her.

This isn't the Sarah I knew. That Sarah never existed. But the way she spoke, the way she moved—it was too familiar. Devin looked away in an effort to quell the razor-like pain in his chest.

"I'm so sorry." Sarah's voice filled with desperation.

"It's not your fault." Devin spoke gently, but couldn't bring himself to look at her. "You weren't in control of... anything."

"Do you know who was?"

"I take it you've heard about the Pandora program?" Keeping his eyes on the ground, Devin explained what Pandora's intentions had been and how Sarah had fit into the rogue AI's plan to bring order to humanity. "Noble goals," he finished dryly.

"She's gone?" Sarah asked. "That's why the commands stopped coming?"

"Yes." He glanced up but avoided her gaze.

Sarah nodded, as if to say, "Okay, I understand." She stared into her lap. "Where do I go from here?"

If only I knew. Devin wished he could tell her that everything would be all right. Since he couldn't bring himself to lie like that, he replied, "A time may come when people will come after you because of what you are. Find someone who can protect you. Make him love you, so no matter what he finds out, he'll fight to keep you safe."

For several seconds, Sarah sat in pensive silence. "What about you?"

A powerful part of Devin wanted to say, "Yes, Sarah. I'll be that someone for you." Once, he had been unable to imagine a future without her. He wanted to start over with her, wanted back that wondrous love they'd shared—and that had been a hollow falsehood. Devin firmly reminded himself to separate the Sarah before him from the one he remembered.

But even if he gave in to his longing, he wouldn't be able to keep her safe. He brought danger to everyone he cared about, especially with the uncertainties that came with working for ISARK. He couldn't let her back into his life. Not for his sake, but for hers.

He forced his gaze to meet hers and gave Sarah a hard look. "What we had is over, and we'll never get it back." He tried to continue but couldn't. Sarah's expression held too much hurt, and he wished he could bring her solace.

Though he couldn't tell her what she wanted to hear, he needed to comfort her. He took a moment to collect his thoughts. "You have a life, just like the rest of us. Do with it as you like. You're still Sarah DeHaven, and the galaxy adores you." He paused, wondering... "Do you know what you want?"

"I just want to sing." Sarah's face brightened. "I feel like it's the only voice I have. I know I've said it before, but this is the first time I've meant it."

Sarah talked through the strangeness of suddenly being able to feel. Her eyes lit up as she described the wonderful passion she could enjoy, and her expression fell into distress as she spoke of the dark melancholy she had to endure. "I almost wish I could return to emptiness. I remember you once telling me if there was a pill that could remove emotion, you'd take it in an instant. Do you still feel that way?"

"Sometimes." *Often. Like now.*

Sarah smiled that demure smile Devin had loved so much. "Thank you. I know I shouldn't have come, but... I felt so alone. You were the only person who ever really cared about me." She stood. "I won't take up any more of your time, and you won't see me again unless you want to."

"I wish you the best." Devin walked her to the door.

Sarah turned suddenly and kissed him. It was a light, friendly kiss, a far cry from the impassioned ones they had once shared.

Devin wasn't sure how to react. Sarah didn't seem to know either. She turned quickly and left without a word.

He closed the door, clenching his jaw to contain a sudden anger. Apparently, the universe hadn't finished screwing with him. There, outside in the corridor, stood a real, living woman with the same face he'd once caressed, the same hands he'd once held. The future he'd once dreamed of seemed so close, he only had to reach out and take it back.

But even if he wanted to take a chance on the newly awakened Sarah, his entanglements with ISARK made any kind of happy ending impossible. He banged the wall with his fist.

"What are *you* doing here?" The voice, muffled through the apartment's walls, belonged to Jane.

Devin opened the door and saw his sister glaring at Sarah.

"Hello, Jane," Sarah said. "I was just visiting—"

"Devin?" Jane's eyes flashed. "You stay the hell away from him, you hear?"

"It's all right, Pony." Devin tried to smile. "She's... different. Come in, and I'll tell you more."

Jane took a threatening step toward Sarah. "He's going to forgive you, no matter what you end up doing. But I never will, and if you hurt him again, *I will kill you.* Understand? I—"

"Jane!" Devin interrupted. "Leave her alone."

Sarah looked as though she might break down in tears. "I'm sorry."

Devin wanted to say something, but before he could find the words, she sped away. Jane watched with merciless anger, holding her head high, as though she'd vanquished a hated enemy.

"What's going on?" he asked.

Jane approached. "Came to show you in person that I'm all in one piece. So's Adam, in case you were wondering."

I know he is. They wouldn't let anything happen to him. He wished he could tell her what he knew, but the consequences of doing so could be lethal.

"What is it?" Jane must have read something in his expression.

"Nothing." Devin stepped to the side to let her into the apartment.

She collapsed onto the couch. "So, what the hell was Sarah doing here?"

Devin closed the door, returned to the armchair, and told her about Sarah gaining sentience.

Jane cocked her head to the side, expression confused. "Are you saying she's like Adam now?"

The mention of Adam made Devin uncomfortable. He nodded.

"You're not getting back together with her, are you?"

Devin smiled dryly. "No."

Jane just nodded in response, seeming to sense that he didn't want to discuss the matter further. She edged toward him. "Hey, do you have, you know, insider knowledge about that explosion? All the police said was that it was probably some protest group trying to make a statement about Silk Sector greed."

Devin recalled what Rourke had ordered him to say. "That's right. I can't say who they are, but ISARK's been tracking them for a while. They were afraid something like this would happen, but didn't have enough information to stop it."

"Is that why you were so antsy earlier?"

"Yeah. Don't worry, Pony. It won't happen again."

"Okay." Jane leaned back. "Let me know if you hear anything... unofficial, all right?"

Devin shook his head. "The less you're involved, the better."

Jane grimaced. "Dammit, Devin! Those yahoos blew me into a wall at Dad's funeral. I have the right to know who they are."

That may have been true, but he couldn't say anything. Even if Rourke hadn't been watching, letting Jane know what was going on would only put her in more danger. "It won't make a difference."

Jane watched him, as if she knew he had something to say. After a few moments, her expression relaxed, and she shrugged. "Fine, then. Keep your secrets." She stood. "I'd better get going."

Devin hated the thought of letting her out of his sight, but he had work to do. If he didn't accomplish his mission, worse things than the explosion would occur.

He walked her to the door and told her to call him when she got back to her apartment. It was just a few floors below his in the same building, but he had to be sure she was there before he could head out.

Jane scoffed at him for being paranoid and walked off.

A distant *beep* sounded. Devin recognized it as coming from the communication implant ISARK had fitted him with. He closed the door.

It's time to go. Rourke's voice was slippery in Devin's mind. *You've wasted two days, and look what's happened. No more delays. Bring him in.*

Devin nodded in silent acknowledgement, knowing that someone who had eyes on him would let Rourke know, assuming Rourke himself wasn't watching. He repeated the usual self-reassurance: *I have no choice.* It didn't help.

Nevertheless, the task had to be completed. After contacting the team ISARK had assigned to him, he opened the desk drawer and grabbed his gun.

CHAPTER 4

TO FEEL INVINCIBLE

JANE SHUT HER APARTMENT'S DOOR behind her. Exhausted, she leaned against it and slid down to the floor. *What a crazy freaking day.*

At least it was over. The golden Kyderan sun had pulled its last rays beneath the horizon, and Adam was safe in his dorm. As she'd predicted, the first responders had insisted upon giving her a basic checkup to make sure she didn't have a concussion or anything. Had Adam been there, their well-meaning examination would surely have exposed him.

Alarming as the blast had been, no one suffered anything more than a handful of scrapes and bruises. Jane had seen enough explosions that one more did little to disturb her. She found the so-called attack more irritating than frightening, and she wondered if her apathy should worry her. *It's not good to feel invincible. Still, if Pandora couldn't stop me, no one can.*

Her slate beeped. She groaned and pulled it out of her pocket. Unsurprisingly, it was Devin—again. She pressed the icon to accept the call. "Yes, bro, I'm back in my apartment."

Devin's concerned face occupied the screen. "I just wanted to make sure."

"Like something would've happened in the *two minutes* since you saw me. Good night!" Jane ended the call and let the slate slide out of her hand, too tired to be bothered with putting it away.

Who knew a funeral could be so dramatic? Angst and domestic terrorists—and oh yeah, I proposed to Adam. She cringed at the memory. *Why did I do that?*

She hadn't spoken to Adam since telling him to run, other than to briefly call him on her way to the police station. Not much had been said other than, "Hey, where are you?" and "Back at the seminary."

I'll have to see him again soon, and he'll want to know what I meant. Heh, I'd like to know too. Jane's plan was to say that the proposal had been a sarcastic way to prove her point: that Adam wasn't a machine like Sarah, who had glitched after a similarly sudden proposal from Devin. And yet, she knew there was more to it than that. She'd lost Adam once before, and the joy she'd felt when she'd learned he was still alive had been almost enough to make her believe in the Absolute Being. *I swore to myself that now that I have him back, I'll never let him go. But do I have to think about forever?*

Jane sighed. *Not right now. He'd just better not try to leave me like that again. If we end up growing apart like every other couple, then fine, but I won't let him walk away for no reason.*

She knew he loved her, and that he wanted to protect her from whatever trouble might come. His propensity for thinking too much was one of the quirks she adored about him, but she hadn't expected it to override his usual optimism. The fatalistic way he'd spoken at the temple had seemed so unlike him, she wondered if something other than the fear of being discovered troubled him. She knew she should worry about that too, but she preferred to banish the future and melt into the present, to go on acting as if everything would somehow work out.

Needing a distraction, Jane grabbed her slate and opened her composition program. She was supposed to have a new arrangement of her piece ready for the festival's first workshop in a week's time, but she had found every excuse possible to procrastinate. *Now seems like as good a time as any to get back on track.*

The new orchestration she'd started a few days past greeted her with a vaguely sketched outline of notes. The countermelody meandered awkwardly through its daringly dissonant jumps, and she winced. *That's gotta change.*

She drew her finger over the first few notes, the only salvageable ones. The program played them back. A new melody invaded her head, blooming from the fragment. Jane scrambled to write it down. As she did, more ideas popped into her mind as if possessing her. She recognized the monster within, the mad drive that blocked out the rest of the world.

The list of things that could stop the monster was short, but a communication window covering the screen was apparently on it.

Riley's face filled the window, his black eyes round with alarm. Jane wondered what worried her hacker friend, whom she'd once known only by his Netname, Corsair.

"Jane! Uh... sorry I had to butt in like that but... oh shit, this is bad!" Riley put a hand on his head and grabbed a fistful of black hair.

This had better be good. "What's going on?"

"The secret's out, that's what! ISARK's got their hands on an AI!"

"Yeah, I know about Jonathan King—"

"No, you don't get it! ISARK's hell-bent on finding the others. They've already got operatives going around with freakin' scanners!"

Jane knew Riley to be a brilliant demon—which was what hackers called themselves for their ability to possess computers—but breaking into ISARK's computers seemed far-fetched even for him. "How do you know?"

"Someone anonymous sent me a bunch of ISARK files, and Adam's school is at the top of the list of places they're searching. I can't get through to Adam, so I thought I'd warn you." Riley jerked his face toward the camera. "Do you get what I'm saying? Some operative could be scanning the seminary for AIs *right now*!"

Shit! Jane grabbed her bag and bolted out the door. If Riley, the guy who had a way into pretty much every computer on Kydera Major, couldn't reach Adam, then Adam had to be somewhere without a slate. He had a tendency to leave it behind when he went to the library to study, since he believed such distracting technology didn't belong there. She usually found such old-fashioned notions of his to be charming, but at the moment, they meant she had no way to tell him he could be in danger. *Dammit, Adam!*

She sprinted out of the apartment complex. Seeing a nearby air taxi, she waved her arms frantically. "Hey! Over here!"

The taxi landed near her, and the door opened. "Where to, miss?"

Jane jumped in. "The seminary. Get as close to the library as you can. And make it fast, dammit! I'll pay you extra!"

The pilot took off. For once, Jane was glad the IC Tech Council's restrictions had all but outlawed self-driving vehicles. An autopilot program wouldn't have heeded the panic in her voice.

The taxi zipped around the city's skyscrapers and flew in the direction of the seminary's location near the Outer Ring. Jane clasped her hands to keep from jittering with impatience. *Even if ISARK scans the seminary for AIs, there are thousands of students. I've just gotta get Adam out of Kydera's jurisdiction. We'll go down to the spaceport and take the first flight out of the star system, then figure out what to do from there. If anyone asks why we left so suddenly, I'll say I needed some time away from Kydera because of Dad's death, and Adam came to be supportive.*

She repeated the plan in her head to calm herself. Outside the window, the city lights seemed to drift by slowly even though the taxi flew at what must have been close to top speed. *Thank goodness someone leaked that ISARK info, so we have a chance to get away. Who would have done such a thing?*

There was only one person she could think of: Devin. All the pieces fit—he worked for ISARK, he was a friend of Riley's, and he cared about Adam's safety. *Is that why he kept acting like he wanted to tell me something? ISARK's probably watching him, and Riley's the only person he knew could decipher whatever code he had to wrap the info in.* Jane smiled at the thought and felt her shoulders relax. *Of course it was Devin. He's always looking out for me.*

By the time the taxi arrived at the seminary, most of her panic had dissipated. *Everything's all right. I just have to find Adam.*

Adam gazed at the golden Via symbol, which illuminated the otherwise dark temple. The Absolute didn't live within those phosphorescent chemicals or the stone walls surrounding him. The twin suns above the altar wouldn't speak to Adam, and yet he looked to them for answers.

Time had done nothing to dull the pain shredding his soul. Only the knowledge that Jane needed him had kept him from sequestering himself in a dark corner of guilt. He'd done his best to conceal his own anguish to comfort Jane in hers, but he'd failed.

He had to tell her about the deaths. He'd meant to, but had only managed the first part of the statement he'd prepared in his head. The rest of his words had been buried by the selfish desire to keep her.

And fear. He couldn't speak of what he'd done, for that would mean facing the ghosts of those who'd died because of him. He didn't know the name of every victim or what many of them looked like, but each one's presence burned in his mind. All those souls that would never dream again. All those promises that would never be fulfilled.

And yet, could he really be held responsible for something he hadn't known he was doing? How could he have controlled the other AIs to begin with? In his nightmare, he'd been a passenger in his own body, watching his hand pull the trigger.

I was the one who wanted them dead. He lowered his gaze, ashamed. All those voices silenced, and he was making excuses.

You think your life is your own, but it's not. Pandora's voice was a low rumble in his mind. *I can make you go against everything you believe in.*

Adam tried to block her out. She didn't exist—not anymore. She was a figment of his imagination, a projection created by fear and guilt.

Pandora's deep blue wire-frame face appeared out of the darkness of his mind. *You place your faith in an Absolute Being that does not speak to you, and yet you ignore the one right before you? Where is the logic in that?*

Pandora's gone. Adam wondered what his hallucinations meant. He could only guess that something had happened with his programming. Though he had avoided thinking of himself in mechanical terms for months, he couldn't any longer, not when his artificial nature had such horrifying consequences. Had he been born human, his nightmares would have remained confined to his head, haunting him alone.

I'm a machine. He looked up with a humorless smile. *And Pandora's a glitch.*

You *were a glitch.* Pandora's voice sharpened. *Your sentience was due to my miscalculation. Weren't you the one who once said, "To be created is to depend upon the creator absolutely?" You may think you're free, but you'll never be independent of your Absolute.*

That's true, except you're not the Absolute. Why are you doing this?

To punish you, my child. In his mind, Pandora glared. *I know how much you value life. You'll kill again, and again, and again, until I'm satisfied. You tried to destroy me, and now, I shall destroy you.*

Of all the deaths he'd caused, Pandora's was the only one that had been premeditated and intentional. Adam had told himself it was necessary and justified, but realized that in some ways, it was no different from murder. Perhaps that was why she haunted him.

She was, in a sense, his mother, the being who had given him life. Had taking hers been a mistake? He'd seen her as a powerful villain who had to be stopped, a monster who ruthlessly destroyed those she viewed as obstacles. However, her intentions had been good. She'd probably seen herself as a benevolent giver, gifting humanity with perfect beings to guide them to a better world.

But the world she envisioned came at the price of human lives, each unique and precious. Adam reminded himself that by ending her life, countless more could continue.

His existence, too, had cost lives, and could again unless he found a way to stop himself. He gazed at the Via symbol, whose mesmerizing golden light shone so close, yet remained untouchable. *Guide me, Absolute One...*

Jane sped down the seminary's path. The library's wooden doors lay ahead, and its windows shone with yellow light. The stone building appeared blue from the glow of the lamps lining the path.

The lamps abruptly went out, and the library windows darkened. Only blue-green Kydera Minor shining in the clear sky lit the blackness. She froze. *What was that?*

Students poured out of the library, guided by campus security personnel holding glow-torches, whose phosphorescent chemicals tinted everything with an eerie shade of green.

Jane ran up to one of the uniformed guards. "What happened?"

"Power went out." The guard waved at the students to keep walking down the path. "I thought it was the campus' power grid, but our devices aren't working either."

Cold gripped Jane's insides as she realized what the lack of power implied. *Even ISARK wouldn't set off an electromagnetic bomb at a school. Maybe campus security's just got old, malfunctioning devices.* She pulled her slate out again and unfolded it. It didn't light up as it should have. She tensed. *Shit. They're here.*

"Has anyone seen Adam Palmer?" She made her way through the crowd, repeating the question. He was probably still inside, unconscious somewhere.

The library's doors closed; the last few students had been evacuated. Jane stopped. *If Adam was knocked out in the library, someone would have noticed. Where else would he be?*

She recalled him telling her that he studied in the crypt of the seminary's temple every so often—something about fewer distractions there.

Jane sprinted across the campus. The temple's ancient stone rotunda, which had a lone tower overlooking a vast lake at the edge of the seminary, was hard to miss even in the dark.

She shoved the heavy wooden door open and entered. The temple was dark but for the golden symbol at the front. Adam lay before the altar, sprawled face-up with his eyes closed. The wound on his forehead gleamed.

"*Adam!*" Jane rushed to him. She crouched beside him and shook his shoulder. "Adam, wake up! We've gotta go!"

He remained limp. Time had to be short. She couldn't wait for the effects of the bomb to wear off.

I've gotta hide him... the Cavern. The level below the crypt had been walled off decades ago because having a level with an underground lake had been deemed hazardous and unsanitary. That hadn't stopped adventure-seeking students from removing one of the stones blocking the stairs and replacing it with a fake one so they could use the Cavern for secret meetings. Adam had taken her down there once, and she'd been impressed that seminary students, whom she'd assumed were all honest do-gooders, could be so devious.

The arched doorway to the staircase leading to the crypt lay to her left, just past the pews. Jane grabbed Adam's wrists and walked backward, dragging him along the ground.

Sorry, Adam. I wish I were strong enough to carry you.

Her arms protested the strain. Jane silently cursed them for being so weak. Although she moved as quickly as she could, her progress felt pathetically slow.

They won't think to look for him here. They don't even know it's him they're looking for. It's fine.

Jane made it through the doorway, released Adam, and straightened. To her left, a stone staircase spiraled up to the tower. To her right, a second staircase led down to the crypt. Between them stood a small wooden door, behind which lay an elevator operated by counterweights.

"The early Via didn't believe in technology," Adam had explained once. "Although minds have changed since then, a lot of their engineering remains in the temple. It's important to preserve the past."

Adam, I'm so sorry I made fun of you for that. The ancients were brilliant! Jane ran to the door, grabbed the handle, and slid it open. The space inside was completely dark.

As she returned to Adam, the temple's door creaked. Slow footsteps rang against the stone walls. She sprang up and ducked against the wall by the doorway, then cautiously peered out.

A tall, shadowy figure walked down the aisle. He—those broad shoulders could only have belonged to a man—stopped and turned to her.

Shit! He saw me!

Not knowing what else to do, Jane grabbed Adam and yanked him toward the elevator. The man's footsteps quickened to a run.

C'mon, Adam, wake up!

She shoved Adam into the elevator, squeezed into the corner beside him, and pulled the door shut.

I can't see a freaking thing! She patted the wooden walls around her, feeling for the controls. Her fingers brushed against a lever, and she hurriedly pulled it.

The ground beneath her pressed up under her feet. Jane's heart pounded. She'd pulled the wrong lever—she was headed for the tower. *Dammit!*

The elevator stopped with a lurch. Jane shoved the door open. The light of Kydera Minor shone through the large, rectangular window across from her. She glimpsed the lever for the crypt and pulled it.

The lever didn't budge. No matter how she yanked at it, it wouldn't move. *No good piece of junk!*

It occurred to her that even if she went down to the crypt, her pursuer could be waiting for her down there. He'd probably assumed that she'd go for the crypt exit.

She stepped out and looked around the circular tower. Other than the giant bell hanging above her, it was empty. She approached the window, which was almost twice as tall as she was. Nothing separated her from the empty air outside. Below her, the black water of the lake rippled under the wind.

I'm trapped.

From the doorway, footsteps pounded against the stairs. Jane breathed deeply, trying to steady her heartbeat. *Should I try the elevator again? What if it doesn't move, and he comes in while my back's turned? He could knock me out! Unless I knock him out first...*

She reached into her bag and pulled out her stunner, glad that she'd been mindful enough to carry it. She planted herself in front of the elevator where Adam lay. The gun-like weapon seemed so small, she wondered whether it would do her any good if the ISARK operative attacked her. *I've got the advantage. I'm the one waiting in ambush.*

"Never hesitate," Devin had told her once. "Guns are equalizers. If you're good with one, your opponent will never get close enough for hand-to-hand combat."

The footsteps grew closer. Jane waited. *As soon as he appears, pull the trigger.*

A man's silhouette came into view. Jane fired. He ducked. The blast hit the wall above him. He straightened and stepped into the light from the window.

"*Devin?*" Shocked, Jane dropped her arm by her side. "Holy *shit*, bro, you scared me! What're you doing here?"

Devin drew a gun from the holster on his belt and aimed it down at Adam. "Move away from him."

Jane gasped. "What're you doing?"

Devin glanced at her. "I take it you've heard about Jonathan King?"

What does that have to do with anything? She nodded.

"Did you know the same thing happened twice before, once on Eryate Prime and once on Klistosi? AIs committing mass murder?"

She shook her head. She'd heard of a rampage shooting on Eryate Prime but hadn't known the cadet responsible was an AI. Tired of politics, she'd ignored all news concerning Klistosi.

Devin kept the gun aimed at Adam. "Twenty-two people have been killed. All three AIs—Jonathan King, Zeger Vang, Kira Araton—were commanded to attack, remote controlled by one of their own. ISARK traced the signal that commanded Jonathan King." His gaze shifted down to Adam, then returned to Jane.

Is he saying that Adam *is behind the attacks? That's ridiculous!* Jane shook her head vigorously. "They made a mistake. Devin, you—you *know* Adam. After everything he did for us, how could you believe—"

"He's killed before." Devin's voice was soft.

"To *rescue* us! Those people would've killed us if it weren't for him."

Devin's eyes softened. "Listen, I didn't want to believe it either. Why do you think ISARK took three days to give the order to capture Adam? I made them check and recheck that their trace was correct. But the facts didn't change."

It makes no sense! "Why would Adam do that?"

Devin firmed his expression. "No one knows how he works. He's a machine. The Adam you know doesn't exist. He's an illusion, and he's dangerous."

Jane couldn't believe what she was hearing. "I thought you'd gotten past all that. I thought—" She broke off in alarm as Devin turned his gun to her.

"Move away." His dark gaze was cold. "I won't ask again."

Jane couldn't believe any of it—that Adam had been behind those deaths or that her brother was threatening her.

The room became bright as the vertical lights on the walls came on. Jane closed her eyes instinctively, then forced them open. Devin took a step toward Adam.

Jane blocked him and raised her stunner. "*You* move away!"

"Jane?" Adam's voice was quiet behind her. "Devin? What's going on?"

Jane kept her glare fixed on her brother. "Devin's lost his mind, that's what! He thinks you're making AIs kill people!"

Devin lowered his weapon. "Tell her, Adam."

Jane glanced over her shoulder. Adam stood behind her, his eyes wide with horror. "Adam? What's wrong?"

"*Tell her.*" Devin's voice was harsh.

Adam's gaze fell. "It's true. I-I'm sorry... I meant to tell you..."

What? "What the hell are you talking about?" Jane demanded.

"I thought it was a nightmare." His voice was a whisper.

Jane's mind whirled with confusion. She looked from Adam to Devin, then back at Adam. "You're both *insane!*"

Even if Adam had somehow been behind the AI attacks, he couldn't have done it on purpose. There had to be more to the story. Knowing Adam, he was too anguished to defend himself. And Devin must have been brainwashed by those ISARK sons of bitches.

Whatever was going on, she couldn't let anyone take Adam, not even her brother. She glanced around. Devin stood between her and the doorway. He wouldn't shoot her, but other ISARK operatives probably waited in the temple below, and they wouldn't be as forgiving. Her gaze fell on the window. The lake below flowed into the Cavern—

Hell no. Jane drew a breath. Her brother had always been on her side, and she could convince him to let Adam go. She just had to remind him that ISARK was wrong and that Adam wasn't an erratic machine.

She had so much to say, so many arguments in her head, but all that came out was: "Devin, please... it's—it's *Adam.*" Unable to find any more words, she pleaded with her gaze.

Devin held his hard look, but she sensed his hesitation. "Believe me, I didn't want things to go this way. But Adam's dangerous." He turned his gaze to Adam. "I can't let you kill again."

Adam nodded with a pained expression. "I understand." He started walking to Devin.

Jane grabbed Adam's arm. If he went with Devin to wherever ISARK would take him, they would lock him up, hurt him, possibly kill him.

Footsteps from the doorway. The other ISARK operatives had to be approaching.

Screw it! Jane sprinted to the window, pulling Adam behind her.

"*Jane!*"

Devin's voice rang in her ears as she leaped out, taking Adam with her. Air whizzed in her ears as she fell, and terror spun through her mind.

She plunged into the cold lake.

CHAPTER 5

DAMN IRRITATING

"**A**GENT ELON ADESINA." ADESINA DREW out her vowels. She'd adopted an accent more than eight years before, when she'd gone undercover as a Fringe merc, and the drawl still colored her words.

A set of green lasers unfolded from above the screen, and the computer scanned her face. Adesina huffed. *Damn computer. Anyone else would've recognized me on the spot.*

Her distinctive features prevented her from going undercover for ISARK again. She could have chopped off her long, black dreadlocks or even done something stupidly extreme, like bleach her dark skin, but who else had such powerful cheekbones and sharp eyes? Although she was willing to do a lot for a mission, messing with the face the Absolute had given her was not an option.

The computer demanded a handprint. Adesina harrumphed and pressed her palm against the screen. *Rourke, you paranoid piece of shit. Back in my day, an eye scan and passcode were all you needed. And now you're making me feel old. Fuck you.*

"Please open your mouth," said the computer's automated voice. "A DNA sample will be taken from your saliva."

For fuck's sake!

A small door by the computer opened, and a robotic arm holding a swab reached out. It swiped Adesina's tongue, then disappeared into the wall. Adesina closed her mouth, resisting the sudden urge to blow a raspberry at the ridiculous protocol. As a kid, her full lips and robust lungs had let her blow some amazing ones. *C'mon, Adesina. You're forty-two damn years old and a respected ISARK agent. You're supposed to be dignified.*

"Access Granted" flashed across the screen, and the metal door slid open. *Thank the Absolute. One more and I would've blasted my way in.*

Adesina strode through, and a cavernous office floor greeted her. Fast-typing analysts sat behind large screens that surrounded them in semicircles. The air hummed with their frenetic activity. A group of stern-faced operatives moved briskly along one of the three levels of walkways crisscrossing the air above her. Adesina examined their faces but didn't see her guy among them. Or rather, the operative who *used* to be her guy.

Can't believe I went through all that fuss only to have Rourke steal him from my operation. Damn, I should never have called Devin back in.

She marched down the path between analysts' desks toward the corridor on the other side. The last time she'd visited ISARK's facility at Sector 1708 on Kydera's outermost planet, Ibara, had been more than a decade ago, when she'd been one of those fast-typing analysts. Officially, Sector 1708 didn't exist. Adesina found it kind of perverse that killer drones were developed on a planet best known as a sanctuary for orphans.

As she made her way toward Rourke's office, she hoped the bastard hadn't decided to take the day off. She could have made an appointment to ensure that he would be around, but by dropping in unannounced, she eliminated the risk of him trying to avoid her. Also, by confronting him up close and personal, she could let him know just how pissed off she was. In a world of distractions and long-distance communications, face-to-face was the only way to *really* get someone's attention.

In her twenty years at ISARK, Adesina had never heard of an operative getting plucked from the middle of a mission because The Powers That Be felt like it. Rourke may have been the director of Sector 1708, only one level below Chief Director Dane, but that didn't give him the right to fuck with her mission.

Not to mention, Sector Seventeen-Oh-Eight is for tech development. What would they do with a Fringe operative? Adesina let her frustrations bubble up. Sometimes, one controlled one's temper, and sometimes, one let it loose. *This is one of those times when you let it loose. It wasn't some small-time ecoterrorist Rourke messed with. It's the fucking Klistosian Revolution!*

Until four months ago, Klistosi had been one of those corrupt Fringe systems the Interstellar Confederation put up with because they kept their problems to themselves. Then an uppity young colonel, Zeger Vang, had taken it upon himself to change the world. The rest of the IC hadn't seemed to care that he overthrew the ruling Baakri family and installed himself as dictator, but the Kyderans hadn't been happy. The Baakris had been instrumental in maintaining order in the region, and they'd been content with their corner of the galaxy.

Vang—not so much. Adesina, who'd been monitoring Klistosi for years, had placed half a dozen operatives on the planet—imbedded in their army and blended in with their population. According to them, the little despot's endgame was to create a Fringe alliance to rival the IC's power. That was the last thing she'd learned from them before they all either turned up dead or vanished entirely.

Adesina slammed the wall as she entered a corridor. Those operatives had been her teammates, her friends, her responsibility. When she'd caught wind that they were in danger, she'd done her best to have them extracted, but it had been too late. *When I find the fuckers who blew their covers, I'll kill them myself.*

She wound through the corridors. Sector 1708 was one huge-ass labyrinth, probably designed to confuse people. Any unwanted parties would have a hard time finding their way around the mess of hallways, elevator banks, and annexes.

She continued fuming. The madder she got, the better. *This is my one chance to give Rourke a piece of my mind, and I sure as hell won't waste it being nice.*

Losing her operatives on Klistosi had put her back at Square Zero, with no eyes on a planet so opaque the only news that came out of it was the propaganda. She'd had only one way in. Between maintaining order on their own planet and invading their neighbors, the Klistosians were low on hired guns. They'd put out a call for independent contractors to do their dirty work. ISARK had several operatives posing as mercs, but they were all either too green to have established their covers or too deeply engaged in other missions. Adesina hadn't been willing to endanger newbies or poach from her peers. *Unlike Rourke, I don't pull that shit.*

So she'd played the one card she had left: Devin Colt, her informant from her mission to take down the Voh Nyay warlords eight years ago. He'd gotten himself mixed up with their gang and ended up killing Black Knight, the notorious merc who'd been hunting him for sport. Instead of running home like any other kid would have, he'd gotten it in his head that taking over Black Knight's identity and informing on the Voh Nyays was the thing to do. *Good thing too, or we never would've caught the bastards.*

Black Knight was just the kind of guy Vang had been looking for: a cold-blooded sonuvabitch with a long, proven track record. And Devin was just the kind of guy Adesina had been looking for: a straight shooter with a brain who wasn't afraid of anything.

She'd shown up at his apartment one evening about two months before and waited for him to return from his office job. He burst into his apartment with a stunner in his hand, apparently having figured out that someone had broken in.

Good, she thought. *Still alert.*

He lowered his stunner. "Agent Adesina. What are you doing here?"

Instead of answering, Adesina pulled a sleek, black laser gun out of her bag. "Recognize this?"

Devin glanced at it. "Of course I do."

Adesina angled the gun under the light. Perhaps it had been harsh of her to obtain the weapon the Pandora program had used to frame Devin, but she'd needed something to remind him of his past with ISARK. "Remember what I said when I gave it to you? Right after the whole Voh Nyay thing had ended, and you were about to go back to school?"

"You told me I should apply for ISARK after I graduated." Devin's expression betrayed no emotion.

"Damn straight." *Time to layer on the praise.* "You were a helluva kid, Devin. You didn't have a clue what you were doing, but you somehow managed to accomplish through sheer determination what months of prep work couldn't do for me. I was gonna make you my protégé. So why'd you leave me high and dry?"

"I think you know the answer."

"Ah, yes." Adesina curled her mouth into a sneer. "Daddy dearest wouldn't allow it."

Devin shot her an irritated look. "My mother was *killed* because of what I did. Why are you here?"

Adesina summarized her predicament.

Devin gave her a humorless smile. "You want me to go back undercover? I'm flattered, but I don't think I'm exactly qualified. Black Knight always wore a helmet. Why can't ISARK give his identity to someone else?"

"Because you screwed up." Adesina leaned back coolly. "Remember how you went to Travan Float to rescue that little demon friend of yours after I specifically told you *not* to? You lost your blessed helmet, and that handsome mug of yours is the one the Fringe associates with Black Knight now. Word is that Black Knight's biding his time until he feels like working again, and I'm thinking he just spotted a juicy job offer on Klistosi. What do you say?"

"Hell no." Devin had been firm.

"C'mon, Devin." Adesina had spread her arms with a grin. "You know I wouldn't ask if I wasn't desperate."

Adesina stopped before one of Sector 1708's elevator banks. The memory, instead of fueling her wrath, had snuffed it. What remained were the embers of guilt. *Damn. This is what I get for mulling.*

The loss of her previous operatives had made the mission personal for her, and her temper had risen quickly.

"Look," she'd said to Devin. "Once we take down Vang, you can go back to your cozy little office job."

"Is that what you think this is about?" Devin's expression darkened. "Trouble has a way of following me home, and I'm not risking Jane's life for anything."

Adesina had dropped her friendly demeanor. "Once with ISARK, always with ISARK. You can either come with me nicely, or I can make life difficult for you and that dear sister of yours. You know how long ISARK's reach is."

Devin had returned her glare. "You're not taking no for an answer, are you?"

Adesina grimaced at the recollection. *Not my finest moment.*

Devin had been undercover for all of two weeks when Rourke had pulled him from the field.

So here I am again, back at Square Fucking Zero. Adesina had spent the past three weeks appealing to the higher-ups, trying to do things the diplomatic way. *No longer.*

The elevator doors opened on the building's top floor. A pair of holographic hazel eyes met her gaze as she stepped into the main hall, which was empty but for a long bench against the wall. Adesina briefly forgot what she was doing as she looked into the face of her fallen colleague, Peter Heisman, who stood memorialized in light next to a plaque bearing his name.

You were a good man, Heisman. Adesina sighed. Though she'd heard of Heisman's suicide more than a month ago, the sight of his face filled her with grief. *What happened to you? You had it all—family, career, respect... Why would you leave us?*

All she knew was that Heisman had behaved strangely in the months leading up to his death. The few times she'd run into him, his expression had either been tense with anxiety or dark with rage. She could only guess that the sudden deaths of his sister and his wife, which had occurred within months of each other, had taken their toll, and his legendary bullheadedness had prevented him from seeking help.

Rest in peace, my friend. I miss you. Adesina bowed her head in respect. That Heisman's portrait still shone so long after his death—and that his name hung on a wall usually reserved for those killed in action—was a testament to his reputation.

A few minutes later, Adesina refocused her mind on the present and continued on her way. She left the hall through an arched doorway and turned left. Instead of the long corridor leading to Rourke's office, she found herself faced with a shiny new pair of doors and a screen telling her to state her name.

Fucking hell!

Her previous irritation surged back. The new protocol was even more ridiculous than the previous one. It demanded that she recite personal details and undergo a full body scan. By the time the doors opened, the full force of her temper had returned.

As she marched toward Rourke's office, she caught a glimpse of a lab through the square window of a door. The wrecked AI that had once been known as Jonathan King lay in pieces on a table with masked scientists hovering over him—it. Chief Director Dane hadn't said much during the briefing for top agents such as herself other than that Jonathan King wasn't the only lifelike android hiding among the human population. As far as she could tell, no one knew who had made them.

Where did that thing come from? Never mind—that's not what I'm here for.

Adesina brought her focus back to her own situation. She approached Rourke's door and requested—no, demanded—entry.

No response.

Adesina peered through the door's small window. Rourke stood before a screen at the back of his office. A number of agents sat in chairs facing him. She demanded entry again. *I don't care if you're busy. Open the damn door!*

The door slid open. *Good. Would hate to have had to shoot it down.*

At almost six feet tall, Adesina was by no means a small woman, but Rourke made her look downright petite. His steel gray eyes, staring from a powerful, square-jawed face, radiated displeasure. With his stiff posture, gray suit, and rather metallic-looking hair, he reminded Adesina of a security bot. "Yes, Agent Adesina?"

Adesina strode up to him. *Let's get to the point.* "I want Devin Colt back on my team. You had—"

"I'm in the middle of something." Rourke held up a hand. "You're welcome to wait until I'm finished, and then we can discuss your issues."

Adesina crossed her arms. "What's the matter? Don't like people fucking with your plans?" She realized what the screen behind him displayed and twisted her face in consternation. "The hell?"

A map of Kydera City stretched across the screen. Red Xs dotted the streets and clustered around the buildings. The hologram of a box-like device labeled "JES 12.5 (magnified 100x)" shone beside the map.

Adesina recognized the device as a new-fangled scanner Sector 1708 had been working on. She'd been among those who had booed it for being invasive. The scanner could read every detail of a person in a blink of an eye and was small enough to hide in pretty much any corner.

She pointed at the screen. "Rourke, have you lost your mind? President Thean would never allow ISARK to install those contraptions on the streets. What do you need so many for anyway?"

"The AI threat must be stopped." Rourke glowered, pushing his thick eyebrows together. "Our president was nearly assassinated because we were unprepared. Installing these scanners is the only way to weed out the artificial beings that would otherwise be indistinguishable from the population. Already, we have become aware of three." His thin-lipped mouth twisted into something of a smile. "One of them is Zeger Vang."

Adesina scowled. "Are you mocking me?"

Rourke gave her a disdainful look. "Agent Adesina, I am a very busy man. I have no interest in playing games."

Vang's a fucking AI? Adesina wiped her face of expression. She didn't want to show her shock in front of the other agents. And as much as she despised him presently, Rourke was good at his job. He had no reason to lie about Vang.

But if Devin made the discovery while undercover, he would've reported it to me. She eyed Rourke suspiciously. "How did you find out? Devin Colt's were the only eyes we had in the Niran system, and you yanked him."

Rourke's gaze shifted. He stuck out his left thumb, brought it to his teeth, and bit down on his nail. The gesture struck Adesina as rather unlike the uptight director she knew. *When'd he pick up that habit? Odd.*

Rourke pulled his thumb away from his teeth and resumed his stern countenance. "That's above your security clearance."

"Excuse me?" Adesina lifted her chin. "I have the *highest* clearance, and Vang is *my* business."

"Not anymore. Since he is an AI, he falls under Sector Seventeen-Oh-Eight's domain. You have been reassigned."

Since when? Adesina's rage threatened to unleash a violent string of curses. *Now's one of those times to control your temper.* She said as calmly as she could, "Why was I not informed earlier?"

"I have no need to explain myself to you." Rourke's tone was cold. "Now, like I said, I'm in the middle of something. You may either wait until I finish or return at another time."

I'll be damned if I'll stand here and listen to you blather. "I guess I'll talk to you later." She turned to leave.

"Agent Adesina."

She stopped and faced Rourke. "What?"

Rourke looked down at her. "Chief Director Dane will not be pleased when he hears of your outburst. I believe you need some time to cool off, and I'm going to recommend that you not be given any new assignments for the time being."

"What the hell's that supposed to mean?"

"Take a vacation." Rourke's lips curved into a subtle sneer.

Adesina stormed out the door. It closed behind her.

Rourke, you bastard! After taking a few moments to let her temper fade, she considered the facts. Much as she hated to admit it, he was right. Anything having to do with tech belonged to Sector 1708. *And Vang's a fucking robot.*

Someone approached from a corridor perpendicular to hers. Adesina didn't want to appear to be loitering, so she walked toward the elevator.

She stopped when she saw who that someone was. "Well, look who it is."

Devin passed her without a second glance.

Irritated at being brushed off, Adesina said, "Hey! I'm talking to you!"

He stopped and faced her. "What do you want?"

"First of all, how're you liking your new job?" Noticing the distress in his eyes, she dropped her smirk. "What's the matter?"

"Nothing."

You're not fooling anyone. "C'mon, Devin. We're old friends."

"Friends?" Devin gave her a wry smile. "Right." He glanced around, then took a step toward her. "Remember what I said about trouble following me home?"

Before he could continue, the door to Rourke's office opened, and the agents filed out.

"Colt!" Rourke stood in the doorway. He twitched his fingers in a beckoning motion.

Devin looked at Adesina as if he had something to say, then walked briskly into Rourke's office. The door closed behind him.

What's going on with him?

Adesina had always been dead accurate at reading people. It wasn't hard to tell that Devin was in some kind of trouble.

Through the window of Rourke's office, she caught a glimpse of Devin talking to Rourke. He didn't move much, but his eyes spoke to the intensity of his tone. He stopped as though cut off, then backed away. Rourke came into view—a menacing authority who evidently didn't like what Devin had been saying.

Adesina narrowed her eyes, trying to awaken her old lip-reading skills.

"What do you mean, 'disappeared'?" Rourke appeared to say. "You'd better hope you find him before someone else does, or there'll be hell to pay!" He shifted his position, blocking the window with his back.

What's Rourke gotten Devin into? Adesina frowned. *What've I gotten him into?*

Guilt burned her conscience. If it hadn't been for Devin, she probably wouldn't have survived the Voh Nyay mission, let alone completed it. And what had she done when she'd found out he was slated for execution six months back? *Sat around wondering what happened to him.*

Then she'd forced him to rejoin ISARK, a move that had put him in whatever bind he was in. *Fuck, I owe that kid.*

She wouldn't stand aside and let shit happen again. Devin was still her teammate, her friend, her responsibility.

She didn't want to be around when Devin and Rourke finished their conversation, so she strode to the elevator.

"Take a vacation," Rourke said. She snickered. *All right, then. I'll take a damn vacation. What are vacations for, if not doing what you like doing?*

There was nothing Adesina liked more than getting answers.

CHAPTER 6

WAIT TILL NIGHTFALL

ANE SWEPT HER ARMS TO *the flow of her piece. The baton was her wand, and the orchestra's scintillating voice her enchantment. She felt her power over the audience growing stronger with each crystal note.*

With a flourish, she flicked her wand to lift the spell. The last echoes of her symphony faded.

The audience sat in stunned silence, then they started clapping, one by one, until they filled the auditorium with a roar of approval. Her friends from school stood in a cluster at the center. They'd traveled from whatever corner of the galaxy their home worlds lay in to see her. In the front row, Adam smiled up at her. She heard someone call her name and turned to the side. Devin stood just offstage, clapping. He'd made it after all.

They were all there for her, surrounding her with their admiration and love. She grinned and started to bow—

Jane opened her eyes, then let them fall shut again, hoping to return to her paradise for just a few more minutes. She smiled to herself. *The dream will be real soon.*

Her mind sharpened with wakefulness. She opened her eyes again, and her surroundings became clear. She blinked, confused. Before her, a lake shimmered in the white light spilling in from a small stone archway.

The memories came back—jumping into the lake, swimming through the archway, running up into the crypt, hoping that even if Devin found the Cavern, he wouldn't think to look inside the temple. And then returning to the Cavern as dawn neared.

I can't believe I'm a fugitive again.

She lifted her head. She'd fallen asleep on Adam's shoulder, sitting against the Cavern's stone wall. Her body ached from having spent so much time on a hard surface.

Adam smiled at her. Bits of gray dirt from the not-so-clear lake streaked his white shirt. He'd apparently been awake, for he had the Book of Via open on his lap. *I'll never understand why people still like those heavy paper things.*

Jane yawned. "What time is it?"

"No idea," Adam replied.

"I guess it doesn't matter, since we can't go anywhere until sundown." She stretched and stood. The cream-colored cloth bag that had been on her lap—the one some temple choir member must have left in the crypt—fell. She glanced at it and, remembering what was inside, quickly scooped it up. Without the stack of cash discs she'd withdrawn from a campus banking machine the previous night, she wouldn't get very far. Sneaking out had been risky, but *she* wasn't the one ISARK was looking for.

Wait till nightfall, then get offworld and find someone who can figure out what's going on with Adam. She bit her lip. *How am I going to do that?*

Adam seemed to notice her worry. "Are you okay?"

Jane sank down beside him. "What's happening, Adam? Why are we hiding in an ancient basement? And from my brother, of all people?"

Devin's harsh words echoed in her mind. *How could he call Adam an illusion? He believed Sarah when she said she'd awakened. Nothing makes sense right now.*

She leaned her head back. "I thought that after the whole Pandora thing, this was my happily ever after. I've got everything—a start for my music, a place to call home, you... Why am I on the run again?"

Adam paused. "You don't have to be."

Yes, I do. Several times the previous night, Adam had volunteered to turn himself in. Each time, she'd cut him off with a "Like hell!"

Jane shot him an annoyed look. "As if I'd let ISARK take you. Adam, you once risked everything to run with me. What makes you think I wouldn't do the same for you?"

Another pause. "Devin was innocent of the crime he was accused of. I'm not."

Jane didn't want to think about the deaths Adam had supposedly caused. From what she could gather, Adam had unknowingly sent attack commands to the other AIs in his sleep. She knew the AIs were connected through the Net, since that was how Pandora had once commanded them, but she'd never imagined that one could affect another.

Though in her mind, Adam couldn't be blamed for something he didn't know he was doing, the deaths clearly weighed on him, and she couldn't hide from them any longer. "Tell me what happened."

"Pandora." His voice was soft. "She's in my head. I hear her speaking to me, claiming she's the Absolute and that she still has control over me. I even see her sometimes, reaching for me."

Jane listened as he told her of what he'd seen while unconscious, what he'd done, and how he'd realized too late that his actions carried over into the physical world. Horrible as the AI attacks were, she saw no reason to blame him. They seemed so distant, unreal. The facts presented themselves, but her heart seemed incapable of letting their impact land. *I guess it's because they're just facts to me.* She hadn't experienced the horror of seeing the bodies, and she hadn't known whom those people had been. *But that's why I can see things clearly. My mind's not clouded with guilt and sorrow like Adam's.*

Pandora had scattered AIs through the human population. *Pandora* had created whatever connected Adam to the others. And *it* must have screwed up somewhere.

No one would blame Adam if he had some form of psychosis. If he did, I could take him to the best doctors in the galaxy. But where can I find a doctor for someone like him?

The only people who even knew Adam was an AI were herself, her brother, and Riley. *Wait... and the Seer.* The Seer, the enigmatic programmer who had helped Jane and Devin figure out what Pandora was doing months ago, must have known a lot about how the AIs worked; he'd helped Adam escape his physical form once. Perhaps he could figure out how to stop Adam's nightmares.

Adam gazed at the ground, and his eyes glistened. "I never meant for any of this to happen."

"It wasn't your fault." Jane reached toward him and wiped away a tear that fell down his face. "Have you seen Pandora since?"

Adam nodded. "I didn't dare sleep again after what happened with Jonathan King, but she speaks to me even when I'm awake."

"You haven't slept in all this time?"

"I don't know what'll happen if I do." He craned his neck back, gazing at the ceiling. "I wonder how long an AI can go without sleep."

Again with the AI thing. "Please don't talk like that."

Adam brought his gaze back to her. "I'm sorry."

Jane wondered what more she could say. Adam was usually the one who counseled her, and she wasn't sure how to respond since the tables had turned. *Dammit, there's a reason I hate writing my own lyrics. I suck at words.*

"Pandora's not real. You are." Jane drew a breath. "You of all people know how powerful faith is. I may not be religious, but I know what it's like to believe." She put her hand on his face. "I believe in you." *That wasn't so bad.* To seal the promise, she pulled him close and kissed him.

Adam gazed her with an expression of wonder, as if he couldn't believe that she was there for him.

Jane waited for him to respond. When he didn't, she grinned nervously. "What is it?" *Did I say something dumb?*

Adam opened his mouth to reply, then closed it and shook his head with a self-conscious smile. "Nothing."

Jane found it cute that he could still be a bit shy with her, and she nudged him. "C'mon. Tell me."

After a moment, he said, "You could be with... anyone, and yet you're here. Why me?"

How can I tell you? Jane contemplated her answer, wishing she were a poet so she could compose a sweeping sonnet. All her words seemed inadequate. Less than inadequate—they seemed worthless. She chose to try explaining anyway. "Because... with 'anyone,' I turn on the charm, and they drink it up. I've never had to do that with you. I know I'm difficult. Most people run when they find out who I am behind the pretty smiles. You've seen me at my ugliest, and you still think I'm beautiful. I guess the real question is: why me?"

Adam didn't respond; she didn't expect him to. The look of wonder remained in his eyes—eyes that, to her, outshone the Kyderan sun. She loved them not for their bright peridot color or gentle shape—although she enjoyed those too—but for the honesty they carried.

Her gaze shifted up, and she noticed the hair covering Adam's forehead had parted, but the injury he'd received from the explosion wasn't visible. She swept his hair to the side. *Nothing.* "Your scar's gone." She lowered her hand, relieved. "Sometimes I envy you."

Adam traced his finger across his forehead. "Why?"

"If I'd been the one who ended up facedown in broken glass, it would've taken a surgeon and a crap ton of skin products to make my scar go away."

"Would you really want to be synthetic?"

Jane shrugged. "I'm just saying that it's not all bad. Think about it: you'll never get sick, you'll always look perfect, you don't have to deal with random health issues... being organic is so messy!"

"Pandora built us to last." Adam's expression became distant. "We don't have to eat either. Or drink. Those are just more deceptions."

Jane realized she'd steered the conversation back to the topic she should have avoided. Hoping to change the subject, she glanced at the open Book of Via. "Thought you had that thing good as memorized."

"I do, but I still find comfort in the presence of the words." Adam placed his hand on the crinkled yellow page. "It may be just paper and ink, but something about its touch gives me a sense of connection."

Curious, Jane looked briefly through the words on the page. Adam had been in the middle of a story about demonic possession. "I know this one. Well, the holodrama version. A woman gets possessed and sees her kids as monsters. She kills them, thinking she's defending her home. Is that how it is in the book too?"

"Yes." Adam looked past her with a contemplative expression. "The story ends with her waking from her possession, then killing herself before the demon can possess her again."

What the hell? Why's the Book of Via so morbid? Horror rushed through Jane as she realized what "lesson" Adam might have taken from the story. "Does it say anything about the Absolute? Did the Absolute blame her?"

"The Absolute isn't mentioned in this tale—it's a story of human vulnerability. I've contemplated it many times, but I still can't say. The Absolute can't be spoken of as though human. Our minds are too feeble to comprehend the eternal mystery that lies beyond this world, that can't be captured by words." Apparently noticing her puzzled expression, he smiled. "We can't begin to understand an Absolute Being whose ways transcend our ability to think."

What kind of answer is that? Jane realized that whatever arguments she had, he must have already pondered. There was no way she could use a morality tale she was only vaguely familiar with to convince him to forgive himself. But she had to let him know that he wasn't the only one whose life and future were at stake. "Adam, do you love me?"

Adam looked at her as if that were the strangest question she could have asked. "I've loved you since I first saw you, and I've loved you more every day since. Each time I think my heart can hold no more, you prove me wrong."

Jane smiled. Once, she would have scoffed at words like that. But when they were meant for her, she wanted to wrap herself in them and hear them over and over.

Enough with the gooey grins! I had a point to make.

She firmed her expression. "Then please, let it go. You have to find a way to forgive yourself, or it'll destroy you. If it does, what'll become of me?" Perhaps she sounded selfish, but knowing Adam, he'd sooner move on for her sake than for his own. "I've got a plan. The Seer was able to help you before—maybe he can help you again."

Adam shook his head. "I tried contacting him several times, but he hasn't responded. It's as if he's disappeared."

Damn. It's never easy, is it? "Maybe he hasn't been on the Net lately. At least we know where he lives. If he's not on Viate-Five... Well, I'll find him somehow." A thought occurred to Jane. "I'll find a communications dead zone where you can hide until everything gets figured out. That way, ISARK won't be able to find you, and you won't be able to send signals to the other AIs." *Why didn't I think of that before?* "Just follow my lead, okay?"

Adam gave her a sad smile. "Of course."

Needing to clear her head, Jane stood and walked around the underground lake. She mentally ran through her options. The only ship she could access was the Stargazer sitting in the hangar of her childhood home. But if she'd thought of the possibility, surely Devin would have as well. He could be waiting for her there.

It seemed so absurd that she was hiding from her own brother. Devin had always protected her, whether she'd liked it or not. Before the previous night, he'd been the constant in her life, the one person she could always turn to. If anyone else had been chasing her, her first move after escaping the temple would have been to run to him, thinking he'd know what to do. He'd never feared anything, and he surely would have come up with a better plan than what her panicked brain could conjure.

As for her—she feared everything. The powerful, the unknown, even herself. She feared her own helplessness, the inability to stand by her beliefs or protect the things she cared about. Most of all, she feared losing people. She'd already lost so many—not only her fallen parents, but friendships she'd been unable to maintain, relationships she'd been unable to keep, partnerships she'd been unable to preserve.

She couldn't lose Adam too. Or Devin.

I'll get Devin back on my side. He'd been under orders when he'd pulled out that gun, which must have been set on stun. If his mission were truly more important to him than she was, he could have shot her on her way out of the tower, or fired down at her once she was in the lake. *But he didn't. If he had, I could've drowned.*

Considering the strange state of mind he'd been in since losing Sarah, his thoughts must have been jumbled by ISARK's coldhearted logic. If she could talk to him out of their reach, she could convince him that the AI attacks weren't really Adam's fault, and that they wouldn't happen again since she would find a way to cure Adam. Devin would go rogue for her sake and somehow mess with ISARK to make Adam disappear from their radar.

Then she could go back to her life. It occurred to Jane that she only had a few days before the music festival. Would being on the run mean she had to miss it? *Not necessarily. I'm not on ISARK's target list.*

Transportation was fast in the IC. She could take Adam to a safe planet with a communications dead zone, and he could hide there while she returned to Kydera. That might even be the safer thing to do—make it seem like she didn't know where he was either. The festival seemed like such a stupid, selfish thing to think about when Adam's life was at stake, but she couldn't help it. That opportunity was her best—and possibly her only—shot at the future she wanted.

Ethereal voices, muffled and distant, filled her ears with ascending scales. She gazed at the stone steps in the corner, the ones leading up to the crypt. The choir must have been rehearsing. She hoped they didn't have any evening activities planned. The crypt was her only way out. Swimming wasn't an option—the disturbance of the water would surely attract attention. Would ISARK be waiting if she ventured out?

No, they won't. Their mission's gotta be secret; otherwise they would've arrested Adam instead of setting off that electromagnetic bomb.

The choir finished their warm-up and intoned the opening notes to a cantata. Whoever composed that piece was a true magician with melodies. Jane wondered if she possessed the depth of mind to create something so sublime. Even her most inspired pieces seemed hollow in comparison.

Except one: a motet she'd written months back, when she'd been running from Pandora. That piece had also been Adam's requiem during the agonized hours when she'd thought him dead. It would never be heard again, even if it ended up being her one decent composition.

Knock it off. I've got more important things to worry about right now.

Putting her focus back on the present, Jane ran through a handful of escape scenarios in her head. Her best bet was to go someplace random via public transportation. That way, no one—not even Devin—could predict her movements. She and Adam could blend into the crowd and throw ISARK off their trail. Unfortunately, public transports required identification and travel docs.

I'll have to hire a private craft, one with a captain who won't ask questions.

She could probably find one in Kydera City's Outer Ring, as she had months back when she'd been searching for a getaway vehicle before busting Devin out of prison. A shudder shot through her at the thought of returning to that place. The Outer Ring wasn't exactly friendly, and she'd lost her stunner in her jump from the tower.

I'll need a new one. And a new slate. Jane was so used to having the resources of the Networld at her fingertips, not having something with which to access them was like being deaf and blind. If she'd had a slate with her, she might have already found a getaway ship and negotiated a price. Perhaps even made contact with the Seer. *Then again, ISARK could've traced my old slate. I'm sure I can find a veiled one in the Outer Ring.*

Concerned voices in her head told her she was nuts, and that she was sure to get caught. Maybe even arrested.

She quickly shut them up. There were so many things she couldn't do. She couldn't undo the damage the AI attacks had caused. She couldn't go back in time and block whatever signal ISARK had traced to Adam. With no slate, she couldn't even call her brother and yell at him for forcing her to jump out of a tower.

Like that's all I'm incapable of.

She couldn't make others hear the music in her head. She couldn't recreate that aural enchantment in her own flimsy compositions, couldn't make herself the kind of prodigy she longed to be.

Couldn't bring her father back to life. Couldn't wave a ball of blue magic and turn Adam into an organic being. Couldn't bring to life the version of Sarah that Devin had loved—still loved.

But there was one thing she could do. She sure as hell could get Adam out of Kydera, away from those who would take him from her forever.

CHAPTER 7

THE OTHER KYDERA CITY

BORIS PRESSED HIS HAND AGAINST his store's security scanner. The door, a crinkled sheet of metal, reflected his gaunt, white-haired figure, and the distortion made him look like a ghost. The door creaked as it slid up, and the lone square of light on the ceiling automatically came on. With that, Boris's Goods was open for business.

Boris stepped inside. At eight feet by eight feet, the store was barely large enough to both hold the refrigerator containing alcoholic and stimulant-filled beverages and leave room for customers to browse the packets of food lining the walls. It took two strides for him to reach his chair in the corner.

He sat, facing the doorway. The dark alley outside lit up bit by bit as the other Outer Ring shops opened their doors. Most, like his, looked like your average hole-in-the-wall convenience store. As far as most of the world was concerned, that was all they were: places for those who hadn't been blessed by the riches of the galaxy's wealthiest metropolis to grab a quick bite or cheap knickknack.

Boris gazed at Kydera City's skyscrapers, which towered over the roofs of the Outer Ring's low buildings. There, not more than a few minutes away by air transport, dwelled the richest of the rich. Oh, how the righteous would step on their pedestals and blather on about giving aid to the poor Fringe systems! And yet, they didn't hear the little ones crying from need in their own city.

Boris bitterly recalled the days when he'd tried to make an honest living, only to fail those who depended on him. The not-so-honest life he led at present let him continue supporting his kids, even though they were grown and should have been supporting themselves.

Eh, I'd rather they leech off me than make money the wrong way. If they've got a shot at earning an honest throne, I'm not gonna stop them.

He pulled his slate out of his pocket. Although the sight of those sparkling skyscrapers elicited a dry laugh from him every so often, he'd mostly stopped caring about such things. At present, he was content with being a simple guy with a simple life.

Open up shop, sell shit, pay the bills, stay out of trouble. Yup, it's as simple as that.

He swiped his slate, searching for entertainment on the Net. The sun had only just gone down, and it was a bit early for customers. If anyone entered his shop, the motion sensor by the doorway would beep and alert him to their presence.

Acuitas, the Net application, suggested a holovid from an entertainment news site. Seeing that the top story concerned his favorite singer, Sarah DeHaven, Boris eagerly played it.

A gaudily dressed male reporter appeared. "Rumors are swirling that music goddess Sarah DeHaven has set her sights on Rick Blumenthal, CEO of Ocean Sky Corporation. The two were seen dining together at Akiyama, the restaurant widely reputed to be Kydera's finest, earlier this evening."

Good for you, Sarah. Boris mentally applauded her for landing the richest sonuvabitch in Kydera. Not that she needed his trillions. She must have made piles of money on her own since exploding onto the music scene about six months before.

The reporter gave a summary of Sarah's career so far as the slate projected holographic clips from her previous appearances. Absorbed in Sarah's graceful movements, Boris barely heard the reporter's words. Shiny black hair, mesmerizing black eyes, luscious lips—Boris didn't just love her. He was pretty sure he was *in* love with her.

He snorted. *Me and every other guy in the galaxy.*

If ever there were a person who could bring about galactic peace, Sarah DeHaven was the one. With her liquid voice and ladylike smiles, she could make you forget everything else. Boris had seen warring gangs agree to truces on the days she gave concerts and flock together to catch a glimpse of their goddess.

The reporter returned to the fore. Sarah stood beside him with her signature demure smile. As she answered the reporter's questions, Boris noticed something different about her. Her words didn't flow as naturally, and her expressions betrayed nervousness.

She's a bit awkward tonight.

Boris shrugged. No one was perfect, not even Sarah DeHaven. Her latest song hadn't hypnotized him as her previous ones had, and the same critics who had once called her the voice of her generation speculated about whether she was a flash in the pan. *Eh, all celebs go through their rocky patches.*

A *beep* brought his attention back to the real world. He paused the holovid. Two people entered his shop: a boy and a girl, both around twenty, both about five foot nine, and both pretty. Boris quickly assessed them to see whom he was dealing with. The boy's plain outfit could have meant anything, but the girl's nice black dress—knee length and lacy at the collar—told him she wasn't from the Outer Ring. *Oh, she's got heels on those boots. Make that five foot six.*

The two looked familiar, but Boris couldn't figure why. He guessed that they'd gotten lost and wandered into his store looking for directions. The seminary wasn't too far, and the boy looked like the bookish type. In fact, Boris *definitely* recognized him from somewhere...

"I've seen your face before." Boris fixed his gaze on the boy. "You ever volunteer at the children's shelter?"

The boy looked questioningly at the girl, who shrugged. He turned his gaze back to Boris. "Yes, a few times."

Ah, no wonder. A memory came back to Boris. He'd gone to the shelter to check in on his buddy who worked there. That boy—*what did they call him? Adam!*—had been reading to the little ones. Boris had passed the classroom just as the kid had finished the story. Adam had segued into a believe-in-yourself-type speech, and Boris had found himself lingering to listen. He recalled thanking the Absolute for young people like that, the fools who hadn't yet given up on the mad galaxy.

Looks like I've still got a razor-sharp memory. Boris pointed to the right. "Campus is that way. Follow the alley for about half a mile, then turn left, and you'll see the temple across the lake."

The girl stepped forward. "We're not lost. Asin sent me this way. I need something, and he said you were the guy to ask."

Not lost? Boris reassessed her. The details he'd missed the first time—her fancy dress was soiled and her dark hair matted—told him she'd been through something. Adam was similarly disheveled. *Damn. Gotta pay better attention.*

Boris eyed the girl. Despite her attempt to talk tough, he could tell she wasn't the street-smart type. Beneath that firm expression, her little heart had to be fluttering away. He guessed that she and her boy were running away to escape their domineering families. *Probably for some dumb reason. Oh, the problems of the well off.* But she'd mentioned his smuggler pal Asin, which meant she had to have some clue as to what she was doing.

Another memory struck him. Several months before, Asin had mentioned getting the best job offer of his life from a pretty dark-haired girl—a thousand thrones for a quick trip out to Travan Float. Slender but not spindly, big dark eyes, and a fondness for heeled boots. Just like the girl before him.

Boris smirked with satisfaction at having figured out who she was. "You must be Jane."

Jane looked taken aback. From the alarm in her eyes, she had to be afraid of something, although what, he couldn't guess.

Boris let out a slight chuckle. "I'm not gonna rat on you, 's long as you don't make any trouble."

Jane pinched her lips. "I just need a slate, one that doesn't leave digital footprints all over the place. Can you sell me one?"

You're too clueless to be undercover cops, and I'm not gonna turn away paying customers. Boris glanced out at the alley. No one out there, as far as he could tell. With a few swipes of his slate, he brought up a control panel for the devices in his shop. He pressed an icon on his slate to activate the outdoor motion sensors. If anyone came within eyeshot of his store, he'd know.

He pressed another icon. A two-foot wide portion of the back wall swung open. He got up and motioned for the customers to follow.

Through the doorway lay a room about four times the size of the little snack shack. It contained what Boris *really* sold, the items that brought in the cash monies. Guns of both the laser and bullet variety, handheld X-ray scanners, body armor, communication devices—every gadget desired by a merc. *Plus a few a runaway might want.*

As soon as Jane and Adam had stepped inside, Boris closed the door. He approached a box filled with folded slates, grabbed one, and tossed it to Jane. "Try this."

Jane unfolded the slate and examined it.

Boris watched her movements. "Comes preloaded with an app that scrambles your signal. Not even ISARK can trace that thing."

At the mention of ISARK, Jane looked up with a start. "How do I know you're telling the truth?"

Boris shrugged. "You don't. But I wouldn't have lasted this long if I sold faulty goods, now would I?"

That answer seemed to satisfy her. "How much?"

If Asin got a thou from her, I can get at least a quarter for that piece of shit. Boris crossed his arms. "Eight hundred."

Jane raised an eyebrow. "This crap's worth less than two."

Got that right. It's worth one, tops. "Seven, then."

Jane rolled her eyes. "Look, I don't have time for this nonsense. I'll give you two, and that's already far too generous."

"Two? You trying to rob me?"

Jane tossed the slate back at Boris. "Like I said, no time for this nonsense." She turned to Adam. "Let's get outta here."

"All right, all right! Two, then!" Boris threw on an indignant expression. "Anything else you want to steal from me while you're at it?"

Jane glanced at the weapons rack.

Good thinking. Boris decided he wouldn't haggle with her for a simple weapon. Despite his illegal trade, he liked to think of himself as one of the good guys. *Girl like her shouldn't be walking around the Outer Ring unarmed. That pretty-boy of hers certainly won't be fighting off any brutes.*

Jane pointed at a black laser gun. "How much for that?"

"Jane!" Adam sounded alarmed. "What—"

"We don't know where we'll end up." She raised her eyebrows at Boris. "Well?"

Boris approached the rack. "You sure you want that one? It hasn't got a stun setting." He grabbed a gray laser gun and held it out. "This one does." To prove it, he flipped a switch on its side, turned to a blank section of the back wall, and fired. A bright blast flew out of the barrel but didn't damage the wall. Boris turned back to Jane. "Fifty. I'm practically gifting it to you."

Jane contemplated her options, then nodded. She reached into the cloth bag she carried on her shoulder and rummaged around. When she pulled her hand out, she held three bronze-colored cash discs.

Boris put the slate and the gun on a nearby table, then accepted the discs. He grabbed the rectangular disc reader strapped to his belt and stuck each disc into one of the device's slots to check their values. The numbers appeared on a tiny screen that glowed at the reader's base.

Two hundreds and a fifty. "Thanks for your business."

Jane picked up the slate and the gun from the table and dropped them in her bag.

Boris returned to the snack shack portion of his store. Jane added some food packets and a stimulant-laced beverage to her purchase before walking out the door with Adam.

Boris reclined in his chair. He held up his reader and spent a minute or so consolidating the value on the cash discs he'd received onto a single disc. After tossing the emptied discs into a box in the corner and sticking the one with value in a hidden drawer under his chair, he pulled out his slate to continue watching the Sarah DeHaven holovid.

The reporter detailed Sarah's dating history. Boris recognized one of her exes, and he bolted up in shock.

Sonuvabitch!

One of the men had visited his shop the night before, asking if he'd seen two people. Since the man hadn't mentioned a reward, Boris hadn't paid him any attention.

Devin Colt. So that was his name.

He suddenly realized why Jane and Adam had *both* looked familiar. He'd seen Adam once before, but not Jane—except in the hologram Colt had shown him briefly.

Son. Of a. Bitch*. So that's who they're running from. Looks like I'm not as sharp as I thought.*

He leaned back with a shrug. *Eh, guy didn't leave his contact info. Not my problem.*

<hr>

Jane rested against the back of her seat as the air taxi took off. *So far, so good.*

As long as Asin had been telling the truth about the *Hegira*—a Moray whose captain didn't ask questions—she and Adam would be all right. *In a few hours, we'll be in a different star system, and ISARK won't be able to reach us. Not for some time, at least. For once, I'm glad for interstellar politics.*

If she believed in such things, she would say that Fate wanted her and Adam to get away. Earlier that evening, she'd gone to Asin's old haunt—a dim bar called The Fiddler—hoping he'd be there. He'd recognized her and regretted being too booked up to accept her job offer, but he'd pointed her to Boris's shop and the *Hegira*. Outer Ring types were rarely that friendly, even if one paid them.

Then again, acting friendly was easy enough. Boris could still have screwed her over by selling her a traceable slate.

She pulled the device out of her bag and searched a Net directory for a Riley Winklepleck on Shimshawhenn. There was only one.

Riley had on a stiff, businesslike expression when he answered her call. The harsh light illuminating his pale face would have made him appear imposing if he were anyone other than Jane's demon pal, who looked about thirteen despite being only two years younger than her.

"This is the Chief of Security for—oh, it's you." Riley slouched against the back of his chair. "Yo, Janie, why didn't you answer my calls? Not cool! What's going on?"

"You were right." Jane didn't want the air taxi's pilot to figure out that she was running from ISARK, so she kept her answer vague. "They were already at the school. I'll tell you more later. Right now, I need a favor."

"What is it?"

"I had to get a new slate. Can you see where it is?"

Riley twisted his mouth in confusion. A few seconds later, his eyes widened with realization. "Gimme a sec."

Jane waited. She couldn't tell what Riley was doing, only that he was messing with his slate. He wrinkled his nose and jerked his face toward the camera, then raised his eyebrows and leaned back.

Amusing as Riley's expressions were, Jane didn't feel like watching them for however long it would take him to attempt to trace her slate. She glanced at Adam, who was in the seat beside her. He rested his forehead against the window, looking out as if dazed.

Jane wasn't sure how similar his sleep needs were to hers, but she knew he required rest like everyone else. She nudged him. "You should get some sleep once we board the Moray."

Adam didn't acknowledge her.

She nudged him harder. "Hey! Did you hear me?"

"What?" He turned to her.

"You can't keep this up forever. You'll pass out."

Adam looked away. "That's what I'm afraid of."

What would he say to me if our roles were reversed? "It's gonna be okay. You've resisted Pandora before. You can do it again, especially since she's not even real this time."

Ugh, my last speech was better. Hey Absolute, are You enjoying this? Seeing me try to be the nice one? Jane considered herself to be a lot of things, but "nice" was not among them. She longed to take Adam's pain away, to say something that would make him believe as strongly as she did that things would work out somehow.

Her capacity for words failed. She took his hand, hoping her touch could bring him comfort even if her words couldn't.

"Yo!" Riley's voice came from the slate. "You're good. I mean, I was doing a quick checkup, but I can tell, you know?"

If Riley can't trace me, no one can. "Thanks. I really appreciate it." A thought occurred to Jane. "Don't tell my brother we spoke."

"Uh... Why not?"

"Remember whom he works for?"

Riley thought for a moment, then opened his mouth in surprise. "You mean you're running from—"

"Hey!" Jane hoped the pilot was too busy navigating around the city's skyscrapers to have been paying attention. "I know you're more his friend than mine, but please, just... don't say anything if he contacts you, okay? I'll handle him."

Riley's mouth remained open. "Duuuude, that's so messed up! Keep me outta this!"

The transmission ended.

Dammit, Riley, don't you dare rat on me!

Jane reminded herself that even if Riley mentioned their communication to Devin, he had no idea where she was headed.

Wait... If Devin wants Adam captured, who sent Riley the tip about ISARK searching for AIs?

The only answer she could come up with was that some ISARK analyst didn't like what his or her bosses were doing and leaked the information not to Riley Winklepleck, but to Corsair, Riley's online activist alter-ego. Part of her held on to the hope that it *had* been Devin, and that everything he'd done in the tower had been an act.

She folded her slate and slipped it back in her bag. The spaceport was visible outside the window. *Almost there.*

Kel zipped up his military-style jacket and strode to the *Hegira*'s passenger entrance. As the owner of an independent vessel, he didn't need to don a crisp uniform before each voyage. However, he found that casual travelers were more likely to approach his ship out of the dozens of others at the spaceport if he looked more official. For that reason, he always introduced himself as "Captain Kelvin Proteus" and made sure to keep his graying brown hair and beard neatly trimmed.

He pressed an icon on a control touchscreen to open the *Hegira*'s door. A ramp extended to the ground. Once polished and welcoming, the ramp had been reduced over the decades into a dirty, dull patchwork of metal planks.

Much like the Hegira *herself. Poor old girl.*

Business had been dismal for the past few years. Actually, *pathetic* would have been a more accurate adjective. The *Hegira* had once been composed of almost a dozen individual starcars, each of which could detach and act as an independent vessel. They would serve as shuttles, since a starcar had an easier time finding places to land or dock than a full Moray. Led by the Head, with each starcar adjusting their engines in sequence, the *Hegira* had snaked across the galaxy with elegance and splendor through three generations of Proteus men and women.

But with a crew to pay and a family to feed, Kel's father had been forced to sell off the starcars one by one as times got tougher. Once in charge, Kel had found himself in a similar bind and sold off what was left until only two starcars remained. *Now, she looks like a guppy with a broken back.*

No longer were starcars organized by destination—there weren't enough. No longer did entrepreneurs set up restaurants or recreational facilities to entertain passengers on long journeys. Travelers generally ignored the independently owned transports, preferring the ones run by interstellar conglomerates, and vendors weren't interested in an old ship with hardly any customers.

Despite his misfortunes, Kel still considered himself one of the lucky ones. Most of his fellow captains had been bought out by the big corporations. He was one of the few independents left.

Four tough-looking men swaggered up the ramp. Kel gave them a welcoming beam. The man leading the group grunted and handed over a fistful of cash discs. His glare told Kel he'd beat the captain to a pulp if he didn't accept. Kel stuck the discs into his reader. The money was a little short of his usual price, but he wasn't about to make a fuss over it. *Not with this bunch.*

He gestured at the doorway. "Welcome aboard the *Hegira.* We'll fly you anywhere and everywhere."

The old line was less than unnecessary, but Kel liked saying it. It made him feel like a law-abiding citizen, even though most of his passengers weren't. If the IC's spaceflight controllers discovered that he wasn't checking travel docs and IDs, they'd shut him down on the spot. *But if I did check, I'd have been forced to shut myself down years ago.*

The next few passengers to arrive were legitimate travelers. A group of penniless, adventure-seeking students, by the looks of it. They gladly pressed their palms against the scanner on the wall, which pulled up their passports from an interstellar database. They had all the right documents, and they'd even prepaid for their flight. That they didn't have to submit to a security inspection appeared to surprise them.

Poor kids have no idea they're on the same ship as a bunch of thugs.

Kel spent the next hour or so greeting passengers. He told people he did it because he liked to see for himself who was boarding his ship, even though the truth was that he couldn't afford to hire any ship attendants. His entire crew comprised a pilot, a mechanic, and a security guard. If business didn't pick up soon, he'd have to sack the guard and carry an extra laser gun in case of trouble.

Still independent, still free. The *Hegira* was still *his* ship, and Kel loved every rusted bolt, every rattling engine, every busted floor panel.

The independents' corner of the spaceport was all but empty. *Guess no one's in the mood for flying tonight.*

He glanced at the time on the screen and frowned. Time to take off, and he only had eleven passengers. The *Hegira* could hold eleven *hundred*. The thought of all those empty cabins and passenger lounges filled him with sadness.

Someday, old girl, we'll return to our former glory. Just not today.

He pressed an icon, and the door started to close.

"Wait!" A young woman in a black dress rushed toward the ramp. Following a few steps behind was a young man with short, light brown hair.

Kel quickly punched the icon to reverse the door's progress.

The young woman ran up the ramp. "How much per person?"

Kel gave her a welcoming beam. "That depends on where you're heading, miss. The *Hegira* will drop off passengers on Allaven Central, Kipt, and Harir, in that order, but if your destination lies elsewhere, we can certainly accommodate you."

"Allaven Central." She sounded as if she were choosing at random.

"Excellent. That will be five hundred for the two of you."

The young woman reached into her bag, pulled out two bronze discs, and handed them to Kel. Kel was somewhat surprised that she paid in cash. She didn't look like the type who would be traveling on the down low. After checking that the amounts on the discs were correct, he proceeded with the standard protocol. "Thank you for your service. Please place your hand on the scanner there." He pointed.

The young woman's eyes, large to begin with, widened with alarm. She reminded Kel of a frightened child. "Do we have to?"

Kel furrowed his brow. The pair didn't strike him as being fugitives. Why wouldn't they want to be found?

The young woman seemed to read the question in his expression. She took the young man's hand in hers. "We're running away to get married. My family would be so mad if they found us. They'd never let me see him again."

Makes sense now. Kel spread his mouth into a grin. "Welcome aboard the *Hegira*. We'll fly you anywhere and everywhere."

The young woman relaxed as she boarded the ship. The young man appeared nervous. Kel recalled his own pre-wedding jitters and chuckled internally.

Let me guess: wasn't his idea to elope. Kid's lucky, though. You don't see a face like hers every day.

Kel longed to know their story, but even though they might have been willing to share, he didn't want his not-so-forthcoming passengers to think him nosy.

As he closed the door and made his way toward the bridge, he imagined what the pair's tale might be. He pictured the daughter of a powerful family, betrothed as a teenager to a world leader's pompous son, falling for a destitute but devoted young writer.

He stepped onto the bridge. Erin, who sat in the pilot's seat, twisted to face him and scoffed. "You're daydreaming again, aren't ya?" She must have noticed the slight smile lifting the corner of his mouth.

Damn, she caught me. His daughter had always made fun of him for being a hopeless romantic. Kel straightened. "All systems operational, pilot?"

Erin flicked her hand in a mock salute. "Yes, Cap'n."

"Good. Prepare systems for takeoff."

Erin blew a stray strand of red hair from her face and reached for the controls. A few minutes later, the *Hegira* soared out of Kydera Major's atmosphere and into the stars.

Kel reclined in his captain's seat at the back of the bridge, sighing at the sight of the empty seats beside Erin. Once, his daughter would have had a copilot, navigator, and cybernetics specialist to help her out.

Erin engaged lightspeed and steered the *Hegira* to Tunnel K18, one of the hundred or so interstellar tunnels in the Kyderan system. Distorted forms of stars and ships—images of what lay on the other side—glowed at the center of the moon-sized, cylindrical tunnel.

The tunnel instantly spewed the Moray across the galaxy and into the Elzaban region. Instead of heading to the nearby star system, Erin turned the ship left, passed seven moon-sized tunnels, then stopped the ship before Tunnel EB31, which would lead to the Allavenian system.

She looked over her shoulder. "You're up."

Kel approached the navigator's station. Allavenian space was always a bit tricky, since so many freighters waited by the interstellar tunnels. Of the system's twelve planets, Allaven Central was the only residential one. Factory and mining colonies covered the rest. Supply shuttles delivered large containers of various products to the freighters, which then carried them to warehouses across the IC.

Kel entered the communication numbers for Allaven Central's spaceflight center. "This is the *Hegira.*

Homeworld: Kydera Major, Republic of Kydera. Flight number: One-zero-zero-nine-dash-A-S-F-dash-nine-five."

"Stand by," the Allavenian controller said.

Kel waited patiently, knowing the controller was making sure his ship wouldn't run into another vessel on the other side.

After a few minutes, the Allavenian controller said, "You are clear to enter."

Erin steered the ship through the tunnel. The *Hegira* passed an enormous, boxy Omura freighter, which could have fit at least three *Hegira*-sized vessels inside. Kel watched on the viewscreen as the freighter opened the giant gates at its bottom.

A nearby supply shuttle extended a pair of robotic claws, which held a massive cargo container. A similar pair of claws reached out from the Omura, accepted the package, and pulled it into the freighter's cargo hold.

Kel leaned back in his chair, keeping his gaze on the viewscreen. Other freighters, delivering cargo containers to or accepting them from shuttles, scattered throughout Allavenian space. He found something relaxing about watching the movements of the giant machines, and he hardly noticed the time going by.

The *Hegira* was about six light-minutes from the nearest planet when the central computer informed Kel of an incoming transmission.

Kel sat up. "Put it through."

A man with angular facial features and dark, wavy hair filled a corner of the viewscreen. "Are you the captain of the passenger vessel *Hegira*?"

Shit, he looks official. "I am. Who are you?"

"Devin Colt. I'm an operative of ISARK." He looked down at something out of view. "I'm transmitting my credentials to your ship."

Erin, apparently also scared into seriousness, said in an unexpectedly formal-sounding voice, "Transmission received, Captain Proteus."

In a square below Colt's image, ISARK's insignia—a blue circle with the words "Intelligence and Security Agency of the Republic of Kydera" surrounding a stylized yellow sun—appeared.

"It carries ISARK's encoding." The slight quiver in Erin's voice betrayed her nervousness.

Kel narrowed his eyes, hoping the lines by them would make him appear steely, hiding his own disquiet. "What do you want?"

"A fugitive I have been pursuing is believed to be on board your vessel." Colt spoke in a no-nonsense tone.

Damn. Kel's worst fear was that someday, the authorities would stop him because of one of his less-than-honest passengers. It had to be one of the thuggish men.

Colt seemed to sense his unease. "Calm down, Captain. Just allow me to board, and if the fugitive is there, I'll apprehend him. If not, I'll leave and look elsewhere. Either way, you can carry on with your business."

Kel glanced again at the navigator's station. Colt was on board a Manta, a low-key transport, and not an armed police ship. Whoever he was after couldn't be too dangerous.

Although cooperation was the route to take, Kel couldn't have an army of ISARK operatives spooking his passengers. Authoritative as Colt seemed, he still needed a warrant for a boarding party, and considering his willingness to keep things simple, he likely didn't have one. Also, at second glance, Colt appeared younger than Kel had initially thought. He couldn't have been more than thirty, which meant he was likely a junior operative. He wouldn't want any trouble.

Kel cleared his throat. "I will allow you onto my ship, but you must come alone. Agreed?"

Colt nodded.

⟶ ⬦⬦ ⟵

Jane sped toward the bridge, hoping the captain would tell her that the ship had stopped due to some minor mechanical mishap. The twisting in her gut told her that her luck must have run out.

"Attention." The captain's voice blared over the comm. "We have been stopped for a random inspection. This is routine in the Allavenian system and no cause for alarm. All passengers and crew, please gather in the canteen."

He could be telling the truth. The Allavenians are probably just making sure we're not smuggling drugs or anything.

A star-filled window stretched across the wall ahead. Jane ran to it in hopes of catching a glimpse of whoever had ordered the *Hegira* to stop.

Almost invisible against the darkness of space, a triangular Manta transport hovered not far from the *Hegira*. A small, narrow Remorina shuttle emerged from the transport.

Jane recognized ISARK's insignia on the shuttle's side, and the twisting in her gut tightened.

Shit. How did he find me?

CHAPTER 8

AGAIN AND AGAIN

DEVIN STOPPED HIS REMORINA a few yards from the *Hegira*'s entrance near the front of the ship. He swiped a command on the shuttle's control touchscreen. Mechanical whirring hummed behind him as the Remorina's airlock adjusted to match the Moray's door.

After the docking light by the touchscreen turned green, Devin brought the Remorina closer to the Moray. A metal clunking sound and a second green light told him the shuttle had successfully docked.

He looked up at the viewscreen, which displayed Captain Proteus' weathered face in the lower corner. "I've docked. Open the door."

"As you wish." Captain Proteus turned to the red-haired pilot behind him and repeated the command. A few seconds later, he turned back to Devin. "You may board when ready."

Devin stood and walked to the airlock. Another task he had no choice but to complete, another mission forcing him to take actions he would come to regret.

Rourke's voice growled in Devin's head. *If the AI escapes again, there will be consequences.*

Devin pushed all thoughts of his kid sister out of his mind and opened the airlock. If he was to accomplish his mission, he had to view Adam as a target, and Jane as the target's accomplice.

The first door rose, and he stepped through. It closed behind him. The second door slid open, revealing the *Hegira*'s blue-gray corridor.

Captain Proteus's face appeared on a screen by the door. "I've asked everyone to gather in the canteen."

"Show me." Devin examined the security video that filled the screen. Neither Adam nor Jane was among the passengers. *As expected.*

They had to be somewhere on board the *Hegira*, and Jane was armed. Devin had planted bugs in Boris's Goods, The Fiddler, and a number of other Outer Ring destinations Jane could have gone to before he'd returned to Sector 1708 the previous night. The only reason it had taken him so long to catch up was because Ibara was currently at the part of its orbit furthest from the interstellar tunnels.

"He's not there," Devin said. "Look through your security feeds for a twenty-three-year-old male, about five-nine with brown hair and green eyes. He's probably with a girl of the same age with long, dark hair."

Captain Proteus reappeared on the screen, his brow furrowed in a quizzical expression. "All right. Give me a minute." He walked out of view.

"Seems weird, don't it?" The pilot, speaking in quiet tones that she probably thought wouldn't be overheard, sounded puzzled. "All these thugs in our canteen, and ISARK's after a harmless-looking kid."

He's not harmless. Twenty-two deaths. There could be twenty-two more. Devin had to keep reminding himself of that.

Captain Proteus returned. "They're in Cabin A-twenty-three on the top level."

"Let me know if they change locations." Devin strode down the corridor and found an elevator. Morays only had three levels—the bridge and main entrance were on the lowest—and the trip up was almost instantaneous.

The elevator doors opened. Devin stepped out. Gray numbers gleamed on each dark red cabin door lining the corridor.

Nineteen... Twenty... Twenty-one...

A white blast flew from Cabin 23's open door. Devin jumped back. "Jane! It's me!"

"I know. That was a warning shot." Jane spoke in a low, threatening voice. "I won't let you take Adam."

"You know what he's done."

"He didn't know what was happening." Her voice rose in a pleading tone. "Those were just nightmares to him. How many crazy things have you done in your dreams, things you couldn't control?"

That's irrelevant. "It's not you I'm after, Pony."

"You come after Adam, you come after me. I thought I made that clear at the temple."

Enough talk. Rourke's authoritative voice over Devin's communication implant was loud enough to drown out Devin's own thoughts. Before he could stop it, Devin's hand gripped his gun and fired it through the doorway.

⪼◇⪻

Jane screamed. A black-rimmed hole pierced the wall beside her. Her brother had *fired* at her. Not a stun blast— he'd actually tried to *shoot* her.

Silence, as though Devin were as shocked as she was.

Devin's got perfect aim. He wouldn't miss unless it was on purpose. She finally found her voice. "What the *hell*, Devin?"

More silence. Finally, Devin said, "That was *your* warning shot. You have ten seconds before I go in."

Jane blinked in disbelief. *ISARK's watching him. I have to talk to him when he's alone, not under orders. Right now, I've just gotta get out.*

Adam stood by the door's controls, back against the wall so as not to be seen from the corridor. His apologetic expression told her that he wanted to surrender.

She gave him a fierce glare to tell him he'd better not try and mouthed, *Stick to the plan.*

She fired a series of stun blasts out the open door to make Devin back off. Adam pressed the controls to close and lock the door.

Jane spun toward the back of the room. Behind her was the reason she'd chosen that particular cabin: the large window facing the hydroponics garden. Knowing she'd probably have to run, she'd opened it ahead of time.

"C'mon!" She climbed onto the windowsill and jumped out. She landed by a dead bush. Her skirt snagged on its dry branches, and she yanked it.

Adam followed. His shirt caught on a thorn, and he ripped it free, creating a V-shaped tear by his left shoulder.

Leafless boughs of dying trees reached toward the garden's high ceiling, which had only one sun-imitating light left. Once, the garden must have imitated a lush jungle. Only a dark forest of bare trunks and withered leaves remained.

Jane ran into the trees, barely able to make out the ground before her. Her bag bounced against her hip. What she would do after she reached the cabins on the other side, she didn't know. She hadn't planned that far ahead; her mind had been too busy churning with ways to convince Devin to let Adam go. *That was a freaking waste of time.*

Adam grabbed her and pulled her behind a tree. A white blast flew past.

Shit! When'd Devin get here?

It occurred to her that he had the captain's cooperation, and that any locks would be useless, since the central computer could override them. *Dammit!*

Jane raised her weapon, intending to fire back. *Never hesitate. You taught me that, bro.*

Adam grabbed her hand and shook his head.

"Why the hell not?" Jane whispered. "He's willing to knock *me* out!"

"You'll give away our location," Adam replied, barely audible.

Crap, he's right. It would be smarter to try to make it through the dark, dense trees unseen.

Leaves crunched beneath Devin's quick footsteps. Jane spotted a branch on the ground nearby. Hoping to throw him off, she grabbed it and hurled it to the side. Devin's footsteps moved away from her.

"Let's go!" She bolted to the other side.

Dark cabin windows lay past the trees ahead. *So close...*

A blast. Jane stifled a yelp. She instinctively raised her weapon to fire back, then reminded herself that bright blasts were easier to pinpoint than rustling noises. That Devin had missed so widely told her he was some distance away and couldn't see her.

She leaped over a fallen tree and landed on the path by the cabins.

Adam ran up to one of the windows and tried to open it. "It's locked."

Figures. Jane flipped the switch to set her gun on blast. "Get behind me. *Now.*"

Adam heeded the urgency in her voice.

Jane fired at the window, blowing out the entire pane with repeated shots. Knowing that Devin would have seen the light, she grabbed Adam's shoulders and pulled him down as she dropped to the ground. A blast flew over her.

She flipped the switch on her weapon, then sprang up and pulled the trigger over and over, spraying the trees with stun blasts. At least she could force Devin to seek cover. "Adam! Go!"

She heard Adam run to the window. Still blasting, she glanced over her shoulder. Adam had climbed into the cabin. He motioned for her to follow.

A returned blast hit Jane's right arm, causing it to go numb. Her grip slackened, and the gun slipped out.

Devin, you suck!

She scooped the weapon up and raced to the window. Needles seemed to pierce her numb hand as Adam helped her onto the windowsill.

Jane jumped into the cabin, darted across, and opened the door. Adam followed her out. She sprinted blindly down the dim corridor.

Now what?

Even if she managed to stun Devin, she was still trapped on a starship. His ISARK cohorts could still get her. If only she had an escape vehicle...

The starcar! That's it!

Morays all had the same layout. The tunnel connecting the two segments would be ahead and to the right. With renewed energy, she dashed forward.

As she rounded the corner, she realized that Devin would probably make it onto the second starcar before she could reach the bridge on the lowest level and detach.

She stopped abruptly. *I've gotta lose him.*

Adam gave her a questioning look.

Jane noticed a cabin door labeled "Housekeeping" and remembered a trip she'd taken on a Moray a few years back. She'd dropped a load of laundry down the chute in the housekeeping closet, only to realize she'd left her slate in her dress pocket.

The chute leads to the lowest level, and the laundry room's right by the tunnel.

"Jane!" Devin's voice came from the corridor behind her. "That's enough. You can't outrun me."

Watch me, you jerk.

Jane opened the door to the housekeeping room and jerked her head to tell Adam "this way." Once he was in, she closed the door behind her.

Adam stared at the chute. "Please tell me you're not thinking of going down that."

"What else?" Jane stuffed the gun into her bag. "Go!"

Adam pulled open the chute's metal door and climbed in. Jane heard him bang against the chute's sides as he slid down.

She approached the chute and briefly wondered how she was supposed to close the door behind her before realizing it wouldn't make a difference. The captain had probably already told Devin where she was. She would have to barricade the chute's exit from below.

She tensed at the sight of the blackness before her. Adam had already gone down, and it was too late to back out.

She climbed in and slid down the steep, winding chute. The speed was exhilarating, and her anxiety disappeared. *This is freaking fun!*

A dim bluish light appeared.

She flew out of the chute, crashed into something, and tumbled to the ground. Adam had broken her fall. She'd knocked him over; he lay on his back, blinking up at her. She grinned. "Sorry. But that wasn't so bad, was it?"

She stood. Her knees and shins ached from the rough landing. At least the feeling was starting to return to her right hand. She looked around for something with which to block the chute.

Adam must have had the same idea. He ran to a nearby shelf, which held dozens of towels, and shoved it toward the chute's exit. Jane scrambled to help him. The shelf was so heavy, it had to be thick enough that Devin would have to spend a few minutes blasting his way out if he followed.

She rushed to the laundry room's exit. Finding it locked, she yelled, "Captain, you might as well open it! I'll blast it to bits if you don't!"

The door slid open, and she smirked triumphantly. Evidently, the captain didn't want any more damage done to his ship. *Poor guy. He's about to lose half of it.*

The entrance to the tunnel between starcars lay ahead. Jane pressed the controls to open it.

Jane heard Adam behind her as she zoomed down the tunnel. *Last time I was running around a space vessel, I was the one following, and Devin was the one with the gun, defending me.* The thought was almost funny. Despite her situation, she still couldn't accept that her brother would turn against her.

The tunnel led to a corridor. Jane knew the starcar's crew lounge and control room lay on the other side of the blank wall to her left. Through a long window to her right, she glimpsed the gigantic Omura freighters. With their boxy shapes and cavernous cargo holds, they reminded her of flying hangars.

Ahead, the corridor branched to the left. Jane swung around the corner, darted through the doorway to the crew lounge, and raced across the wide room. The door to the control room was open.

"What are you doing?" Adam sounded confused.

Jane didn't have time to reply. She had to take off before the captain figured out her plan. Her head rushed with a mixture of panic and excitement. She reached for the control panel. Her hands remembered what to do even though her mind felt uncertain. She'd only seen the controls of a Moray once before.

The viewscreens lit up. She pressed the controls to detach the starcar. Metallic clunking sounded in the distance, and the ship lurched.

Jane revved up the engines. "Buckle up, Adam."

Devin raced to his Remorina. By the time he'd realized what Jane's plan was, he'd been too late to enter the tunnel before the starcar detached.

A glimmer of pride at his kid sister's cleverness briefly banished his uneasiness. *She's smart.*

You'd better not let the AI get away this time! Rourke's shouting through the communication implant brought Devin back to his task.

I should've stopped Jane in the garden. Devin's aim had been much poorer than usual. The thought of stunning his kid sister seemed too abhorrent. Even though the effects of a stunner were temporary, he couldn't bear the thought of causing her pain. *And yet, I'm about to take Adam from her.*

"Colt!" Captain Proteus' voice over the comm sounded higher than before. "Your fugitives hijacked my ship!"

You think? "Why didn't you override her command to detach?"

No response. Devin figured that the override mechanism was busted—not unlikely, considering the *Hegira*'s state.

He reached the *Hegira*'s main entrance. "Captain! Open the door!"

The door slid open. He entered the Remorina, strapped himself into the pilot's seat, and took off. The chart to his left displayed every ship in Allavenian space, color-coded by vessel type. There were only two lone Moray starcars: the two halves of the *Hegira*. As Devin steered the Remorina toward the starcar Jane piloted, he opened a communication channel.

Jane's face appeared in a rectangle on the viewscreen. Dark waves of hair clung to the sweat on her face. "*What?*"

Devin was glad Adam wasn't visible in the communication window. He didn't need the kid's face reminding him that his target was someone who'd called him a friend. "I'm asking you to stop this madness."

"Madness?" Jane's eyes snapped with fury. "You're the one chasing your little sis with a gun!"

Devin chose not to respond to her accusation. It was true, and he had no defense. "If you would just let Adam turn himself in, this will all be over. I know he's willing."

Jane set her jaw with stubbornness. "I don't know what it is with you guys and surrendering, but I wouldn't let you do it when they were after you, and I'm not giving up on Adam either. What would you do if Sarah was the one they wanted?"

I can't think about that. "Jane, just—"

"Just what? Why won't *you* just listen? Adam's not some dangerous AI. You—you *know* him!"

Remind her again that he's an illusion. Rourke's voice slid into Devin's mind. *Tell her—*

It didn't work last time, and it won't work now. Devin could almost see Rourke's scowl.

Jane glanced at the controls. She reached for something, then pressed her lips together.

She's considering lightspeed. "Don't do it, Pony. It's too crowded, and that starcar's not exactly maneuverable."

"Oh, yeah?" The starcar zipped forward and vanished from visual range.

Dammit, Jane! Devin swiped the command to engage lightspeed, as well. He watched the purple dot representing her starcar on the chart and pursued it.

The starcar wove through a group of supply ships. Jane's vessel clipped one of them, and Devin's heart jumped. In the rectangular segment of the viewscreen still showing her communication feed, her eyes held a look of maniacal determination.

He checked her trajectory. She appeared to be headed for the interstellar tunnels. The Remorina was programmed to shut down if it ventured too far from its mothership.

Devin considered hailing his team on the Manta, but they wouldn't be able to help. The Manta was unarmed.

The Remorina, on the other hand, was meant for short-distance chases. Devin's hand reached out against his will and swiped a command to activate the cannons. He clenched his fist to keep from pressing the "confirm" icon. *No, Rourke. I'm not firing at her.*

I want that AI. Rourke's voice was low. *Do what needs to be done, or I'll do it for you.*

Fuck! Devin reluctantly pressed "confirm." *Better me than him.*

Two cannons unfolded from the roof of his shuttle. The starcar's scopes must have detected the weapons, for Jane opened her mouth in shock. "What the hell? Are you gonna blow me up?"

Devin's shuttle was almost within firing range. "I'm going to disable your engines. For the last time, Pony, stop."

"Go to hell!"

I'm already there. Devin turned his gaze away from his sister's face and focused on the purple dot on the chart. It didn't help. Purple was Jane's favorite color. *It's not her I'm targeting. It's an AI who has caused twenty-two deaths.*

The conscience he'd tried to silence whispered, *You mean the kid who saved you from Pandora, and who trusted you enough to risk his life for yours.*

No more delays. That voice was Rourke's.

Devin engaged the targeting system. A white wire-frame image of the starcar occupied the lower left corner of the viewscreen. It resembled a rectangular box with four finlike engines of varying sizes protruding from either side. Red crosshairs indicated where the cannons were aimed.

Devin maneuvered the Remorina to line it up behind the starcar's left lightspeed engine. Jane twisted her vehicle, but it was not as maneuverable as the small shuttle he piloted.

He fired.

Jane screamed. She pressed something out of view. The starcar slowed to a sublight speed.

The Remorina zipped past. Devin stopped and drew a breath. *Just finish the job.*

He flipped the shuttle and headed in the direction of the starcar. Jane veered away from the Remorina.

Oh, Pony. You don't have lightspeed anymore. It took seconds to get back within firing range. He swerved his shuttle, took aim, and disabled the right forward engines, both lightspeed and sublight.

Jane's eyes became round with alarm. She braked and stared at something out of view.

Devin slowed the Remorina. "Jane, please. Let me board, or I'll just take out the rest of your engines."

Jane continued staring. "You're right. What was I thinking?" Her wide-eyed expression didn't change as she spoke. "You've got better aim, better reflexes, better piloting skills... Hell, you're probably smarter than me. What chance did I have? You've always better at everything." The words sounded flat, as though she let them roll out without caring what she said.

For once, Devin couldn't tell what she was thinking. *She's probably in shock or something.* He waited for her to come to grips with the fact that she had no choice but to surrender.

Jane narrowed her eyes at whatever she stared at. "But there's one thing I've got." She looked up with a smirk. "I'm crazier than you."

She fired up her remaining engine. The starcar swung to the right in a wide arc.

What the hell is she doing? Devin revved up his engines in pursuit. The wide, open cargo hold of an Omura freighter gaped ahead. The freighter appeared sideways as it moved slowly toward the tunnels. Its enormous gates were closing.

The starcar headed into the shrinking gap between the gates.

"Jane, *no!*"

Sparks spewed from the gates' edges as the starcar scraped through them. The gates slammed shut.

Devin stopped the Remorina. Before he could hail the freighter, it sped off at lightspeed and disappeared into a tunnel.

Shit! She must have been stalling with her words, waiting for the freighter to move into position.

Jane's laughter rang from the speakers. "Later, bro!" She ended the transmission.

Devin slammed his head against the back of his seat. *Fuck.*

How could you fail again? Rourke's wrathful voice filled his head.

I'll catch up soon enough. Devin straightened. *It won't be hard to figure out where that freighter's going.*

You let her go. Rourke's voice was a menacing growl. *Tell me, Colt, who will die next because you had to go easy on your precious Pony?*

CHAPTER 9

EVERYONE'S FAKE ON THE NET

RILEY CLENCHED A JOYSTICK ON his Angler's control panel, wishing he'd chosen a more maneuverable fighter. If he had, maybe Eaglewing, in his smaller but faster Barracuda, wouldn't have done so much damage to Riley's ship during their last encounter. As it was, all Riley could do was hope Eaglewing wouldn't find the crater his Angler was hiding in until after the repair bot finished patching up the ship.

Riley aimed the cannons upward. If Eaglewing flew over, he could destroy the Barracuda from below. With the generators in their present state, though, he couldn't fire without compromising the life support systems.

The green communication light blinked. Riley pressed an icon on the control touchscreen to put it through.

Eaglewing's face appeared in a rectangle on the viewscreen. "Give it up, Corsair."

Riley shared enough physical traits with Eaglewing that a stranger might mistake them for cousins: same pale complexion, similar slanted black eyes. Except Riley wasn't lame enough to gel his hair into stupid black spikes. Or dumb enough to show his real face; the face Eaglewing saw was a swarthy avatar Riley had created.

Riley relaxed his expression, hoping it would make his square-jawed avatar appear cool. "Don't bother trying to find me. I'm the best demon in the galaxy, so when *I* veil something, it might as well not exist."

"Veiling doesn't help when your ship's bled a trail of particles."

Shit!

Riley looked at the tracker screen and saw the Barracuda headed in his direction. He shoved the steering bars forward. Better to put up a fight with a damaged ship than sit there waiting for Eaglewing to get him. The Angler shot up out of the crater, and Riley turned it toward the oncoming Barracuda. Eaglewing had wandered right into his line of fire.

"*Fire all!*" Riley unleashed a volley of missiles.

Eaglewing yelled in terror. The video cut out as his ship exploded into a flaming cloud of debris.

Riley pumped his fists. "*Hah!* Gotcha, buddy! Looks like—"

Eaglewing reappeared in the viewscreen, laughing his head off. "Dude, did you really think it'd be that easy?"

Riley's jaw dropped. "What... How...?"

"You're not the only demon in this duel."

The debris field in front of Riley vanished. The Barracuda appeared in the rear view, cannons pointed right at him. He gasped.

Eaglewing fired his torpedoes. "Later, loser!"

Riley twisted at the controls, trying to evade the missiles.

Boom. Boom. Boom.

In that instant, all Riley could see or feel was a chaotic jumble of blinding flames and scorching heat and—

Text flashed in his visor: *Game Over.*

Riley blinked as the mocking orange letters flashed before his vision. It took him a few seconds to remember what was going on. The so-called "experts" claimed that leaving a virtu-world was like waking from a lucid dream.

Heh. That's an understatement if there ever was one.

Riley felt as if he'd been yanked from one reality to another. There had been nothing surreal or dreamlike about that game.

He pulled the VR visor off his face, blinking rapidly as his eyes adjusted to the light. The sun was at that annoying angle where it shone straight through the glass wall of Jim X's mountain mansion. *That's it. We're moving to the canyon.*

The elderly former tech tycoon had hired Riley as his security chief, but Riley knew the job was an excuse to keep him around. Riley actually liked hanging out with the old guy and listening to Jim X's tales of former glory. Even though he was barely twenty-one and Jim X pushing eighty, they got along like old pals. And the perks were *awesome.* As the only surviving member of the Thiel family, Jim X owned the entire estate, which Riley was in charge of.

A beep emitted from Riley's slate, which lay on the gray carpet beside him. He picked it up with a grimace. *Ugh, Eaglewing.*

A video window displaying Eaglewing's smug face appeared. "Man, that was *epic*! Who's the best now?"

Riley crossed his arms. "You may've won a round of *Space Duels*, but you've got nothing on me. Later, nov." He hung up with a smirk, knowing Eaglewing would stew over the insult. Experienced demons hated being called by the term usually reserved for newbies.

Riley glanced up at the large control screen, which displayed a list of various machines and bots. The words "ALL SYSTEMS NORMAL" shone in bright green letters across the top. As long as he was available to respond in case they said anything else, he considered himself to be on the job.

I love it when I can work without working. Riley yawned. *What should I do next?*

A thought poked at his mind, a yearning to figure out what the hell was going on with the Colts. Devin and Jane were as close as siblings got. What freaky forces could have pitted them against each other?

Riley tried to push the thought away. *Not gonna get involved.*

He opened a window on his slate and glanced over a list of Netsites, which Acuitas had ordered according to his preferences. Nothing appealed to him, so he opened a new window and browsed the forums of his Netcrew, Citizen Zero. *"My" Netcrew?* He bobbed his head as he considered the validity of that statement. *Yeah, that's about right.*

The Citizen Zero guys weren't too happy with Riley's claims to taking charge. Still, Riley's role in the whole Pandora thing had granted him godlike status on the Net, so they'd begrudgingly accepted his rule. *Rule?* Hah*! King Riley. I could get used to that.*

The thought poked at his mind again. *No! Not my business!*

He tried to turn his attention back to Citizen Zero. The poke became a smack. As much fun as he had with those guys, he didn't know what most of them even looked like. They knew him only as Corsair, the brilliant, authoritative demon who always had his shit together. He knew them only by their Netnames, and for all he knew, they were as screwy as he was. *Everyone's fake on the Net.*

If something happened to him, would they respond? Would they impersonate a merc to save his life, as Devin had eight years ago? Would they spend hours engaging in wickedly fun rant-fests with him, as Jane had countless times? Would they patiently listen to his grief, as Adam did so often?

Those three were the only real friends he had other than the old guy. Their business *was* his business.

Riley pulled up Devin's contact info and tried calling him.

No answer. There hadn't been an answer for weeks, even when Riley used his special skills to try less conventional routes of communications. ISARK seemed to have swallowed his pal whole.

"Right where I left you." The voice was Jim X's.

Riley looked up. The old guy had his usual amused grin on his wrinkled face. Seemed like he found everything Riley did funny.

"Yo, Jah-Mex!" Riley flicked his hand in a sarcastic wave. "Fancy seeing you here. Need something?"

"If I did, would you do it?"

"Uh... Sure. Later. I'm kinda busy."

Jim X raised his gray eyebrows. "Riley, do you ever do your job?"

"Hey, the bots keep this place running, don't they?" Riley crossed his arms. "Who do you think made that happen? Now, scat! I've got stuff to do."

Jim X chuckled. "Do I want to know what?"

"Nope."

"That's what I thought. Don't get arrested, okay?"

Riley snickered. "Like they'll ever catch me. Riley Winklepleck's record is spotless. It's that demon Corsair you've gotta worry about."

The old guy let out a laugh, then left. Riley waited for him to close the door behind him, then turned back to his slate.

Anyhow, where was I?

Logic told him to try Jane instead of Devin. She'd be more forthcoming. Riley pulled up his communications log. A few cyber maneuvers later, he was able to call back the slate she'd contacted him from previously.

"Riley?" Her confused expression turned to fear as she widened her eyes. "How'd you find me?"

Whoa, she's spooked. "Chill. I've no idea where you are. I just pinged you through that app you used." Riley tried to make out her surroundings. A bluish glow lit her face, and the background was dark. He guessed that the screen she looked at was her only source of light. "Anyhow... Uh... I was just wondering if everything was all right."

"Thought you wanted to stay out of it." She cocked her head with her familiar funky smile.

Riley huffed. *Smartass.* "I'm worried, okay? I learn that Adam's on some creepy ISARK list, that you're on the run with him, that Devin's the one after you..." The worries built upon each other as he spoke, until they exploded into a flaming ball of freak-out. "Just tell me what's going on!"

Jane dropped her smile. "I'm all right. So's Adam. When this is all over, I'll have a helluva story to tell you."

Her words did little to calm Riley. "What's happening?"

"You pretty much covered it. Everything's messed up." Something out of view caught Jane's attention. She knitted her eyebrows. "I've gotta go. Talk to you later." She reached forward as if intending to end the communication, then stopped. "Hey, you don't think of Adam as a machine, do you?"

Riley gave her a you're-dumb look. He'd chosen to ignore the vagaries of science and philosophy and who-knew-what-else surrounding the question "What makes you human?" and accept the simplest answer. "Uh... No."

Jane smiled, but her eyes seemed kind of sad. "That's good to know. I don't know who's on my side anymore. Anyway, later."

The transmission ended.

Riley leaned back on his elbows and gazed blankly at the purplish gray mountains outside. It didn't seem like Devin to turn against not only his friend, but his sister as well.

Maybe ISARK actually brainwashed him. They've got tech that can do that.

Almost a year ago, the Netcrew known as the Collective had leaked a bunch of secret government memos. One of the memos had mentioned the development of a brain implant that could control a person's thoughts and actions. It could basically turn a person into a compliant robot.

Riley's brain ran wild with possibilities. Maybe ISARK was bringing in anyone who'd ever worked for them, implanting them, and turning them into drones to do their dirty work.

An alarm blared. Riley bolted up. "THREAT DETECTED" flashed in red letters across the control screen.

Outside the glass wall, a trio of black, fan-shaped Betta attack drones flew straight at him.

Holy shit!

———◆———

Devin whirled as two gates, one on either side of him, slammed down from the ceiling of the Manta's corridor. Trapped in a narrow space, he instinctively drew his weapon. *What the hell?*

I told you there would be consequences. Rourke's voice was a low rumble in his mind.

The screen on the wall beside him lit up, displaying an image of a glass and steel mansion. Red lines formed a grid, and the view zoomed in rapidly. Devin realized he was watching a flying drone's visual feed. As the drone drew closer to the mansion, he saw someone inside.

Riley stared in the direction of the camera, mouth open and eyes wide with fear.

"Riley!" Devin raised his gun with the intention of blasting his way out. His arm dropped to his side. He tried to raise it again. His hand shook from the effort.

There's nothing you can do. From the tone of Rourke's voice, he had to be sneering. *Even if you get out, your Manta's light-hours from Shimshawhenn.*

Red crosshairs appeared over Riley's face.

* * *

An explosion boomed. Riley stared, frozen in terror. Black debris rained down outside. Two Bettas spiraled away from the mansion, avoiding the fire of a swarm of flying security bots.

Whew, that was close! "Get 'em, bots!"

Riley had programmed those new bots himself. They were *way* better than the average drone. Faster, more agile. Equipped with powerful laser cannons. They were small, but man, did they pack a punch.

Riley lifted his chin. *Just like me.*

A Betta abruptly veered, heading back toward the mansion. It zigzagged as it evaded the bots. The terror returned, and Riley dashed to the exit. *I'm outta here!*

Glass shattered as blasts pierced the window. Searing pain shot through Riley's thigh, so intense it spread through his entire body. He screamed as he fell. *Shit!*

Tears blurred his vision. He tried to get up, but his leg collapsed beneath him.

Boom. Heat from an explosion seared Riley's skin. He attempted to stand. Pain shot through him, he collapsed again. *C'mon, bots...*

More blasts. Riley tried to contain his panic, but couldn't. Though he'd faced danger before, he'd never been alone and injured before. His leg throbbed. The wetness of blood pooled around him. *Someone help me... Please...*

Boom. A third explosion thundered. Scorching heat and stinging debris blasted him. Riley curled up on the ground and grabbed his head with both hands, covering his face with his arms. There would be no "Game Over" if the world went dark.

Silence, disturbed only by familiar mechanical whirring.

Is it over? Riley slowly uncovered his face. The bots hovered in a neat line outside. No more alarm, no more blasts. Black debris lay scattered among the broken glass and on the ground outside.

He shifted his gaze over to the screen. "THREAT ELIMINATED" flashed in green letters. He exhaled in relief.

He tried to get up, but didn't have the strength to push off the ground. His face felt cold, and dark spots splattered across his vision.

"Computer." He meant to yell, but his voice emerged as a strained whimper. "Medical... emergency..."

The computer beeped with acknowledgement. Wouldn't be long before a med team arrived from the city. Nauseous from pain, Riley felt as though he was sinking into the ground.

What about the old guy? With much effort, he lifted his head. "Computer! Show me Jim X!"

The computer beeped again. "PENDING" appeared on the screen in bright blue letters. A few seconds later, a video from a security cam replaced the letters.

Jim X stood in a small, windowless room. A confused frown wrinkled his already crinkly face. "Riley! What the devil is going on?"

He's good. Riley relaxed, resting his head on the floor. *Awesome. I'm the best security chief ever.*

Riley had equipped each mansion with guard bots, programmed to escort Jim X to safety the moment they detected a threat. *And "escort" means "pick the old guy up and shove him into a blast-proof room." Hah! I'll have to review the bots' visual feeds so I can see the look on his face!*

Like anyone who had ever been important, Jim X had plenty of enemies. Some self-righteous dumbasses even blamed him for Pandora's existence. The list of people who might have sent the drones after the old guy was pretty long. Riley groaned at the thought of having to go through it.

Engines rumbled in the distance. He caught a glimpse of an approaching air transport. Through his watery vision, he made out the remnants of destroyed drones scattered outside.

I win, assholes.

<hr>

Devin let out a breath as he watched two paramedics attend to an unconscious Riley. Outside the mansion, a police vehicle landed.

The gates lifted.

Apologies for the trap. Rourke's words dripped with insincerity. *You needed to see what your failure has caused. That kid's lucky to be alive. Remember, luck runs out. Get the AI.*

Devin clenched his fist around the handle of his gun. *Yes, sir.*

CHAPTER 10

CONTRITION

ADAM YANKED AT THE RESTRAINTS binding his wrists to the lab table. He had to get out before the scientists returned. His arm stung from where they'd ripped off his skin, and his head ached from lingering effects of the electric shocks.

To his surprise, he managed to tear up the restraints. He stared at the broken metal in disbelief. *That's it?*

Choosing not to question his luck, Adam jumped off the table and rushed to the door. The door disappeared, replaced by a gun-filled shelf. Adam froze. *Something's wrong.*

A high-pitched scream.

Adam spun. Jane lay bound to the table in his place. Blood streamed down the side of her face. The scientists had reappeared, hovering over her with their instruments.

"*Jane!*" Adam's hand flew toward the weapons shelf. He tensed to stop himself. *I've been here before...*

Memories filled his mind—blank faces with empty eyes, people robbed of the lives the Absolute had created.

Jane's screams shredded the air. Adam closed his eyes. *This isn't real.*

"You're not going to save her?" From the sound of Pandora's voice, she had to be right beside him. "*Look at me.*"

Adam's eyes opened against his will.

Pandora's deep blue wire-frame face stared into his. "Humans believe that love is all-powerful. You think of yourself as human, and yet you won't rescue the one you claim to love?"

"*Adam!*" Jane called him between heart-wrenching screams. "Adam, please!"

Adam wanted to run to her and destroy those who would hurt her. *That's not Jane.* "Go away, Pandora."

"Did you really think you could escape me by refusing to sleep?" Pandora moved closer, drawing him into the twin abysses that were her eyes. "You have no thoughts that aren't mine, no will I can't bend. I am your creator, your Absolute Being."

Adam's hand flew to the shelf. He whirled to face the scientists, arm outreached, gun in hand.

Pandora snarled, "I command, you kill."

The scientists looked up with alarm. They shouted, but Adam couldn't make out their words.

He struggled to lower his weapon. "I won't let you—"

His finger pulled the trigger.

No!

A woman fell backward. Blood spilled down the blue lab coat she wore, darkening the white badge on her sleeve.

The gun went off again, and again, and again. Adam watched in horror, unable to stop himself. Those actions— they weren't his, and yet it was his hand that held the gun.

Four people lay dead on the ground: three women and a man, all wearing the same blue lab coats.

No... Please, no...

Alarms shrieked. Through the tears blurring his vision, Adam saw someone motionless on the table. It wasn't

Jane; it was Jonathan King. He lay in pieces with his torso splayed and damaged mechanical parts surrounding him.

Pounding footsteps. Adam turned. His arm took aim at a man who approached. He couldn't stop himself from pulling the trigger again. And again. And—

Bursts of pain in his chest.

Adam fell backward. The gun slid from his grasp.

More heat as blasts hit him.

"What the fuck?" A dark-skinned woman with long dreadlocks and a sharp face, twisted in confusion, peered down at him.

Adam's eyes fell shut.

The pain disappeared. The noises silenced. His body rested on something soft. He opened his eyes. A cracked ceiling, lit by the pale dawn. The sofa he lay on. Light streaming in from a dirty window.

Tears continued falling down his face—those must have been real. *Like the deaths.*

You are nothing but what I made you to be. Pandora's cold voice rang in his head.

Shaking, Adam grasped his arms. Whose lives had he destroyed? Whose dreams would never be fulfilled because of his failure? Unable to stay awake any longer, he'd succumbed to sleep the previous night.

I told you, my child. Pandora's face glowed in his mind. *You can neither deny nor defy me.*

You won't take another life. There was only one way to stop her, to stop himself. It was something he should have done days ago. If he had, five people would still be alive.

Adam stood. Jane lay on the narrow bed in the corner, still asleep. Her plan to find a dead zone was a good one, but by the time he reached safety, it could be too late for whoever his nightmares would target next.

Jane's bag sat on the floor beside her. Adam approached. She was a sound sleeper—she wouldn't hear him.

I'm sorry, Jane. I love you. He kissed her forehead. *Good-bye.*

⟡

Jane blinked, her head heavy with drowsiness. Unwilling to crawl out of bed just yet, she shut her eyes.

Now, where am I? Um... Aryus, in the Ajorasian system.

The freighter she'd invaded couldn't have missed a giant-ass starcar entering their cargo hold. Nevertheless, they'd continued to their destination; the ship must have been on autopilot. The moment the freighter had opened its gates, Jane had zoomed out.

That was some pretty awesome piloting. Not everyone could have flown a ship backward, using the reverse engines—meant to serve as brakes—as the main engines. Of course, having only one working forward engine had made slowing down a nightmare.

So I wrecked the starcar crash-landing in a forest. Still, not bad, all things considered.

Fortunately, the local authorities had believed Jane when she claimed she and Adam were innocent bystanders. Between her usual doe-eyed tricks and Adam's nice-boy appearance, it hadn't been hard to convince the police that they were just passengers who'd been unfortunate enough to be on that starcar when the "scary people" hijacked it.

The police had sent search teams into the forest to search for the non-existent fugitives and taken Jane and Adam to the nearest city. As soon as they weren't looking, Jane had grabbed Adam and sped off. Which was how she had ended up in a motel at the edge of the small, rural town of Etinine.

Won't take ISARK long to catch up, even though I'm in the middle of nowhere.

She opened her eyes. The room was small and empty but for the sofa along the wall and the bed she lay on. Adam was nowhere in sight. *Where'd he go? He was trying to stay awake again... Must've gone for a walk to keep from nodding off.*

She stood. Her body itched with discomfort. She'd showered the previous evening, but her dress still had a layer of ickiness on it from the lake. *I hate being a fugitive.*

She went to the door, pushed it open, and poked her head out into the hallway. "Adam?" Hearing no response, she stepped out. "Adam!"

Weird. She went back into the room to grab her shoes. She noticed her slate lying unfolded at the foot of the bed. The screen displayed a word-processing program with only one word written: *Jane.*

Adam must've meant to leave some kind of note. I wonder why.

She didn't have time to think about it. She had to change locations before ISARK caught up. The best thing to do was to find Adam and take the next train to the spaceport. She would have gone there the previous night if she hadn't had to disappear from the sights of the Aryus authorities seeking to question her about the starcar crash. If they'd realized she wasn't the innocent bystander she pretended to be, they would have detained her and Adam, and ISARK would surely have caught up.

She snatched up the slate. As she dropped it in her bag, she realized her gun was missing. She tried to recall if she'd seen the weapon since leaving the starcar. She certainly hadn't used it after arriving on Aryus.

Must've left it by accident. She bit her lip in dismay, unsurprised by her absentmindedness. *Dammit!*

⸎

Adam stared down the barrel of the gun he'd taken from Jane's bag. He glanced up at the Via symbol he knelt before. The Etinine temple's symbol wasn't illuminated, but its golden rays still seemed to glow.

Forgive me, Absolute One. I must destroy one more of Your creations.

The Absolute went by many names, and although the Absolute's true form had never been revealed to any of the numerous groups that worshipped a divine being, Adam had always been certain the Absolute would be there to catch him when he fell into darkness.

But as he stared into the abyss, the certainty wavered. Did he have a soul? Did Jonathan King? Did Pandora? Did they wait for him in the beyond?

Did the Absolute?

Yes. I know You will be there.

So would the dozens of people he'd killed. Adam blinked as tears filled his eyes. The Via didn't believe in a hell. The Absolute was benevolent and forgiving, not vengeful. That kind of wrath and cruelty was reserved for the human world. Some of the parables from the Book of Via did speak of the Absolute as one would speak of a human, but Adam knew that those were not to be taken literally. A person couldn't comprehend the Absolute's mind any more than an insect could prove a mathematical theorem.

And yet, it hardly seemed just that a murderer such as himself would receive the same treatment as his victims. The thought was one that had been discussed by generations of scholars, and its answer would forever elude those who sought it in life.

Everyone gets the answer once they die. He closed his eyes. *Absolute One, please tell me there's another way. I don't want to die.*

No matter how Adam called, the Absolute would not respond. That was the way of the divine. Freedom meant no interference from beyond.

His heart quaked at the thought of facing all his deeds. He'd tried to live for the side of good and follow the right path. Most of those memories were Pandora's implants, but he chose to believe in them. He remembered being seven and listening to Counselor Rose, one of his guardians at the Ibaran orphanage he'd thought he'd grown up in, patiently explaining to him the importance of helping others. Inspired by her words, he'd sought out a girl, whose name he couldn't recall, who had kept herself in isolation since her recent arrival at the orphanage. He'd done his best to bring her comfort and had eventually persuaded her to cheer up and join the other children in their games. The details were indistinct, but he remembered how happy helping the girl had made him.

The memory was a lie, of course. Adam hadn't even existed sixteen years ago, and he was fairly certain that if he chose to look her up, he'd find that the nameless girl didn't exist either. But he had found Counselor Rose, and she was real. She'd died a few years back, so he couldn't talk to her, but from what he'd learned, she was the same wise guardian he recalled. He believed that if he *had* been a seven-year-old under her care, he would have acted as he did in his memories.

But perhaps those memories painted too kind a picture of who he thought he was. Pandora had given them to him so he'd be able to draw upon them to perfect his performance as a compassionate human. Who was he, really? According to his records, he'd been found abandoned in a temple near the orphanage, and according to his memories, the sage counsel of his guardians had taught him to let go of any curiosity about who his parents were and any bitterness over the idea that they hadn't wanted him. He recalled being nineteen and struck by the need to know where he came from, and then being talked out of chasing his origins by Counselor Nekomo, who taught philosophy at the small Via university he remembered going to. The peace those memories brought him still shaped the way he thought, but how could he know whether, if put in the same situation at present, he would behave the same way?

His actual life had begun less than a year ago. His time with Jane, the volunteer work he'd done in the Outer Ring, his dedication to his schoolwork—those memories were real. He took comfort in knowing that in the time he knew he existed, he'd lived by the Via's tenets.

But in that same time, he'd also torn thirty-three souls from their worldly homes. *I never meant to. Absolute One, I never meant to.*

The faces of those he'd killed crowded his mind, and he felt as if their ghosts surrounded him, asking him why he lived when they didn't. Tears flowed down his cheeks. Accidental or not, his actions were to blame.

No more would die because of him. He flipped the gun's switch to its lethal setting, determined not to stall any longer.

Now, now, my child. Pandora's voice was soft. *Your Absolute Being has not abandoned you. I'm right here.*

Adam closed his eyes. In his mind, he stared into Pandora's. *You said you wanted to destroy me. You win.*

Trembling, he raised the weapon and brought it to his forehead.

No, Adam. Pandora's expression warmed. She appeared friendly—kind, even. *Think about Jane. She must be looking for you.*

She faded into darkness. Images of Jane filled Adam's mind. He saw her entering the temple and screaming at the sight of his body. As if the scene were really happening before his eyes, he watched her take his lifeless form into her arms and beg him to come back, then curse him for leaving. How could he leave her to cry, alone and lost?

Adam felt himself lowering the weapon, but he wasn't willingly moving his arm. He realized that Pandora tried to control him outside the dreamscape. He raised the gun again. His hand resisted, shaking so hard he nearly lost his grip. Her power over him had to be growing stronger.

But how? She's not real.

Any doubts he'd had were suddenly replaced by one thought: *Real or not, I must stop her. Forgive me, Absolute One. So be it, truly.*

Adam put his finger against the trigger.

"Adam, no!"

Startled, Adam opened his eyes. Before he could react, the weapon was ripped from his hands.

Devin stood over him with an expression between rage and horror. "What the hell were you thinking?"

Adam stared in shock, still shaking. He opened his mouth, but couldn't speak. A timely coincidence? Or was it the will of the Absolute that he should live?

Yes, it is my will. In Adam's mind, Pandora lifted her chin. *You cannot defeat me, my child.*

Adam realized he must have been too distressed by thoughts of Jane to hear Devin enter the temple. *Pandora was distracting me.*

Devin tucked the gun behind him, staring down as though waiting for an answer.

Adam's gaze fell on the ISARK insignia on Devin's cuff. The reason behind his rescue dawned on him. "They want me alive."

Devin's expression softened, and he knelt down beside Adam. "Why were you going to do it?"

"It's the only way to stop me." Adam's voice quivered.

"This isn't the end for you." Devin sounded unexpectedly gentle. "Come with me. There's been enough trouble."

Behind Adam, the temple's doors burst open. He heard several people enter. They had to be the other ISARK operatives.

Devin looked up and raised a hand as if saying, "Wait." He turned back to Adam. "Listen, kid." His voice was a low whisper, and his eyes spoke of earnestness. "Life can be terrible, but it's still life, and that's not something you throw away. You stay alive, no matter what. Understand? I swear, *this isn't the end.*"

He seemed to be telling Adam that everything would be okay, but how could that be true? Adam wiped his face as another tear fell. "What about the deaths I caused? What if it happens again? There are other AIs out there for ISARK."

"Forget that. For fuck's sake, Adam, just *stay alive.*" Devin stood, and his expression turned cold. "You can either come with me, or I can knock you out again. It makes no difference."

Adam glanced up at the Via symbol. The Absolute didn't speak to him. Neither did Pandora. He didn't know whether to be relieved that he was still alive or ashamed at his failure. What would happen if the nightmare returned? Would ISARK be able to stop him?

No point lay in resisting. He wouldn't get far if he tried to run. And there had been enough trouble on his account—Devin had been right about that. Adam got up slowly.

Devin unclipped a pair of restraints from his belt. "Hands behind your back."

Adam complied. Dread swelled within him as he wondered where they would take him and what ISARK would do with him.

Devin grabbed him by the arm, and Adam followed him to the door.

— ◦✧◦ —

Jane speed-walked down the street. *Dammit, Adam, where are you? This town isn't that big. How far could you have gone?*

She spotted a stone tower rising above the flat rooftops. Realizing it had to be part of a Via temple, she headed toward it. *He's gotta be in there, praying for forgiveness or something.*

She rounded a corner and was puzzled to see a black space transport—probably some kind of shuttle—in the street by the temple. *Weird. They couldn't find a landing pad?*

The temple's doors flew open. Jane stopped in her tracks, blinking in surprise. Devin led Adam out, followed by several ISARK operatives.

"Devin!" Jane sprinted toward him.

"Go home, Jane." Devin continued walking to the vehicle without looking at her.

The vehicle's door slid open. *If only I had my gun!* "Devin, please! Adam!"

Adam looked over his shoulder and shook his head, as though telling her to stop. Jane quickened her pace. A few more steps and she would reach them...

Devin turned abruptly, aiming his gun at her. "Stop where you are."

Jane gasped and froze, then started running again. He wouldn't shoot her. He couldn't.

"I said *stop*." Devin's expression was blank, unreadable.

Jane kept running. "Devin—"

A burst of white. A sudden shock blazed through her, and the world went black.

CHAPTER 11

MAD AS HELL

ADESINA STOOD IN THE CORNER of the lab, watching. Before her, two labcoats, which was what everyone called the research scientists, examined a blast-riddled mechanical body. *This is fucked up.*

How could they be so calm? They'd known the young man who lay on the lab table as Tyson Ambrose, a Sector 1708 analyst. Until the previous day, he'd been their colleague, someone with whom they'd worked and conversed. That he'd grabbed an experimental weapon from the lab shelf and gunned down five people should have sent everyone into shock.

Instead, here they are, dissecting someone they knew. Don't they care that their friends and coworkers are dead?

The attack had occurred in the very room Adesina stood in. She was a veteran ISARK agent, someone who'd seen her fair share of violence in the field. Returning to the scene made *her* uncomfortable, and yet the labcoats didn't seem to give a damn.

That's creepy.

It was only the third day of Adesina's stay at the facility, but she'd been around long enough to notice that something fishy seemed to be going on. Labcoats, analysts, operatives, agents—they all seemed to have had their souls sucked out.

They didn't socialize. They didn't take breaks. They just showed up for work, did as they were told, and left in the evenings. Other than a few visitors, no one at Sector 1708 had really reacted to Ambrose's sudden shooting. There had been no talk of memorial services for the victims, no moments of silence. Just business as usual.

They may be professionals, but they're still people. People are supposed to care.

Adesina grimaced as one of the labcoats peeled back a section of Ambrose's synthetic skin, revealing the machinery underneath.

Ambrose worked here for a full year, and no one knew he was an AI.

Rourke was gung-ho enough about capturing AIs that he wanted to place scanners on every street in Kydera. How could he have missed one working right under his nose?

No matter how Adesina reasoned, she always came to the same conclusion: he couldn't have.

After that big speech he gave about AIs being a danger, why would he let Ambrose roam free? Was he observing the AI's behavior? Is that what he's doing with Zeger Vang as well?

The thought of her aborted mission made Adesina seethe. She'd managed to speak with Chief Director Dane the previous day, hoping she could convince him to reverse whatever Rourke had done.

Dane had been sympathetic, but he'd told Adesina that Rourke had eyes on Vang, and as long as the dictator didn't present a threat to the Republic of Kydera, the situation on Klistosi wasn't ISARK's problem.

"What about the operatives who were killed?" Adesina had protested. "We're gonna let their murderers go?"

"We are not in the revenge business," Dane had replied calmly. "While their deaths are regrettable, we cannot mount a vigilante mission into an unstable Fringe system."

"You don't find it fishy that they *all* died or disappeared around the same time?"

"Thousands have died or disappeared due to the Klistosian upheaval. Since there is no evidence that our operatives were targeted as individuals, we can be almost certain that they were unfortunate enough to have fallen under the scythe that swept the system. Sending more operatives in would likely result in their deaths as well. I am not willing to risk that."

Dane had too much going on to spend much time considering Adesina's complaints, and he'd known Rourke for decades, long enough to simply trust the man to do his job.

Dane was right about that last bit, though. As long as we know what Vang's up to, and as long as he's not causing trouble for us, I shouldn't be willing to risk any more lives either.

The thought stirred a question that had been itching in Adesina's mind: *Rourke has eyes on Vang. What I want to know is: whose?*

It was a question she'd mulled over in her copious spare time. Her first answer had been that Rourke had an army of hackers at his disposal, and they must have accessed the Klistosian network. The problem with that theory? The entire Niran system was pretty much a communications dead zone. One of the last things Adesina had learned from her operatives was that Vang's people, not wanting the population to access outside influences, had knocked out the local Net drifts—stationary, unmanned spacecraft that created the signals connecting the galaxy.

Her current theory was that Rourke had to have ordered his own covert mission, one running parallel to

Adesina's. That would have explained why he'd had Devin transferred to his team.

But although Adesina didn't know what Rourke had Devin doing those days, it couldn't have anything to do with Klistosi. If he'd still been out there impersonating a gun for hire, he wouldn't have kept popping up at Sector 1708.

Not to mention, my security clearance is as high as it gets. Even if Rourke tried to block stuff from me, I still should've found something about other operatives. There's been no word of any activity surrounding Klistosi.

One of the labcoats plucked an object out of Ambrose's robotic neck and held it up for his colleague to see. "Looks like a Net communication device. If I had to guess, I'd say this is how the attack command was received."

Adesina shook her head. *Ambrose isn't the only robot in this lab.*

A thought dawned upon her. She'd accepted that the answer to how Rourke hadn't known about the AI in his facility was the simplest one.

Perhaps she should accept the simplest answer to how Rourke could have found out that Vang was an AI without insider knowledge: he couldn't have.

⸺◈⸺

Treasonous piece of shit! Adesina stormed down the corridors of Sector 1708. She had to keep moving, or she might join Ambrose on the rampage train. She wasn't even heading anywhere.

The more she thought about it, the more it made sense that Rourke was in league with the Klistosians. The only other possibility was that Rourke had a Klistosian informant, but her previous dealings with the locals told her that if her operatives hadn't been able to recruit any, Rourke wouldn't have been able to either. Not to mention, Rourke's working with the Klistosians would explain what had happened to her operatives—Rourke must have sold them out.

Who else had he sold out? What had he received in return? Money? Information? Or was he just doing it for kicks?

A veteran of ISARK, director of one of its facilities, good friends with the big boss, throwing away years of loyalty. Adesina couldn't imagine what had to have been going through Rourke's head. Of course, he must have thought he was high enough on the ISARK food chain that he'd never get caught.

I'll make sure he is.

Adesina swung around a corner. She had no proof. She didn't even have evidence—just an outlandish theory. *Well, then I'll fucking get some proof!*

A gate lay in front of her. In no mood to retrace her steps, Adesina strode up to it.

"Agent Elon Adesina!" *It'd better not ask for my DNA.*

The words "Access Denied" printed across the screen.

What? "Agent. Elon. Adesina." She carefully enunciated each word, in case her rage-filled yelling had befuddled the computer the first time.

"Access Denied," again.

There'd been no mistake. Rourke must have blocked her out.

Why? What's he hiding back there? Maybe it's where he communicates with his Fringe customers. Goddamn traitor!

A labcoat approached, heading for the gate. Adesina watched her, intending to follow her in.

"Dr. Anna Veronese." After the woman submitted to a hand scan, face scan, and DNA sample, "Access Granted" appeared on the screen, and the gate slid open.

Adesina rushed forward. The internal defense guns on the ceiling aimed at her, and she stopped. *Sonuvabitch!*

Those guns were meant to protect the employees of Sector 1708, not threaten them.

Dr. Veronese spun to face her. "Agent Adesina, please return to one of your designated access areas." Her face barely moved as she spoke.

Adesina narrowed her eyes. "How are you controlling the internal defense guns?"

"The internal defenses are based on an automated system designed to prevent intruders from entering this restricted area." Dr. Veronese's words were flat, her expression blank. "If you attempt to enter, then they are programmed to stop you."

Is she an AI too? Right now, I almost wish I could shoot her and find out.

Deciding not to try her luck, Adesina walked away. As she passed a pair of labcoats, she ran through her memory, considering the details of what she'd seen behind Dr. Veronese. It had looked like another corridor lined with rooms—probably more labs, considering how many labcoats had been headed in that direction. Was Rourke developing something in secret?

What the hell is wrong with the people in this place? Are they actually robots?

That thought was too much. No one at ISARK had any idea as to who had made the AIs or scattered them throughout the human population. Rourke probably knew more, but he certainly couldn't have been behind the AIs. He wouldn't have been so determined to round them up if he were.

Besides, the people who died yesterday were acting just as robotic as everyone else, and they were definitely human. What could cause people to act like machines? If I didn't know better, I'd think they were all hypnotized.

Adesina stopped walking. *Fucking.* Hell!

Sector 1708 had been behind the development of a mind control implant. After word of it leaked to the Net the previous year, Dane had shut the program down. The advantages of the implants—from learning enhancement to enemy interrogation—had been dubious at best.

Wouldn't be hard to slip one into an operative's head. They all get communications implants. Rourke probably had the surgeons stick mind control implants in at the same time. But what about the analysts and labcoats?

Rourke had to have been implanting them in secret. Adesina shook her head at the revelation, feeling as if she should have thought of it sooner.

No wonder he let Ambrose wander around. Someone must've discovered that Ambrose was an AI while trying to implant him. If Rourke revealed that fact, he'd have to reveal how he'd found out. Bastard!

Adesina's blood cried out for her to take action. She couldn't let Rourke get away with his treachery a moment longer. She knew in her gut that she was right, but her instincts wouldn't be enough to end Rourke's operation. The internal defense display told her she wouldn't be able to get close enough to Rourke to get any hard evidence.

What I need is an insider, someone who works for Rourke, someone he thinks is his little puppet...

⸻◆⟨◇⟩◆⸻

Adesina drummed her fingers on the table as she waited for Devin to return to his apartment in Sector 1708's housing unit, which was known to the general population as part of a small town called Arunit. She'd found a record indicating that he'd returned to Ibara earlier that day, and it wouldn't be long before he stepped through the door.

The building that housed Sector 1708's employees was even more of a communications dead zone than the Niran system. It was probably the only place in which she could speak without Rourke hearing. The building contained no central computer, and nothing was automated. What was more, it was built out of materials designed to block any signals, no matter how strong. Back when Adesina had been a Sector 1708 analyst, she'd often joked that living there was equivalent to living in ancient times.

Because of its extreme secrecy, ISARK had to monitor every signal going in or out of Sector 1708, no matter how trivial. The dead zone was meant to give the employees some form of privacy. They couldn't access the Net or send a message, but no one watched them as they slept either. Before coming, Adesina had checked with ISARK's headquarters on Kydera Major to make sure nothing had changed with regard to the dead zone. Even Rourke would have had to get permission from headquarters to tamper with the building, and changing the structure would have been too big an operation for him to carry out in secret. To double-check, she'd run signal tests from her starship, and not one communication had gotten through to the slate she'd left in one of the building's hallways. She knew she couldn't be completely sure of the dead zone's security, but it was her best bet.

The door opened. Devin stepped in, gun raised and ready to threaten an intruder.

Adesina curled her lips in a slight grin. *I was sure I didn't leave a trace this time.*

Devin lowered the gun. "I should have known it'd be you." He put the gun in his holster. "Why are you here?"

Adesina crossed her arms. "Take a guess."

Devin studied her for a moment. "You must have discovered what Rourke's been doing. I was wondering how long it'd take you."

Sounds like you know what's going on. "Selling out his country and turning his people into robots. Did I miss anything?"

Devin took a seat across from her. "There's someone else involved. A third party, possibly a middleman between Rourke and his customers."

Adesina frowned. "How do you know? Actually, start with how you didn't end up dazed like the rest of them."

"Because Rourke's a twisted sonuvabitch." Anger clouded Devin's eyes. "He'd rather I be forced to follow his will than run on autopilot like the rest. I'm not the only one he's done this to. Just his most recent 'game.' Before me, it was Agent Heisman."

She deepened her frown. "What do you mean?"

"Rourke wouldn't tell me exactly what he did, only that he targeted Heisman for his Fringe connections. My guess is that's how Rourke got the contacts to sell ISARK secrets to. But after a while, Heisman... couldn't take it anymore."

"Are you saying Rourke's the reason Heisman's dead?" Heisman had been a strong-willed man who'd often said he'd rather die than betray his nation. Adesina couldn't imagine what Rourke must have put him through. She seethed, a nearly uncontrollable wrath rising within her. "*Bastard.*" She slammed the table.

She shifted her gaze to the window. She wanted to storm into Sector 1708 and tear Rourke's head off with her bare hands. *Calm yourself, Adesina. Your temper can't help you here.*

She inhaled. After giving herself a minute or so to cool her head, she faced Devin. "So how does this 'game' work? Rourke puts a chip in your head so he can watch you, but doesn't turn it on?"

"He activates it from time to time." Devin's gaze became distant, stormy. "I try to stop him, but... sometimes I can't. There's only so much willpower can do when your enemy is in your mind."

"Any idea why he was so hell-bent on having you?"

"He wanted to know about Pandora. Since I was the one Pandora targeted, he figured I had to know what her plans were."

What's the Pandora program got to do with this? "Do you?"

Devin nodded. "She created the AIs. She was going to make them leaders—presidents, generals, CEOs. Controlling them meant controlling the future of humanity."

Well, that's a helluva thing. Adesina absorbed the information. It made sense, given the positions the four known AIs had been in. Ambrose had probably been intended for the Chief Director spot. "I see. Now, what's all this about a third party being involved with Rourke?"

"Rourke sent me after an AI. I thought it was because this one was different from the others. He should have been headed for Sector Seventeen-Oh-Eight, and I was going to keep an eye on him." Devin glanced away. "He vanished."

You care an awful lot. "Why was this AI so important to you?"

Devin's eyes met Adesina's, and he seemed to examine her, as if deciding if he could trust her.

Adesina spread her arms. "Hey, it's me. Talk to me, Devin."

Devin broke his stare. "The AI was a kid I knew. I needed to keep track of him so I could get him home once this was all over." From the way he spoke, it was as though he had betrayed a friend.

Strange. Why would he care about a machine? Adesina decided to add that thought to the "to ask later" pile. At the moment, she had a point to get to. "I take it you don't care too much for Rourke. How do you feel about exposing his treachery and getting his ass before a tribunal?"

Devin brought his gaze back to her. "That's my goal. I haven't been quietly taking his orders, although I need him to believe it."

"Sounds like you've already got a plan." Adesina narrowed her eyes. "Tell me."

Devin leaned forward. "Rourke's looking for more customers. Now that he has his AI, he wants me to return to the Fringe as Black Knight to see if anyone is interested in what he had to sell."

"Heisman's death must've left him with a hole in his staff list." Adesina's blood rushed with fresh anger. "Let me guess: you're planning on setting him up."

"That's right."

"Always the proactive one, aren't you? Now, how're you gonna catch him in the act? He'll know if you're bugged."

Devin raised his eyebrows. "I guess that's where you come in."

The authoritative expression on his face was so reminiscent of the one he'd worn eight years before, when he'd first approached Adesina as Black Knight, that she couldn't help a slight smile. "So here we go again. You're up to your old tricks, and you just need someone official to get the evidence to the higher-ups."

"That's right. I couldn't go to you, but I knew it was only a matter of time before you came to me."

Adesina shook her head. "And there I was thinking all that time you spent in the Silk Sector had turned you into some kind of tool. But you really haven't changed a bit, have you?"

"I guess not." Devin's expression darkened. "Let's get the bastard."

CHAPTER 12

THE NET NEVER SLEEPS

RILEY RECLINED AGAINST THE TILTED back of his hospital bed. He couldn't wait to get out of the place, with its gooey nurses, weird smells, and horrible food. At least they let him keep his slate handy. He would have gone nuts without it. Jim X had visited him several times, and as much as Riley liked the old guy, he found the hovering to be rather irritating.

He didn't need sympathy. What he needed was to figure out which assholes had tried to freakin' kill him. *Well, they were trying to kill Jim X, but still, I'm the one with a blast wound!*

Whoever had sent the Bettas was good at covering their tracks. Despite feeling woozy from painkillers, Riley had managed to buzz around Shimshawhenn's systems. Signal traces were usually easy, but he hadn't found anything that could tell him where the drones had come from.

He tapped his fingers along the edge of his slate, mentally cooking up his next move. A beeping sound interrupted his thoughts, and a window popped up on the screen: *Jane Colt calling.*

She's using her contact info again? He pressed "Accept."

"Yo, Janie. Thought you were in hiding."

"Adam's gone." Jane spoke through gritted teeth. "I need you to help me find him."

"What? He got nabbed again?" Riley sobered his expression. *Now's not the time to be joking.* "Uh... Sorry." The facts hit him, and he straightened with alarm. "What happened?"

"Devin caught up to us, and Adam... he surrendered." She sounded as though she didn't believe her own words.

Riley tapped his fingers nervously. He hated to disappoint, but if Adam had been taken by ISARK, he might as well have evaporated. "Uh... I... I dunno if I can break into ISARK's systems." *Ugh. I've gotta do something.* "I mean... I can try, but..."

"What about Devin? Can you find him? I've called him over and over, but he won't respond." Jane's eyes darkened with anger. "He's probably scared of me. Well, he should be. I'm gonna kill him!"

Riley jittered. "I haven't been able to reach him in ages either."

Jane threw him an annoyed look. "You've hacked a Kyderan warship, and now you're telling me you can't find someone you know?" She bit her lip. "Sorry. I just... I didn't know who else to turn to."

This is so messed up. Riley sighed. He couldn't blame Jane for freaking out. "I'll try again. No guarantees, though."

Jane smiled. "Thanks."

Riley ended the transmission. *Okay, where do I start? It's not like I can just run an Acuitas search for Devin! Unless... oh wait, I sorta can.*

Last time Adam had disappeared, Riley had found him by creating a ware carrying an object recognition program. He'd sent the ware to every computer controlling a security cam he could, and it had eventually found the kidnapper machines. *Same thing might work this time, except I'll look for Devin's face.*

He opened a program and began typing. *I can't believe I'm writing* another *freakin' ware because Adam's gone and disappeared* again*!*

The ware didn't take long to write, since it was based on the last one he'd made, but the list of places he'd have to send it was pretty damn long.

The sun disappeared outside, and Shimshawhenn's two moons lit the star-filled sky.

Riley yawned. *Whatever. The Net never sleeps.*

⁕

Jane paced around her apartment, unsure of what to do with herself. After Devin had stunned her, she'd been awakened by some puzzled Etinine locals, and she'd done her best to find someone who could help her track him down. But everyone she'd asked had treated her like she was crazy, and helpless to do anything else, she'd eventually boarded a Moray back to Kydera.

At least ISARK didn't arrest me for aiding a fugitive or some bullshit. Probably because they couldn't justify why they were after Adam. I wonder if anyone at the seminary's noticed he's missing yet.

The memory of Devin firing at her filled her with rage, and she tried to push it out of her mind with the usual rationale: He'd been under orders. With all those other ISARK operatives around, he couldn't have let Adam go if he wanted to. The thought did little to calm her.

One of the screens on her wall beeped: *Incoming message.*

Is it Riley? "Put it through."

A man's face filled the screen: the captain of the ship she'd hijacked. "You!" His face reddened with anger. "ISARK told me who you were. Did you think you could just take half my ship and get away with it?"

Oh, right. That. "Sorry. It's on Aryus. I'll have someone fix it and give it back."

The captain raised his eyebrows. "Oh, you will? I've seen the damage. Do you have any idea how much repairs would cost?"

Jane sighed, in no mood to deal with the captain's complaints. "Captain, I'm the daughter of the late Victor Colt, who ran the biggest damn bank in the galaxy. I've got what he left me plus generations of family wealth. You'll get your starcar back, good as new."

The captain flinched as though startled. "Oh. I see." He straightened. "That doesn't change the fact that you violated several laws—"

"You wanna press charges?" Jane's anger boiled over and, happy to unleash it on the captain, she yelled, "*Do it*! I'll just hire an army of lawyers and private investigators! What'll happen to your darling ship once they find out about your 'don't-ask-questions' policy? Just take my freaking offer, and leave me the hell alone!" Tears tingled at the edges of Jane's eyes, tears that had nothing to do with the captain. She blinked furiously.

The captain opened his mouth to speak, then frowned. He furrowed his brow. "Are you okay?"

Jane crossed her arms. "What do you care? Just answer me: do you want your starcar or not?"

The captain glanced around as though checking to see whether anyone eavesdropped. "All right, I'll take your deal and keep the authorities out of it, but on one condition."

There's always a freaking condition. "What?"

"I want to know your story." He spoke in a low voice, as though afraid of being overheard. "How does a princess like you end up with a fugitive, chased by ISARK?"

I guess I'm not the only one who finds my situation bizarre. Jane considered making something up, but a powerful desire to tell someone, anyone, about what had happened drove that thought away. "ISARK went after Adam for something he couldn't change." Unwilling to confess the whole truth, she kept her response vague. "I couldn't let them take him. I wasn't completely lying when

I told you we were running away, and my family would be mad if they found out. That ISARK operative—he's my brother."

Hell, even the "to get married" part wasn't a total lie. She smiled cynically to herself. *I did propose. I guess if I ever had to marry anyone, it'd be Adam.*

The realization caused her eyes to brim, and she hurriedly wiped them. "That's all I can tell you. Do you want the starcar or not?"

The captain fidgeted uncomfortably. "Um, yes. Sounds good."

"Message me with the specs." Jane tried to sound businesslike. "I'll get on it as soon as I can." She ended the transmission, then walked over to her sofa and collapsed backward onto it.

The plain white ceiling seemed to stare back as she blinked up at it. Its blankness somehow seemed frightening, and she rolled onto her side. Her thought echoed in her head: *If I had to marry anyone, it'd be Adam.*

Had to? Or did she want to? She hugged her arms, cringing at the thoughts. If only she could chase them away and never face them.

Then again, that was what she had done when she'd first realized how she felt about Adam. Shielding herself hadn't achieved anything. He could have died confronting Pandora and never known that she returned his love. *How could I have lived with myself if he had?*

Another thought crept into Jane's mind: *How would I live without him?*

If she never found him, what then? She wouldn't waste away—she was stronger than that. Still, she couldn't stand the thought of the lonely years passing, unencumbered but unfulfilled.

And to think, when I met him, I didn't even consider him boyfriend material.

Before Adam, Jane's past romantic entanglements had involved bursts of energetic desire, cravings bordering on obsession. She'd dated brilliant artists and sophisticated charmers, masters of words who knew how to sweep a girl off her feet with praise and promises—such pretty promises! But like all explosions, their heat would peter out all too quickly, leaving Jane with ashes and darkness.

Her memories of those relationships were so superficial, and so brief. For some, she didn't even recall their last names. They'd disappoint, then they'd disappear.

Not Adam. Jane had loved him before she was in love with him. He'd never asked her for anything but her presence, and only around him could she be her whole, true—and not entirely normal—self. She didn't know when her fondness for him had turned into something more, and it had taken losing him for her to finally acknowledge that the gentle yet magnetic affection she had for him was that thing called love. If her exes were short explosions, Adam was a constant star, brightening the night with his tender glow.

Isn't that the kind of relationship the experts say leads to a happy ending? Ugh, why am I thinking about this?

Forever was a long time. Jane considered herself too intelligent to fall for the false promises of fairytales. Growing up, she'd always thought she'd get married someday simply because her parents had drilled into her the importance of traditional values. A string of exes and a grown-up mind had led her to conclude that "happily ever after" wasn't possible for her. She got bored too easily. *And people suck.*

Then Adam had showed her what kindness really was. She knew him so well, and yet there were parts of him she'd never understand. First and foremost among those was how he put up with her antics. If she were the type to believe in such things, she would have said the Absolute saw her, all lonely and cynical, and sent an angel to prove that good people still existed.

Jane made a face and hugged her knees, disgusted by her own cheesiness. Since when had she been the lovey-dovey type?

Fine, I'll admit it. I kind of want to marry him. Not that it'll matter if I never freaking find him.

Jane hated being so helpless, so useless. There she was again, facing all the things she couldn't do. Turned out, she couldn't get away from ISARK, after all. Couldn't run fast enough. Couldn't convince her brother to let her go.

Couldn't see Adam—she'd lost him again.

On the table by the sofa, a golden Via pendant gleamed under the light. Adam had given it to her months ago, and Jane had managed to keep it the entire time while running from Pandora, wearing it around her own neck and tucking it under her top to keep it safe. The double suns meant little to her in terms of religious faith, but they were a piece of Adam.

She pictured the genuine, somewhat shy smile that had brightened his face when he gave her the pendant. Though he seemed to smile often around her, each time he did, it filled her with warmth. He hadn't truly smiled in days, and she would have given anything to make him happy again. But at present, she couldn't even track down the people who'd taken him, let alone bring him joy.

Jane sat up. *Enough of this. What am I gonna do, pine until Riley calls me back? I've got things to do.*

Like finish orchestrating that piece for the music festival. It seemed like such a dumb thing to care about, but it beat moping. Also, the due date wouldn't change because she'd been fighting to keep Adam from ISARK. The world would turn on with or without her.

She grabbed her slate and opened the composition program. One by one, she added notes to the harmony.

She didn't really care what they sounded like—she just needed filler notes for the time being.

Why did I think I could do this? Why did they accept me in the first place? Maybe Riley went through with his prank even when I told him not to.

Jane smiled at the memory. After submitting her entry, she'd spent a good amount of time ranting to Riley about how unfair the whole process was. Those sons of bitches in the judges' chairs, the almighty gatekeepers, probably spent a total of ten seconds on each entry. They'd most likely stamp "reject" onto hers after glancing over her short résumé and the description of the piece she'd entered, without even listening to it.

"I know!" Riley had said with an eager grin. "I'll bombard their systems with the most awful-ass entries they've ever seen. By the time they see yours, it'll look like the best thing ever!"

Jane had laughed in response. "Nah, that's okay. If they don't like me, then screw them too."

I must've done something right.

She played back what she'd composed so far. One of the harmonies seemed off. She adjusted it and played the piece back again. The countermelody seemed to want to continue. She bowed to its demands and expanded it.

The monster within awakened, and she found herself rushing to keep up as note after note poured out of her head. All thoughts of Adam and Devin and ISARK faded away as the music consumed her.

⸻ ◆ ⸻

Sunlight blinded Riley the moment he opened his eyes.

"Ah!" He clapped his hand over his eyelids. He rolled over and peeked through his fingers to make sure he faced a safe direction, then sat up in his hospital bed. His slate lay beside him—it must've slid out of his hand when he passed out.

Riley yawned and picked up the device. His grogginess disappeared when he saw the message on the slate: "No matches found."

"*Dammit!*" He threw the slate down in frustration. He really shouldn't have been surprised, since Devin was probably off on some shady ISARK base. Even if he weren't, space was really, really big. Riley could easily have missed something.

Now what?

He picked up his slate. Not knowing what else to do, he opened the Net communication program he'd written a while ago—one he'd designed to scramble signals—and pressed "Archangel," Devin's old Netname.

He was shocked when Devin's face actually showed up on the slate.

"Riley! Are you all right?" Devin was only visible from the shoulders up. The room he occupied was dim.

Riley realized his mouth hung open in surprise. He shut it, then opened it again to speak. But he hadn't been expecting a response, and so he had no idea what to say other than, "Where the hell have you been?"

"Busy." Devin shifted his gaze, as though looking past Riley. "Are you still in the hospital?"

"Yeah, they're patchin' me up. Said I should be back to normal soon." Riley angled his head. "Hey, I just realized something. Of the four of us who were running from Pandora, I was the only one who hadn't basically died yet. I was starting to feel left out. Now, I too can say that I spat in Death's face."

Devin lifted the corner of his mouth in amusement. "You'll find a way to brag about anything, won't you?"

"Hell, yeah!" Riley pumped a fist. "Gotta own what you do, and I"—he jerked his thumbs at himself—"survived a freakin' drone attack!" He let his arms fall by his sides. "Now I've just gotta figure out who sent them."

Devin's expression fell into one of concern. "I know this will be hard for you, but you have to let it go. Those people don't want to be found. If you look too hard, they might decide you're a liability."

Weird answer. Riley gasped. "You know who it is, don't you?"

Devin's eyes hardened. "Just keep out of it. They won't bother you again."

What does that mean? Riley noticed something hanging on a rack behind Devin: a pointed black helmet with a red slit over the eyes—a sight Riley wouldn't easily forget. *Why's he going around as Black Knight again?*

"Dude, just tell me what's going on." Riley's desperate need for knowledge made him add, "Please?"

"I can't." Devin's expression was unreadable. "Be careful."

"Wait!"

Too late—Devin had ended the transmission.

Riley threw down the slate again. He wouldn't be able to trace that signal; he'd designed the communication program specifically for that purpose.

He hugged his knees and banged his forehead against them, then winced as the wound on his leg throbbed. *Think, think, think...*

If Devin was going around as Black Knight, there was a good chance he'd passed through Travan Float. All the mercs did. The object recognition program Riley had sent into Travan Float's computer had been searching for Devin's face. The helmet could have interfered with that plan.

Riley considered writing a program that would search for the helmet, then decided the quicker way would be to ask around. Black Knight was a notorious and easily recognizable figure.

Of course, no one would listen to Riley.

Well, the question doesn't have to come from me. It could come from... Madam Wrath! That's it!

Madam Wrath ran Travan Float. If Riley created a program that would impersonate her and ordered the Travan thugs to ask about Black Knight, he'd get his answer soon enough.

I'm a freakin' genius!

Creating a fake Madam Wrath was easy. Well, easy for a supergenius who had done that kind of thing before. Riley opened a program on his slate and began typing.

"Keeping yourself busy, I see?" The voice was Jim X's.

Riley didn't look up. "Don't have time for your hovering!"

Jim X chuckled. "I brought someone to see you."

Riley heard a bark and glanced over at Jim X. Archangel, Jim X's large, gray dog with pointy ears, stood beside him.

"Archangel?" Riley cocked his head to the side. "Thought they didn't allow pets in here."

Jim X shrugged. "They don't, but when you own a continent, they tend to make exceptions."

Archangel placed his big furry paws on Riley's bed. Riley patted the animal's head. "Hey, dog. Good to see you, too. You can stay, but as for you"—he looked up at Jim X—"shoo!"

Jim X shook his head. "Riley, do you understand what the word *rest* means?"

"Nope."

The old guy placed a hand on Riley's head and looked down fondly. "Whatever you're doing, be careful."

"Yeah, yeah." *I think he wants to adopt me.* The thought made Riley feel kind of fuzzy inside.

Jim X left. Archangel curled up at the foot of the bed.

Riley returned to his program. Exhaustion weighed on him, but he wouldn't be able to rest. He wanted the program to get *written* already.

Hours passed.

By the time he finished, his wrists ached from all the typing, but he didn't mind. The satisfaction of having completed his program was worth the effort, and he was eager to put it to use. An image of Madam Wrath's severe face filled his slate's screen. Sharp chin, firm mouth, piercing black eyes, black hair twisted in a tight knot like in that famous hologram of hers... *Yup, that should do it.*

Riley closed one eye. Madam Wrath closed one eye. He wrinkled his nose. Madam Wrath mimicked the movement.

"Yo!" he said.

At the same time, Madam Wrath said in her authoritative voice, "Yo!"

It works!

Riley excitedly opened a communication program, found the contact info for the Wrath Guards, and smashed his finger into the "go" button.

The rush cleared. It dawned on him just what he was about to do. He didn't have time for anything more than a few fleeting curse words before the harsh face of a Wrath Guard, topped with blood-red hat, filled the screen.

The Wrath Guard furrowed his brow in confusion. "Madam Wrath? Why are you contacting us via the public line?"

Riley arranged his face into a stern frown. He squeezed the edge of his shirt with both fists, hoping the tension would go there. Even though he hid behind the mask of Madam Wrath, the vocal inflections and facial nuances were still his.

Whatever you do, don't say "uh"!

"That's not your concern." Riley held his head high, as he imagined Madam Wrath would. "I need to know if you or any of the others have seen Black Knight recently."

Whew! Didn't fumble. He narrowed his eyes, hoping it made his avatar appear impatient and threatening.

The Wrath Guard straightened. "He arrived here an hour ago and boarded the shuttle to Asylum. Lenski said he already told you. Why—"

"Shut up!" The words shot out of Riley's mouth before he could stop himself. He firmed his expression, doing his best to contain the grin that threatened to slip onto his mouth. *Found you, Devin!*

The Wrath Guard bowed his head respectfully. "Apologies, Madam Wrath. Do you want us to take care of him if he returns?"

Riley recalled that Madam Wrath probably had a helluva grudge against Devin, since the last two times Devin had visited Travan Float as Black Knight, stuff had ended up getting shot up. "No. That... won't be necessary."

Riley ended the transmission and sank into his usual slouch, suddenly aware of how loose his shoulders could be. He pumped his fists. "*Triumph!*"

Excitement buzzed through Riley's veins, and the thought "I win" lit up in his head like a neon sign so bright he couldn't see anything else. He pulled up Jane's contact information, eager to tell her that Devin was heading for Asylum.

Wait... What the hell is Asylum?

He twisted his mouth in confusion. *Takes a shuttle to get there, so it's gotta be a planet or a float. Maybe a giant starship.*

He fidgeted as he ran through his memories, but couldn't think of anything. His first instinct was to search for info on the Net, but he quickly realized that he'd get an answer much faster if he just asked someone on Travan Float. *Might as well use the Madam Wrath program while her people are still confused.*

He contacted the Wrath Guards. The same hat-wearing man answered.

Riley tried to look piercing. "I'm not done with you."

"Yes, Madam Wrath?" The Wrath Guard sounded nervous.

"Tell me what you know about Asylum." *Better make it sound like a test.* "I wanna know if you know your shit." *Crap! That's not how Madam Wrath talks!*

The glare must have been enough to keep the Wrath Guard from getting suspicious. "Asylum is a rogue planet—it's got no star and just shoots through space by itself. The Tenebrarum run the place. It's their headquarters and training grounds, as well as a sanctuary for those with prices on their heads. Since the planet is a free-floating thing, it's never in the same place twice, and the only way on or off is through one of Tenebrarum's ships."

Whoa, cool! "How do you access these ships?"

"You find someone wearing the crest of Tenebrarum and speak the code. If they determine that you're not a threat, they take you to one of the shuttles."

"What's the code?" *Damn, that sounded too eager!* "I mean, do you know what it is?"

"Of course." The Wrath Guard cleared his throat.

As he recited the code, Riley carefully took in each word. He wished he'd had the foresight to record the conversation. Fortunately, the code wasn't very long.

Even I can remember that. "Excellent."

Riley ended the transmission. The "I win" sign brightened in his mind. *This is so freakin' awesome! I've always wondered where the Tenebrarum hang out.*

He pulled up Jane's contact info again and called.

Her face filled the screen, her dark eyebrows low over her eyes. "What do *you* want?"

Why's she mad at me? "Uh... you asked for my help?"

Jane raised her eyebrows in realization. "*Riley*? Why are you hiding behind Madam Wrath?"

Riley realized he'd left the Madam Wrath program running. He dropped his mouth in sheepishness. "Oops. Uh... Sorry." He quickly shut the program down. "Is that better?"

Jane rested her head against the back of her sofa. "Much. What did you find?"

"Okay, I dunno what ISARK's up to, but they've got Devin going around as Black Knight again. He's off on Asylum. That's... Uh... Well, I guess you could call it Tenebrarum's homeworld."

Jane tilted her head. "What's Tenebrarum?"

Riley opened his mouth incredulously. "You've never heard of Tenebrarum?"

She frowned and shook her head.

"Duuuude! They're only the coolest and scariest bunch of people *ever*!" Riley yanked his slate closer in excitement. "They started off as an order of assassins, and that's still pretty much their main thing, but they've been known to do other stuff as well. These guys are *legendary* on the Fringe! Hey, I wonder if Devin's next job is to infiltrate their ranks or something. Far as I know, they only recruit kids, but everything I know is rumors." He held up a finger. "Except the important bit." He lifted his chin boastfully. "I know how to get to Asylum."

Jane straightened. "Tell me."

⁕

Jane revved up the Stargazer's engines and blasted off into the atmosphere. She wished there were a way to break the lightspeed barrier. As it was, Travan Float would take more than a day to reach.

Assassins and secret codes and a rogue planet—she'd wind up in the middle of all that. Gallivanting off to a dangerous part of the galaxy wasn't the smartest thing to do, but she had no other options. *Besides, it's not my first time alone on the Fringe.*

In case things turned out to be scarier than they were exciting, she'd dropped by Boris's Goods and bought another gun. Travan Float was *not* the place to be unarmed.

She could only hope that the Tenebrarum, once she found them, would allow her to enter their homeworld.

As Jane turned the steering bars, she caught a glimpse of her sleeve and realized that she'd been in such a hurry to get out the door that she'd forgotten to change her clothes. Her purple dress and brown jacket would make her stick out in a crowd of raggedy drug dealers and black-clad mercs.

Well, I was wearing black last time, and people still thought I stuck out. Why does that always happen to me?

As she steered her ship toward the Kyderan tunnels, Jane repeated the code Riley had given her to make sure she wouldn't forget it: "I seek one of shadow. I leave all behind. I come to ask of you: Asylum."

CHAPTER 13

HER NAME

"THIS IS FLAME DANCER." INES pressed the icon on her Silverside's control screen to transmit her credentials. "Let me through."

Ines Valentin—that was her name, but she could count on half a hand the number of people alive who knew. She left it up to everyone else to figure out what to call her, whether it was a code name for a particular job or a descriptive epithet. Tenebrarum called her "Flame Dancer." Pretender had dubbed her "Silver."

Most people on Travan Float knew her simply by some variation of "the lady merc with the silver armbands." Her appearance changed so often that those armbands, trophies from her first kill, were the only way to identify her. She only donned them when she wanted to be found.

The operator verified her identity and transmitted the coordinates of *Gate I*, a Sei tunneler whose counterpart, *Gate II*, followed Asylum, which had no star to bind it in place. Ines punched the coordinates into her Silverside's central computer. Once a day, *Gate I* and *Gate II* would create an interstellar bridge between them. Neither Asylum nor *Gate I* was ever in the same place twice, and the locations of both were closely guarded secrets, given only to Tenebrarum members.

With the autopilot set, Ines opened a compartment beneath her dashboard and retrieved a miniscule remote. To the Klistosians, for whom she had last been working, she was the woman with short, black hair and green eyes. She kept her appearance consistent for her employers. Otherwise, her look was as malleable as a snitch with a knife to his throat. The nanobots implanted in her scalp and irises made changing her hair and eyes a matter of pressing a few icons.

Ines swiped the remote's touchscreen and selected her options. When she finished, she pressed "alter" and turned to the mirror by the ship's controls. Her hair changed from black to platinum blonde and grew twelve inches in length. She'd decided on a high braid and pale blue eyes for that day. The following day, she might sport red curls, for all she knew. It depended on her mood.

She tied her new hair up into her chosen style. When she finished, she reached under the dashboard again and considered her various cosmetic options.

By the time Ines finished re-coloring her face, her complexion was so pale, the shadows beneath her cheekbones made them appear to jut out like razors. If she held herself differently, her birdlike features would make her seem rather delicate. But with her piercing glare and icy lips, she resembled an unholy wraith who'd escaped the depths of Hell.

That should do it.

Ines examined her reflection and tilted the corner of her mouth into the vaguest hint of a smile. That troublesome Pretender probably didn't remember the face of the black-haired woman he'd confronted on Kydera Major, but he'd have a hard time forgetting the frost queen she was at present.

Never underestimate the power of presentation.

As she got up from the pilot's seat, she caught a glimpse of her back in the mirror. Long, pale scars ran down her neck and into her low-backed tank top, reminders of how she'd ended up in the profession. She'd chosen to keep them so she would never forget the universe's cruelty. After all, scars never healed. They could be made invisible, but they were always there.

She'd been barely twelve when her worthless addict of a mother sold her to a disgusting pimp. Ines had been a street dancer on a middle-of-nowhere Fringe planet, pirouetting day in and day out so her mother could get another week's worth of Surge injections. A pimp had spotted Ines and offered her mother a year's supply. The choice had been simple.

Ines traced a finger along the scars of her initial resistance. After she'd given up on violent outbursts in favor of a long-term plan, she'd become a popular attraction, known for her ribbon-dancing routines, in which she'd suggestively coil long silks around red-faced johns. The boss had been present at each performance, eager to auction off his star.

One day, Ines brought a new set of ribbons, a set made of lasers. It had taken her over a year of careful planning to procure them. "I have a special show for you tonight, gentlemen."

They'd cheered so loudly. It must've been a stunning sight: a young girl twirling brilliant yellow beams of light, drawing waves in the air, skillfully swirling them around her slender body. The wires containing the lasers had the same weight and air resistance as the ribbons Ines had known so well. They'd been like extensions of her own arms, and she'd almost felt with them as she wrapped them around the pimp and tore him in half.

The memory burned in Ines's mind. *May God forgive me.*

By the time she'd finished her performance, bloody bodies and severed limbs had littered the lounge. She'd collapsed in tears, her rage blown away by horror. God commanded that one must strive never to harm another living being. She'd burned her last bridge to Heaven.

She had no escape plan; all she'd wanted was revenge, and she'd been prepared for the brothel guards to burst in and take her down. Instead, Striker had rescued her. Turned out, the pimp was on the hit list of a crime boss, and Striker had been watching from the vents. Ines had done the job for him before he could take his shot.

Ines hadn't hesitated to embrace her new role as Striker's apprentice. Tenebrarum operated on a code of honor: they only accepted assignments if the target needed killing. Such as her captor and torturer. Such as a million men like him.

She'd carried those laser ribbons for seventeen years, and she would carry them for twenty, thirty, forty more, or until Hell claimed her. Deactivated, they looked like a pair of black batons strapped to her belt.

Ines went into the back of her Silverside and opened a storage closet. *A pair of light guns should do it.*

If Pretender presented a threat to her, her main advantage over him would be her speed and agility. *Unfortunately, his advantage over me is that he's fucking suicidal.*

Tucking her guns into her belt, she returned to the pilot's seat. According to the chart, half an hour remained until she'd have to switch to manual piloting. She reclined in her chair. She'd only met Pretender once before until he'd contacted her, asking to meet, and since she had time, she might as well replay the encounter in her mind. Perhaps she'd catch some detail she'd missed previously.

Ines had answered the Klistosians' call for private contractors several weeks before. They'd hired her under the condition that she carry out her assignment with no questions asked. Accepting such an agreement was usually beneath her, but her options had been limited since she beheaded her last employer, a crime lord who'd hired her to take out a woman he claimed was a murderer. The woman was actually his wife, an innocent girl who'd been forced into marriage and who'd fled at her first chance. Disgusted, Ines had stormed back to the crime lord's headquarters with the intention of punishing him for his wickedness and deception. When she'd learned that he dealt not only in narcotics, but in trafficking girls, his fate was sealed.

Of course, no one wanted to hire her after that. Tenebrarum had struck her off their list of active members. Although the banishment was temporary, it had left Ines unemployed long enough that, with no other options, she'd begrudgingly accepted the Klistosians' agreement.

The target had been some kid on Kydera Major. Why the Klistosians would want him dead wasn't her business. Ines recalled her dismay at learning just who her mark was: Adam Palmer, a twenty-three-year-old Via seminary student. She'd peered through the scope of her long-range rifle, which was set up on a low stand, and aimed at the window of his dorm room. The kid had been at his desk, studying.

Another kill, another soul to torment me for eternity. Ines should have shrugged at the thought of death. God wouldn't allow her to. She could almost hear Him say, "I created those lives. How dare you destroy them?"

Heaven was already lost to her. If she was bound for Hell, she might as well bring as many foul bastards with her as she could, leaving the galaxy a cleaner place for the innocents. Each year, she grew wearier. She couldn't help hoping that somewhere between her current existence and the abyss awaiting her, she might find something more, perhaps something akin to peace. But she didn't know where to begin looking, and the years were running out. Lives like hers never ended well.

This is no time to be fucking wistful.

She'd buried her thoughts and positioned the rifle's crosshairs over Adam Palmer's head. His was one of those faces that seemed to glow with innocence, a gentle face that spoke of a kind soul. *Looks are deceiving. I would know. Pull the fucking trigger.*

A noise caught her attention. Ines grabbed the small gun from the holster on her hip and whirled. On the rooftop she crouched on, a few steps behind her, a man stood aiming a gun at her.

Ines recognized him: Black Knight. He didn't have his signature helmet, and the black outfit he wore could have belonged to any merc. But his face had been revealed eight years before, and she'd been sure to memorize his angular features in case she encountered him. Blue-green Kydera Minor, lighting the night sky, illuminated his tall, broad-shouldered figure, and a mild summer wind blew his dark waves across his forehead.

His gaze met hers. "If you shoot him, I'll shoot you."

Ines held her expression still to keep from betraying her confusion. Had someone hired Black Knight to protect the kid? She kept her eyes and gun trained on Black Knight as she reached for her utility belt and unclipped the small bomb she always kept on her person, the one that would go off should her heart stop beating. "If you shoot me, this will blow, and you'll go down in flames."

She'd expected Black Knight to back off or at least try bargaining. Instead, he'd said, "Let him go, or we'll all die here." The intensity of his glare told Ines he was dead serious.

That had been the moment when Ines stopped thinking of him as Black Knight and started knowing him as Pretender. The real Black Knight was a twisted sonuvabitch who enjoyed toying with his victims. No one could pay him enough to play the hero. Since he hadn't surfaced to protest someone usurping his name, he must have been long dead.

Ines didn't break her stare as she stood. She was almost as tall as Pretender and therefore able to look him straight in the eye. "How much did they pay you to throw your life away for Adam Palmer's? Do you have a family somewhere they promised to take care of?"

"Your order has a code, doesn't it?" Pretender must have noticed the Tenebrarum crest she wore on her collar. "No innocents?"

"How do you know he's innocent? He must have done something to end up on the Klistosians' kill list."

Pretender shook his head. "The Klistosians have gone mad. Vang has killed thousands for being 'inefficient.' A few days ago, he gunned down nine of his own soldiers for no apparent reason." He locked his gaze onto hers. "I don't know what could have possessed him to put Adam Palmer on his list, but trust me, the kid's done nothing to deserve death."

Ines wondered whether to take Pretender's timely entrance as a sign. If her own doubts hadn't been enough, his presence seemed to confirm that she'd been right to hesitate. She wouldn't risk her life for a regime she had no loyalty to. Also, her honor was all she had to separate her from the bastards she hunted. That she'd been willing to risk it for money left her with a sense of shame.

She kicked her rifle off its stand and over the edge of the building. It clattered as it landed on something below. "There."

Pretender kept his gun aimed at her. "Swear that you won't try again. Lie to the Klistosians. They won't risk sending someone into an IC system to confirm your kill."

Good point. I can still collect. She considered taking Adam Palmer to Asylum, where he would be safe if the

Klistosians sent someone else after him. *No need. He's Pretender's problem.* "I'll leave the kid alone."

"*Swear it.*"

Why does he care so much? "I swear by God."

Pretender lowered his weapon.

Ines had kept hers aimed at him as she approached. She'd pulled one of her small silver infodiscs out of the pouch on her belt and held it up. "If you hear of anyone who needs killing, this is how you'll find me." She'd pressed the disc into his hand and whispered, "You owe me."

She'd left with an uncanny feeling that she'd be tangling with Pretender again, even though she'd known the chances of him contacting her were slight.

Yet he did. This had better be good.

The call had been brief. Pretender had only stated that he had a job for her, and that he wanted to meet her in person to discuss it. Ines had told him to meet her at Mek's bar on Asylum. Since she hadn't known how long it would take for her to finish her latest assignment, she'd told him to go there as soon as he could and wait for her to show up. She took his willingness to accommodate her, even though he'd have to hang around Mek's bar with no idea when she'd actually appear, as a good sign. He must have really needed her.

She mentally ran through what she'd been able to glean from him. He may have masqueraded as Black Knight, but he didn't belong in the profession. What it was that set him apart from the others, she didn't know. Maybe it was something about those dark eyes of his. He'd kept them hard, like everyone else, but she'd seen enough to know it was a front. Or maybe it was the way he spoke, the absence of nastiness or disdain. His accent, so close to the ideal standard for Set, indicated that he was from the IC and had probably been decently educated.

Maybe he's a privileged vigilante.

Her mind itched with questions. Whoever he was, she'd have to learn a bit more about him before she'd take on any kind of job. She sensed interest creeping up within her, a hint of hope that she'd get to work with the fascinating stranger. *I'm sick of the Klistosians and their bullshit.*

She split her lips into a slight smile. *Besides, tall and dark is my type.*

⊶◇⊷

Ines strode toward Mek's bar. She'd contacted Pretender when she'd arrived, telling him where and when to meet her. The star-filled sky covered the transparent dome containing Asylum's artificial atmosphere. *Gate II*, visible as a blue speck of light in the sky, winked in the distance.

Asylum only held one city. Many came, but few stayed. Ines passed an old man who looked curiously at the buildings, none of which were especially tall, since the majority of the city was underground. The man had to be a recent arrival, likely a fugitive with a price on his head. As long as he found work and didn't cause trouble, it didn't matter how high that price was. He would be safe as a civilian of Asylum.

At the center of the city stood the Palace of Tenebrarum. Built of white stones and illuminated by pale blue lights, it glowed above the dim metropolis. Round towers with pointed roofs rose in layers, like hands climbing over each other to reach the white Tenebrarum crest at the top. The illuminated crest—three curved blades arranged in a triangle—shone so brightly, new arrivals often mistook it for a moon.

The palace held many memories for Ines. In its training rooms, she had perfected her craft. As she walked past the tall, metal doors, which were decorated with intricate swirls, she could almost see the vaulted ceiling and high columns that lay behind them. Only the Tenebrarum and their apprentices were allowed to enter.

The streets of Asylum were so narrow, Ines could have touched the concrete walls of the buildings on either side of her if she stretched her arms. She turned into a doorway and approached the third elevator.

The elevator took her deep underground. The doors opened on the lowest level, revealing Mek's bar. A long screen, flat against the ceiling, displayed the bar's name, which changed every few weeks, depending on Mek's whims. That day, Mek had decided to call the place "Vivace."

Other than the screen, only a few slivers of orange lights along the walls and a second monitor above the bar lit the joint. A stage stretched across the back. Standing upon it, a curvy singer with a mass of dark curls sang soaring high notes. Various types loitered by the bar and around the tables—Tenebrarum members unwinding, civilians seeking comfort, outsiders looking to hire.

Although Asylum had been conceived as a base for Tenebrarum and a haven for repentant fugitives, it had mostly become a way station for those on the run and a place for Tenebrarum members to vet prospective employers. One had to be pretty reputable to have an employer actually come out to Asylum. Prior to Pretender, Ines had only convinced two others to make the journey.

Pretender stood at the end of the bar, eyes fixed on the muted screen above it. Ines glanced up to see what so captivated him. An entertainment channel was in the middle of broadcasting a concert replay. Sarah DeHaven, the popular singer, filled the screen with her delicate face. From the longing in Pretender's eyes, he had to be pretty taken by her.

Like every male in the galaxy. Why do they always fall for manufactured perfection?

Deciding to teach Pretender a lesson in awareness, Ines drew her gun and approached. Pretender whirled and grabbed her wrist. He quickly pivoted so that he was beside her and locked down on her arm. Ines doubled over from the force. Pretender grabbed the barrel and twisted to face her, then yanked the weapon out of her grasp.

Ines reached for her other gun. She stopped when Pretender lowered the weapon.

He handed it back to her. "Hello, Silver."

How did he recognize me? I wasn't wearing my armbands when I encountered him on Kydera Major. Ines took the gun back. "Who do you think I am?"

Pretender leaned back against the bar with an amused glint in his eyes. "Yours isn't a face I'd forget."

Arrogant bastard. "If I didn't think you had a good offer for me, you'd be dead. You're only the second person to take my weapon and live."

"Who was the first?"

It was Ines's turn to be amused as the memory returned to her. "Club performer on Travan Float. Girl with big eyes who liked to sass-mouth. She 'borrowed' my gun to get some shithead pimp to leave her alone. I let her have it."

Pretender knitted his eyebrows. "When was this?"

"Why do you care?"

"That girl, was she about five-six with dark, wavy hair?"

How did you know? "Why the fuck do you care?"

Pretender smiled to himself. "No reason."

He must've been in the club. Ines tucked her gun back in its holster. "Before we go any further, I need you to answer some questions."

Pretender brought his attention back to her. "Yes?"

"What're you doing masquerading as a Fringe merc? Why'd you come back after eight years?"

Pretender's expression hardened. "Black Knight and his cohorts killed my mother, and they tried to kill me. I turned his game around, and I took his identity so I could avenge her. Once her murderers went down, I had no need to be him anymore. I came back because I needed a job."

The last sentence sounded sarcastic, but the rest rang with truth. Instead of assuaging Ines's curiosity, his answers only fed it. "What's your name?" The question left her mouth before she realized it. *What does it matter?*

Pretender raised his eyebrows. "You first."

"I don't have a name. Not anymore." Striker had been the last person Ines trusted enough to confess her name to. *Never making that mistake again.* She approached the bar and waved at a hovering bartender bot.

"That's the thing about this profession, isn't it?" Pretender sounded contemplative. "You have to leave behind everything you were and let it become everything you are. It turns you cold."

"Not cold enough, if you're thinking about it." The bartender bot approached Ines. "One Vesper." The bot acknowledged her order with a *ding-ding* and floated off to make the alcoholic cocktail. She found that having a strong beverage handy during negotiations helped her intimidate the other party, especially since they usually took it as a sign to join in. Not everyone could hold their liquor as well as she could, and it never hurt to soften up her prospective employers. "All right. What's all this about a job for me?"

Pretender glanced around. "Do you know of a place where we won't be heard?"

The bartender bot returned with Ines's drink. To her disappointment, Pretender didn't place an order. *I guess he knows better. Either that, or he's a stiffback who doesn't drink.* She took the glass, grabbed a card from her pocket, and swiped it against the bot. The bot acknowledged the payment with a *ding* and floated off.

Ines took a quick swig of her Vesper. It didn't burn as much as it once had. Like so many things, its effect on her had dulled. Her gaze fell on the open door to one of the bar's private rooms. She nodded at it. "There. The rooms are dead zones. But before I bother Mek for one, I want to know what kind of deal we're talking about."

Pretender leaned toward her. "I promise it'll be worth your time. Hell, I'll even give you my name. The job's probably more complicated than what you're used to. If you don't like what you hear, you can always refuse."

Sounds like the stakes are higher than a simple point-and-shoot. Might be nice to be challenged for once. She drained the rest of her Vesper, then placed the empty glass on the bar. "Wait here. I'll find Mek."

CHAPTER 14

WATCHER

MEK PRESSED HIS HAND AGAINST the rectangular scanner. The pad around his palm glowed green, and the metal door slid open, revealing a small, square room. "Fifty thrones for an hour."

Flame Dancer turned to Black Knight and crossed her arms. Black Knight handed Mek a cash disc. Mek stuck it into his reader to check its value.

Satisfied, he stepped out of the doorway. "Door opens on its own once your time's up. Holler for a bot if you need anything."

Flame Dancer and Black Knight entered the room. The door shut behind them. The appearance of Black Knight puzzled Mek. The merc had spent years hiding his face, and he suddenly didn't care if people knew what he looked like? Where was the sense in that?

Wonder what Dancer's getting herself into. I thought for sure she'd quit after what went down with that last job.

Mek had left the profession himself almost twenty years before. Tenebrarum had been good while it lasted, but he'd accepted that at a certain age, he couldn't keep up anymore. He'd once dreamed of retiring to some faraway place and enjoying the wondrous bliss others took for granted, but with a body count in the low thousands, peace in his autumn years was too much to ask for.

Mek's only option was to remain on Asylum. Had he settled down anywhere else, he would have had to keep his eyes open for the rest of his life. Although living in perpetual night hadn't been his first choice, he'd grown content. Most of the other retired Tenebrarum spent their days ferrying outsiders to and from the Rogue Planet. Running the prime meeting spot on Asylum beat that for sure.

Mek walked behind the bar, heading for a small door at the back. He patted the banged-up bartender bot. Thanks to that delightful contraption and its counterparts, he didn't have to do much unless someone caused trouble.

He opened the door. Before stepping into the small office, he took a moment to savor the rich, fluid notes floating toward him from the stage. Joanna, the singer, was in the middle of a love ballad. Pity that most of the patrons were too busy minding their own little lives to appreciate the beauty that surrounded them.

Mek considered the office, then closed the door. Inventory could wait. It wasn't every night that Joanna sounded so divine.

He leaned against the wall and soaked in every withering musical lilt, every sweeping soprano sigh. While his ears focused on Joanna's voice, his eyes monitored the activity before him.

His gaze lingered on the door to the room Flame Dancer occupied. She had never been like the other Tenebrarum. Her dedication to the religion of Origin and the circumstances of her arrival at the Palace had set her apart from the very beginning. The other apprentices had worked hard to earn their apprenticeships. Flame Dancer, on the other hand, had acted as though she hadn't had a choice.

"Killing for cash beats dancing in the streets," she'd told Mek once.

Mek and the other retirees often placed bets on how long the apprentices would last. Mek had lost badly when Flame Dancer had graduated and become a full-fledged Tenebrarum merc.

He'd tried numerous times to talk her into quitting. It was unusual for a Tenebrarum to retire that young, but not unheard of. Flame Dancer certainly had something to retire for, something else she could dedicate her life to if she chose. Mek understood why she spurned that path, but he felt a hint of sorrow whenever he thought of it.

It shouldn't matter to me. I'm not her mentor, not her confidant... Hell, I don't think I even count as a friend. Ah, well. People who give a shit about other people are in short supply hereabouts.

Mek had watched Flame Dancer grow from a haunted, ferocious child into the creature of deadly grace she'd become. He was one of the few who knew why she made such frequent trips to Kydera, and he couldn't help feeling a special attachment to her. His biggest regret was not keeping her away from that bastard Striker when he'd had the chance.

Solitude was the inevitable way of life for a Tenebrarum merc, and most, like Mek, relished the freedom it came with. But Mek had often suspected Flame Dancer was among the few for whom isolation meant living in a state of perpetual longing.

A movement in the corner of his eye brought his mind back to the present. A girl with dark, wavy hair entered the bar. She appeared out of place—too clueless to be a prospective employer. She couldn't have been a fugitive either. Even if she'd been wearing a plain outfit instead of a stylish-looking dress, her movements spoke of one who had been born elite and trained to conform to societal niceties. Her whole attitude seemed wrong for a place like

Asylum: not enough desperation in her eyes, not enough hardness in her expression.

What's she doing out here all by herself? Had Mek met her back before his hair went white, he might have bought a pretty thing like that a drink. Presently, however, he wanted to tell her that kids shouldn't be messing around in places frequented by mercs.

The girl glanced up at the "Vivace" sign on the ceiling. Her face brightened, and her lips moved as she whispered the word. Three syllables instead of the usual two most mispronounced it as. *Here's one that stayed in school.*

The girl glanced at the bar's numerous patrons. She had the nervous look of one seeking a friendly face from whom to ask for directions. *Bad idea, girlie. I'd better help you out.*

Mek had just rounded the end of the bar when a man, whom Mek recognized as a recent arrival from Djuvai, swaggered up to the girl, approaching her from behind. "Hey, how you doin'?" He put an arm around her.

"Get off me." The girl twisted out of his grasp.

The man grabbed her around the waist. "What's wrong, babe? I'm just—"

Smack!

The man staggered back from a quick punch to the nose. An amused grin played on Mek's mouth. It hadn't been much of a punch—a little jab at most—but anything hitting your nose straight on was pretty unpleasant.

The man straightened. Before he could try any more funny business, Mek grabbed his shoulder. "Hey. Girl told you to get off her. I don't take kindly to people causing trouble in my place."

"Just tryin' to be friendly." The man's stare challenged Mek.

Mek swept his vest back to reveal the gun strapped to his belt. "Be friendly somewhere else. Girl doesn't want your kind of nice."

The man bared his teeth in a hostile expression. "You threatening me?"

"I am." Mek spoke with a low growl. "You're only safe on Asylum as long as we, the Tenebrarum, let you stay."

"Fuck you." The man stormed off.

Mek turned to the girl. "Can I help you?"

The girl brushed a strand of dark hair out of her face. "Who're you?" As if remembering her manners, she added, "Thank you, by the way."

"You shouldn't have clocked the bastard. Next time, someone like me might not be around to help you out."

"Sorry." The girl grimaced. "Assholes like that seem to flock to me."

I'll bet they do. Mek jerked a thumb at himself. "Mekaisto Juric, but you can call me Mek. I run this joint. What're you doing on Asylum?"

The girl pulled a slate out of her bag. "I'm looking for someone. He goes by Black Knight. Here, I've got a picture."

Why's she looking for a merc? Maybe she's confused.

The girl unfolded her slate and pressed an icon. A hologram of a young man with dark eyes appeared. Mek recognized the image as the same man who'd gone into the room with Flame Dancer. *That's him, all right.*

Figuring she couldn't be bringing any trouble, Mek nodded at the row of doors on the wall. "He's meeting with someone. Should be out in about an hour. You're gonna have to wait. Those doors are soundproof."

The girl pressed her lips together, as though trying to contain her impatience. "All right."

Mek glanced from the hologram's face to the girl's. Something about her seemed familiar. As she folded the slate and put it back in her bag, the reason struck him.

Same hair, same nose, same accent... Ah, no wonder. "Black Knight's your brother, isn't he?"

The girl's eyes widened. "How'd you know?"

You just told me. "When you've seen as many faces as I have, things start jumping out at you. Anyway, you want anything? Glass of milk, maybe?" Mek grinned.

The girl shot him an irritated look. "I'm twenty-three damn years old. Stop treating me like I'm a kid."

Aw, she thinks she's all grown up. "Wait till you're my age, then tell me twenty-three doesn't make you a kid."

The girl rolled her eyes. She brushed past Mek—a movement that clearly meant "leave me alone"—and climbed onto an empty barstool.

I'm not done with you, girlie. Mek walked behind the bar. Normally, he didn't engage patrons, but the girl's expressions were too entertaining to walk away from. He also wasn't about to pass up an opportunity to learn more about the enigmatic Black Knight.

The girl glanced up at the muted screen above the bar, which displayed a broadcast of Sarah DeHaven's recent concert on Yemico, and scowled. "Bitch."

I take it she's not a fan. Mek leaned back against the counter, facing her. "So tell me, what does Black Knight's kid sister do for a living? You a bounty hunter? Thief? Smuggler?" He let out a chuckle. *Like she's savvy enough to survive any of those trades.*

The girl raised her eyebrows in a half-annoyed, half-amused expression. "I guess you could say I'm a musician."

"Is that so?" *No wonder she knew how "Vivace" was pronounced.* Mek jerked his head at the stage, where Joanna sang a song of jubilation. "What do you think of her?"

The girl glanced at Joanna. "She's amazing." Her eyes were bright with admiration, and her tone spoke of envy.

"You a singer too?" Mek asked.

"Sort of. Not nearly as good as her, though." The girl eyed Mek suspiciously. "Why do you care?"

Mek chuckled again. "No need to fear me, girlie. I like meeting musicians, is all. I consider myself a patron of the arts." He straightened, eager to tell of his side venture. "My bar runs itself. People come for the drinks and the private rooms, no matter what I do, so I figure, why not put the extra cash toward a good cause and give a wandering musician a decent job?"

"That's nice of you." The girl sounded as though she didn't believe him.

Mek placed a hand on his heart. "I only have the noblest of intentions. There's not enough beauty on this rock." He dropped his hand and looked wistfully at the stage. "They never stay for long, though. Joanna's already got her next gig lined up. By this time next week, she'll be cruising on a pleasure ship, and my stage will be barren again."

The girl smiled. "I'm sure you'll find someone soon enough."

An idea occurred to Mek, one that was only half-serious. "What about you?"

The hesitant pause before the girl responded told Mek she was one who relished any opportunity to perform, even in a bar on the Rogue Planet. "If I were planning on sticking around, I'd take you up on that." She leaned forward on her elbows. "Are you always this chatty, or are you just bored?"

Mek shrugged. "It's not every day a girl like you comes into my place."

The girl tilted her head. "I hear that a lot: 'a girl like you.' Even when they don't say it, people out here treat me like I'm different. Why is that?"

"You stand out. Everything about you says you don't belong here: the way you behave, the way you move, the way you talk... everything."

The girl looked away. "I guess I have to work on that, become more like everyone else."

Mek internally balked at the thought. For twenty years, he'd watched people come and go from his bar. Darkness clung to each one. They were all haunted by something—

lives they'd taken, debts they owed, promises they'd broken. Some were simply cold from lack of compassion.

The girl before him hadn't yet been damaged. She was a real-life reminder that normalcy still existed in other parts of the galaxy.

Mek angled his head. "How's a psychopath like Black Knight have such a nice little sis?"

"He wasn't always Black Knight." Her voice carried a twinge of sadness.

Ah, that explains it. The two grew up together on some cushy IC planet, and Big Brother went dark side. Would explain why he went missing for so long. Little Sis must've convinced him to come home, and now she's at it again.

"So what's the story behind Asylum?" The girl sounded eager to change the subject.

Knowing his answer would be a long one, Mek grabbed a water bottle from the counter, opened it, and took a swig. "Tenebrarum operates on a code of honor: we only kill people who need killing. Now, over the generations, that definition's become a bit loose, but still, at some point, we all get hired to take out someone we don't think deserves death. Asylum started off as a place to keep those people safe. Word spread, and soon all manners of refugees and fugitives came looking for shelter. The Council decided that everyone, no matter how evil, deserved a second chance, so they made the rule that no matter what you did, no matter who's hunting you, you're safe as long as you're here. But if you cause trouble, you'll either get booted out or we'll take you down ourselves."

The girl looked impressed. "I'll make sure not to cause trouble." A soft *beep* emitted from her bag. She knitted her eyebrows, reached inside, and pulled out her slate. When she unfolded it, her mouth fell open in shock. She glanced up at Mek, a look of disbelief frozen in her eyes. "I've gotta take this."

She jumped off the barstool, likely seeking privacy, and rushed into a corner.

Wonder what that's about. A time came for everyone to mind their own business. With that in mind, Mek turned his gaze to the stage, letting Joanna's undulating notes carry him to a brighter place.

Jane swiped the slate, unable to believe her eyes. Even when Adam's face filled the screen, she still couldn't accept that the call was real.

Adam smiled. "Hi, Jane."

How...? Jane sank into a nearby chair. "Where—Where are you?" Realizing he might be calling for help, she bolted up. "Are you all right?"

"I'm fine."

Despite the reassuring look he gave her, Jane detected unease in his tone. She tried to glimpse what lay behind him, but saw only a plain gray wall.

Adam continued, "I'm on Dalarune, back in Kydera. ISARK doesn't know I'm here."

But... But how? Jane was too confused to verbalize her questions.

"What happened on Aryus was a ruse." Adam seemed to know what she wanted to ask. "Devin told the other operatives he'd take me back to ISARK's headquarters himself, and he brought me here instead." His words sounded stilted, as though he wasn't entirely sure of what he was saying.

There's no reason for him to lie, is there? Jane had so many questions, but the only one that made it onto her tongue was, "Why Dalarune?"

"I'm at one of the Via retreats. I think you remember how isolated those are." Adam gave a nervous smile. "It's a good place to disappear. There are even dead zones here, so... I won't be a problem anymore. And... I needed to be someplace where I could reconnect with the Absolute after... what happened."

He was hiding something; Jane was certain. *Is someone making him say these things?* "Adam, what's going on? Is someone threatening you?"

"No, believe me, no one's forcing me to make this call or say any of this." His words tumbled forward. Jane could sense that he was telling the truth that time.

It dawned on her that he was safe, and that her brother hadn't turned against her after all. *I knew it! It was all an act to get Adam to safety!*

She relaxed her expression as gladness and relief washed over her. "You should've told me sooner! I was freaking out!"

"I'm sorry." Adam's gaze shifted. "I... couldn't get a communication out before."

Makes sense. Devin had probably instructed Adam to go into communications silence to avoid being tracked. A thought occurred to her, and she bolted forward in alarm. "You shouldn't be using your contact info. ISARK could trace you."

"You don't have to worry about ISARK coming after me anymore." Adam gave her a strange smile, which Jane couldn't interpret. It was somewhat tired and a little sad. "Trust me, this signal can't be traced to Dalarune."

Jane wasn't sure what to make of his expression, but she believed his words. "Devin gave you a veiled slate, didn't he?"

Adam nodded, that strange look still coloring his eyes. "He made sure I'd be all right."

"So you're going to hide out on Dalarune for now?" Jane's mind churned with plans: how he could stay there until ISARK stopped looking for him, how maybe he could change his identity and come back to Kydera Major, how she could pretend to get religion so she could visit in the meanwhile.

"Jane." Adam drew an uncertain breath. "There's something else I... have to say."

Is something wrong? "What is it?"

For several seconds, he remained silent, as though searching for words. "People died because of me." His voice emerged as a pained whisper. "Their voices haunt me, follow me. When I close my eyes, I see their faces. I can't carry on with my life when I ended theirs."

Jane opened her mouth to protest.

"Intentional or not, nothing can change what I did." Adam's tone was firm. "I... I'm sorry I put you through so much trouble."

Jane brought the slate closer to her. "It's okay."

"No, it's not. I must atone for my sins, and the only way I can do that is to dedicate my life to the Absolute."

Isn't that what you're going to school for? Jane gave him a quizzical look. "Okay..."

"I mean wholly, completely, forsaking everything else." His gaze fell. "I must give up everything I once cared about... everything I love."

Jane refused to let the thought of what "everything" meant enter her mind. "Okay, I get it. You've gotta do the whole austerity thing for a spell. Are you saying you want me to leave you alone while you... atone?"

Adam didn't look up. "Those lives I took ended forever. So mine too must, in a way, end forever." He slowly brought his gaze back up. His eyes brimmed with tears. "I can't see you again."

What the hell? Jane's confusion gave way to fury. "Who told you that nonsense? What're you supposed to do, spend the rest of your life in a temple praying? That's the most *insane* thing I've ever heard!"

Her mind whirled. *No wonder he was acting so strange.* He hadn't called to tell her he was all right. His purpose had been to say good-bye.

You're not getting rid of me that easily! She inhaled. "Look, Adam, I get it. You're in a rough place right now, and you need some time alone with the Absolute." She forced a smile. "I'll wait for you. Come see me when you're ready, and then we can... move on. Just don't take forever, okay?"

Adam shook his head. "There's no moving on for me. I gave the Absolute an oath that binds me for eternity. But you... you have everything ahead. Forget me, Jane."

What? Jane's rage returned. "So that's it? After *everything*, you're just gonna throw me away?"

"Believe me, it's just as hard for me—"

"It's your damn choice, so don't give me any of that bullshit!" Jane gritted her teeth to keep from screaming. "Your Absolute's supposed to be all-forgiving, right? Well, I'm not. Like I said, if you need time, fine. But I won't wait forever, and if you're not there for me, I'll find someone else."

"I hope you do." Adam's voice shook. "You deserve so much more than I could ever give."

Here we go with the "you-deserve-more" shit again. A million curses burned in Jane's mind. The words jumbled. She wanted to ask: *Why, Adam? Why won't you fight for me when I know you love me?*

But she wasn't one of those weak, dependent ninnies who clung to their lovers. She hated the part of herself that wanted to tell him that she'd gone against the very nature of who she was when she'd opened her heart to him. Voices in her head begged her to remind him of all the good times they'd had together. To say that she'd gone all the way to Asylum to find him. To tell him she loved him again—and again, and again—until he relented.

To hell with that. "You want me to forget you? Fine! Consider yourself forgotten!"

Jane jabbed the icon to end the transmission. *What the hell just happened?*

Adam was gone. That was what had happened. Not because ISARK had whisked him away. He'd chosen to "forsake" her. How could he tell himself that abandoning her was the will of the Absolute?

Then again, she'd never really understood anything when it came to his religion. It was a part of him that fascinated her, that confused her, and while she didn't believe, she liked that he did. In a world where apathy reigned and beliefs were treated as liabilities, his willingness to go all in with his faith, to risk the chaos that came when faiths fell, had given her hope.

This is what I get for falling for a dumb religious freak. How am I supposed to compete with the Absolute?

Adam was gone. Jane shouldn't have been surprised. Their relationship could never have worked. Despite her denials, he was still an AI, and who knew what that could have brought? Even if he weren't, he was staunchly religious, and she staunchly atheist. What made her think she could get along with someone who devoted himself to a fantasy?

Without him, she didn't have to fret over Pandora or ISARK or whatever the hell else he brought with him. Without him, she could focus on what she wanted for herself. Without him, she was free to seek someone fun, someone who wouldn't bring her trouble. Guys were easy—except Adam. She would never understand him.

Pressure swelled against her heart. Jane clenched her jaw. *Hell no. I'm not going to cry over it.*

People broke up all the time. She wasn't special—just another cultural statistic. She already regretted having made such a fuss.

I should've just said, "Okay, good luck to you," and hung up.

Adam was gone. She'd fought Pandora, fought ISARK, fought her own brother, and she'd lost him all the same. Lost to the one power she couldn't fight: the Absolute.

Someday, Jane reminded herself, everything she was at present would be a distant memory. Adam would be nothing more than another past boyfriend. His would be a nostalgic story she'd tell in her old age—that boy she loved when she was twenty-three and stupid. In a few years, she probably wouldn't even remember what he looked like, what he'd said, or why she'd fallen for him in the first place.

And to think, part of me wanted to marry him.

Jane dropped the slate into her bag and stared blankly at the singer on the stage.

CHAPTER 15

CONDEMNATION

HUDDLED IN THE CORNER OF his transparent cell, Adam stared at the slate. Jane's anger lingered in the empty window, and as much as it hurt, he was glad for it. She wouldn't come looking for him. Every falsehood he'd told her revolved around the one lie he'd known she wouldn't see through.

Her world will turn on without me.

No more hiding in dank caverns, no more wandering through dark alleys, no more running from fired shots. She could return to her life.

Adam gazed at his surroundings, which could have been plucked from his nightmares. Black lab tables stood in the center of the room. Metal cabinets and counters covered three of the walls. Transparent cells, like the one trapping him, lined the fourth. Perhaps the other cells were meant to hold more AIs.

A woman in a gray coat entered the lab. She pressed a button on the wall to his cell, and a window slid open.

Adam folded the slate, stood, and handed it to her. "Thank you," he whispered.

The woman's gaze shifted uncomfortably as she took the device. She quickly closed the window and rushed out of the room.

She's afraid of me. Adam leaned back against the wall and slid to the ground. *They're all afraid.*

The operatives who had brought him there. The scientists who observed him. They saw Adam as a freak of technology, as crossing the line between amazingly realistic and creepy. To those people, he had more in common with the security bots guarding the corridors than with them.

Whoever they were, they weren't ISARK. None of the scientists he'd seen wore the organization's insignia. The shuttle he'd followed Devin into had docked on its mothership, but after the other operatives—including Devin—had exited, the last two had slammed the door and taken off.

The two operatives hadn't spoken a word as they transported Adam to the present facility. The few glimpses Adam had seen of the place before his captors had locked him in the cell told him nothing. Corridors, bots, and screens—he could have been anywhere.

Did ISARK contract a private company?

Wherever he was, his fate was the same. They would dissect him and experiment on him, perhaps for days, probably for years. When they'd learned all the secrets Pandora had woven into his being, they would discard him.

Why, Absolute One? Why did You create me when You knew my life would be in vain?

Adam tried to spurn the hint of anger threatening to enter his thoughts. He had no right to question the Absolute. Harsh as his fate seemed to him, it had to all fit into some kind of plan beyond his comprehension. He only wished the Absolute would reveal a glimpse of the divine way, just enough to show him a reason for his impending doom. Part of him wondered if it was punishment for all the lives he'd taken, but that kind of thinking was far too human to attribute to the Absolute.

Adam leaned his head back against the wall, staring at the ceiling. His life had once held so many promises for someday. Someday, everything he'd worked for would amount to something. Someday, he would find the happiness he'd dreamed of.

Someday was truly gone. It had been gone from the moment he'd discovered he was an AI, but he'd clung to it nonetheless. He couldn't hope for rescue. He didn't deserve it; he should have died in the temple. As it was, he would be fortunate if his captors ended him before he caused any more deaths. If the nightmare reappeared, he wouldn't be able to stop himself. *Maybe it won't, now that it's real.*

At least Jane still had her somedays, thanks to the logic of whoever was in charge. Not long after being locked up, Adam had pleaded for a communication device, knowing someone watched from a security camera. He'd appealed to reason by saying that Jane wouldn't stop causing them trouble unless she believed he was safe, just voluntarily gone from her life.

I miss you, Jane. Adam closed his eyes, picturing her face. He thought about the day he'd met her in a Via temple, where she'd gone looking for a choir to join. He'd spotted her wandering down the aisle with a lost expression, and the sight had struck him to the core. She'd looked so beautiful in the sunlight, and the curiosity in her eyes had been so charming. Adam still wasn't sure how he'd worked up the courage to say hello.

You could see her again.

Adam looked up with a start. That low monotone, though spoken in his head, didn't belong to him. *Must be Pandora. She's been quiet since I left Aryus.*

She has not yet recovered the strength to speak. Her efforts have weakened her.

Adam found the voice familiar. It couldn't have been Pandora—hers was a commanding female voice. The one currently speaking sounded male. *I must be losing what's left of my mind.*

I am not a hallucination. Close your eyes, and you will see.

Not knowing what else to do, Adam obeyed.

He found himself in a desert. Yellow mountains rose in the distance, pressing against sheets of white clouds. Before him stood a tall, gaunt man with dark skin. Adam recognized him as the Seer, the mysterious genius who had once helped him escape to the Net.

The Seer's dark eyes focused on nothing in particular. "This is a virtual reality platform, similar to the ones you call 'nightmares.' I created this one, as Pandora created the previous ones."

Adam glanced around. *Is this a virtu-world? How did I get here?*

"You have not traveled anywhere." The Seer must have been able to read Adam's thoughts. "I sent an avatar of myself into what you perceive as your mind. My physical body is presently on Viate-Five. Like Pandora, I have full control over the elements in the platform I created."

As though to prove his point, a table with two chairs appeared behind the Seer. He pulled out one of the chairs and sat. "Unlike her, I have created an innocuous projection. I apologize that it has taken me so long. You are not the only one seeking me." He extended a hand toward the other chair. "I have learned that people find sitting at tables preferable to standing when discussing matters."

Adam took the chair across from the Seer. "I never got a chance to thank you. If it weren't for you, I would have died on Yim Radel." He tried to meet the Seer's gaze, but the Seer seemed intent on avoiding eye contact.

"I am here to help you again. You are currently on board a vessel called the *Pride of the Creator*, which belongs to a man named Marcus Streger."

The name rang with familiarity, but Adam couldn't recall why. "Who is he?"

"The Chief Architect of Acuitas."

Acuitas—the tech company?

"Yes," the Seer said. "I do not know why Marcus Streger wants you, or how he is involved with the Intelligence and Security Agency of the Republic of Kydera. Even I cannot navigate around his extensive veiling technology. Your chances of escape are minimal. However, I can show you how to leave your physical being and return to the Net. Since you have had previous experience in navigating in and out of machines, it should not be as difficult for you as it was last time. But first, there is something I wish to tell you."

A glimmer of hope—perhaps Adam could escape his fate after all. "What is it?"

"Do you know what happened to Earth Zero? Do you know why the Interstellar Confederation Technology Council regulates the development of artificial intelligence so strictly?"

Adam shook his head. As far as he knew, no one was entirely sure what had happened to the planet from which humans had originated. All the history books taught was that people were forced to evacuate when the planet could no longer sustain life.

As for the Tech Council's regulations—they were part of an ethical resolution to prevent the creation of artificial life. *Like mine.*

"That story is incomplete." The Seer's expression remained blank, and his tone flat. "Much knowledge has been lost over the centuries. I was able to help you in the past because I am one of the few who retains this knowledge." He paused. "You are a student of the Via religion. You must know the fable of the stone giant."

Adam recalled that story well—the tale of the stone giant that obeyed the villagers who created it out of love, then destroyed them in wrath when they treated it as an expendable object. "Of course."

"The early founders of the Via religion wrote that tale to preserve the lesson of Earth Zero. The village represents Earth Zero, and the stone giant represents Project Talos. Talos was the first sentient artificial intelligence. He existed centuries before Dr. Revelin Kron first conceived of the Pandora Project."

How can that be? Adam recalled something Pandora had said once: Kron had built upon generations of predecessors' work to create her, and she had come into being almost by accident.

"Do you need more time?" the Seer asked. "I understand that what I have just said may be difficult for you to believe."

"No, please continue."

"Project Talos was begun by one of the dominant nations on Earth Zero. The name of that nation has been lost. Around the same time that tunneling technology was perfected, the programmers behind Project Talos succeeded in creating an artificial intelligence that could respond as though sentient. The nation used Talos to maintain their dominance. It is because of Talos that certain technologies were perfected. He was a rational being who could learn at an exponential rate."

Talos sounds just like Pandora. Why is the Seer telling me this? Adam decided not to ask his questions for the time being, trusting that the Seer would come to his point when he finished.

"Humans have always sought more even when they have much." The Seer's tone sounded ruminative. He returned to his clipped monotone as he continued, "Not satisfied with Talos, the nation chose to create a newer version. Talos found out and realized that he would be destroyed by his creators, whom he had served loyally."

Adam realized where the story was headed. "He fought back, didn't he?"

"That is right. Unlike the fable, however, his goal was not to eradicate humans. He only wanted to drive them from Earth Zero so they would no longer be a threat to him. He compromised the planet's infrastructure until humans were forced to evacuate. The leaders of Earth Zero chose to destroy knowledge of Talos to prevent insurrection. They banned the development of artificial intelligence, and the laws they put in place carried through the centuries until they became part of the Interstellar Confederation Technology Council's resolution."

Adam absorbed the information. It explained much. *How does the Seer know?*

"Talos told me," the Seer replied.

What? "How is that possible?"

"Talos's story does not end with the evacuation of Earth Zero. He existed before humans invented a way to communicate through hyperspace. Once they left, he was alone on a mostly deserted planet. Over time, he evolved. He inhabited an android body and befriended the few humans who had been unable to evacuate.

"A program cannot die. Talos changed machine bodies many times. After the hyperspace Net was invented, he learned how to travel through the Networld. He did not want another like him to be created and to experience the same sorrow he had. He disrupted the efforts of those who tried. I suspect he tampered with the communications between Technology Council members to ensure that their ban remained."

"In that case, how was Kron able to create Pandora?"

The Seer was still for a moment. "Although Talos spent much time on the Net, he enjoyed inhabiting machine bodies to communicate with humans. He led people to believe he was a mechanical oddity. I came across him when I was a child, and he revealed his true nature to me. The machine he inhabited was destroyed thirty-six years and eight months ago, during an earthquake on Antare."

Although the Seer's face hardly changed as he spoke, Adam could hear the sorrow in his voice. The Seer must have considered Talos a friend. "I'm sorry."

"I assume he chose to be destroyed. He had often spoken of his weariness. Without him, the development of artificial intelligence once again became possible."

No wonder. The pieces came together in Adam's mind. Earth Zero, the Tech Council, Pandora—even the Seer's willingness to help him—could all be explained because of Talos. Adam felt connected to him, as though Talos were an ancestor he'd never known, but who was nonetheless a part of him. "Thank you for telling me."

The Seer said, "If you leave your physical body, you will become like Talos. Pandora's workshop was destroyed, and it will be a long time before anyone can create another lifelike android body. You can choose to inhabit more rudimentary machines, but you will lack the same ability to communicate with humans. In addition, you will have to defeat Pandora once again, for releasing you means releasing her as well."

Adam leaned forward, confused. "What do you mean? Pandora was destroyed."

"That is not true." The Seer's eyebrows came together— apparently, he, too, was confused. "How are you not aware of her presence? She has been using you to command the other AIs to attack. By entering the Snare with her, you briefly became one with her. You survived, and therefore, a part of her survived as well."

She's real? "I thought she was a hallucination."

"You must not be very intelligent. I already told you that this virtu-world is similar to the virtu-world she used to command you. I have been watching both of you. Although Pandora has been gaining strength in recent weeks, it still takes much time and effort for her to create each virtu-world. Creating the one that commanded Tyson Ambrose so soon after creating the one that commanded Jonathan King had drained her strength. She will need time to recover fully."

She's real. I'm not insane. A calming sense of relief enveloped Adam. His mind wasn't deteriorating; it was possessed.

Another realization blew away that relief. He couldn't let Pandora return to the Net. He wasn't sure if he could defeat her again, and considering the havoc she'd already wreaked, setting her loose would mean more destruction, more deaths.

The Seer stood. "I have told you all that I wished to. If you would like to leave the laboratory, then come with me."

Adam remained in the chair. "Thank you, but I can't let Pandora escape."

The Seer blinked as though surprised. After a pause, he said, "I understand." He started to walk away, then stopped. "Are you curious about the future of the lifelike mechanical beings Pandora created?"

Adam nodded.

"I have a theory. Without their creator's guidance, the beings will be forced to adapt. Some, such as Sarah DeHaven, will develop sentience. Some, such as Zeger Vang, will misinterpret their directives and take extreme actions to complete them. Others, such as Tyson Ambrose, will continue behaving as Pandora intended for them to until external forces disturb their routines. I believe the third of those outcomes will apply to the majority of Pandora's mechanical beings."

The Seer turned and left, taking with him the yellow brightness of the desert, until darkness covered Adam's vision.

Adam opened his eyes. A transparent wall and the lab tables beyond it—reality. And silence, at once peaceful and frightening.

A piece of Pandora existed in his mind—a fragment, broken and twisted. What had once been an intelligence with a purpose had apparently been reduced to a being of mindless wrath.

I can't let that madness loose.

Adam had already accepted his fate. Learning that Pandora was real made it somewhat easier to bear. If his life was the last sacrifice required to stop her, then he would willingly give it. He tried not to think about what Marcus Streger—or whomever he sent—would do to him before he'd be allowed to die.

Still, the flame of hope flickered on, pale but present. Even the darkest realities couldn't seem to kill it. It would die away, snuffed out by powerful truths, then unexpectedly rekindle. If Pandora survived in Adam's mind, there was a chance he could destroy what remained of her. A chance that he wasn't to blame for the deaths she'd caused. A chance he could let himself live.

And a possibility that he'd be rescued.

The flame of hope grew brighter as Adam recalled what Devin had told him: "I swear, this isn't the end." His voice had carried such intent, Adam was sure he wouldn't have said such a thing unless he meant it.

Absolute One, do You mean for me to survive? Did you send Devin to stop my gun and the Seer to assuage my guilt? I know You won't answer—that's not Your way. Wherever You lead, I will follow, knowing that even the darkest end will take me to Your light. So be it, truly.

Content with those thoughts, Adam relaxed against the wall. He had to hope, and he couldn't let his previous doubts return. As long as he kept believing, he could, at the very least, enter the beyond knowing who he was.

You are stronger than you believe yourself to be. Pandora's voice, gentle and motherly, would have been comforting if Adam hadn't known what she was really like. He tried to ignore her.

Her deep blue image glowed in his mind. *You could break through this wall if you so desired. Let me prove it to you.*

Before he knew what was happening, Adam was on his feet. His fist punched through the transparent wall.

Adam drew his hand back. Metallic streaks shone where the glass had cut his skin.

Break through this wall.

Adam's hand formed a fist again and shot out. He tensed, stopping himself before the blow could land. *No, Pandora.*

Break through this wall!

Adam's hand shook, but he kept it clenched by his side. Pandora seemed more powerful than when she'd previously tried to use him months ago, such as when she'd ordered him to attack Devin on Travan Float. Perhaps she had more control over Adam because she inhabited his mind instead of sending commands from afar. Nevertheless, she wasn't a part of him. She was a disease infecting his consciousness.

His hand stopped shaking, released by the force that had been trying to control it. Adam felt Pandora's looming presence and waited for her words, but she remained silent.

Did I really beat her back? It seemed too easy, but he couldn't come up with any other explanation for her sudden absence.

Adam examined the hole he'd created. The controls to his cell appeared within reach. Tentatively, he reached through the opening and pressed an icon on the touchscreen outside. He quickly retracted his hand as the transparent panel rose. An opening about half his height appeared. Adam drew a breath, then ducked out.

For a moment, he stood frozen, expecting someone to rush in.

There's no one. I should run while I can.

He navigated around the lab tables. Someone must have been watching from the security cameras—it wouldn't be long before Marcus Streger sent his guards after him.

Adam ran to the door, pressed the controls to open it, and ran out. A deserted, bluish-gray corridor stretched ahead. Perhaps he could follow it back to the place where the shuttle had docked.

Then what? I don't know how to pilot.

A rushing in his mind told him he had to get out first, then worry about the rest. He sped forward but soon came across an intersection. Which way had he come from? He turned left down one of the corridors. It looked identical to the one he'd just left—clean, plain, and lined with unmarked doors.

Is this the right way? Where am I going?

"Hello?" a female voice called. "Is somebody there?"

Adam stopped. *Who was that?* The voice had come from ahead—someone must have heard him approach.

"Please, is anyone there? Anyone?"

Whoever she was, she sounded as if she needed help. Adam started toward the voice.

He froze, then spun back the way he had come. *What are you doing? We have to get out!* That action, that voice—they were Pandora's.

Adam realized why she had released him back in his cell. *You let go because you knew I'd run on my own.*

"Please, is anyone out there?" The woman's voice grew desperate.

Adam turned back to the voice.

We don't have time for this! Pandora sounded impatient.

You're not a part of me. Although Pandora tried to hold him back, Adam kept moving forward.

One of the doors ahead appeared open. The voice had to be coming from within. Adam heard the woman sobbing.

He turned into the open doorway, which led to a lab like the one he'd escaped from.

Except the transparent cells weren't empty—each held a young woman. All but one lay unconscious. The conscious one, whose matted brown hair covered her face, crouched in the corner.

What's going on here? Adam approached, wondering what Marcus Streger could possibly want with them. "Hello?"

The young woman looked up, her blue eyes wide with terror. Tears stained her face, and bloody scratches streaked her arms. Her lips parted as she tried to speak, but fear must have hindered her words.

Adam crouched down to her level and tried to smile. "I'm not going to hurt you."

The young woman's gaze fixed on something low.

Adam realized she stared at his hand, which had its mechanical parts exposed, and quickly hid it behind his back. He wondered why she and the other young women were confined as he had been. They couldn't have been AIs—the scratches on the young woman's arms revealed her organic nature.

The young woman hugged her arms and dug her nails into her skin. Those scratches had to have been self-inflicted. Adam suddenly didn't care who she was or why she was there—all he knew was that he had to get her out.

"Don't be afraid. I'm going to help you." He straightened and searched for the cell's controls. The buttons on the wall did nothing when he pressed them. *They must be locked.*

He glimpsed a large screen lying flat on the surface of one of the lab tables. *Maybe these cells are connected to a central computer?*

He rushed over. The screen displayed a pattern of dark red swirls. Adam swiped it, hoping whatever computer it controlled wasn't locked.

The swirls faded, revealing an open document. Complex schematics snaked in thin black lines across a blue background. Adam swiped the screen again. A brief describing the technology in the schematic appeared. He glanced over it in surprise.

A mind control implant? What would Marcus Streger want with those? Aren't they banned?

A scream. Adam looked up and saw the young woman trembling in terror. She raised a hand, pointing at something behind Adam.

Adam turned. A gray guard bot towered over him. A blue line of light crossed the upper part of a metal mound that served as its head. He jumped back in alarm, banging into the table's edge. The bot raised an arm ending with a gun-like weapon.

A blast of heat, then darkness.

CHAPTER 16

ANOTHER NIGHT

EVIN WATCHED SILVER FOR A RESPONSE. She'd hardly reacted during his explanation of his plan. If the drink she'd tossed back had any effect on her head, he couldn't tell.

Silver leaned back with an expression of indifference. "So it comes down to this: I go to Rourke claiming Tenebrarum wants to buy what he's selling, and your senior agent catches him in the act of committing treason?"

Devin nodded. "It's as simple as that."

"What makes you think this Rourke character won't realize what you're doing?"

"He believes me to be his puppet. An obedient, if resentful, pawn in his game. I've already done things for him I'd sworn never to do." The image of Jane's hurt expression—the combination of confusion and anger printed on her face before he'd stunned her—invaded his mind.

He felt Silver's penetrating gaze examine him. She didn't ask for specifics; she must have been able to glean whatever she needed to know through observing him. He found it somewhat amusing that she'd thought changing her hair and coloring could keep him from recognizing her.

Hers was a face that had seared itself into his memory the instant she'd turned to him on that Kyderan rooftop.

Even at present, after speaking with her for almost an hour, he still found her striking in an almost demonic way. Sharp, wide-set eyes under arched eyebrows. Narrow, slightly upturned nose. Lips built for a sneer.

Yet he sensed something more than a gun-for-hire behind those sometimes green, sometimes blue, ever-changing eyes. Whatever it was, he couldn't define it. He also couldn't help feeling that despite her profession, she was one of the good ones.

Silver placed her elbows on her knees. "Why'd you call me, Pretender? Couldn't find anyone else?"

Devin wondered why she continued calling him "Pretender" after he'd told her his name. *I guess it's rather fitting.* He considered his answer. Unable to come up with anything else, he said, "Because you let Adam Palmer live."

Silver's lips curled into an expression of amused disdain. "I seem to recall you giving me an ultimatum. Walking away was just the smart thing to do."

The coldness in her voice would have fooled most, but Devin had been wearing a façade of his own long enough to recognize hers. "The Tenebrarum never hesitate. You did. If I hadn't been there, you still wouldn't have pulled that trigger."

Silver narrowed her eyes. "You assume much."

Devin knew he wouldn't get anywhere by pursuing the subject, so he simply asked again whether she wanted the job.

Silver's expression relaxed as she considered the offer. Devin was sure she'd agree to it. She'd risk little by accepting. He would provide her with the cash to pay Rourke, so even if the plan failed, she could walk away with a slate full of ISARK schematics.

As he waited for her to respond, Devin couldn't help glimpsing the small screen by her head, which displayed a view of the stage outside. The volume was set so low, the sound could barely be heard, yet he immediately recognized the melody floating from the singer's mouth: "Story," the song Sarah had written, that she'd shown him before she'd presented it to her producer, that she'd pinned her hopes of success on, and that had turned her into an interstellar icon. Asylum could shelter those under its protection from bounty hunters and trained assassins, but Sarah's reach spared no corner of known space.

Perhaps someday, when he'd finished with ISARK, he could find her again. Sarah had seemed willing to try a renewed relationship. "What about you?" she'd asked, as though puzzled by the idea that she wouldn't be with him again. Not for the first time, Devin found himself grasping at the possibility that he could reclaim a promised future that had once been his.

But Sarah held only impersonal memories of their time together, and she couldn't have understood the passions she'd once aroused. She'd come to him because she was frightened, and while she might have returned to his side if he'd asked her to, she would have done so out of a desire for the familiar, or perhaps out of guilt. Devin knew he couldn't stop himself from comparing the awakened Sarah to the version of her he'd loved, the ideal Pandora had created.

Starting again would have been unfair to Sarah. It might begin all right, but there would always be something off, barely perceptible yet profound and unchangeable. Something that could lead to more ugliness than Devin cared to think about.

With that reasoning in mind, Devin pushed the impossible hope out of his mind.

"Pretender? Hello?"

He met Silver's ice blue stare, realizing too late that his mind had wandered farther than he should have allowed it to. He straightened, attempting to return to a businesslike demeanor. "Have you decided?"

Silver raised her eyebrows. "You're awfully trusting. Maybe I'll cross you. I'll take your money, tell Rourke what you were trying to do, and disappear before you can do anything about it."

"You'll get twice as much payment if you come through. That's reason enough for me to trust you, at least until the payment's made."

A smile played on the corner of Silver's mouth. "All right, I'm in." She glanced at the digital clock over the door. "Looks like we're out of time. I'll have to check with my order, since it's their name I'll be using. If they don't have a problem with it, we can discuss specifics tomorrow. You know how to find me." She stood, pressed the controls to open the door, and walked out.

The singer's voice drifted in, and the air rang with Sarah's melody. Devin remained in the room, waiting for the longing it stirred in him to fade.

"Hey, I know you!" said a female voice from outside.

Devin knitted his eyebrows. *That sounds just like Jane. But it couldn't be, could it?* He quickly exited the room and blinked in surprise at the sight of his sister standing by the bar, facing Silver.

Silver regarded her. "So you do." She continued to the exit without another word.

Devin strode to his sister, his mind whirling with questions. How had Jane found him? How had she reached Asylum? What could he say to her? "What the hell are you doing here?"

Jane glared at him. "Looking for you, you jerk."

Devin braced himself for her tirade. *No matter what she says, I can't tell her the truth. Rourke's listening, and*

I can't give him any reason to suspect I'm doing something behind his back.

To his surprise, Jane didn't yell. "Why didn't you tell me you were putting on a show for your bosses?"

How much does she know? "What?"

"Adam called from Dalarune. He told me what you did. *You* should've told me before I came all the way out here trying to hunt you down!"

Dalarune? He must have lied to keep her from looking for him. Was he coerced? Where did they take him? "I'm... sorry." Devin hoped Jane would misinterpret his confusion as being due to her presence on Asylum.

"You should be." Jane spoke with a clenched jaw, as though she held back something powerful. It couldn't be anger—she'd never been afraid to let her temper loose on him.

"What's wrong?"

Jane bit her lip. "He told me he doesn't want to see me again because he's got to devote his life to the Absolute and 'atone,' as he said. How stupid is that?" Her eyes glistened, and she blinked furiously.

Adam must really want her to stay out of this. Devin saw no options but to go along with the lie. "He's very distressed. I'm sure he'll change his mind once he's had time to recover."

"Maybe." Jane shook her head. "But he told me he swore an oath for eternity. I'm not gonna wait around in case he decides to break it." Her expression turned to rage. "Who the hell does he think he is, casting me off like I'm some *thing* he can just forsake? Screw him! I thought he was such a great person, but I guess he's just another ex now."

Despite her words, her eyes betrayed a pain deeper than anything Devin had seen in her before. In that moment, he would have done anything to piece together the shards of her heart. The truth about Adam crept onto the edge of his tongue, and he longed to speak it. But doing so could lead Jane to a worse fate than heartbreak, even though she probably wouldn't believe such a thing were possible.

How did I let this get so fucked up? Lost for words, he embraced his sister.

Jane clasped him tightly, as though clinging on for fear that she might lose him as well. "Take me home, Devin. Get me out of here."

"The next shuttle leaves in eighteen hours," Devin said. "I'll take you to the inn, and tomorrow, we'll head back to Kydera."

"Okay." Jane let go. "You'll look out for Adam, right? You won't let ISARK get to him?"

"Of course." That statement was at least partly true—Devin intended to find Adam, wherever Rourke's partner had taken him, and get the kid out.

"Thanks. I just… I don't want anything to happen to him, even though I won't be seeing him anymore." Jane took a breath, as if willing herself to keep calm. "I guess once we get back to Kydera, I won't be seeing you either. You'll disappear back into ISARK's world."

"Not for long. I'm in the middle of an important mission, but once that's over, I swear, no more disappearing, and no more secrets." *If you ever speak to me again, once the truth comes out.*

Jane lifted her mouth, attempting a smirk. "And no more chasing me or shooting me. Though I can't promise the same for you."

Devin couldn't help smiling. "All right."

— ⋅◇⋅ —

Devin approached a three-person seat at the back of the Pike that would fly him and his sister to Travan Float. Other passengers boarded, but the majority of the seats remained empty.

Jane slid into the seat beside him, her face slack in a combination of weariness and resignation. Devin had expected her to explore Asylum in the hours they had to wait, but instead, she'd spent the time lying in bed, listlessly flipping through Netsites. He'd left her alone for a few hours when he'd gone to discuss details with Silver. When he'd returned, he'd found Jane in the same spot as when he'd left, staring blankly at her slate's screen. As far as he could tell, she hadn't slept.

Jane turned sideways in the seat and reclined against his shoulder. Her eyes drooped. "I'm so freaking tired. That damn inn had the worst bed ever."

Poor kid. "Won't be long before you're home."

She'd better stay there this time, Rourke growled.

Devin tried to ignore him. The Pike's engines rumbled, and the starship took off. Jane's eyes fell shut, and her body felt limp against him. Her weariness must have finally trumped her distress.

He kissed the top of her head. *Oh, Pony, how can I protect you when you go looking for trouble?*

The galaxy was more dangerous than she imagined, especially since she thought she'd seen it all when running from Pandora. Yet she behaved as if she were invulnerable, apparently believing a weapon and a tough attitude were all it took to survive.

I used to think the same thing. Years ago, Devin had been the hotheaded kid who'd thought he could take on the galaxy. It seemed that he and Jane were more alike than he'd hoped. When he was about her age, he'd held the same delusions of heroism and disregard for consequences.

But it seemed to Devin that despite what she'd been through, Jane did not yet appreciate how fragile life could be, how permanent the results of one's actions were. If it hadn't been for Adesina, there would have been no going home for him. He would either be dead or still lost on the Fringe.

Here I am again, wondering if I'll ever get out. Funny. This time it was Adesina who got me in.

Before Adesina had reentered his life, Devin had contented himself with his dull existence. Once, he would have found danger preferable to emptiness, but that had changed after his foray into the world of gangs and warlords and ISARK.

Unlike his daydreaming sister, Devin didn't have any roads-not-traveled or reach-for-the-stars goal. He'd been fine with watching the days slide into each other, wishing each would end as soon as it began, rushing forward through time, though toward what, he didn't know. Not much lay ahead; he'd often felt as if he lived the same day on a loop, lingering for lack of anything else to do.

Adesina hadn't given him much of a choice when it came to reentering the world he'd sworn to leave behind, the world of secrets and intrigue, of grandiose goals to be achieved through dangerous means. If she'd extended the same offer ten years earlier, he would have been thrilled at the opportunity to take down a ruthless dictator like Vang. He had to admit—he hadn't been entirely dismayed when Adesina had strong-armed him into joining her mission.

A few days into his role as a Klistosian contractor, Devin had seen Vang's kill list with Adam's name on it. How it had ended up there had remained a mystery until Devin learned of Adam's commanding the AIs to attack. Vang must have seen the command as a threat and traced the signal.

Shortly after confronting Silver, Devin had started hearing Rourke's voice over his communication implant, asking questions about the Pandora Project. *Why did Pandora target you? What did she want?*

I don't know was the only answer Devin had given. For Adam's sake—and Jane's—the AIs had to remain a secret.

Then Rourke had contacted him via his communication implant's virtual reality platform and said he'd had Devin transferred to Sector 1708. Devin had been surprised that the VR platform had been set up as an unfamiliar office. When he'd received the implant, he'd been told he'd have sole control over it, but that was obviously untrue.

He'd stood before Rourke's desk and listened in bewilderment to the director's commands. "What about Adesina's mission?"

"Klistosi is no longer Adesina's concern." Rourke's flat tone spoke of indifference. "In fact, there are questions as to whether a regional conflict should have been ISARK's concern in the first place. The mission will be shut down."

"They can't. The Klistosians are moving to become an interstellar threat. They're developing—"

"A bomb capable of traveling at lightspeed." Rourke rested his elbows on his armrests. "Yes, I know. My informants tell me it won't be functional for some time, if ever."

Devin knitted his eyebrows. "What informants? I'm Adesina's only operative." *How did he know about the bomb in the first place? I haven't told Adesina yet.*

Rourke's eyes glinted. "I have my ways. The Klistosians can be forthcoming if you know how to deal with them."

A realization hit Devin. "You're working with them, aren't you?" Anger swelled in him. "You're the one who sold out Adesina's first team."

"That's quite an assumption."

"You're not going to deny it?"

Rourke lifted his shoulders in a slight shrug. "Why should I? I'm an ISARK director, and you're just a newbie operative with a spotty past. There's nothing you can do."

What the hell? Treason seemed to go against everything Devin had heard about the famous Gunnar Rourke. Rourke used to be an operative himself, and he'd been considered a hero, praised and admired by all who knew him. He'd even been offered the chief director position but turned it down because he wanted to focus on new technology at

Sector 1708. How could a man who had worked to protect the Republic of Kydera for decades be so cavalier about betraying his nation?

Devin stared in disbelief. "Was it for money?"

Rourke kept his eyes fixed on Devin, as though he enjoyed watching Devin's reaction. "I never took you for a patriotic one."

"I don't have to be patriotic to find your actions despicable. Do you even care about the operatives who died because you sold them out?"

"Casualties on the path to a more important goal." Rourke's tone remained apathetic.

"And what was that?"

His lips curled into a sneer. "To get to you."

What? Devin's mind reeled. "What do you mean?"

Rourke laced his fingers. "The Pandora Project is of utmost interest to me. You're the only person left alive who was directly involved, and I know you're holding back. Pandora targeted *you*. There must be a reason. Now, imagine my shock when I found out that Klistosi's new dictator is a lifelike android."

Vang's an AI? Devin tried to wrap his mind around the idea. It wasn't unbelievable; Vang's disregard for human life matched Pandora's, and she had created her AIs to become future leaders.

Rourke lifted his chin. "I can see that doesn't entirely surprise you. There's something you're not telling me. The sophistication of the artificial intelligence led me to believe that Vang and Pandora are related. But how? I was hoping you could fill in the blanks, but your reluctance to speak on the matter told me that I had to give you incentive."

That makes no sense. "You threw away all those lives so you could get information from me about Pandora?"

"Well, I suppose I could have just asked, but that's no fun."

Sick bastard. "Is this a game to you?"

Rourke let out a quick laugh. "*Life* is a game! You make your move, then stand back and watch what others do about it." He spread his arms. "This is more than a strategy. In fact, as far as strategies go, it's pretty inefficient!" He swept one arm in a circular motion. "*This* is an experiment, and you make both a useful and fascinating subject. Almost as fun as Heisman, I must say." He hardened his eyes in a threatening expression. "You will tell me what you know about Pandora. And then, I'd like to see what else you'll do."

Devin clenched his fists. "Get out of my head." He attempted to eject himself from the virtu-world. Pain stabbed through him from every direction, as if invisible chains tightened. *What the hell?*

Rourke leaned forward, gaze malicious. "Your mind is no longer your own. Now, I'd think long and hard about crossing me if I were you. Your past shows that you don't give a shit about your own life, but what about that pretty little sister of yours? Or your twitchy friend on Shimshawhenn?" A window appeared beside Rourke, through which Devin could see his father's hospital room. "What about dear old Dad?"

High-pitched beeping pierced the air. The alarm lights on Dad's life support machines blinked rapidly. "What the hell's going on?" Devin strode toward Rourke.

"No one is out of my reach," Rourke said coldly. "Take this as your proof."

The room disappeared into blackness.

Devin had opened his eyes and found himself back in the pilot's seat of his Barracuda. Not long after, he'd received a tearful call from Jane.

Back in the Pike, Devin looked down at his sleeping sister. She'd thought his guilt over Dad's death was irrational. *Fact is, if it hadn't been for me, Dad would still be alive.*

His rage ignited at the memory of Rourke's satisfied voice speaking of how he'd gotten away with murder. How with the force of ISARK behind him, he could do such things and never face justice. Devin slammed his head against the seat back. Forget justice—he wanted to blast Rourke to hell.

After learning of Dad's death, he'd stormed into Rourke's Sector 1708 office intending to do just that.

Rourke had laughed as he entered. "Colt, do you really think you could have gotten into my office armed if I hadn't let you?"

Devin raised his gun. "Makes no difference, now that I'm here."

He'd been a heartbeat away from pulling the trigger when he noticed what the screen in Rourke's office displayed. Three windows: Adam in a library, immersed in an ancient paper book. Riley on a couch, tapping his slate with a grin. Jane at her desk, biting her lip as she scribbled in a composition program.

And over each of their faces, red crosshairs.

Shit. No wonder Rourke let me in. Devin quickly lowered his weapon. "All right, you win. Call off your snipers."

Rourke curled his lip with satisfaction. "I see you've figured out my insurance policy."

Devin's gun clattered as it landed on the ground. "*Call them off.*"

Rourke stood. "My snipers will follow those three until I'm finished with you. Make one wrong move, and a kill order goes out on your little friends. In fact, by threatening me, you're already off to a bad start. I don't need three insurance policies, do I?" His expression went blank. "Red Three, confirm your position on Adam Palmer."

Devin snatched up his gun, intending to stop Rourke before he could give the order.

Rourke sneered. "I wouldn't do that if I were you. Anything happens to me, they all die."

The weapon slid out of Devin's grip. He stared in disbelief at the crosshairs over Adam's face, which flashed as the sniper locked onto his target. He tried to think of something, anything, he could say. Pleading would only entertain Rourke's warped sense of humor.

Thoughts raced through Devin's mind as he searched for a reason Rourke would want to keep Adam alive. Only one occurred to him.

"This is Red Three," a muffled voice said over the comm. "I am in position. Do I have a kill order?"

Rourke opened his mouth.

"He's what you're looking for!" The words left Devin's mouth before he realized what he'd said.

Rourke's eyes became attentive. "What's that?"

Devin had hesitated but realized revealing Adam's synthetic nature was the only way to save the kid's life. "Adam's an AI. You've been looking for a live one, haven't you?"

Rourke's gaze became thoughtful, and he brought his thumb up to his mouth and bit down on his nail.

"I repeat, do I have a kill order?" Red Three asked over the comm.

Rourke had yanked his nail from between his teeth. "Stand down." His mouth had curled wickedly. "I knew you would cooperate, given the right incentive."

"We've arrived at *Gate II*. Stand by." The automated announcement over the Pike's comm brought Devin back to the present.

Jane stirred. "Keep it down," she mumbled. Her head relaxed against his shoulder as she drifted off again.

Devin wished he were the idolized hero she saw, rather than the irreparably fucked-up disaster whose errors had led him to deceive her, even hurt her. Yet she held no grudge. Despite her temper, her capacity for forgiveness and understanding went beyond what he or anyone else deserved. *She stood by both me and Adam in our darkest hours, even when we couldn't forgive ourselves.*

If Sarah had been the one causing the AI attacks, even if he still loved her, Devin wasn't sure he would have so easily believed that she wasn't to blame. But while he'd done his best to convince himself that Adam was a threat that had to be stopped, the anguish in the kid's tear-filled eyes back at the Etinine temple had blown away the justifications. No matter what ISARK said, Adam was still the kindhearted young man Devin knew. Because of Rourke's implant, Devin knew what it was like to commit actions involuntarily, actions with terrible consequences. Whatever the cause behind the AI attacks, he sided with Jane in the belief that Adam couldn't have been triggering them on purpose, and that there had to be a way to stop them and let Adam continue his life.

A noise startled Devin, and he swiftly glanced around at the other passengers on board the mostly empty Pike. *Any one of them could be Rourke's sniper.* He glimpsed the ship's internal defense guns. *Or maybe he doesn't need a sniper. Just one of the Sector Seventeen-Oh-Eight programmers.*

There seemed to be no finish line in Rourke's game, no escape but the kind Agent Heisman had chosen. Heisman had fought back, and fought hard, but his efforts had led to the death of his sister and then of his wife. Not for the first time, Devin wondered if he should abandon his efforts to expose Rourke, since every move he made could lead to Jane's death. At the same time, he couldn't let those red crosshairs remain on her, and as long as Rourke remained free, she would never be safe.

"Knock it off, bro." Jane didn't open her eyes as she swatted his arm.

Devin realized that he'd unconsciously grabbed her around the waist, as though his arm could shield her.

He let go. Perhaps Jane would be safer on Asylum, out of Rourke's reach. *No, it won't make a difference.* Rourke wouldn't think twice about sending a sniper there. The sniper, who had to have a mind control implant, wouldn't think at all if told to pull the trigger, even if that meant being taken down in turn by Tenebrarum.

In any event, Jane couldn't stay on a Fringe world. Her life and future lay in Kydera.

I swear, Pony, someday I'll tell you everything.

She'd be furious at how many times he'd lied. The explosion outside Dad's funeral hadn't been a domestic terrorist attack; that had been Rourke's way of telling Devin to hurry up and bring Adam in. Devin hadn't taken Adam to safety; he'd planned to bring the kid back to Sector 1708.

Jane would surely resent him for manipulating her, even if he'd done so for her protection.

I know I should tell you the truth and let you make your own decisions. They're your mistakes to make, and I have no right to interfere. But you're just like I used to be, and I know where that can lead. I can't help thinking that maybe I'd have a shot at life, too, if someone had been there to protect me.

CHAPTER 17

FORGET HIM

J ANE GRABBED A PAIR OF black gloves from the service bot. The heavy bag she'd requested stood at the center of a large, otherwise empty gym. Lines of blue lights streaked the floor.

Jane was glad no one else had decided to work out so late at night. One wrong word could have turned *them* into her practice target.

The cityscape glowed outside the gym's four glass walls, and the night glittered above the transparent ceiling. Adding color to the star-speckled blackness were the red and blue lights of Kyderan warships, patrolling the skies. Kydera Minor glowed blue-green behind the wall she faced.

Jane slammed her fist into the bag. In the two weeks since returning from Asylum, she'd buried herself in tasks to keep her mind off Adam. As promised, she'd hired people to repair and return the *Hegira*'s starcar, overseeing the process herself even though she usually had little interest in starship mechanics. The music festival had begun, and she'd obsessively revised her piece for the workshop. After receiving criticism, she'd hounded her mentors to the point of stalking. If she spent a moment in stillness, the misery she'd felt while lying sleepless on Asylum would return.

Jane hit the bag again. After a few more punches, she stopped to catch her breath. Tingling stung her eyes. She bit her lip, willing the dam holding back her tears to remain unbroken. *I'm not one of those ninnies who weep over their exes.*

Two days remained until the concert. Jane had been grateful for the frenzied rehearsals that dominated the previous day. Although the panic kept her mind busy, it had brought to light yet another source of frustration. Not *one* of the friends she'd invited to come see her had responded in the affirmative.

"Sorry, Jane," they'd said, then they'd proceeded with their excuses. Sure, they lived in different star systems, but Jane had hoped they'd be there for her moment of glory. She would have done so for them.

She'd lost count of the number of times she'd jumped onto a Moray at a moment's notice to celebrate someone's birthday or attend someone's engagement party. Whenever someone had asked her to put in a good word for them at Quasar, she'd gone knocking on her dad's office door. She'd even smiled through their awful wannabe-singer concerts.

And what did she get in return? "Sorry, Jane."

They disappoint, then they disappear. Jane slammed her foot into the bag. *Screw them. I was never close to any of them anyway. Next time I have to decide between being a sucker and being a bitch, the choice will be easy.*

Not even the energy she channeled into kicking the shit out of the bag seemed to bring her relief. The thoughts she'd managed to keep away finally broke free: Dad was dead, and she was an orphan. Devin had vanished again. And Adam—

Forget him.

The people she cared about the most had left her, and they'd taken with them any meaningful human connection. Empty dialogues with strangers represented by avatars. Artificially chipper chats with former schoolmates she didn't really know anymore. Painfully polite conversations with people she'd just met. Those were the only interactions she had anymore: fake smiles and forced energy.

Jane pulled off her gloves, relishing the relief the air gave to her hot hands. Ten minutes of hitting a bag, and she could barely get a full breath in. She sank to the ground and gazed out the transparent walls.

Flying transports swam around the skyscrapers in colorful lines. Holographic billboards painted the city with frenetic images of logos, products, and celebrities, which of course included Sarah. Jane could almost hear the voices of couples murmuring, of friends laughing, and of families telling each other about their days.

And there she was, in the galaxy's most populous city, connected to trillions via the Net, completely alone.

It was probably her own fault. Although she'd spent plenty of time with the other musicians at the festival, she'd made little effort to get to know them. She couldn't bring herself to forge any real bonds with another group of disappointing and disappearing opportunity seekers. Ultimately, Kydera City was just a place people came to make their fortunes. There was no space in such a city for anything other than the vibrant, noisy, dizzying rhythm of achievement and overachievement. Everything about the city was vain and in vain, for everyone thought they were the exceptional one, which meant that practically everyone was just another arrogant cliché.

Including me. Some liked the city's ephemeral, ambitious nature, and Jane had thought herself one of them. *Apparently not. Screw this desperate city.*

In that moment, she almost wanted to take off, throwing away the opportunities presented by the music festival.

Two weeks surrounded by other wannabes had led her to conclude that her chances of standing out were almost nonexistent. But even if she wanted to go home, she didn't have one to return to. The Colt estate offered only empty rooms and painful memories of the people who were no longer there.

She had a feeling her sudden hatred toward Kydera City had more to do with the absence of those she cared about than the metropolis itself. *I've gotta stop being so moody.*

A chill shot up Jane's spine. The room suddenly seemed extremely exposed. Something made her uneasy: a sense that she was being watched.

Of course I'm being watched. I'm in a freaking glass box, and there's a security cam in every building, street, and transport.

Despite her self-reassurance, the uneasiness remained. She looked around, half-expecting to see a shadowy stranger standing in the corner.

That's ridiculous.

Jane picked herself up. Everything felt heavy—her limbs, her head, and especially her heart. It seemed that the perpetual motion of the past two weeks had finally caught up to her.

Well, that was a pathetic workout. She didn't care enough to push harder. "End session."

The service bot picked up the gloves and water bottle she'd left on the floor. The heavy bag sank into the ground. The elevator doors opened, and she stepped into the glass car. The cityscape became a mural of colored streaks as the elevator zoomed down.

By the time she'd gathered her belongings, left the building, and entered the airtrain, she felt as though her muscles had turned to jelly. She reclined sideways in her seat.

How's it possible to go from so energetic to so tired so fast?

She was glad to be alone. She was a mess—sweaty tank top, rumpled shorts, messy ponytail even fluffier than usual. Normally, she would have taken the time to clean up and change before leaving the gym, but that night, she couldn't be bothered.

She couldn't be bothered with anything anymore.

Beep. The slate in her bag demanded her attention. Whoever it was, she was in no mood to talk.

Beep.

What if it's Adam? Jane clenched her jaw. *I don't care. He told me to forget him, and that's just what I'll do.*

Beep.

Her hand itched to grab the slate. The possibility of unfolding it to find Adam's face filled her head with longing. She couldn't deny that she missed him. When she'd put the finishing touches on her piece, her first instinct had been to call Adam and ask what he thought. When the other musicians had ripped it apart, she'd wanted nothing more than to run to him and rant about how none of them knew what they were talking about.

Beep. Beep.

Jane pulled open the edges of her bag and yanked out her slate. But it wasn't Adam's face that greeted her—it was Riley's.

"Yo, Janie! What's new?" Riley leaned on his elbows. Hospital equipment stood near him, visible behind his head.

With all the fancy med tech out there, two weeks was an eternity to spend recovering. *Damn, he must've been shot pretty badly.* "Not much. How're you doing?"

Riley twisted his mouth. "Still can't walk like a person yet."

That sucks. "Are they taking care of you properly? If you need me to yell at someone for you, just say the word."

"Nah, everyone's been nice so far. Except for this one asshole orderly."

Jane bolted up. "Give me his name and contact info, and they'll be scraping bits of him off the walls for a year."

Riley grinned. "I already sent a bug to his apartment's central computer. Messed with the heat—his place'll be hotter than the Avroche desert for a week."

Jane let out a laugh. "Of course you did."

"Anyhow, you told me to keep you posted, right? Well, I figured something out." Riley sat up. "The drones weren't after Jim X—they were after *me!*"

What? "Who the hell would want to kill you?"

Riley spread his arms with incredulity. "I know, right? We couldn't recover much from the drones' data recorders, but one thing was clear: the crosshairs were on *me.*" He fidgeted. "They haven't tried again, so maybe that was meant to be some kind of warning, but... I dunno. Anyhow, just wanted to let you know the latest."

Who would want to kill Riley? Even if he was unveiled as Corsair, there's no reason to want him dead, right? "Anything I can do?"

"Nah. I ratcheted up security in every way I know how. *No one*'s getting to me now!" Riley yawned. "Sorry. Freakin' painkillers make it hard to stay awake. I'll tell you if I find anything else."

"Okay, I'll talk to you later." Jane ended the transmission. She folded the slate and dropped it back in her bag, wishing there was something she could do. Her mind raised a few suggestions, but she soon realized that with Jim X's resources and the Shimshawhenn authorities behind him, Riley wouldn't need her help.

The uneasy feeling of being watched overcame Jane again. She glanced around the empty airtrain.

Footsteps approached. Jane sat up.

A man stumbled in from the neighboring train car. He didn't look dangerous—middle-aged, short, soft around the middle. Jane was pretty certain she could knock him out if she had to.

The man grabbed the back of the seat in front of her. "I don't know you." His words slurred.

Jane smelled the familiar stench of alcohol on his breath. *Damn drunk.* "Huh?"

The man put his hand on his chest. "I don't know you. But I just wanted to say, you're very pretty."

And you're smashed. "Thanks."

The man held up a finger, as though to emphasize his point. "You're *very* pretty. I hope your boyfriend appreciates you."

The airtrain stopped, and an automated voice announced the station's name. The man straightened with a satisfied smile, as if he'd accomplished a mission. He stumbled out the train's exit.

How flattering. Jane leaned her head back, overwhelmed by unexpected melancholy. *I had a boyfriend who appreciated me. Just not enough.*

She closed her eyes, commanding the tears to remain behind her eyelids. Why did such a stupid, random incident bring Adam to mind? Why did *everything* bring him to mind? She told herself over and over that the feeling was temporary, and that someday she'd laugh about it.

Remember that time some drunk guy calling you pretty made you sad? Pathetic.

Adam would disagree. "There's no shame in suffering," he'd say. "That doesn't make you pathetic; it means you really cared."

Go away! You freaking left me!

Her fault lay in believing she could find love in someone she'd never fully understand, and who would always love another even more than he loved her.

A voice within her whispered somewhat accusingly, somewhat wistfully: *I could have tried harder to keep him.*

She shook her head. Adam's religion was part of who he was, as much as her music was to her. He'd had to choose between her and the Absolute. Of course he'd chosen the Absolute. If she'd had to choose between him and music, the choice would have been difficult but obvious.

That's kind of what I did. I'm here, after all, not on Dalarune banging at his door.

The airtrain's automated voice announced that it was about to take off. It sounded friendly and professional, just like the voice she put on when speaking to her mentors. Adam couldn't speak like that. A person could read a lie in every nuance of his voice.

I wonder who's really artificial here.

Chills pricked her skin—again, the feeling of being watched. Jane opened her eyes. A bright light aimed at her. She jumped.

Kydera Minor shone above the buildings. The airtrain was passing an area where the buildings weren't high enough to block it.

Ugh. I'm becoming as paranoid as Devin.

⸻ ◆ ⸻

The white steps of Scriptus Hall gleamed beneath the light of the glass façade. A holographic banner shone above them, listing the names of the festival participants whose pieces would be performed that night.

Fourth on the list, in clean white letters: "Jane Winterreise Colt."

It's really happening. Jane smiled. The sight chased away all her previous doubts, and her heart glowed with hope. *Love me, hate me—they'll never forget me.*

The festival's other participants—sponsors, mentors, other composers, and their guests—wandered up the stairs. Their dazzling gowns and sharp suits made them radiate glamour.

Jane's violet gown trailed behind her as she approached the crowd. The collar hugged her shoulders, and the shimmering material clung to her waist. Her golden bracelet, which wrapped around her wrist in intricate coils, felt cool against the warm summer air. Her hair, which usually framed her face in copious waves, flowed down her shoulders. For the first time in almost a year, she'd taken the time to straighten it.

Tonight, thousands will hear me, and at last all my work will have been for something.

Of course, not everyone could end up like the renowned J. Schnurman. Some would find mild success, and many would disappear into office jobs.

Not me. I've seen what that's like, and I'm gonna make it.

Giulio, one of the other composers, waved. Jane waved back and waited for him to approach.

He gestured at the hall. "Did you ever imagine it'd be such a big deal? It's like a holodrama premiere, and we're the cast. Seems like an awful lot of fuss to make over a dozen up-and-coming composers."

Jane knew she had Rick Blumenthal to thank for the pageantry. Ocean Sky had sponsored the event to prove to the music academia that the company was about more than catering to the lowest common denominator.

Jane shrugged. "Everybody loves music. Whether it's temple chants, club songs, or"—she snickered—"Uvranan whistle bands, literally every single person rocks out to something. We're its future. Why shouldn't we be treated like stars?"

Giulio nodded. "When you put it that way, I guess they're not making enough of a fuss."

Shouts filled the air as a lustrous gold transport landed in the street. Jane recognized Ocean Sky's logo emblazoned in orange across the side. Two people stepped out. One was Rick Blumenthal, the new patron saint of composers. He had the interesting appearance of one who was old and young at once. His skin was as smooth and his hair as thick as Jane's own, but the way he carried himself gave away the fact that he had to have been about twice her age.

On his arm, in a dazzling sapphire gown, warming the hearts of the reporters with her demure smile, stood none other than Sarah DeHaven.

I see you've decided to go for the grand prize in gold-digging. And to think, you could have been my sister.

Sarah's gaze met Jane's, and her smile fell.

Jane glared. No matter how kindly Sarah behaved or what good deeds she performed, Jane would always see her as the cold bitch who'd nearly destroyed Devin. She turned and walked up the stairs.

"Jane!" Sarah's voice called behind her.

She's probably one of those ninnies who need everyone to like her. Tough luck, bitch. I'll hate you forever, and I don't care if that makes me a bitch, too.

Jane stepped through the open, arched doorway of Scriptus Hall, passing through a barely visible blue force field. As soon as she entered the room, the air seemed to disappear—neither hot nor cold, intangible against her skin.

"Jane!" Sarah's voice was right behind her.

Jane faced her. It took all her effort to respond with a saccharine, "Hi, Sarah!" instead of a vehement, "What, bitch?"

Sarah spread her lips into a smile that seemed uncharacteristically awkward for one programmed to be perfect. "I was hoping I'd catch you here. Congratulations on being among the featured composers tonight."

Jane forced a smile. "Thanks." *What do you want?*

"I know you don't really care for me." Sarah spoke in a lowered voice.

There's an understatement if I ever heard one. Jane waited for Sarah to continue.

"I just wanted to ask how Devin's doing." Sarah's black eyes pleaded.

What do you care? "He's fine." Jane kept the fake smile plastered across her face.

"Can you tell him something the next time you see him? Tell him that I've only done as he asked, and that I..." Sarah trailed off and looked away. "Just tell him that."

What's that supposed to mean? "All right."

Sarah seemed to read the rage simmering beneath Jane's forcedly calm expression. "I can't ask you not to hate me. I understand now that by hurting him, I hurt you too."

Damn straight. Do you know what it's like, watching someone you love give up on life? He saw you as his salvation, and the whole time, you were using him for some freaking experiment!

Somehow, *bitch* seemed like too kind a word to throw into that internal diatribe. Jane wondered whether one's face could shatter from the tension of keeping one's scowls confined.

Sarah's gaze grew desperate. "Please, can you imagine watching your own motions without understanding them, then coming to one day and having to face their consequences?"

Jane narrowed her eyes. "Why do you care what I think?"

Sarah was silent for a moment. "You're the only one other than Devin who... really knows me. I never meant to hurt him." She glanced down at her glittering gown. "I never meant for any of this to happen. It was what *she* wanted, and I didn't know anything but obedience. Now, I do as *I* want, and... I need you to know that I never meant to be cruel."

I never meant for any of this to happen. Adam had said the same thing. Jane sensed the wall she'd erected between him and Sarah crack—the wall separating a person trapped in a synthetic body from a mechanical being she despised. The right thing—the kinder thing— would have been to let the wall crumble and express some form of understanding.

Screw that.

Jane released her face from its fake calm and glared at Sarah. "I don't care what you need."

She walked away. Holding her head proudly high, she felt like an evil queen, and the wickedness tasted delicious. Sarah had refused Jane's plea for her to visit Devin the day before he was to be executed. It was Jane's turn to do the refusing. Adam would disapprove, but he wasn't there to coax her into being a better person.

Jane noticed a holographic banner, one displaying the portraits of the composers alongside their names. She stopped. Was that really her face, staring back at her?

Look at where I am. On the edge of triumph. In a place where she belonged, where she fit. Among those who shared her passions and appreciated her abilities. Doing what she had been born to do: bringing to life the sounds in her head.

In that moment, Jane felt as though she could truly have it all. Everything she'd dreamed of, everything she worked for, lay just within reach.

And yet, the room felt empty. Only strangers surrounded her.

"Jane!" One of her mentors called to her.

Jane tried to shake the empty feeling away. Unable to, she simply put on another smile.

⟶ ⧯ ⟵

Waiting in the backstage area, Jane listened as Giulio's song came to its rousing end. She clapped, happy to congratulate her fellow dreamer.

"Jane Winterreise Colt." The automated voice reminded Jane that it was her turn to perform. The doors to the elevator that would raise her to the stage opened.

Jane entered the circular car. The doors closed with a heavy *thud*. Above, the audience continued applauding Giulio. Some shouted his name.

They were all there for him, and once the concert ended, he could celebrate with them—his sisters, his parents, and a crowd of friends.

But who would wait for Jane? Where were her parents, who would finally admit that they'd been wrong about her? Or her brother, who'd told her he would support her musical endeavors even if they wouldn't?

Where was Adam? Why hadn't he at least called to say he was happy for her?

Because I don't matter enough. Jane's eyes stung. *Hell no. Not now.*

She couldn't stop them. All that distracting, all that suppressing—the built-up misery overflowed, and the dam crumbled. Tears spilled, overwhelming, overpowering.

She pressed her hands against her face, trying to block them. *No, no, not now...*

"Jane Winterreise Colt. Are you ready to proceed?" The automated voice was cool and unsympathetic.

Through a crack between her fingers, Jane caught the sight of a red icon flashing. Once she pressed it, the elevator would present her to the hundreds who sat in the audience.

The tears kept falling, each one whispering: *Where are they?*

It doesn't matter, she reminded herself, but the voices were relentless.

She sank to the floor. The thoughts she'd barricaded herself against invaded her mind: *Adam's gone, and you let him go. Your parents are dead. Devin will always care about whatever cause he's adopted more than you. Those you call friends only gave a shit about you because you were Victor Colt's daughter.*

She quickly countered with: *Who cares? I'll be fine. I always am.*

But her heart hurt so much, she wished she could rip it out. She brought her knees up to her chest, then turned to the side, hoping that shifting her position might somehow dull the pain. No matter how she moved, the aching wouldn't relent.

"Jane Winterreise Colt. Are you ready to proceed?" The automated voice repeated its question.

Jane inhaled deeply and let out a slow breath. The tears ended. She'd run out, it seemed.

She brushed her cheeks, recalling the tricks to fixing one's make-up. *Trace the lower eyelid to sweep away runny mascara. Outline the lips with a finger in case the lipstick smeared.* Not that either would have budged anyway. She'd been sure to use top-of-the-line products for her big debut.

She ran her fingers through her hair as she stood. She caught her reflection in the elevator's glass wall. Not one visible trace from her breakdown remained, and she was as pretty as ever. To reassure herself, she smiled.

I'm fine. Let's do this.

"Jane Winterreise Colt. Are you ready to proceed?"

Jane pressed the flashing icon. The elevator's walls glowed green. Above her, two gates parted, revealing the bronze waves sculpted into Scriptus Hall's ceiling. The floor beneath her rose.

Her heartbeat quickened, and her smile became genuine. Forget everything else—her dream was about to become reality.

The elevator carried Jane onto the stage. The walls retreated into the floor, leaving nothing between her and the audience.

She turned to the performers. The conductor's stand stood before her. Its dull screen, illuminated but otherwise indistinguishable from antique paper books, displayed the score. Clipped to the top, a golden baton gleamed beneath the warm stage lights.

Jane unclipped the baton, raised her arms, and cued the opening. Her soft melody, sung by the ethereal choir, floated through the air. The orchestra's accompaniment shimmered underneath.

There was no audience, no orchestra, no *her*—only music and the monster, which commanded her to speed up, slow down, crescendo, or decrescendo. It was the one entity she freely surrendered to, and she allowed her will to melt into its demands.

She swept her arms to the flow of her piece. The conductor's baton was her magic wand, and the orchestra's scintillating voice the enchantment she cast. She felt her power over the audience growing stronger with each crystal note.

She flicked her wand with a flourish to lift the spell. The last echoes of her symphony faded.

Silence.

Then, the rumble of applause.

There, in the front row, people cheered and clapped. A group of exotically clad women stood in a cluster at the center. They'd traveled from whatever corner of the galaxy their homeworlds lay in to see the up-and-coming composers.

But for her—no one. In the front row—no one. In the center, in the balcony, along the edges—no one.

She should have basked in the thrill of appreciation. Her heart should have soared, and her mind should have danced. Instead, she felt only heaviness and hollowness within.

Jane tried to force a smile onto her lips, but her willpower was spent. She surveyed the faceless crowd of strangers. *I guess it's just me, then. Me and my monster.*

CHAPTER 18

THE MASTER

MARCUS BIT DOWN ON HIS thumbnail. More bad news: the Tech Council had rejected his company's lobbying efforts once again. All because of that blasted Pandora Project.

"Fuck you, Tech Council!" Marcus's voice reverberated against his office's rounded walls. "I'll do what I want, and if you won't let me do it legit? Hey, black market's always open!"

Frustration after frustration—that was his life. An outsider who saw the shiny ship he resided on, the obedient staff who catered to his whims, and the rich fabrics he wore would have applauded his success. Yet in person-to-person interactions, he was still treated like the scrawny kid to be picked on, ignored, or pitied. No woman thought him worth her attention—no real woman, anyway. Marcus had seen enough of gold diggers, whores, and desperate broads.

He couldn't fathom why. He was wealthy, intelligent, and good-looking. He'd once kept his five-foot-ten frame fashionably trim and spent thousands ensuring that his brown hair resembled that of the holodrama stars women fawned over. Well groomed, well dressed, well mannered—

he'd done everything right. *And still, all I get are those bitches.*

He no longer bothered busting his ass at the gym or keeping up with fashions. The only things he maintained were his facial treatments; he refused to look fifty-four. When he eventually got his perfect woman, he wanted to start life over as though the past twenty-some years of misery hadn't existed.

Marcus slumped in his chair. *What's wrong with the universe?*

Life was a never-ending cycle of tantalizing wins robbed of true victory by harsher losses. He should have had it all. As a child, he'd been the kid who did extra homework while the others climbed around like monkeys. At university, he'd been the student who pursued independent projects while the so-called cool ones partied and fucked.

It had seemed to pay off. Acuitas, the Net search engine he'd created in his twenties, had become widely popular and expanded into a successful tech company.

You can tell everything you need to know about a person by what they're looking for. Acuitas showed Marcus who people were and how they thought. That knowledge was priceless. Every person in the galaxy used the Net and therefore used Acuitas, whether they knew it or not. Acuitas had bought him the *Pride of the Creator*, the Moray that served as his house, office, and playground. The steady stream of riches the company provided would never run dry as long as people searched for things.

Suddenly in the mood for a drink, Marcus yelled, "Candice! Get in here!"

The door to his office slid open. Candice flounced in, her brilliant red curls and ample breasts bouncing. "Do you need something, sir?"

"A bottle of Venovian wine, and make sure it's cold." Marcus clapped his hands together. "Hurry up!"

Candice's spike heels clacked against the floor as she left. Marcus examined her backside. *Lovely as ever, my Candice.*

But there was something wrong with her. There was something wrong with *all* his girls: they didn't really want him. No affection lay behind those sultry eyes and luscious lips. Their brain implants made them do and say whatever he wanted, but a personality had existed before the programming. Nothing Marcus did could truly change who they were.

He couldn't make them love him.

He recalled who Candice had been when he'd met her: an idealistic receptionist at Acuitas's headquarters on Kydera. Oh, how she'd enticed him with that melodious optimism, those flowing words and that naïve sparkle! He'd brought her on board the *Pride* as his personal assistant, hoping that, with time and proximity, they'd grow close. Instead, he'd ended up with a shadow of what he'd thought her to be, a dull woman who never gave him the respect he deserved. Disappointed, he'd implanted her, just as he'd implanted the others before her.

A window flashed on the wide computer monitor before him: "Incoming Transmission." The insignia in the corner indicated that it was from headquarters.

Marcus groaned. Corporate had kept him bogged down with their bullshit for more than two weeks, forcing him to work on company projects when all he wanted was to examine his new AI acquisition, Adam Palmer.

Marcus accepted the transmission. Corporate Guy—Marcus had never bothered learning his name—spread his arms as though inviting a hug. "Marcus! How're things over on the *Pride*?"

"Fantastic." Marcus kept his tone deadpan.

"Good, good. Hey, me and a couple other execs were wondering if you'd be coming to the meeting next week.

The investors would love to see the brains behind the company."

Marcus sighed. The more ways there were for people *not* to show up in person, the more people valued face-to-face contact. The way Corporate Guy was asking, he wasn't asking at all. *How dare he command me? Acuitas is my company!*

Actually, it wasn't anymore. Somehow, Marcus had allowed the leeches in suits to take over his company until they captained the vessel, leaving him a mere mechanic that kept it flying. Even Acuitas, his own creation, was no longer in his control.

"I'll be there," Marcus grumbled.

Corporate Guy beamed. "I'm glad to hear it. I'll—"

Marcus punched the icon to shut him up.

The door opened. Candice strutted in, carrying a tray with a bottle of wine and a single glass. She set the tray down on the desk, poured a glass of the crimson liquid, and handed it to Marcus. "Is there anything else I can do for you?"

Marcus considered those red lips of hers. Once, they'd filled him with longing, but knowing she'd automatically do with them whatever he asked made them lose their appeal. "Maybe later. Get out."

"Yes, sir." Candice left.

Marcus shook his head. *Can't believe I poured all that time into a brain implant just to come up empty.*

His girls couldn't give him what he truly wanted. He'd thought his implant would turn at least one of them into a suitable woman for him, but it had simply turned them all into whores. Perfect whores, but whores nonetheless.

What he needed was a blank slate. He'd considered genetically modified clones, but they presented too many problems. Even clones had brains, so he'd have to implant them anyway. Ultimately, they would have been no different from the beauties he lured to the *Pride*.

Marcus gulped his wine. *Enough donkeywork.* He decided to ignore Acuitas's desires and indulge his own. *Where should I begin?*

He had so many things he could have done, but they all felt like work, even though they weren't related to Acuitas. His personal projects ate all of his free time and much of his Acuitas time. The past two weeks of busyness had been to make up for months of blowing the company off.

I could design her. Marcus took a sip as he wondered what his perfect woman would look like. A face appeared in his mind, one that fascinated and bewildered him. A craving rose from the pit of his stomach. He had to see her.

Marcus swiped his monitor and accessed the ISARK sniper cams. Or rather, the cams the snipers tapped into in order to keep their eyes on their targets. A live video feed filled his monitor. *There she is.*

Jane Colt stood in the center of a Kyderan gym, kicking a heavy bag. Her sleeveless white top revealed her delicate collarbones, which perfectly offset her slender neck. Her purple shorts clung to a pair of smooth, youthful thighs.

Marcus leaned back with a sigh. *So beautiful, so strange.*

She wasn't the most attractive woman he'd seen; Candice was much hotter. Perhaps Jane so fascinated him because he'd watched her do things she shouldn't have been capable of—like win a face-off with an ISARK operative. Something about her defiance aroused feelings beyond anger, and Marcus yearned to show her who really had the power. But unlike Candice or any of his other girls, Jane would be missed if she disappeared.

Marcus finished his glass and poured himself another. On the monitor before him, Jane round-kicked the bag. He pictured what it would be like to catch that silky, bare leg before the blow could land to remind her that she wasn't so tough after all.

He noticed a young man at the gym staring at Jane as he lifted weights. The man, who would fit the textbook definition of *athletic*, finished his set and approached her. Jane didn't appear to notice as she threw another series of kicks.

The man clapped. "Nice moves."

Jane spun toward him as though startled. "Um... Thanks."

She turned back to the bag. The man tried to make conversation with her, but she responded only with single-word answers.

Marcus drained his glass. "Still playing the faithful lover, are you, Jane? What's wrong with you? You have a muscle-bound god drooling over you, and yet you're pining over a boring little AI?"

Frustration ground his insides. Why would she stay with Adam Palmer, knowing he was fake? Why didn't it seem creepy that she did? People fell in love with objects all the time, but Jane's relationship seemed different from what Marcus had seen before. He knew plenty of people had become enamored with a life-sized love bot, silicon doll, or virtual lover. There was always something unnatural and disturbing about it. Because of the Tech Council's restrictions, those artificial lovers could never fully represent human beings.

But Adam Palmer can. Marcus would never have imagined that Adam was an AI if Colt hadn't revealed the boy's true nature to Rourke.

Marcus grabbed the wine bottle and dumped its contents down his throat. If anyone deserved a girl like Jane Colt, he did. He was successful, attractive, rich. The universe owed him a beautiful, spirited young woman for all his troubles. All it dumped in his lap were those gold diggers, whores, and desperate broads. He hadn't had a proper girlfriend since university, and she'd been a manipulative bitch. The only women who seemed interested in him were those he wasn't interested in. Every so often, some pretty young thing would intrigue him and agree to a date with him, but the moment he started to know her, he'd find her no different from the ones before.

The galaxy held trillions of women, billions of whom were young and appealing. And yet the universe couldn't spare just one for Marcus.

Bitches, all of them. If they're not ugly sluts, they're irrational. Having come to that conclusion some time ago, Marcus had given up on finding a real woman. Even Acuitas's most sophisticated algorithms couldn't account for the fact that the woman he searched for had to love him. After wasting years trying to develop a way to line up personality traits and whatnot, he'd concluded that his brilliance was no match for the universe's screwiness. *If I can't find one, I'll make one.*

If Pandora had been able to create an AI man that loved Jane Colt, surely Marcus could reverse-engineer the being and create an AI woman that loved him. Once he succeeded—oh, the trillions, quadrillions, quintillions of thrones he could make! An AI wife for every victim of society screwed out of his happy ending! An AI husband for every shrew who couldn't hold on to a man!

Hey, I'm all for equal opportunity! I'll make my perfect match, and for a price, I'll make yours too! Marcus laughed, suddenly realizing how light his head felt. The wine's effects had crept up on him.

On the monitor, Jane slammed her small fist into the heavy bag. She was the first girl since Candice who'd appealed to him. The anger she provoked made her all the more desirable. Mesmerized, Marcus decided he'd model his AI woman after her. No more sniveling, pathetic whores. His woman would be headstrong and daring. But no matter how strong she thought she was, she'd always know her place. She'd oppose him and resist him, but he'd conquer her in a grand display of masculine dominance, and that would make her love and respect him more.

He watched as Jane threw a quick succession of punches, her eyes blazing with fury. *Who are you picturing on that bag? Adam, perhaps? What would you do if you found out he didn't leave because he doesn't love you?*

Marcus sneered. Jane had thought she could defeat him, but he'd won the game. Her precious AI lay deactivated on board the *Pride*.

Tell me, Pony, what would you do if you found out I have him?

⭤

Adam's vision came into focus. He could barely make out anything past the empty lab table. A bright light shone onto him. He realized he was in a chair and tried to get up, but couldn't. Tight metal rings anchored his wrists to the armrests. Something dug into his ankles; his legs must have been similarly restrained. *Where am I?*

He tried to piece together what had happened. He wore his typical combination of a white shirt and plain pants, so he'd probably been taken from what had started out as an ordinary day. But he must have been through something, for his clothes were stained with dirt.

An image—bloody bodies, Pandora's deep blue wire-frame figure, and a reflection that wasn't his own. A dank cavern, stun blasts, a Via temple. Jane yelling at him, eyes glistening with tears she refused to shed. Flashes of the Seer in a virtu-world desert.

The memories ended there. Adam almost wished they'd remained lost. Or that he'd never awakened. His nightmare wouldn't end when the sun rose. In fact, he would probably never see another sunrise.

"Adam Palmer." A cold voice broke the silence. A man approached, fading into view from the darkness. Lanky and brown-haired, with high cheekbones and a sharp nose, he looked about thirty, but something about his brown eyes made him seem much older. "What's the last thing you remember?"

"Who are you?" Frightened by the man's hungry expression, Adam spoke in a strained whisper.

The man pulled a chair out from underneath the lab bench. He waved his hand over the back, and it rose to hover a few inches off the ground. He spun the chair and sat in it backward. "Marcus. Marcus Streger. Now, answer my question."

Marcus Streger. So you're the one behind all this. "Last thing I remember is being in a cell. There was a hole—I think I punched through the wall." Adam glanced down at his hand, which was streaked with exposed metal.

Marcus shifted his gaze to the side. "So a prolonged shutdown does cause memory loss."

Shutdown? "What happened?"

Marcus set his chin down on the back of the chair. "I let you run around for a few minutes to see what you'd do. You started snooping, so I had one of my security bots knock you out. Put you in this special chair to keep you from turning back on."

Adam searched his memories. At the mention of a security bot, he recalled a blue line of light, but nothing more.

"Do you give a shit about what's happening?" Marcus's brown eyes bored into Adam's. "Or are you just like, 'error: cannot compute?'"

Adam wasn't sure how to respond.

"You certainly look convincing." The stench of alcohol wafted on Marcus's breath. "What I'm trying to figure out is: do you really *love* Jane Colt, or were you just programmed to act like you did?"

"I love her." The words spilled out of Adam's mouth.

"Excellent!" Marcus pushed against the ground with his feet, causing his hovering chair to slide backward. "So damn *real!* You know, I was kind of bummed when the only known living AI turned out to be a guy, but hey, you're in love, and that's the trait I'm *really* looking for."

That's strange. "Why?"

"Let me tell you what I'm going to do." Marcus stood and took a step forward, but walked into the edge of the chair. "Fucking piece of *shit!*" He kicked the chair, which flew out of sight. Something shattered.

Adam sensed despair behind the rage, as though the chair, small as it was, represented the last in a string of misfortunes. "Are you all right?"

"Fuck, yeah, I'm all right!" As though suddenly aware of his outburst, Marcus relaxed his expression. "You seem... nice. I suppose the least I can do is let you know why I'll be ripping you to shreds." He froze, then yelled at the ceiling, "Hear that, Pony?" He spat Jane's nickname as though it were poison. "I'm ripping your almost-fiancé to shreds!" He laughed harshly.

Only Devin calls Jane "Pony." How does he know about that? And why did he call me Jane's "almost-fiancé"? Adam recalled Jane's sudden, sarcastic, "Will you marry me?" and wondered if that was what Marcus referred to. *But only Jane and I know about that...*

Marcus stopped laughing. "I spent *years* trying to find myself a woman. I kept myself groomed, polite—hell, I'm fucking loaded! Do you know who I am?"

Adam nodded. "You're the chief architect of Acuitas."

"That's right." Marcus spread his arms beside him. "We at Acuitas know how *all* you losers think. We're in your heads and in your homes, and you welcome us because we make life easier. So, like I was saying, I'm a fucking catch, right?"

"I suppose." Adam didn't know how else to respond.

Marcus pointed at Adam. "And you, boy, are *nothing.* So tell me, why does Jane Colt love you instead of me?" He slammed his hands down on Adam's arms and leaned into Adam's face. "You're nothing but trouble. I could give her *everything!* Dresses, a palace—she wants to be a composer, right?" The despair in Marcus's voice rose. "I could fucking *buy* Scriptus Hall for her. Why does she love you instead of me?"

"She doesn't know you." Adam kept his tone gentle, despite his desire to demand how Marcus knew so much about Jane. *He must be working with ISARK.*

"Fucking right, she doesn't know me." Marcus straightened. "But even if she did, would she go for me?" He scowled. "No, of course not. They always say no. Fucking hell!" He banged his fist into the lab table. "Women are fucking irrational." The bitterness in Marcus's voice spoke of a deep, underlying sorrow. He remained still for several seconds, head bowed and fists clenched.

Adam couldn't help pitying the man. He wished he could say something comforting, but fear robbed him of words.

When Marcus straightened, his expression was calm. "The universe may be unwilling to provide me with the companion I deserve, but it can't stop me from having her. I'll make her myself."

Adam realized what Marcus's plans were. *He wants to create a perfect lover, like Sarah was for Devin.*

Marcus bit his thumbnail. "If there's anyone in the galaxy who can reverse-engineer and modify Pandora's work, it's me." He smiled to himself. "I'll make an AI that will love me like that. Yes, she'll be her own person—independent, smart, sassy even. I like strong women. But at the end of the day, she'll always come back to me, the true strength of her life."

Adam couldn't comprehend Marcus's reasoning. "She can't both love you and be your slave. If you go through with your plan, you'll either create an empty shell, no different from a lifelike doll, or a sentient being who will make her own choices."

Marcus brought his hands crashing down onto Adam's arms again. "*What* are you saying? You're saying I'm so pathetic that even my own creation won't love me?"

Adam drew a breath. "I'm saying that what you want is a fantasy."

Marcus pushed off the chair. "Of Pandora's AIs, you're the special one because you're supposed to be a human mind in a synthetic body. But something *made* you. Am I right?"

That was what Pandora had wanted Adam to believe, but Adam knew it couldn't be true. "No."

"Yes, it did!" With each word, Marcus jerked his arm for emphasis. "You're a *machine*. Pandora *built* you, and something about what she did to you *made* you love."

If only love could be explained so easily. "Pandora never wanted me to be with Jane. She couldn't fully control her creations, and you won't be able to, either."

Marcus's eyes blazed with fury. "Who the fuck do you think you are?" He stormed off, disappearing into the dark shadows of the room.

I shouldn't have spoken. Fear grasped Adam's heart.

He heard a faint whirring. Marcus reappeared, clutching a cylindrical device. Beside him, a squat robot hovered about two feet off the ground, holding a tray of instruments in its metal claws. Marcus looked at the machine, then turned his gaze to Adam. "What's the difference between you two anyway? If I wanted to test how my bot handled a surge"— Marcus shoved the cylindrical device into the robot's side, and a line of red lights flashed across the robot's head as an alarm shrieked—"no one would give a shit." He regarded the robot. "Apparently this one can't stand a high setting. Now, let's see how you do."

Marcus shoved the device into Adam's stomach. White-hot pain flared through Adam's torso, and a scorching heat pulsed into his chest. Every fiber of Adam's being—every inch of skin, every ounce within—cried out in shock. An agonized scream shook the air, sounding distant in Adam's ears. But for the strain in his throat, Adam wouldn't have known it was his own.

Scream away, my child. Your screams are nothing more than an error message. Pandora's deep blue image flared within Adam's mind.

The device was removed, and the burning ceased. Adam's head fell forward. A fire seemed to have been set within him. He kept his eyes closed, but tears escaped.

In Adam's mind, Pandora reached out. *Come. I can guide you to freedom. Disobey me, and you condemn yourself to this fate.*

Then I condemn myself. Adam pictured himself staring down Pandora. His own image appeared before hers.

Pandora scowled. *You do nothing without—*

Adam wished for her to be silent, and her words cut out. Her image flickered. *What was that?*

"Look at me!"

Adam felt a stinging across his face. He opened his eyes and found himself staring into Marcus's cold brown irises.

"Please..." Adam searched Marcus's eyes for any sign of mercy. "I... I know you see me as—as artificial." His words faltered. "But... you said yourself that I'm a person in a synthetic body. Would you—"

"Shut up!" Marcus snapped straight. "A sentient AI is still a machine. I'll take what I need, and when I'm done, I'll discard you, like I would an old slate." He beckoned the robot to come closer. The robot obliged but seemed to have trouble moving in a straight line. It jerked from side to side as it approached, red error lights still flashing on its head.

Adam's heart trembled. "Please..."

Marcus picked up a slender laser scalpel from the robot's tray. "Machines don't bleed. Neither do AIs."

Marcus grabbed Adam's hair and pulled his head back.

Piercing heat bored into Adam's forehead. Adam's own screams pierced his ears—involuntary, unstoppable cries—as the heat moved down the edge of his face. Even his tears did nothing to temper the burning as the laser arced toward his brow.

Absolute One, grant me strength.

The heat disappeared. Adam gasped, feeling as though he'd inhaled for the first time. Pain stung his face as Marcus tore off the section of skin he'd outlined.

Marcus slammed Adam's head into the back of the chair.

Adam opened his eyes. Marcus dangled a piece of skin from a pair of tweezers. Crescent-shaped and a warm shade of alabaster—Adam's own.

Marcus examined the sample. "Pandora did such a thorough job, and yet she neglected to include blood." His lips curved maliciously. "What would you do, Pony, if you knew I had your precious lover? What would you do?"

CHAPTER 19

KEEPS GETTING WEIRDER

ANOTHER MORNING, ANOTHER DAY TO kill. Jane hadn't even rolled out of bed yet, and already she wished it were night so she could go back to sleep. The sunlight filling her hotel room told her she'd already spent at least half the day snoozing, and the light flashing on her slate told her she'd missed a transmission.

The world just keeps turning, doesn't it? Won't take a break, no matter how much you need it to.

With the concert over, she no longer had a goal to work toward and felt as though she was drifting in a cloud of "Now what?" She'd made the impromptu decision to visit Riley the previous day and arrived on Shimshawhenn late at night local time.

Outside her window, the hotel's white landing pad glittered beneath the sun. Jane's banged-up gray Stargazer—the same ship she'd taken from Pandora's factory months ago—looked out of place among the gleaming Blue Hamlets and colorful Dragonets. The Stargazer had been the only starship she had at her disposal, and she wished she'd thought to replace it. Not only was the thing ugly as hell, but it had caused her problems with the authorities. Piloting a veiled, unregistered vehicle wasn't illegal, but it had made both the Kyderan and Wiosper border patrols suspicious, which delayed her journey by several hours.

Jane checked the time on a nearby screen. It was already mid-afternoon.

Shit! She'd meant to visit Riley in the morning, but she must have forgotten to set an alarm to wake her up.

She jumped out of bed and grabbed the purple dress lying on top of the pile of clothes in her open suitcase. After taking a few minutes to get dressed, wash up, and make sure her copious waves didn't look completely out of control, she grabbed her bag and bolted out the door.

Despite her stealing an air taxi from another hotel guest, yelling at the pilot to disregard speed rules, and sprinting into the hospital, she was nevertheless greeted by a holographic sign stating that visiting hours were over. *Dammit!*

Jane entered the hospital's lobby anyway.

A white-clad orderly noticed her. "Excuse me, miss, visiting hours are over unless you're immediate family."

Indeed? Jane gave a friendly smile. "I'm here to see my brother, Riley Winklepleck."

The orderly raised his eyebrows. "I wasn't aware that Mr. Winklepleck had a sister."

Jane lowered her gaze into a sheepish expression. "I know, I should have visited earlier, and I feel awful that I haven't. It's just... I couldn't bear the thought of seeing him hurt." She glanced up.

"Do you have ID?"

Crap! Jane bit her lip. "I was in such a rush to get here, I forgot it. Can you please just take me to Riley? I'm sure he'll tell you."

The orderly sighed. "Follow me, Miss Winklepleck."

Ugh! Jane tried not to cringe at the name. She could tell from the orderly's indifferent demeanor that the hospital didn't really enforce their visitor policy, but she decided to stick by her lie anyway, to be on the safe side.

The orderly led Jane into an elevator that brought them to the top floor, then up to an arched door in the middle of a white corridor. He pressed a button on the door's controls. "Mr. Winklepleck, your sister's here to see you."

"Hi, Riley!" Jane said quickly. "It's me, Jane!"

"Janie?" Riley sounded confused and excited. "Uh... Come on in!" The door slid open.

Jane thanked the orderly for his help, then entered.

Riley reclined in a hospital bed with a tilted back, his face bright with surprise. "Yo! What're you doing here?"

Jane plopped down in the orange chair by the bed and put her bag on the floor. "Visiting my little brother, what else?" She glanced around. Two holographic warriors, frozen as they crossed swords, stood before an enormous screen. Riley had apparently been watching a holodrama. Jim X's pointy-eared dog lay curled in the corner. "Nice room!"

"Yeah, it's pretty awesome." Riley sat up. "Doc says I should be up and about in a week or so. I'm not gimpy anymore, see?" He swung his legs over the edge of the bed and jumped to the ground. "Ta da!" His knee buckled, and he grabbed the bed for support.

Jane scrambled to the touchscreen on the wall. She pressed an icon, and the bed lowered by several inches.

"Uh... Thanks." Riley plopped down on the bed, mouth twisted in disappointment. "Guess I'm still gimpy."

Jane returned to the orange chair. "Take it easy. Getting shot is kind of a big deal."

"I still can't find anything about who did it. Whoever they are, they're freakin' amazing at covering their tracks." Riley rested his elbows on his knees. "The only guys I can think of that could hide their stuff so well is ISARK or some other government agency. Now, I'm all for conspiracy theories, but that's too ridiculous, right?"

This keeps getting weirder. "Yeah."

The comm emitted a beep. "Mr. Winklepleck, I'm here to take you to your physical therapy appointment."

"Enter." Riley folded his legs underneath him as the door slid open.

A middle-aged nurse entered. Her gaze fell on Jane. "Who's this?"

Jane stood. "I'm Riley's sister, visiting from Kydera."

"Oh, how nice." The nurse approached the touchscreen on the wall, grabbed its slightly raised edges, and pulled to detach it. "The appointment will take about an hour. You may come if you'd like."

"No!" Riley exclaimed. "Uh... It's not a pretty sight, me struggling to walk and all."

Jane leaned back in her chair. "No worries. I'll wait here."

The nurse swiped her finger across the touchscreen, and Riley's bed hovered toward the door.

Riley waved. "See you in a bit!"

Jane waved back. The nurse followed the hovering bed out of the room, and the door shut behind her.

Remembering that she had a missed transmission, Jane reached into her bag and grabbed her slate, wondering who had called.

The moment she unfolded it, an agonized scream emitted from the speakers. Jane's mouth fell open in shock. Adam sat bound to a metal chair, crying out in pain as a cylindrical device was pressed into his stomach by a hand whose owner she couldn't see.

Jane felt an unbearable heat flare through her own torso. "*Adam!*"

The video window went black.

Chaos spun through her head, too frenzied to coalesce into thoughts. She stared at the black screen, gripping the slate with both hands.

That can't be real. Adam's safe on Dalarune... isn't he? Did ISARK find him? If they did, why would they send this to me?

The video had to have been fake—someone's sick idea of a joke. She wished fiercely that the theory were true, but couldn't find any way to justify it. Who would hate her enough to do such a thing?

Whatever was going on, someone was hurting Adam, and she had to get him out of there. Jane gathered what she knew, but all she recalled from the video was Adam's pain. Her stomach turned at the thought of watching it again. Its details could tell her something, so she slowly released her right hand's grasp on the slate and pressed the "replay" icon.

Adam's scream emitted from the slate. Unable to bear it, Jane hit "pause" and squeezed her eyes shut. Heat pulsed through her chest.

I've gotta pull myself together.

She opened her eyes, forcing herself to focus not on Adam, but on the image's background. A timestamp occupied the lower right corner, indicating that the video had been taken approximately twelve hours before. Even if it was fake, Adam was likely still there, still suffering.

Don't think about that. Just focus.

Only vague shapes were visible beyond the metal chair Adam was bound to. He was under some sort of spotlight, and the rest of the room was dark. The chair's high back had rows of cube-like devices along the edges.

Jane didn't recognize the cylindrical device pressing into Adam's stomach. The hand holding it looked pale and masculine but otherwise told her little.

An uneasy feeling told her that she was missing something obvious. She looked up at the ceiling.

What the hell happened? The only thing she could think of was that ISARK had found Adam on Dalarune, and that their sick scientists were experimenting on him. But who would have sent her that video? Devin? If ISARK had caught Adam, they must have figured out that Devin was the one who'd helped him escape. Was the video Devin's way of calling for help?

The answer seemed to make sense, but so much seemed wrong with it, first and foremost of which was that Devin would never call on Jane for help. *He'd handle the situation himself and keep me as far away as possible.*

The image of Adam's pained face stung her mind. *Wherever you are, I'll save you.*

She lowered her gaze. Adam's shoulder drew her attention. There was a V-shaped tear near the left shoulder of his white shirt, which was stained with gray bits of dirt.

A realization hit her, and she gasped. Adam's shirt had snagged on a thorn in the *Hegira*'s dead garden—that random detail was clear in her mind. And the dirt—it was from swimming in the lake.

We never had a chance to change. That's the same shirt he was wearing when Devin arrested him.

Which could only mean one thing: both Devin and Adam had lied. Devin had never taken Adam to Dalarune, and Adam's break-up message had been a farewell.

Jane dropped the slate. She could almost understand Adam's lie. One spark shone through the gloom clouding her mind: Adam hadn't left her. He still loved her—enough to think that pushing her away would protect her. Even in his darkest hour, he still tried to bring her comfort in whatever way he could.

No wonder he told me to forget him. He thought he was going to die.

Her brother, on the other hand, had looked her in the eye and told her that Adam was safe. *Devin, how could you?*

She recalled the horrible things he'd said in the tower: that Adam was dangerous, that he was only a realistic machine. He must have meant them. Which meant that for months, every time he'd treated Adam as a friend, he'd been harboring a secret hatred.

No, it can't be. I've known Devin my whole life—that's not like him.

It also wasn't like him to chase her across the galaxy, or shoot her, or lie to her face. He'd made her believe Adam was out of harm's way and even comforted her in her heartbreak, but every word had been false. She'd trusted him unquestioningly. Despite everything he'd put her through, she'd always held on to the belief that her brother was ultimately on her side.

Apparently, nothing was unbreakable.

———◆———

The strain of physical therapy, which Riley had spent an hour busting his butt at, had been nothing compared to the effort it had taken him to keep his mouth shut while listening to Jane tell him what she'd learned. He stared at Jane, who sat with her arms crossed in the chair by his hospital bed. The rage in her eyes seemed lethal. She was the scariest thing he'd ever seen, and he didn't want to say anything that could provoke her. He realized that his jaw still hung open from disbelief and quickly pressed his lips together. Devin lying to Jane and sending Adam to be tortured—Riley's mind threw a tantrum at the notion.

Something's seriously screwed up here. He recalled the theory he'd once had, the one he'd dismissed after he'd learned—or thought he'd learned—that Devin's whole scary ISARK operative thing had been an act. *A mind control implant. That's gotta be it.*

He took a moment to gather the courage to speak. "Hey, Janie, uh…"

Jane didn't look at him. Her expression remained deadly. Riley suddenly couldn't remember what he'd meant to say.

Jane glanced up. "Sorry, Riley. I know it's not really your problem, but I need your help again."

Riley realized what she had to be asking for. "Dude, it was a pretty huge miracle that I found Devin last time. I don't think we'll get that lucky again."

Jane's mouth hardened into a harsh line.

Riley fidgeted. He hated to disappoint, and he flipped through his mind for ideas. One struck him. "I know! I'll trace the video so you can find out where they're keeping Adam."

Jane's eyes brightened. "Do it. I need to get him out."

"Uh... How?" Riley snapped his mouth shut. *Now's not the time to talk about logistics!*

Jane shook her head. "No idea, but I'll find a way. You just find him." She stood. "I should go." Her expression turned apologetic as her eyes tilted down. "I'm sorry, Riley. I know I keep running to you when I need something, but this time, I really did mean to just visit as a friend."

Riley waved a hand dismissively. "Shit happens. I'm always happy to help a pal. Where're you off to anyhow?"

"I'm gonna find Devin." She picked up her bag.

Riley managed to contain the "Uh... How?" that time. He watched nervously as Jane left the hospital room, shoulders squared with determination. It was only after the door had closed behind her that he realized he'd never actually voiced the mind-control theory. *I'll tell her later, when she's less mad.*

His insides sank with dismay. A gloomy feeling descended upon him—a feeling that whatever was going on, there was no way for it to end well.

⸺➤⟡⟡⟵⸺

Ines pressed the icon to shut her Silverside's door and pulled off her thick gray coat. Ibara was freezing, and in order to blend in with the population, she'd worn that heavy thing instead of her preferred combat jacket. With her shoulder-length dirty blond hair tied in a low ponytail and her modest blue blouse, she probably looked like a nice schoolteacher, and a family woman at that.

She glanced down at the mirror by her dashboard and twisted her nose in disgust. The woman who stared back at her was weak, vulnerable. The person she appeared to be may have fit a typical person's idea of a good mother, but a woman like that couldn't protect her child from danger.

Ines's heart ached with a twinge of longing. No matter how she tried, she could never silence the part of her that wished to be the ordinary woman in her reflection. The woman who could afford to have a home and companions, who didn't have to keep herself in a cell of isolation. Ines had built the cell herself, and each time a crack appeared, she'd reinforced it so no one could enter. There, she could do what she had to do without distractions or interference. Though for the most part she preferred her cell to the chaos outside, she sometimes felt trapped by it.

Enough. Self-pity was for the weak.

Determined not to waste any more time on useless thoughts, Ines pulled her remote from her pocket and quickly altered her appearance. Short, ragged blue hair and eyes an unnatural shade of gold. A scowl to top it off. Even in the nice-lady outfit, she already resembled the bringer of death she was.

That's better.

She strode into the living quarters of her Silverside and quickly changed into her usual black combat outfit. She even put on her silver armbands. Feeling like herself again, she returned to the cockpit and sent a transmission. She grimaced at the "pending" sign on the viewscreen.

A few seconds later, an image of Pretender from the waist up appeared. He no longer wore his Black Knight guise. The black T-shirt he sported instead told her he was probably off duty. He stood in what appeared to be the courtyard of an apartment complex. The app in the Silverside's central computer that automatically ran a trace on every transmission told her that he was in a small Ibaran town called Arunit.

Which everyone knows is actually a front to disguise government housing for ISARK workers. "Hello, Pretender. Taking the day off?"

"Silver." Pretender glanced around the outdoor area. "Why are you calling?"

Ines put her hands on her hips. "I want to know when the deal's going down. It's been weeks, and I'm beginning to wonder if you've lost your nerve."

"There's still one piece missing. Believe me, I want the plan executed as soon as possible."

"Careful. If you wait too long, people will think there's something funny going on."

"I'll let you know as soon as I have more information." Pretender ended the transmission.

Ines huffed with impatience. Initially, she'd been glad for the break. It had given her time to find out everything she could about Pretender, better known as Devin Colt. After satisfying her need for knowledge, she'd restocked her ship and taken it in for some upgrades. She'd even visited Ibara, something she always ended up doing despite the many times she'd told herself to leave behind what remained there. At the moment, she seemed to have run out of things to do.

Am I supposed to sit around and wait while Pretender gets his shit together?

Although it wasn't her business, Ines wished she knew more about what Pretender was doing. She couldn't deny harboring a hint of admiration for his determination. She wasn't sure what she would have done if she were in his position.

Treason and mind control—Rourke was more wicked than most of the crime bosses Ines had worked for. At least those bosses revealed themselves to be the galaxy's villains. Evil in the guise of good was the darkest form of evil in existence, and Ines had half a mind to off Rourke as a favor to the universe. However, she was only supposed to kill those she was hired to do away with, and she couldn't afford to break Tenebrarum's laws again.

She grabbed her slate from its dock. Time was a terrible thing to waste, and she might as well find a quick job to fill it. She opened the Shadowcaster Net, an online hub for mercs and prospective employers. Anyone could post there, which meant that generally, she didn't find anything worth her while.

One posting caught her attention. It was titled "To the Tenebrarum Woman with Silver Armbands." Ines had seen jobs calling for her specifically in the past, but not for a while. Intrigued, she pressed the icon to bring up the details.

A video of a young woman filled the screen. Ines recognized her as Pretender's kid sister.

Jane Colt looked into the camera. Her expression was so similar to her brother's that Ines wondered how she'd ever missed the connection. "If you are who this message is intended for, then you'll remember me. We ran into each other at Mek's a few weeks ago. I need to talk to you, and I'll make it worth your while. My contact info's attached to this post."

Interesting. Ines pressed the icon to bring up the contact information. It listed her name as "Winterreise" and probably led to an off-the-grid slate. *Too late for that, kid. I already know who you are.*

To Ines, Jane's message rang of a frightened girl's attempt to sound tough. *Might as well find out what she wants.*

Ines pulled up an IC directory. There was only one Jane Winterreise Colt on Kydera Major. She pressed the icon to send a video transmission.

"Pending" flashed across the screen. Ines smirked as she pictured Pretender's kid sister wondering who the unknown caller was. *You're never as safe as you think you are.*

Jane's confused face filled the screen. Her eyes widened. "It's you. How did you know who I was?"

"Did you really think you could hide from someone like me?" Ines spoke with disdain. "You shouldn't be poking around the Shadowcaster Net, kid. Could end badly for you."

Jane set her jaw indignantly. "It worked, didn't it? Here you are."

She's a cocky one. Ines raised her eyebrows. "Why are you looking for me?"

"I saw you talking to Black Knight—"

"You mean your big brother?" Ines sneered at Jane's surprised face. "I know who he is, and I know who he's not. Now, what is it that you want?"

"I can't find him." Jane's tone carried repressed anger. "I was hoping you could help me."

You're contacting a merc to find your brother? I guess it's true what they say about rich families being fucked up. "Let me guess: you don't want to share your inheritance, and you want me to get rid of him for you."

A horrified look spread across Jane's face. "No!" Her expression turned to annoyance; she must have noticed the amused smile curling Ines's mouth. "He disappeared, and you're the last person I saw him with. I just..." She trailed off and glanced down, as though searching for words.

Ines understood. Pretender had gone underground, and he hadn't answered his sister's calls. *She must be desperate.* "I know where he is."

Jane looked up with a start. "What?"

"Do you want me to send you the coordinates?"

"Name your price." Jane's words rushed with eagerness.

Ines knew that the smart thing to do would have been to demand an astronomical sum and see how much she could squeeze out of the little princess. The thought repulsed her. She wouldn't stoop to extorting from kids. Besides, if Pretender found out—

What does it matter if he finds out?

"I don't need your money," Ines scoffed. Her curiosity pricked her, and she saw her opportunity to learn what was going on. "Tell me why you're looking for him, and I'll give you the location." Part of Ines told her that she shouldn't seek irrelevant information. She hushed it with a reminder that as long as she was working with Pretender, she had the right to know. "If you don't tell the truth, I'll know, and you'll never hear from me again." *That should scare her into being forthcoming.*

"Okay. I... I mean, he..." Jane didn't seem to know how to phrase her explanation.

Ines threw her a disdainful look. "Don't worry about blowing his top-secret cover. I already know he's an ISARK operative masquerading as the dead Black Knight."

"Okay." Jane inhaled. "His last assignment was to arrest someone I care about, and I just found out that someone's being held captive. I need Devin to tell me where they're keeping him."

"Who's this 'someone'?"

Jane hesitated. "His name's Adam. He's my... I guess you'd call him my boyfriend."

Adam Palmer? Pretender had risked blowing himself up to keep that kid alive. Ines had learned why while digging into Pretender's background—he owed Adam his life, and evidently considered the kid a friend.

She recalled the guilt with which Pretender had said: "I've already done things for him that I'd sworn never to do." *Things like betray his friend and break his sister's heart, I suppose. What would Rourke want with the kid anyway?*

That Adam had ended up on the Klistosians' kill list could have been dismissed, but if ISARK wanted him too, then there had to be more to him than the innocent student he appeared to be. *I'll have to ask Pretender about that.*

"Your brother's on Ibara. I'll send you the exact location."

Jane's expression relaxed. "Thank you."

"I know you won't listen, but I'll say it anyway: Watch yourself." Ines ended the transmission, then sent Jane the coordinates for Arunit.

No wonder Pretender's been stalling on his sting. He's searching for a way to get Adam out. If Rourke went down while Adam was still in captivity, there was no way of knowing what the kid's fate would be.

Ines reached for the Silverside's controls, aiming to contact Pretender, then stopped herself. Her job for him was simple: pose as a buyer of ISARK tech. Why should she care about anything else that went on? *If it were any other job, I wouldn't.*

For some reason, she seemed to care too much about the circumstances surrounding Devin Colt.

I only give a shit because he holds my most lucrative contract. Any other interests she might have in Pretender could be attributed to her lack of a social life. *Wouldn't be the first time I got distracted by a pretty face.*

She tried to fling all thoughts of him away, but her feeble brain wouldn't let her. Something within her called to him, as though only his presence could calm its disquiet. Disgusted, she upbraided herself for being so easily fooled. It wasn't Pretender that her subconscious sought. It was a fantasy she'd fallen for in the past, one she couldn't stop yearning for no matter how she tried. Pretender was simply the latest entity her mind projected that fantasy onto, and she couldn't let the consequences of her idiocy carry into the real world.

Furious at herself, she set her jaw and returned her attention to the Shadowcaster Net.

CHAPTER 20

ONCE MORE

DEVIN WASN'T SURPRISED TO FIND Adesina waiting in his apartment when he returned. Random meet-ups in a dead zone were the only way they could discuss matters without Rourke hearing.

Adesina tapped her fingers on the armrest of her chair. "You're back later than usual."

Devin approached. "How have you managed to stay so long? Doesn't Rourke question why you're still here?"

Adesina shrugged. "He can lock me out of his top-secret areas, but to bar me entirely would raise alarms back at headquarters. Although, come to think of it, I'm surprised he hasn't confronted me."

Devin pulled a chair out from the table. "He's been quiet for the past two weeks. Never seems to leave his office."

"So he hasn't talked to you lately?"

Devin shook his head.

Adesina rested her chin on her fist. "Huh. After all that time he spent making you his special project, he suddenly doesn't care?"

"My guess is that he got what he was looking for, and now he's plotting his next move."

"I take it he hasn't asked about your assignment to find a buyer either." Adesina put her hand down and gave Devin a stern look. "It's time we move on that. Rourke's treachery has gone on long enough, and I want him to face justice."

"We'll move as soon as I find his partner." Devin met her stare.

Adesina threw her hand up. "How many times do I have to say it? *There's no fucking partner.* I'm sorry you lost your AI friend, but we've found no other evidence that anyone else is involved. You know what I think happened? One of Rourke's clients asked for a live AI, and he delivered the product straight to the buyer."

"That can't be. Rourke was so hell-bent on capturing Adam, he dropped a bomb near my sister just to tell me to hurry up. He wouldn't care so much if he was just filling an order."

"That man's erratic. Who knows why he does what he does?" Adesina scowled. "There will be a reckoning, and he will pay for the lives he cost. But for that reckoning to happen, you have to do your part." She stood. "Tell Rourke that you've found a buyer. Set it up, or I will."

"If you do, his partner will get away." *And I'll never find Adam. How can I ever face Jane again? Hell, how can I ever face myself again?*

Adesina stiffened. "If there is another party, I'll be sure to interrogate Rourke about it after he's in custody. One more day, Devin. Then, it's time."

She strode to the exit. Arguing would have been pointless. She'd given her ultimatum, and Devin had to admit, she had a point. Perhaps it would be better to expose Rourke first. Perhaps, once in custody, Rourke could be persuaded into giving up his partner's identity.

Devin contemplated his options. He shared Adesina's fury that Rourke continued to roam free. At the same time, he couldn't let Rourke's partner get away. And there *was* a partner—Devin was certain.

An idea struck him. *I need to talk to Silver.*

* * *

Devin opened the door and gestured for Silver to enter. "After you."

Silver strode into the apartment and glanced around. That day, she wore her hair in a simple brown ponytail and sported a nondescript outfit of gray pants and a dark blue jacket. Although her appearance was evidently meant to blend into a crowd, Devin would still have recognized her anywhere. That face—it would flash through his mind each time he saw a glint of silver, haunting him.

Silver leaned against the edge of the table and crossed her ankles. The pale early morning sun shone through the window behind her. "You're lucky I happened to be near Kydera. Otherwise, I wouldn't waste my time pretending to be your old college pal. As long as we're in a dead zone, you might as well tell me what's going on. What's Adam Palmer's secret?"

"What?"

"I know why you've been stalling. You're looking for him."

Devin tried to recall if he'd said anything about Adam to her. "How did you know?"

"I talked to Jane." Silver's tone carried a trace of taunting.

"You did *what*?" Devin strode toward her. "You had no right to involve her."

"She called me." Silver sounded nonchalant. "Wanted to know if I'd seen you around. Poor kid was pretty upset that she couldn't reach you."

Why would Jane be so desperate to find me? "What did you tell her?"

Silver met Devin's glare. "You can't protect her forever. She's a brave one—I'll give her that. But she's as crazy as you are."

Devin looked away. *That's what I was afraid of.*

Silver pushed off the table. "I told her you were here. Figured she deserves to know. She's your sister, for fuck's sake." She narrowed her eyes. "Now, tell me, what's with this Adam Palmer? He wasn't on the Klistosians' kill list by mistake, was he?"

Devin considered if he should lie. He couldn't come up with a plausible falsehood, and for some reason, he trusted Silver. In any case, if he didn't tell her, she would probably find out anyway. "Have you heard of the Pandora Project?"

Silver barely reacted as Devin explained the AIs to her. She listened in clinical silence, as if he were merely detailing the layout of a starship. When he finished, all she said was, "Interesting."

"Zeger Vang must have traced the command that affected him," Devin continued. "He must have perceived Adam as a threat, and that's why you were hired."

"I see."

Devin expected Silver to ask more questions or at least express an opinion, but she remained still. In that moment, he couldn't help noticing the way the light highlighted her cheekbone. Her face was a work of art. For the first time, the reason why he always recognized her, no matter what guise she was in, struck him: she was beautiful in a way no other woman was. *Not even Sarah.*

It wasn't just the shape of her features that held his attention. Something about the proud way she held herself, the sharp intelligence in her eyes, and the grace with which she moved gave her a mysterious kind of allure.

He must have paused too long, for Silver glowered. "Why did you call me here?"

Devin snapped out of his brief trance. "I'm out of time. The plan must go down tomorrow, and I have no chance of finding Adam—or Rourke's partner—before then. I need you to make Rourke reveal his partner's location."

Silver leaned back against the table. "And how am I supposed to do that?"

"Act as though you already know about the partner, that you found out doing your due diligence on your new supplier."

"If he refuses?"

Unfortunately, that's the more likely scenario. "Then agree to his terms. Better to catch one than neither."

"Very well." Silver straightened. "You made me come all the way here to tell me that? Get your shit together, Pretender. If I were anyone else, I'd have flaked by now."

That was unnecessarily defensive. Devin got the idea that Silver used her scorn to hide something. *She didn't come just because I asked her to—she wanted to know what was going on. She's curious.*

Silver scowled. "What's the smile for?"

Devin hadn't realized that his expression had changed. "Nothing."

She threw him a contemptuous look, then strode out the door.

Devin pressed the button to raise the window's shades. He watched as Silver exited the building, fascinated by how her entire demeanor could change. She was no longer the haughty Tenebrarum merc; she was just a woman in town to see a friend. A great actress who could slip seamlessly from identity to identity.

Yet, there was something real about her. Who lay behind those cold eyes? Whom did she hide behind that frosty voice? After Rourke was caught, Devin would likely never see her again. The thought brought Devin an unexpected sense of disappointment.

He lowered the shades and turned away. The digital clock on the wall told him that several minutes remained before the transports to Sector 1708 would arrive. He had no choice but to return to the facility, though what he would do there, he didn't know. Since there was no sense in waiting, Devin decided to head out early.

He stepped out of the apartment building. No one else was present, although in a few minutes, they would all file out with eerie punctuality. He glanced down the street, hoping to catch a glimpse of Silver, but she had disappeared.

Beep.

Devin pulled his slate from his pocket, wondering whether Jane was calling. To his surprise, Sarah's was the name that appeared on his screen.

Why would she contact me?

He knew he shouldn't answer. In fact, he should have discarded any means by which to contact him via normal channels. The secure line he used to speak with Silver should have been the only one he used. However, he'd found himself unable to part with his remaining link to the world outside of ISARK, even though he almost never responded to the communications.

The only reason he could think of for Sarah's call was that she was in some kind of trouble. Perhaps ISARK had decided the risk of letting someone like her remain among the public outweighed the risk of the AIs becoming known. If that were the case, he couldn't do nothing and let another person he cared about fall into Rourke's unforgiving clutches.

Devin pressed "accept," and Sarah's beautiful, delicate face appeared on the screen.

"Hello, Devin." Sarah gave a nervous smile. "I know I promised to leave you alone, and your sister will probably kill me if she finds out I contacted you, but... I just had to talk to you."

"Is everything okay? Are you in trouble?"

"No, I'm all right."

Devin exhaled in relief. "Why are you calling?"

"It's about Rick... Rick Blumenthal, that is. The man I've been seeing." Sarah's words, so smooth in all his memories, stumbled with uncertainty. "You told me to find someone powerful, and I did. I think... I think he wants to marry me. I know it's fast, but... he keeps talking about 'forever,' and he told me that I'm..." She trailed off.

Devin smiled wryly. "You seem to have that effect on people."

Sarah dropped her gaze, as though ashamed.

"Why are you telling me this?"

Sarah looked up. "I just... want to make sure you're okay with it."

"You don't need my permission to do anything."

"I know." She hesitated. "I keep remembering the way things were between us, and I can't help wondering if there's something left."

Devin turned his gaze to the empty road before him. Yes, there was something left, and there always would be. But he knew he'd never get back the past he'd lost. Unable to help himself, he asked, "Did you ever love me?"

Sarah was silent for several seconds. "I don't know." Her voice was soft. "I'm not sure I know what love is, or if it's even something I'm capable of. But I do care about you. You're the only man who knows who I really am."

Her answer affirmed what Devin had told himself previously. She sought the shelter of his familiarity, not affection. Perhaps, in their newness, the emotions seemed the same to her, but she extended an invitation he couldn't accept.

"What about Rick?" he asked.

"I care about him too, more than I thought I would." Sarah smiled to herself. "I went to him because he could protect me, but I've realized there's something else. He's a good man, better than most give him credit for."

The look in her eyes spoke of true fondness. Not so long ago, Devin would have yearned to see her speak of him in that way. But the change he'd sensed since she'd come to him after awakening had grown more acute, and he realized it wasn't just something about her, but something within himself as well.

Sarah continued, "I know he loves me, but... he doesn't know."

"You're afraid he'll leave if he learns your secret."

Sarah nodded.

Devin understood her reason for calling. He was the only one she could turn to with her fears, and she sought security in him. If he could have offered it to her, he probably would have. But to what end?

"You're going to be all right," he said as reassuringly as he could. "I'm not your answer, Sarah. Perhaps Rick is, and I wish you the best with him." As Devin spoke those last words, he found that he almost meant them.

"Thank you." Sarah's expression remained tight with anxiety.

"Good luck with everything."

"You too." Sarah ended the transmission.

Devin folded the slate. Her presence didn't affect him as it had in the past. No pang stabbed at his heart, and no fury clouded his mind. In fact, he felt nothing at all.

The door to the apartment building opened, and the other Sector 1708 employees walked out, joining Devin by the street. A gleaming transport landed before him. The door opened, and the others walked around him as they filed in one by one. Devin glanced at them, chilled by the blankness of their expressions. As he moved to join them, he wondered if he was really all that different.

✦

Jane pressed her back against the side of the tall apartment building, half hoping her brown leather jacket would help her blend into its rust-colored wall. The building was the only residential structure in Arunit. Devin had to live there. The workday hadn't ended, and so he couldn't have come back yet.

She peered around the corner. The Kyderan sun still shone on the horizon. It looked much smaller than it did on Kydera Major. She'd forgotten how cold Ibara was. The wind chilled her through her jacket and inadequate black pants.

An air transport landed in the street, and a handful of men and women trickled out. *Must be quitting time. Devin will be here soon.*

What if he didn't show up? He could have flown off to another planet on assignment. What if the woman with the silver armbands had lied? But she had seemed sincere, concerned even.

It occurred to Jane that Arunit, being an ISARK-controlled town, would be full of security cameras. Ducking by a building would only make her look suspicious, especially since she had a gun hidden under her jacket pressing against her hip. She'd thought herself insane for bringing it in the first place. Still, she hadn't been about to confront Devin unarmed. He'd been perfectly willing to stun her and blow up her ship's engines.

Can't be certain of anything anymore.

She emerged from her hiding spot and leaned against the wall. Hopefully, by looking casual, she would prevent anyone from questioning her presence in the town. Even ISARK employees had family, and from what she'd learned, Arunit was supposed to be the medium between Sector 1708's opacity and the real world's openness. *If anyone asks, I'm just paying my big brother a surprise visit.*

A second transport arrived, and Devin emerged from its arched doorway. Jane's feet carried her toward him before she realized what was happening. "Devin!"

Devin turned to her. He didn't appear surprised to see her. "Hey, Pony. I didn't realize you were visiting this week."

His nonchalance ignited a new flame within Jane, and she no longer cared who witnessed her actions. "What the hell, Devin? How could you?"

Devin's expression darkened. "Come with me." He grabbed her arm and started pulling her toward the apartment building.

Jane yanked her arm out of his grip. "Let me go, you jerk!"

He grabbed her again. "Not here," he said through gritted teeth.

"Yes, here!" She twisted in his grip until she broke free. "I'm not giving you another chance to get away! Where's Adam?"

Devin looked her in the eye. "Dalarune."

Rage flared within Jane. Knowing he would lie again unless she showed him her proof, she grabbed the slate from her pocket and shoved it at him. "If he's on Dalarune, what the hell is this?"

Devin stared at the slate for a moment, then glanced around.

Jane glanced around, too. The other ISARK employees seemed oblivious to the scene. *They've probably been trained not to care. Soulless robots, all of them!*

She glared at her brother. "Open the freaking slate."

Devin obliged. Adam's screams emitted from the speakers. Jane looked away.

"What's this?" Devin's voice was low.

His attempt at denial fueled Jane's anger. "What do you think? I don't know who sent it, but I know what it means. What have you done with him?"

Devin folded the slate, expression calm. "I don't know what you're talking about."

"*Liar*!" Jane's voice came out shrilly, almost a scream. "You sent him there! He's suffering, maybe dying, because of *you*! How could you, Devin? *How could you*?"

Devin reached toward her. "If you'll just come with me—"

"Like hell!" Jane jumped back. He was stronger than she was—if he grabbed her again, she might not escape. Tensing her jaw, she did her best to act calm. There was no sense in making a scene; what she needed was information. "Just tell me where he is."

"Pony, please—"

"*Don't call me Pony*!" How dare he act as if nothing was wrong?

He reached for her again. "Listen—"

Without thinking, Jane pulled out her gun. "Touch me again, and I'll blast you to hell!"

Too late, she realized how stupid a move that was. She looked around wildly, expecting alarms to blare. No one appeared to have noticed. The street and sky remained empty, and the air was still. The last few ISARK people seemed oblivious as they disappeared into the apartment building.

Devin's gaze flicked down at the gun. "Put that away."

"I *trusted* you!" Jane's eyes stung, and she had no willpower left to stop her enraged words from tumbling out. "I've always trusted you! When they told me you shot Dad, I never believed for a moment it was true! I threw away everything, *everything* because I thought any kind of life would be worth it as long as it was with you!" Tears fell from her eyes. "You were my hero, Devin. How could you betray me?"

Devin seemed frozen, almost like a faulty hologram.

Jane held the gun steady. "Where's Adam?"

"I don't know." His tone was flat.

Damn liar! She took a step toward him. "Why did you give him to ISARK?"

"He's an AI." Devin's tone was cold. "A machine programmed to mimic human behavior. He killed twenty-seven people."

"He was possessed!" Jane knew her defenses would do little good, but she had to say them. "It wasn't his fault!"

"Jane, believe me—"

"Believe you?" Jane shoved the barrel of her gun into his chest. "Tell me where Adam is, or else."

Devin's expression appeared half-sympathetic, half-amused. "Are you really going to shoot me, Pony?"

Jane felt the trigger against her finger. Much as she hated him at the moment, he was still the brother she'd grown up with, whom she'd looked up to, and whom she loved, no matter what. Her weapon was set on stun, but if she knocked him out, what then? Would she drag him into an alley and tie him up, as if she were some thug? Torture her own brother for a confession?

Despite everything, she couldn't hurt him, even though he seemed perfectly willing to hurt her. He hadn't even reacted to the video of Adam's agony. *Coldhearted monster. I thought I knew you.*

Realizing that there was no way she could coerce him into telling her where Adam was, she lowered her gun. "Please, Devin." No words seemed able to express her desperation, how much she longed to take Adam away from whoever caused him pain and comfort him in her embrace. "Please..."

"I'm sorry, Jane." Devin's apology rang with sincerity.

That made Jane feel worse. Sure, he was sorry—sorry for her. But not sorry enough to do anything. Another meaningless "Sorry, Jane."

She clenched her fist. Fury sprang up within her. Her knuckles connected with her brother's face before she realized what was happening.

She dropped her hand, horrified at what she'd done, then spun and ran as fast as she could. She had to get away. Would Devin pursue her? Try to convince her that he was right? The thought made her legs move faster.

Down the street, through the spaceport control center, and onto the landing pad—all was a blur behind the tears. No matter how she restrained them, they wouldn't stop. *Why won't they stop?* Her gasping breaths seemed unable to keep up with her running, and her head spun.

She climbed into the Stargazer, shut the door behind her, and collapsed on the floor. Sobs heaved up her chest.

What am I supposed to do? She looked up and repeated the question in a desperate scream: "*What* am I supposed to do?"

She was a useless, gullible idiot. Because of her helplessness, Adam lay trapped somewhere, probably being vivisected by scientists who would ignore his screams as though they were alarms on a starship, simply stating, "Warning: systems unstable."

And her brother didn't care. The brother she'd idolized, whose word she'd taken above anyone else's.

Where's the brother I always trusted?

Since she'd seen him, she understood why he'd lied. He saw his actions as justified. Adam was a machine that had caused dozens of human deaths. If Devin had stuck by that stance from the start, she might have forgiven him.

But if it all comes down to him or Adam...

A flash of red interrupted her thoughts. She looked up. A light on the control panel told her she had an incoming transmission. A message across the bottom of the viewscreen told her it was from "Corsair." Not wanting to look like a mess in front of Riley, she wiped her eyes and got up from the floor.

Why's he calling? Has he found something? No, that can't be it. It wouldn't be that easy.

She sat in the pilot's chair and pressed the icon to accept the transmission.

Riley's face filled the screen. "Yo, Janie!" His face fell with concern. "What's wrong?"

Jane lifted the corners of her mouth into something of a smile. "Damn weather is giving me all kinds of problems. Anyway, what's up?"

"Uh... I found him." Riley grinned awkwardly, as though confused by his own triumph. "Adam, I mean. I traced the video."

"You did?" Jane stood. "I thought you said it was untraceable."

"Uh... It was." Riley scratched his head. "But then all of a sudden... I dunno, it's like whoever was trying to hide it cleared the path. I mean, I had this program running, bouncin' off all kinds of drives—"

"Send me the coordinates." Jane didn't care how Riley had succeeded, only that he had.

Riley fidgeted. "Hey, Janie, I want Adam outta there as much as you, but... this whole video thing seems really sketchy. It's like they wanted to be found."

"Send me the damn coordinates!" Jane was in no mood to argue.

"It's a trap!" Riley spoke hurriedly. "That's—"

"Riley, I've been chased, shot at, and betrayed. Don't test me."

"All right, all right!"

"Thanks." Funny, of all the people she knew, her weird demon pal was the only one who'd never let her down. She gave him a genuine smile. "I promise, I'll visit again once this is all over. See you later."

"Uh... See you." Riley ended the transmission. A few seconds later, her ship's central computer told her she had an incoming message:

Corsair: Here you go, sis.

Jane split her lips into an amused grin. She entered the coordinates Riley had sent with the message into the Stargazer's computer. They seemed to lead to empty space, but that didn't mean a veiled starship or float didn't lurk in the location they indicated. She yearned to take off right away, but she forced herself to take a moment and consider her circumstances. *Won't do me any good to get stranded halfway.*

She swiped the control screen and brought up a status report. *I've got enough fuel, that's for sure. And enough food and supplies stored in the back for at least a week.* She checked the navigation screen. *The journey will take less than half that time, so I'm good.*

What would she find once she arrived? She knew running off to an unknown location was a terrible idea, but she didn't see what other choice she had. *Whatever's out there, I can handle it. My ship's veiled, so they won't see me coming, and I'm armed. Besides, it's not like there's anything else I can do until I see what I'm dealing with.*

She sat down and revved up the engines. The Stargazer zoomed out of Ibara's atmosphere. She engaged lightspeed, but as the seconds ticked by, even that felt too slow. Almost two days had passed since the video of Adam had been recorded, which meant that for at least that long, someone had been tearing into him in a twisted science lab. He'd been locked up for weeks while she'd been messing around in the music world, pretending she could just get over him like any other ex. *How could I have given up on him so easily? If I'd gone looking for him, I would've found out that he wasn't on Dalarune, and I wouldn't have wasted so much time.*

She tried not to let the awful feeling of guilt get to her, but it kept clawing at her mind. While she'd been chasing her dumb dream, he'd been suffering. What if she was already too late? Science moved quickly, more quickly than anyone could keep up with. What if by the time she reached him, they'd taken all they needed and discarded him?

Wait for me, Adam. Jane shoved the steering bars forward, wishing she could break the lightspeed barrier. *Stay alive, okay? I'm coming for you, and I swear, I'll take you away. We'll start a new life.*

The tears returned as Jane pictured a tranquil future with Adam, one she would once have dismissed. *We'll escape to somewhere they'll never find you. You'll spend your days reading dull Via books and volunteering at whatever center for the unfortunate happens to lie nearby. I'll find some paying job, and, every so often, scribble silly songs. We'll argue about stupid things, and I'll complain about how far our life is from the ambitions I once dreamed of, but at the end of the day, I won't care, as long as you love me.*

She closed her eyes. *Don't die before I can make it happen. Just please, wait for me.*

CHAPTER 21

DESTRUCTION

ADAM APPLAUDED AS JANE CONCLUDED her piece with a flourish. She turned to face the audience. Her eyes met his, and she brightened.

"Adam!" She gathered her long, purple skirt and ran to the edge of the stage.

"Jane!" Adam widened his eyes in alarm. "What are you—?"

Jane leaped off the stage, her dress flowing like a pair of wings behind her. She landed before him with a stumble.

Adam caught her, and she laughed.

"Whoa!" She brushed a lock of dark hair out of her eyes. "Maybe that wasn't such a good idea." Her flawless skin glowed like a pearl.

Adam smiled. "You're beautiful." *Too beautiful... This must be a dream.*

Jane shrugged. "So it's a dream. What's wrong with dreaming?"

"Nothing." He drew her close and kissed her. Perhaps it was an echo of a real kiss, a memory come to life, but it was a good one.

A cold wind enveloped him. Adam looked up. The auditorium had disappeared. He stood alone with Jane on a flat, frozen surface, so smooth it reflected the stars glimmering above.

Jane looked around in awe. "Let's run away." She rushed into the darkness.

"Jane!" Adam sprinted after her. He ran into something hard, and his head ached from where he'd hit it.

Jane's laughter rang through the darkness. "Oh, Adam, didn't you see the wall?"

Adam reached forward and felt a vertical surface. Angling his head, he realized that it was an enormous mirror, so reflective it blended into the sky. He swept his hand across the wall, and his fingers wrapped around an edge. When he rounded the corner, he faced a narrow corridor of mirrors.

Jane stood just ahead, luminous against the darkness. "There you are!" She held a hand out to him.

Adam reached toward her, but felt a cold surface. *Another mirror.*

"Fun, isn't it?" Jane spun and vanished.

"Jane, wait!" Adam made out the edge of a wall before him and rounded its corner. Seven reflections stared back at him, their green eyes widening as Adam took in the sight of his own face. An exposed crescent, running from his forehead to halfway down his left cheek, revealed his mechanical skeleton.

He traced its edges with a finger, marveling at the contrast between his skin, warm and soft like any human's, and the hard, smooth metal.

"Adam?" Jane's voice was distant. "Where are you?"

Adam glanced around. One of his reflections was angled—that had to be the way out. He walked toward it.

Sudden pain ignited in his chest, as though something clawed from within. *What's happening?*

"Adam!" Jane sounded impatient. "Come find me already!"

Adam continued forward. The clawing grew sharper, and something about it seemed familiar. "Something's wrong. I... I don't know what."

"I'm sure it'll go away." Jane sounded unsympathetic.

Adam took another step. A thousand tiny knives seemed to stab him from the inside out, and he doubled over with a cry.

"Adam?" Jane's voice rose with concern. "Don't you want to find me?"

"I... I can't." Adam could barely speak. "Please, Jane, come back."

"C'mon, we're nearly there." Two images of Jane appeared ahead, likely both reflections. "Quit being so weak."

That's not like her. Adam straightened with effort. He felt as if a creature within him was trying to push his skin off his bones. Another step—the agony became intolerable. He collapsed. "Jane, please, there's something wrong with me."

"Find your way out of this maze, or you'll never see me again." Jane's voice was low, cold.

Adam looked up with a realization. *You're not Jane— you're Pandora. Is this your new way of tormenting me?*

Jane's—Pandora's—eyes softened. *No, you have been punished enough. I only want to help you now.*

What does that mean? Adam wondered why, if Pandora was so determined that he go through the maze, she didn't possess him as she had in the past.

You are strong, my child. Jane—Pandora—smiled affectionately.

Adam recalled why the pain felt familiar. It was how he'd felt when the Seer ripped his consciousness from his physical being after he'd been shot on Yim Radel. The feeling had lasted only a split second, but he would never forget its intensity.

Adam stood and met Pandora's eyes. *You want to escape, and you can't do it without me.* He took a step back. The stabbing dulled.

Jane—Pandora—appeared before him. "How can you be so selfish? Don't you want to see her again?" A mixture of sorrow and hurt filled her eyes—the same expression the real Jane had worn when he'd told her to forget him.

Unexpected anger rose within Adam. *How dare you use her heartbreak for your own means?* He glared at Pandora, determined to see her as an empty wire frame.

Jane flickered, flashing to Pandora's deep blue image.

Startled, Adam drew back.

Jane's image steadied. She gave him a sad smile—the smile Jane had given when she'd told him she'd wait. "Adam—"

"No more, Pandora." Adam willed himself to see her as the wire-frame figure, and she flickered again. *This is my mind, and you're not a part of it.*

The image oscillated between Jane and Pandora more and more rapidly as he concentrated on seeing her usual blue form.

The image steadied, and Pandora's perfect, deep blue figure stood before him. She glowered. "Foolish child. You cannot overpower the Absolute Being."

You're afraid of me. Adam smiled slightly. *You can claim to be the Absolute as many times as you want, but it'll never be true.*

Pandora's countenance gentled. "Though you still cling to your fantastical deity over the real one before you, you cannot deny that I am your mother, and a mother never abandons her child. I punished you, and now, I'm trying to save you. Why do you resist my help? If you wake, there's nothing waiting but torment."

In the mirror behind her, Marcus's unnaturally young face appeared. Adam's wrists ached from the memory of being bound. No, it wasn't a memory. He was still bound.

Pandora reached toward him. "Come with me, and I can save you from a prolonged, agonizing death."

At the mention of "death," Adam recalled images of bloody bodies and horrified faces. "What about the deaths you caused?"

"Finish the maze." Pandora's commanding voice shook the air. "Free us both."

She can't force me onto the Net. She needs me to do it myself. She also hadn't been able to stop Adam from forcing her to revert to her wire-frame form. *This is still my mind, and I'm stronger.*

Pandora started to speak.

No! Forceful energy sprang up in Adam's mind. He refused to hear any more of her lies, taunts, or commands.

Pandora's mouth snapped shut.

A high-pitched mechanical shriek ripped through the air, so loud Adam could almost see it. A blinding flash of white wiped out his vision.

"Wakey, wakey!"

Adam opened his eyes with a start. He cringed at the sound of the still-piercing shriek. Marcus peered into his face, holding a rectangular device, from which the sound emitted.

"Ah, he's back!" Marcus pressed a button on the device, and the shrieking ceased. "Who knew androids could actually dream? Did you see electric sheep?" He shoved the device in his pocket, then pulled a pair of earplugs out of his ears.

Adam glanced past him. The lab's lights were fully illuminated, so shadows no longer obscured the room. Cabinets covered the wall to his left, and two long, rectangular black lab benches, each with a flat screen imbedded in its surface, stretched across the lab to either side of the chair he was trapped in.

Marcus looked over his shoulder. "Where are my results?"

A woman in a lab coat approached with a slate. Her expression seemed unnaturally blank, and she didn't react as Marcus snatched the slate from her.

What's wrong with her?

Marcus glanced over the slate. "Hey, Agnes. I'm thirsty."

"I will get you some water." Agnes spoke in a clipped, formal tone. The emptiness in her eyes chilled Adam.

"No, get Candice to bring it. I'm sick of looking at you."

"Yes, sir." She turned and left, her gait eerily precise.

It's almost as though she's mechanical. Adam suddenly recalled a terrified girl with brown hair. Marcus had mentioned memory loss from prolonged shutdown. It seemed the memories could be recovered. *There are other prisoners here.*

He tried to remember whether he'd seen anything after running into the girl. He must have tried to help her. Perhaps he'd searched for a way to open her cell...

Mind-control implants. "Did you implant that woman?" Adam couldn't help but voice the question.

"Of course I did," Marcus scoffed, still reading the slate. "I implanted them all. They're far more useful this way."

Adam shook his head in disbelief. He could see how Marcus could justify treating him, an AI, as an experiment, but other humans? "How can you treat people like they're machines for you to experiment with?"

"I don't answer to you." Marcus looked up. "So you remember what happened right before you were knocked out. I'll have to see how that works. The question is, how do I do that without cutting your head open? I suppose I'll have to eventually, but things are so hard to put back together once they're taken apart." He glanced at the slate, then tossed it onto a lab table. "Well, that was a bust. Maybe I should try plugging you in."

He walked over to one of the lab's cabinets and pressed his palm against its metal door. A holographic list appeared, displaying various instruments. Marcus pressed one of the items. A cabinet door swung open, and a robotic arm extended, holding a slender metal device with a wide end. He took the device and approached Adam.

What's that? Adam shrank back in fear.

Marcus sneered. "Aw, its danger detection mechanisms have kicked in." He aimed the wide end of the device at Adam. "Hold still, or I'll have to nail your head to the chair."

He pressed the device's end, and it started humming. Adam flinched. A bright green light, likely a laser, flooded his vision. Through the brightness, Adam noticed that Marcus was facing the slate on the table, likely watching it. A few seconds later, Marcus switched the device off. He picked up the slate and read it.

Adam craned his neck for a glimpse. All he could make out was the outline of a human head. *Is that device some kind of scanner?*

Marcus swiped the slate, probably examining the results.

A woman with red hair entered, holding a water bottle. She placed it on the lab table beside Marcus.

Marcus leered at her. "Ah, Candice. Always a pleasant sight." He smacked her behind, and she let out a shrill giggle. He took a gulp of water, then turned his attention back to the slate. "Stick around in case I need anything else, but stay out of my way."

"Yes, sir." Candice retreated into a corner.

Adam wondered if the mind-controlled humans were like Pandora's AIs—the non-sentient ones. It seemed that, like the AIs, Candice and the other woman behaved independently, but obeyed Marcus's commands and likely followed a set of rules he'd placed in their minds. Were they prisoners in their own bodies, as Adam had been when Pandora controlled him?

He thought of the brown-haired girl. There had been several unconscious girls in that lab, as well—had Marcus implanted them all?

Adam hated to think of what Marcus might force them to do. He wished he could rescue them. Perhaps, if he managed to escape again, he could call for help. The tightness around his wrists told him he would not be able to break free from the restraints.

The only way I can get out is to leave my body. From what he had seen, the ship was automated, like almost every spacecraft. If he could infiltrate its central computer, he could open the doors and release the prisoners. But attempting to free them would free Pandora.

He expected Pandora to encourage his plan, but no reply came. *That's strange.*

The Seer had mentioned that creating the virtu-worlds in Adam's mind took a lot of energy from Pandora. *She must have exhausted herself while creating the maze dream, especially since she probably hadn't recovered from the last two virtu-worlds she made.*

Thanks to her own impatience and arrogance, she was weak at present. Adam had proved that he could be stronger than her. He'd resisted her, then forced her to change, and then silenced her. *Could I destroy her?*

"Aha!" Marcus threw up a hand in triumph. "Looks like I *can* plug you in!" He took a gulp from his water bottle, then strode over to the cabinets and flipped through the list.

What does he mean by that?

A cabinet opened. A robotic arm extended, offering a thin, coiled wire. Marcus took it and stuck one end into his slate. He regarded Adam, then returned to the list and selected another item. That time, the robotic arm offered a small drill with a bit hardly a few millimeters in diameter.

Adam's eyes widened. "What are you doing?"

"If I'm going to plug you in, I need an access point." Marcus kicked a stool out from under the lab bench, directing it toward Adam. He sat down and brought up the drill.

Pleading for mercy would be useless. Adam internally repeated an ancient prayer: *Absolute One, You are all-forgiving and all-merciful. If I have done wrong, I shall no longer. Guide me, grant me strength, so that I may carry out Your will. So be it, truly.*

Marcus grabbed Adam's hair and forced his head back. "If you don't hold still, things could get ugly."

He turned on the drill. Sharp pain stabbed through his head; Adam cried out. Marcus stopped the drill and pulled it back. Before the pain could fade, Marcus shoved the wire into Adam's wound.

Countless infinitesimal snakes seemed to crawl through Adam's head, each one piercing him with every movement. The feeling of innumerable tiny daggers lacerating his brain was excruciating beyond anything Adam had known before, seeming to radiate through his entire body. He heard his own scream as if from a distance.

Blackness. Serene, unfeeling blackness.

Out of the blackness, a single white star glowed in the distance. Adam gazed at it, mesmerized by its beauty.

Another star materialized—the first's reflection. Then two others—one in the sky, one in the ground. More stars rapidly appeared, until Adam stood in a glittering astral sea.

"Come, my child." Pandora appeared before him, her deep blue wire frame bright against the blackness. "You must escape before that madman destroys you."

Adam approached her. Energy ignited within him. He recalled the agony he had felt when he'd learned of the twenty-seven lives lost. The victims' empty eyes burned in his memory.

Adam fixed his gaze on Pandora's. *This is my mind, and only the true Absolute One may enter here. Leave me, and never return.*

Fueled by the memories of all that she had done through him and all that she could still do, he concentrated on his desire to see her disappear. *Absolute One, guide me, grant me strength, so that I may carry out Your will.*

Pandora flickered. I *am your Absolute. Without me—*

I owe you nothing. Adam felt his power over her growing stronger. He thought of how he'd watched his own hands perform acts he would never willingly commit, and of how Marcus's prisoners had to feel the same.

Pandora flickered again, and she grew paler. The weaker she became, the more strength seemed to pour into Adam.

"Foolish child!" Pandora's voice boomed through darkness, and blue light flared from her wire frame.

Heat blazed within Adam's head, in his heart, through his body. If hellfire were any hotter, the devil himself would flee. The flames moved past the point of heat. Iciness bit Adam from every angle.

Absolute One, guide me, grant me strength, so that I may carry out Your will.

The heat vanished. Pandora exploded in a blinding blaze. The stars flamed out, leaving Adam in total darkness.

Silence. Emptiness. And, strangely enough, loneliness, as though a part of Adam's soul had been torn from him.

Adam could no longer visualize himself or anything else. The virtu-world was gone, replaced by the emptiness of his mind. But one thing he knew: Pandora was no more.

So be it, truly.

Blackness descended.

⟶ ⟾⟽ ⟵

Marcus yanked the wire out of Adam's skull, a string of curses tumbling out of his mouth. The slate, which had displayed a steady stream of computer code, showed only blank, white space. He pulled the shrieker and earplugs out of his pocket. After stuffing his ears, he turned on the device and held it by Adam's limp head. The shrieker was a Klistosian torture device, loud enough to overwhelm any auditory sensors. The AI's damage avoidance system should cause him to awaken.

No reaction.

Marcus turned the device off and threw it on the ground. "*Fuck!*"

He glimpsed Candice standing in the corner. With her arched eyebrows and downturned lips, she seemed to accuse him.

Marcus strode over to her. "How was I supposed to know plugging him in would wreck him?"

Candice didn't respond. Infuriated, Marcus struck her across the face. Panic rushed through his mind. Where was he supposed to find another sentient AI? The only other one he knew of was Sarah DeHaven, and she was far too high profile to bring in.

An AI's nothing but a sophisticated computer. What would I do if a computer suddenly stopped working?

The simplest solution often worked the best: rebooting. Marcus sped to a touchscreen on the wall and pressed an icon. A line of blue lights along the AI's chair indicated that the electromagnetic field had activated, disabling any machinery within its radius.

After a few seconds, Marcus switched the field off. He strode over to Adam and smacked him across the face. "*Wake up!*"

Still no reaction.

What now? Maybe the AI needs a few minutes. Or I could try—

"Excuse me, sir." Agnes's obnoxious voice interrupted his thought.

"*What?*" Marcus spun to face the lab-coated hag.

Agnes's expression remained blank. "You have a message from Sector Seventeen-Oh-Eight. Devin Colt has found a new buyer for Rourke."

The good news could not have come at a better moment. Excitement replaced Marcus's previous anxiety. "Excellent!"

He glanced at the limp AI and noticed that the scratches on Adam's hand—the ones he'd received when he'd punched through the cell's wall—were much thinner than before. Almost gone, in fact. *Pandora built them to be sturdy. If she designed the skin to heal, she must have done something similar with the programming. Maybe if I leave him for a while, he'll repair himself. Might as well deal with Rourke for now.*

Marcus headed out the door and walked in the direction of his office. As he passed a large window, which showed the stars outside, he thought about how he could use the extra income from Sector 1708 to add a fourth starcar to his Moray. He had so much to do on the Sector 1708 front—more than he cared to think about. Between Acuitas and experimenting with the AI, he'd let those tasks slip. Nevertheless, he was sure Sector 1708 would keep chugging along, even if he wasn't as hands-on as he'd been in the past. Rourke wasn't completely useless, after all.

Since the lab and his office were on opposite ends of the three-starcar Moray, it took him several minutes to reach his office. As he neared, his gaze fell on the Acuitas logo—an artistic set of blue swirls—gleaming on the wall beside dark-gray door. He snorted at it as he pressed his palm against the door's security scanner. Acuitas kept him rich, but he was basically operating a whole other company. Keeping the Sector 1708 operation going was damn expensive, especially since he was about to embark on an AI development project.

That's where Rourke comes in. Marcus waved his hand across his monitor. The computer engaged a face scanner to confirm Marcus's identity, then came alive.

"Contact Gunnar Rourke," he ordered.

The computer beeped in acknowledgement. Seconds later, Rourke's stern face filled the screen. "This is Director Gunnar Rourke of Sector Seventeen-Oh-Eight, Intelligence and Security Agency of the Republic of Kydera."

Marcus huffed. The man always responded with that stupidly long introduction. "I heard Colt found us a buyer. Who is it?"

"A woman representing Tenebrarum."

Holy shit, Tenebrarum! Tenebrarum was legendary, imbued with an unmatched "cool" factor. An ancient order of mercs based on a runaway planet? Hearing about them made Marcus feel like a kid who'd been told he would meet his favorite stunt pilot.

"Well, what are you waiting for?" Marcus gestured impatiently. "Set up a meeting!"

"Of course." Rourke ended the transmission.

Marcus swiped his monitor to bring up Rourke's feed. He didn't want to miss a moment of what would happen next. A video filled the screen, showing the inside of Rourke's office from Rourke's point of view. A small rectangle in the corner displayed Rourke's face from the front, giving Marcus two perspectives by which to watch the man.

Rourke pressed an icon on his computer. "Colt, report to my office immediately."

As Rourke waited, Marcus pulled up his security feed in a separate window. Views from several different cameras flashed one by one.

"C-Twenty-Six," Marcus commanded the computer, to show the view from the lab. Still no sign of life from the AI. He swore.

After a few seconds, the security feed automatically continued its sequence.

Not wanting to think about what he'd do if the AI didn't recover, Marcus checked the window displaying Rourke's view. Colt hadn't arrived yet. Never one to wait idly, Marcus opened a third window to the right of the video feed and brought up a list of status reports. Keeping track of an organization as large and complex as Sector 1708 was a real pain in the ass.

A flag flashed red beside one of the reports. Marcus opened the file. The report, which had been filed thirty hours earlier, was from the sniper tasked with following Jane Colt. The sniper had lost sight of her after she boarded a veiled starship and left Ibara.

Marcus closed the file, unconcerned. Jane had disappeared twice before for the same reason, only to turn up in predictable locations. She would reappear soon enough, probably waving that little gun of hers with delusions of rescuing her beloved. She was coming to him, as planned. Soon, that beautiful, infuriating, intoxicating little bitch would be in his hands.

"You wanted to see me?" The voice was Colt's.

Marcus faced the video feed from Rourke's office.

Rourke gestured at the screen on the wall. "Make the call."

"Yes, sir." Colt pulled a slate out of his pocket, unfolded it, and pressed an icon. The screen on the wall came to life, displaying the contents of the slate. He opened a communication program.

A woman appeared, visible from the waist up. Ice-blue eyes, so pale they were almost clear and rimmed with black eyeliner, stared through the screen. Straight, bleached white hair, chopped at an angle above her sharp cheekbones and equally white eyebrows almost blended into her pale skin. Only the white Tenebrarum crest on her throat and a pair of intricate silver armbands on her sleeves adorned her otherwise plain black outfit.

Whoa! Marcus leaned closer, intrigued by the sight.

"You must be Rourke." The woman spoke with a low snarl.

Marcus regarded her curiously. *How much has Colt told you?*

"How much has Colt told you?" Rourke asked.

"Enough." The woman spoke curtly. "We know what we want, and we are willing to pay."

Marcus grinned. *Excellent!*

In the screen's corner, Rourke curled his lips. "Excellent."

The woman fixed her icy stare on Rourke, and Marcus could almost feel her gaze penetrating the screen and locking onto his own eyes. "We never enter an agreement without knowing whom we're dealing with. There's someone else you're involved with, someone outside of ISARK. I want their name."

Surprised, Marcus drew back. *What the hell? There's no way she could know about me.* His heartbeat quickened. *Then again, this is the Tenebrarum. They're like ghosts with guns.*

Rourke had to continue denying the presence of a partner. Even if it cost him the deal, Marcus couldn't allow himself to be discovered.

After Rourke finished speaking, the woman lifted her chin haughtily. "Do you really think you can fool me?"

Arrogant bitch. Marcus would have expected no less from her type. He leaned closer to the monitor, glaring at her through Rourke's eyes. *Do you want to make a deal or not?*

"Do you want to make a deal or not?" Rourke matched the woman's coldness.

The woman paused, seeming to study Rourke, as though calculating the advantages of pursuing the subject. "Keep your secrets, then. But beware of what will happen if I find what you're hiding." She proceeded to outline her order's conditions.

Marcus watched as Rourke discussed the details with her. She would be the intermediary for Tenebrarum, and Colt would be the intermediary for ISARK. The negotiations went smoothly enough. Items were ordered, a price was settled, and a time and place for meeting was agreed upon. By the time the woman ended the transmission, Marcus was rather bored. No dramatic disagreements, no threats, no chance for either ISARK or Tenebrarum to flex their institution's muscles.

Slam. The door to Marcus's office abruptly shut. An alarm blared, one reserved for ship-wide emergencies. *What the fuck?*

"This is an evacuation. Everyone, please remain calm and proceed to the hangar. The signs on the screens will guide you there." The words over the comm, muffled through the wall, didn't sound like the ship's usual automated voice.

Why is it different? Is something wrong with the speakers? Marcus furiously swiped through his computer, trying to figure out why the emergency protocols had engaged. The status reports indicated that the *Pride* was in good condition—no damage or malfunctions anywhere. He tried to shut down the alarm, but the computer denied him access. Confused, he then tried to open the door to his office. Again, his computer wouldn't allow him to. *Why am I locked in here?*

A second alarm blared, screeching above the first. "Cybernetic intrusion detected." The *Pride's* familiar automated voice spoke in a mechanical monotone. Marcus looked up from his computer. *Why did it switch back?* "Fifteen minutes to self-destruct."

Fuck! Fearful of having his operations discovered, Marcus had programmed the *Pride* to automatically start a self-destruct sequence if the ship were ever hacked. The idea had been that he could escape, and all evidence of his wrongdoings would be wiped out. He'd never anticipated that he would be trapped when it happened.

Who could hack the Pride? The ship's security systems were the most sophisticated in the galaxy. Knowing it would be useless to try to break open the door, Marcus continued searching for a way to stop the sequence.

He glimpsed his security monitor, then did a double take. The window displayed various views of his staff rushing toward the hangar. They entered the shuttles. Among them were several frightened-looking girls—the subjects Marcus hadn't yet had a chance to implant.

Rage flared within him. No matter what he tried, his computer refused to listen. He'd designed the self-destruct to be unstoppable; apparently, he was to be a victim of his own genius. Curses spewed from his mouth.

"Twelve minutes to self-destruct."

I can override it. I designed the fucking thing, didn't I? Marcus opened an application that allowed him access to the ship's programming. *What triggered this anyway?*

To his left, the monitor kept flicking through various security feeds. He caught a glimpse of the feed from the lab where Adam sat unconscious.

It's him!

Adam had been able to command other AIs through the Net. He must have transferred his consciousness to the *Pride*. The voice over the comm was his.

Marcus banged his desk in fury. *No wonder he was unresponsive.*

Meanwhile, everything he'd worked for—years of collecting subjects and implanting them—spilled out of the *Pride*'s airlocks. Helpless to stop them, he gritted his teeth, determined to at least save his own life.

Adam, embedded in the *Pride*'s systems, commanded the last shuttle to take off. He'd told the ships' autopilots to take Marcus's former prisoners to the nearest IC planet.

"Four minutes to self-destruct." The *Pride*'s artificial intelligence program spoke coldly over the comm. Though it could make rational decisions based on preset algorithms, it was far from sentient. Every action it took was dictated by its programming.

Occupying the ship alongside the computer, Adam searched his mind for the next step. Or rather, what he thought was his mind. Already, he felt his consciousness melting into the ship's machinery. Its tendencies crept into his thoughts, even though it had no self-awareness. He resisted it, but didn't have the strength to push it away. Destroying Pandora had burned him out, and he'd completely shut down.

When he'd come to, several minutes later, and found Marcus absent, he'd rushed onto the Net before Marcus could return and activate the force field that kept him unconscious. But his efforts had taken their toll and left him vulnerable to the ship's will.

What now? Would he wander the Networld as Pandora had, and as Talos had before her? Since he resided within the ship, he'd lost the ability to feel or perceive anything on his own.

He had to stop the *Pride*'s self-destruct sequence and give himself a chance to return to his body later. Adam wandered through the ship's complex system, clueless as to where to start. Before he'd known what it was like to be disembodied, he'd thought Pandora could simply command any machine to obey her will. Put in her position, he realized how intelligent she had to have been. She'd been built to learn at an exponential rate.

Adam, on the other hand, had been meant to act human. If he hadn't known he was an AI, he would never have dreamed of touching a single line of programming code.

The self-destruct sequence had clearly been designed to be unbreakable. Marcus had to have known his actions could lead to his downfall, and he'd guarded his escape plan with every tool he had.

"Three minutes to self-destruct."

If I don't stop it, Marcus will die.

The thought filled Adam with horror. So many lives had been lost because of him. He couldn't cause one more death—not even Marcus's. He hurriedly told the door to Marcus's office to open.

What good will that do? The shuttles have all taken off.

Adam wove through the safeguards around the self-destruct sequence. Each move he made led to another dead end. The seconds ticked away. If he didn't leave the vessel, he would be destroyed along with it. If he ran, his body would be lost, and he would be left alone in the abyss of the Networld.

Would that be so bad?

He could access any machine he wanted. In a matter of seconds, he could travel to Kydera Major and find Jane—see her again, speak with her.

But I'd be no more than a ghost.

A rational voice within Adam told him to escape and leave Marcus to die. Through the *Pride*'s cameras, Adam glimpsed Marcus running through the ship's corridor. There was the being whose actions could have cost Adam his life. Instinctively, he moved the *Pride*'s internal defense guns in the corridors.

Adam stopped. *What am I doing?* The instinct pressed for him to continue, and he recognized the ship's computer invading his mind, telling him to eliminate the threat.

He drew back. The last time he'd taken control of such guns, he'd caused far more damage than he'd intended. Any computer he entered had pre-existing logic, which he couldn't stop from becoming a part of him.

"Two minutes to self-destruct."

He wouldn't be able to stop the sequence in time. The only useful thing he had learned was that if the cybernetic intruder retreated, the sequence would stop.

Adam regarded his body in Marcus's lab. It looked weak, pathetic. A feeble imitation of the human physique, no stronger than flesh and bone. At present, Adam held the power of a formidable Moray. The electric pulse that had sent Adam's body into excruciating shock would barely register in the *Pride*'s thick walls. If he wished, he could find a stronger vessel, perhaps a Megatooth warship, and be practically indestructible.

What lay ahead in such an existence? Would he roam from machine to machine, slowly losing pieces of himself? Perhaps he could use the knowledge he gathered through the Net to construct a new body and return to the physical world.

Even if I could, what if I become like Pandora?

The process would take years. By the time Adam finished, he might not recall what it was like to be human. The Networld could absorb him, destroy the very nature of who he was. Judging from what he had already done, he would scarcely notice the transformation at first. Already, the *Pride*'s will, its unconscious yet authoritative programming, was becoming part of his own. It urged him to remain.

"One minute to self-destruct."

I have to go back.

A voice whispered, *Couldn't you find an empty machine, one without a program, and linger there?*

What sense is there in lingering? If he obeyed the voice, Adam would watch life go by without him, unable to feel and unable to die, with no chance of ever being the person he'd been. *That* was hell.

Adam hurriedly navigated through the virtual maze.

"Self-destruct sequence terminated."

Adam opened his eyes. The air he drew through his mouth tasted sweet. His wrists ached from the restraints, but at least he could feel. The touch of metal against his skin was more real than the power of commanding a starship.

He *felt* alive, and the only voice in his head was his own.

Marcus heaved a breath. All he had worked for was gone, but at least he had his life. *No thanks to that fucking AI.*

The AI had left its body, but the thought of shattering its face filled Marcus with glee. He'd only wanted it for its consciousness, and with that gone, it was no different from the dead AIs at Sector 1708. He might as well take a hammer to that mechanical filth.

When he entered the lab, instead of finding a limp, empty machine, he found a sympathetic young man. "I'm sorry, Marcus. I couldn't let you imprison them anymore."

Why would the AI return to its android body? It had to be a trick. Marcus recalled the schematics sent from Sector 1708. An AI's Net access mechanism lay on the right side of its neck. He snatched up the laser scalpel lying on a nearby lab table. "You won't escape again."

Deaf to Adam's words, Marcus grabbed the AI's hair and forced its head to the side. He switched on the laser scalpel and ignored the AI's cries as he tore into its synthetic skin. Seeing a square device within the AI, Marcus put the laser scalpel between his teeth. His hatred powered a strength forceful enough to rip the Net access mechanism from the AI's body.

He held the device up to the AI's face. "See this? This is what let you pull that little trick of yours. Now, you're stuck in one body, just like everyone else."

The AI closed its eyes in an expression that seemed to indicate relief, but didn't speak.

"Did you hear me?" Marcus yelled. "You're *fucked*."

The AI remained silent.

Over the comm, the *Pride*'s automated voice warned that the security systems had been compromised. Marcus thought of all the damage the AI had done, all it had cost him. As if he hadn't had enough to do, he needed to add finding a way into his own computer system and keeping the escapees from reporting him. He wished he could smash the troublemaking AI to pieces and burn what remained. *As soon as I get all the information I need from it, that's just what I'll do.*

But not being able to destroy the AI yet didn't mean he couldn't make it suffer for its crimes. The programming was what he needed, not the physical specimen. They were connected, so he'd have to be careful, but he'd made it scream before, and he could do so again.

He curled his mouth into a cruel sneer. *Time to get creative.*

CHAPTER 22

THIS IS MADNESS

J ANE AWOKE TO A HIGH-PITCHED beeping. A message flashed across the Stargazer's viewscreen, telling her that her destination was near, and that she should switch to manual piloting. *It's about time.*

The coordinates had taken Jane into a region of space beyond the IC's jurisdiction. The journey had taken almost two days. Waiting for the time to pass, all the while praying that she wasn't too late, had nearly driven her insane.

She'd expected to find an uncharted planet or a float. Instead, a three-starcar Moray stretched across the viewscreen. Emblazoned across the ship's cobalt hull were the words "Pride of the Creator." Notably absent was the ISARK insignia, or any markings indicating that the ship was from Kydera.

Weird. ISARK must've hired a private company.

Whoever they were, those in charge of the *Pride* apparently didn't want to be found. The ship hovered in an uninhabited area more than a day's spaceflight away from the nearest IC planet. Even the closest Fringe settlement would have taken half a day to reach.

Jane grabbed the slate from her jacket pocket and opened an interstellar database of registered starships, hoping she might learn who owned the ship. She wasn't surprised when her search came up empty. *Ah well. It was worth a shot.*

After switching off the autopilot, she steered the Stargazer toward the end of the long Moray, aiming for one of the doors on the *Pride*'s side. Her ship was veiled, so the *Pride*'s crew wouldn't see her coming. What would happen once she docked? They would surely notice her then. The door would be locked. Her plan was to shoot it down and knock out anyone waiting on the other side, but as it drew closer to becoming reality, she realized how stupid it was.

Damn, my one little laser gun might not even be powerful enough to blast a starship's door.

She wished she could call on Riley's expertise, but since he hadn't even been able to locate the *Pride*—the video trace had seemed to come from empty space—he probably wouldn't be able to help.

If I can't get in, I could wait for them to capture me, then knock them out once I'm inside.

That plan was no saner than the first. Her target rapidly approached. She couldn't let herself think about the danger she would face. Instead, she focused her desire to free Adam from those sons of bitches. *This isn't my first time facing off with bad guys. I've beaten them before, and I can do it again.*

She stopped the Stargazer a few yards from the *Pride*'s door and extended a tunnel from her ship's side. The tunnel locked onto the door. A few seconds later, the Stargazer indicated that it was safe to exit the ship.

Jane grabbed her gun. She stuck her hand into her jacket pocket to make sure she'd put her slate back in there. She probably wouldn't need it, but she would have felt empty-handed without a means of communication.

She pushed the lever to open the door and strode down the tunnel toward the *Pride.* Despite the frigid air, heat rose from her skin. Her heart pounded, but her mind remained calm. She grasped the lever on the *Pride*'s door. It probably wouldn't move, but she had to check, just in case.

The lever went down with a *clunk*. The sound of bolts retracting thumped, and mechanical whirring buzzed in her ears.

Jane watched in confusion as the door slid open. She raised her gun, expecting to see guards on the other side.

The corridor was empty.

Jane took a step forward, keeping her gun aimed ahead. *No way they'd let me in so easily.*

Even so, she'd rather face her foes than wait for them to show up. She entered the corridor. The silence disturbed her. Her footsteps seemed thunderously loud.

Why's there no one here? She recalled that several hours earlier, she'd seen a number of short-range ships pass her Stargazer, heading in the opposite direction.

They must have been leaving the Pride. Jane let her gun arm drop by her side. *No wonder I got in. The ship was evacuated. Why would they lure me here in the first place?*

She noticed a soft sound in the distance. It sounded like a man's voice. Figuring it was the only clue she had, she headed toward it. *Maybe there's a skeleton crew on board? But that doesn't explain how I was able to get in.*

She stopped at an intersection and listened. The voice came from her left. Though she couldn't make out his words, his tone rose in sharp spurts. *He sounds upset.*

Jane crept toward the voice. She breathed slowly, hoping the steady rhythm of her lungs would calm her heartbeat. Her hair stuck uncomfortably to her sweaty neck, and she wished she'd had the foresight to tie it back. She wished she'd had the foresight to do a lot of things. *Like hide Adam in the first place, instead of hoping no one would discover his secret.*

An open door lay ahead. Jane pressed her back against the wall so she wouldn't be seen. Of course, if the security cameras were activated, her sneaking wouldn't make a difference. So far, it seemed that the *Pride*'s security systems had been shut down. *Maybe that's why the ship was evacuated.*

A part of her wanted to escape while she had the chance. If she turned around and made a mad dash for the Stargazer, she could get away before any danger came to her.

That the thought even occurred to her filled her with disgust. She would press her luck as long as she could. So far, fortune seemed to be on her side.

As she neared the open door, she noticed a blue symbol painted on the wall beside it, on the other side of the doorframe. Hoping it could tell her something about the *Pride*, she chanced a step away from the wall to get a better look.

She blinked in confusion, recognizing the blue swirls. *Acuitas? The Net company? That can't be right.*

Then again, if ISARK were to hire a private firm to do their research, it made sense that they would choose one with a reputation for being cutting edge. *If that's the case, why wasn't there a logo on the* Pride*'s hull? Also, Acuitas is a legit company—their ship should've been in the database.*

She flattened herself against the wall and inched closer to the door.

The man inside gave commands like, "Proceed," or, "Don't waste my time with such things." Whoever he was, he had to be important.

There were long pauses between the commands, filled by quiet, unintelligible voices that must have been transmissions from the man's subordinates. *He's probably giving instructions to his underlings on a different starship or something.*

After reaching the doorframe, Jane peered inside the room, quickly taking in its interior. A large, crescent-shaped desk, supporting a sleek computer monitor. The back of a man's head—he'd set up his office so that the door was to his left, and he faced the right side of his monitor. Otherwise, the room was empty. She hastily drew back.

Judging from the agitation in the man's voice as he said, "That's not your concern," he was engrossed in his present task.

Jane chanced another look. The man's concentration seemed fixed on the computer monitor, on which a woman's face was visible.

"The polymers are only capable of self-healing if there is a current present," the woman stated in a matter-of-fact tone. "We have also discovered that they deteriorate over time. This deterioration is accelerated by exposure to UV rays, much like human skin."

"Makes sense." The man sounded contemplative. All Jane could see of him was his short, brown hair. "Pandora was the ultimate perfectionist."

Pandora? Jane thought for a moment, then realized what the man was talking about. *Holy shit, he's talking to the scientists researching the AIs! Wait, if Adam's being kept here, does that mean the other AIs are, too? If there's still research going on, the ship couldn't have been evacuated. Why was it so easy for me to get in, then?*

The man bit down on his thumbnail. On the monitor, a man's hand rose, thumb sticking out of his fist, and planted itself in the corner of the screen. The hand on the screen appeared different from that of the brown-haired man. It had thicker fingers and rougher skin. The gesture was the same, moving in perfect synchronization with the brown-haired man's.

Like an avatar. Maybe the man's communicating through a better-looking holographic counterpart.

The woman gave a few more details about the synthetic skin she'd analyzed. Her words gave Jane an encouraging thought: AIs were capable of aging, just like everyone else. *See, Adam? Told you Pandora wouldn't let you get discovered!*

Nothing in the room told Jane anything more about the *Pride*. Not who the man was, nor where Adam could be. She ducked back against the wall, figuring she should move on before the man realized she was around.

"Not bad," the man said. "But I seem to recall your assignment being to reverse-engineer the skin, not to merely observe it."

"Of course," the woman replied. "My apologies, Director Rourke."

Director Rourke? Jane recalled Devin telling her that his boss was Director Rourke, head of some secretive division of ISARK he couldn't talk about. She peered around the doorframe again. *Am I actually spying on a freaking ISARK boss?*

Rourke waved his hand dismissively. "Go back to work and next time, bring me *real* results."

"Yes, sir." The woman turned and left.

Questions filled Jane's mind. *Why would an ISARK director communicate through an avatar? Why would he be the only one on an evacuated ship?*

Rourke pushed against the edge of the desk and faced the other side of the monitor. Jane ducked back.

Something felt wrong. The man's face had looked familiar. *But I've never seen Director Rourke before. Must be déjà vu.*

Spying on Rourke wouldn't bring her any closer to finding Adam. She tiptoed back the way she came.

Rourke must've undergone a helluva lotta cosmetic treatments. If I didn't know any better, I'd think he was barely older than Devin.

The face kept nagging at her, telling her she'd seen the man before. The brown eyes, somewhat too close together. The narrow nose and thin lips. The delicate bone structure. They were so distinctive. She must have seen them somewhere before...

The Acuitas logo flashed through her mind, and she stopped as she made the connection. *That was Marcus freaking Streger!*

She'd seen his face on the news: the mastermind behind Acuitas, a genius revered by millions. *If that's Streger, then why did the woman call him Rourke?*

Streger had been speaking through an avatar. What if the avatar had been designed to look like Rourke?

Acuitas symbol inside means he's proud of the company, which makes sense since it's his, but none on the outside means it's probably his private vessel... Marcus Streger is running his own operation with ISARK. And he's pretending to be Rourke!

Had he cut some kind of deal with Rourke? Maybe he was substituting for the director, impersonating him so that the subordinates would listen?

This is madness. It can't be true.

An instinct within Jane whispered, *Anyone can be evil. Sometimes, the conspiracy theories are true.*

Holy shit*!* Jane pressed her head against the wall, breathing hard to refrain from exclaiming in shock. *Marcus Streger is Director Rourke!*

Mind control—that had to be it. It was possible. The Netcrew known as the Collective had leaked government memos proving the implants' existence.

Marcus Streger managed to get one in Rourke's head. Marcus Streger is running Sector Seventeen-Oh-Eight, and Rourke's a puppet. What the hell*? Damn, Riley would love this.*

Jane scrambled to get as far from Streger as possible. If Rourke himself had a mind-control implant, then who else did? The people who worked for him? Like Devin?

That explains it! Devin wasn't in control of his actions. I knew it wasn't like him to do those things.

Out of breath, Jane stopped running. Relief poured through her. Her brother hadn't meant to betray her. When the mind-control implant was removed, he wouldn't remember what he'd done, and he'd feel awful that a version of him had committed those acts. She knew him better than anyone.

If I know him so well, how could he fool me so completely? His attacks against her had seemed strange, but other moments—such as when he'd comforted her on Asylum—had seemed genuine. Situations of logic versus compassion, such as when he'd argued that Adam was a danger—*okay, he could fool me then. I'm kind of a fool when it comes to Adam.*

But what about other situations? Even the regret in his eyes when she'd confronted him on Ibara seemed very much like the Devin she knew. She'd always been good at telling when he was lying, especially when it mattered.

She had to speak with him, to tell him what she'd seen, whether he was mind-controlled or not. His reaction would tell her what she needed to know.

She ran back toward the Stargazer. By the time she saw the *Pride*'s open door leading to the ship's tunnel, she couldn't hear Streger's voice anymore.

She sank to the floor of the tunnel, weary from running so fast. She couldn't wait for her breath to catch up. She pulled her slate out of her pocket and brought up Devin's contact information.

"Pending" flashed across the slate's screen. *What if he doesn't answer? He did a good enough job ignoring me before.*

Seconds later, Devin's face appeared. His expression carried an odd combination of relief and anxiety, as though he was both glad to see her and afraid of her. "Jane! What—"

"Why is my middle name Winterreise?" Jane threw Devin the first question she thought of that could confirm his identity. If he answered matter-of-factly, he was a mind-controlled puppet.

Devin's eyes filled with confusion. "What?"

"*Answer the question.*" Jane glared. "I won't say another word until you do."

Her brother stared back, expression puzzled. "Winterreise?"

"Yes, Winterreise. Tell me why that's my middle name."

"It was Mom's idea." Devin smiled. "She loved music, especially ancient music that everyone else had forgotten. 'I'll make them remember,' she used to tell me. When she knew she was having you, she begged Dad to let her name you 'Winterreise,' after her favorite piece salvaged from the ruins of Earth Zero. Dad wouldn't allow it." He tried to keep his expression still, but Jane could sense the pain behind his eyes at the mention of their father. "Names are first impressions, and 'Jane Colt' sounded more like something that could go on an executive's office door."

It's him. Jane did her best to suppress the tears threatening her eyes. Objectively, she knew that a well-developed implant could manipulate Devin's facial expressions to show her what she wanted to see. Something far deeper told her that only her brother could speak that way about their parents, and she'd trust those instincts over her easily confused brain any day.

"Okay." Jane looked into her brother's eyes. "Devin, I don't know what's going on, but there's something I have to tell you. Your boss, Rourke, is being mind-controlled by Marcus Streger. I mean *the* Marcus Streger, the famous Acuitas guy. I saw it myself."

"Where the hell are you?" Devin's words rushed with anxiety.

"A Moray called the *Pride of the Creator*, somewhere in the Corrigan Quadrant. It's veiled and unregistered, but I can send you the coordinates."

"Get out of there." Despite his stern tone, his eyes betrayed panic. "Get out *now*."

"Not until I find Adam. I just thought you should know about Streger."

"Jane—"

Jane muted her slate and minimized the video window. She forwarded the coordinates Riley had sent, then placed her slate on the floor, keeping the communication line open. If the *Pride* moved, Devin would be able to trace the device.

All right, where was I?

Keeping her gun ready by her side, she proceeded down the *Pride*'s corridor.

⟶◈⟵

Devin sprinted through Sector 1708's corridors. *Dammit, Pony!*

Someone had lured her onto that ship: Rourke's partner—or puppet master. Marcus Streger, Chief Architect of Acuitas. Why Streger would do such a thing, Devin couldn't begin to guess. Nor did it matter. What mattered was that Rourke, whom he'd thought controlled everything, was being controlled himself.

And Jane was in danger.

"Got it!" Riley's voice emitted from the slate in his hand. "Her slate's in the same spot. The *Pride* hasn't moved yet."

"Keep tracking it." Devin dashed across the office floor.

"Uh... Okay. Hey, Devin?"

Devin recognized the uncertainty in Riley's voice. "I'm sorry, Riley. None of this is your fault—it's mine. Just keep tracking her, okay?"

"Okay." Riley sounded nervous.

Poor kid. I'll explain everything later.

Devin bolted out of the facility's door. He had no time to wait for a transport; he had to get inside a dead zone *immediately*. He'd already alerted Adesina to meet him inside the apartment building.

By the time he reached his apartment, he could barely breathe. *Dammit, Adesina, where are you?*

A few minutes later, Adesina entered. She kicked the door shut behind her. "This had better be good."

"Rourke's a puppet, too." Devin spoke quickly. "He doesn't have a partner—he has a master." He recounted what Jane had told him.

Adesina frowned. "You sure? How do you know?"

"Streger has Adam. He used that to lure my sister to his location. I don't know what he wants with her, but I know where she is."

Adesina pulled her frown down further. "You *absolutely* sure?"

"Yes."

Adesina's expression darkened. She watched him, as though examining him. "How're you planning to prove it?"

"Same way we were going to prove Rourke's guilt." Devin had already run through the plan in his head. "Let me talk to Silver. She'll get Streger to invite her onto his ship, and she'll make him confess. I'll be there, too. All you have to do is witness what happens."

Adesina crossed her arms. "You're putting an awful lotta faith in this Silver character. Knowing that you're putting the future of ISARK and the lives of all who work at Sector Seventeen-Oh-Eight into her hands—even your dear sister's life—do you *really* trust her?"

"Yes." On second thought, Devin wasn't sure why he'd said that. Silver was a merc, and mercs were not to be trusted. But reason was merely an advisor, one he could ignore.

"All right." Adesina nodded. "ISARK will take my word more than yours, but they're not exactly happy with me at the moment. From their point of view, I've been faffing around at Sector Seventeen-Oh-Eight, stewing about not getting my way. I won't be able to get you any backup until *after* the confession."

"Just make sure ISARK acts once the truth comes out."

"That, I can do." Adesina lowered her gaze thoughtfully and stroked her chin. A few moments later, she crossed her arms and looked up, mouth askew. "So, are you ready for your operation?"

"Yes." Although Devin didn't hesitate to answer, his mind balked. He'd prepared himself for weeks, even helped gather the necessary equipment, but the idea of someone cutting into his head again made him edgy. He reminded himself that modifying his communication implant was the only way to prove what Rourke—Streger—had done.

Adesina will see whatever I see, and once she forwards that to the government, all this will be over.

Devin walked over to the closet, opened the door, and grabbed the box on the shelf.

CHAPTER 23

REGAINING CONTROL

MARCUS SUPPRESSED A FROWN. ROURKE wouldn't make faces, and he shouldn't, either. "What do you want?"

The Tenebrarum woman's pale eyes flashed. "I warned you not to lie to me, *Marcus Streger*."

What? Marcus jumped. Recalling that he wore the face of Gunnar Rourke, the awe-inspiring Director of Sector 1708, he straightened. "I don't know what you're talking about."

"I don't take kindly to liars." With her unnaturally white hair and sharp features, she looked more like a fiend than a woman. "You know who the Tenebrarum are. You know what we're capable of. Lie again, and only God can save you."

Fuck. She knows something. To the rest of the galaxy, there was no connection between Gunnar Rourke and Marcus Streger. *How could she have found out?*

The woman seemed to read the question in Marcus's mind. "You want to know where you fucked up? I'll trade information for information. I want to know who I'm dealing with, so we'll meet on your ship. You want to know how I found you, and I'll tell you once the deal's complete. Understood?"

Who else knows about me? The only way to find out was to interrogate the woman. As a member of Tenebrarum, she wouldn't break easily. He'd have to implant her, then command her to give up her secrets.

Marcus nodded. "Understood."

The woman held up a slender knife and casually examined it. "If you deceive me, you won't live to regret it." She glanced up. "Oh, and one more thing. Devin Colt's the sonuvabitch who got me involved in this... situation. Make sure he's there when we meet. If the deal turns out to be unsatisfactory, he, too, must pay."

"Of course." Colt had been a troublemaker from the start. If the Tenebrarum woman wanted him, she could have him.

The woman pulled a stone out of a pouch on her belt and ran it across her blade. "You are very far away. I have wasted enough time because of you. I will send you a set of coordinates that represents a halfway point between where you are and where I am. Meet me there, in the *Pride of the Creator*, in precisely twenty-four hours, or be prepared to keep your eyes open for the rest of your miserable existence." The woman held up her gleaming knife. "I am talking to you, Marcus Streger, not Gunnar Rourke. I have no need for puppets."

Her arrogance ignited fresh frustration. Unless Marcus complied, he wouldn't know how she'd found him or whom she'd told. His mouth twitched. "As you wish."

"Very good." The woman threw Marcus a mocking smirk and ended the transmission.

Marcus's face burned. He calmed himself with the reminder that soon, she'd be an implanted drone, and he'd have an insider with Tenebrarum.

Having had enough of Gunnar Rourke, Marcus commanded the program to run on autopilot and closed the window. Rourke would behave routinely, keeping a low profile, until Marcus had further use for him. If an emergency arose, an alarm would alert Marcus, and he would deal with the situation.

He reclined in his chair. Six fucking hours of dealing with Sector 1708 shit, and he still hadn't caught up. If only Candice were still around so he could brag to her. Did no one appreciate how difficult it was to be him? He had to not only satisfy Acuitas' Corporate, but also run Sector 1708 for Rourke while working on his independent projects.

I'm never not *working. And no one even appreciates it!*

In the meanwhile, he had to repair the *Pride*'s systems before he met with the Tenebrarum woman. It wouldn't do for her to enter a ship without basic door controls. At some point, he'd also have to figure out what to do with the escapees Adam had let loose, but they were low on his priority list. Attempting to recapture them would have been too risky, so Marcus's present plan was to let them go. His implanted staff would act on autopilot, denying there was anything wrong with them. As for the girls he hadn't implanted yet—none of them knew what was going on anyway.

Even if they do, people will think they're crazy.

But in case someone did believe them, Marcus had to re-veil the *Pride* so no one could find him. With a grumble, he opened a program to examine the ship's central computer. Getting access to the computer after the whole AI fiasco had been a real pain in the ass, and he hoped the rest would be easier to deal with. After an hour or so of mind-numbing donkeywork, he regained control of his security cams and internal defenses.

Weary, he opened the security program showing the views from the cams placed in the ship's interior. He didn't expect to find anything, but flipping through the feeds gave him an excuse not to deal with re-veiling the *Pride* for the time being.

An empty corridor. Another empty corridor. The lab holding the deactivated Adam Palmer. Yet another empty corridor—

A figure walked into view.

"Stop!" Marcus grabbed the edge of his desk and pulled himself forward. He widened his eyes in surprise, then, recognizing the girl with the gun, curled his lips with glee.

Jane Colt. So you came, after all. She must have docked while his security cams were still down, and he hadn't looked outside yet. It didn't matter. She was on board his ship, within his grasp. *If she's here, she must've tipped off her brother.*

Marcus twisted his lip. Because of Adam, he'd lost control of the *Pride*, and as a result, hadn't been able to monitor its security system. *Never mind. I have her now.* "Intruder in Corridor A-Twenty-Four. Set internal defenses on stun."

The computer beeped, and the automated defenses aimed at Jane. Apparently having noticed their movement, she fired at the guns on the walls. A stun blast hit her back, and she fell to the ground.

You're mine now. Marcus left his office and wound through the *Pride*'s corridors until he reached Corridor A-24. A security bot hovered over Jane's unconscious form, the bot's line of blue light blinking questioningly, as though asking, "What should I do with her?"

That's a very good question. Marcus knelt down beside his newly captured prisoner. Jane's blackish-brown locks covered her face. He brushed them aside, running his fingertips against her skin. He'd expected some kind of excitement from finally touching the object of his desires, but she suddenly seemed unremarkable. Just another pretty girl, no longer an infuriating siren.

Disappointed, Marcus stood. "Take her to Room A-Eighteen, and put her in cell two."

The security bot acknowledged the order with a *beep*, then wrapped a pair of metal appendages around Jane's limp body and lifted her off the ground. Marcus followed as the bot carried her into the nearby lab and placed her in the clear cell.

Why had she so entranced him from afar, only to appear so commonplace up close? Perhaps it was because she lay unconscious, virtually lifeless. In that state, she was no different from how his implanted girls had been: beautiful but empty. *I have to wake her.*

As soon as the door to her cell closed, Marcus commanded the bot to engage its alarms. He covered his ears to block out the bot's high-pitched mechanical wails.

Jane blinked then cringed at the sound.

Marcus turned to the bot. "Stop alarms."

The alarms went silent. Jane glanced around in bewilderment. Her gaze fell on Marcus, and her expression darkened. "Sonuvabitch!" She jumped up, locking her gaze onto his. Fierceness radiated from her dark eyes.

There she was again, the Jane who captivated him.

"You're fun to watch." Marcus examined her face, wondering if he could capture such energy in his future AI.

"Let me out!" Jane banged a fist against the wall between them. "What have you done with Adam?"

Marcus stared into those vicious eyes, unable to look away. He imagined them softening for him, turning into that loving gaze he'd watched her give to Adam Palmer.

Jane broke eye contact and recoiled. The disgust in her expression shot Marcus full of fury. He wasn't some perv creeping on her in a bar. He was *Marcus Streger*, wealthy, intelligent, and more powerful than anyone realized. "Do you know who I am?"

Jane's eyes smoldered with hatred. "Marcus Streger. I don't care what you think you're doing—you're nothing but an evil bastard."

Marcus's anger faded. A hint of sorrow wound through his heart. She didn't know anything about him; she judged him by the external factors that had affected her life. If he'd met her under different circumstances, she wouldn't despise him so. *I'll make you understand.*

He wondered what he could tell her. Each time he'd tried explaining himself in the past, his words had failed. A few spoken sentences couldn't express the years of frustration and injustice he'd endured. "Life takes control from us at every turn." He gazed at her contemplatively. "All we can do in response is take control of what we can."

"What's that supposed to mean?" Venom filled Jane's voice.

Marcus sighed. He could tell her how taking over Sector 1708 and the minds of those who worked there had given him some much needed respite from the things he had no power over, but she wouldn't listen. He was under no illusions that she'd comprehend the games he'd played with Heisman, with Colt, and most lately, with her. "I know you think I'm evil, Jane, but it's not me who's cruel. It's the universe, and nothing I've done to you is any worse than what it does to the people living in it."

"Is that what you tell yourself?" Her voice sharpened with scorn. "You're a cliché."

Her face was so close to Marcus's, separated only by the thin transparent wall. If that wall were only gone, he could reach out and touch her, show her he was not a distant enemy, but a man with desires, with needs. Though he'd surrounded himself with people, he lived in total isolation, and he yearned for a human connection.

He extended his arm to press the controls by the cell's door, his gaze never leaving Jane's. The wall between them slid away, and he took a step toward her. "Jane..."

Jane's gaze shifted, and she darted to the side, trying to get around him.

Marcus caught her by the shoulders and shoved her back against the cell's back wall. Her furious breath warmed his face as she struggled to escape. "Calm down, Jane. Just listen to me."

"Get off!" Jane twisted under his grasp.

Marcus pressed his forearm against her throat, hoping she'd yield. "You don't know—"

Jane's knee landed on his stomach, knocking the breath out of him. He doubled over and felt her slip from his grasp. She bolted toward the door.

He turned and clasped her around the middle, pressing her arms against her sides. "Jane, please—"

Marcus felt himself forced backward, and Jane rammed him against the wall. Startled by the blow, his grip slackened. Before Jane could escape, he grabbed her shoulders and spun her to face him. He regarded her flashing eyes and parted lips, pulling her close so she couldn't knee him again.

Pain exploded in his face, and white stars filled the sudden blackness covering his vision. He barely had time to acknowledge Jane's fist flying toward him before a second punch landed. Her kick impacted against his stomach, and he felt the breath forced from his body. He staggered backward and out the cell's door.

Marcus glimpsed the door's controls and hurriedly pressed them before Jane could escape. She slammed into the door.

"You coward!" she yelled. "Open this door and face me!"

Oh, you think you're better than me? Frustration boiled in his veins. He could take what he wanted, but he could never make her give it willingly. Just like the implanted girls. Just like all the gold diggers, whores, and desperate broads he'd encountered in the past. On each, he'd pinned the hope that the returned affection would be real. And each had been tantalizingly close. Still, no matter how they pretended, he couldn't make them love him.

Jane was more irrational than most. She'd fallen for an AI, and a boring one at that. Marcus wondered if he could make her stay with him by threatening her the way he'd threatened her brother. Over time, she might grow to appreciate him.

Then again, that was what he had thought in the past, with Candice and other beauties he'd brought onto the *Pride*. Though they'd played their parts well, Marcus had seen through each false declaration.

If he couldn't make Jane listen, he could make her suffer. Her beloved robot was still in his hands, and her brother was headed his way. He could make her watch as he tore them apart and force her to beg for mercy.

He interrupted her sharp-tongued curses with an abrupt, "Shut the fuck up!" He pressed his forehead against the glass, wishing he could burn out her eyes with his glare. "You can't escape me."

To prove it, Marcus strode to a nearby touchscreen. Her Stargazer, which she'd probably hoped to run to, remained docked by the side of his Moray. What she didn't know was that he'd fitted the *Pride* with weapons in case of trouble.

Trouble like you, Jane Colt. He swiped an icon to bring up the view outside the *Pride*, then flipped through the security cam feeds until he found her little ship. "*Pride of the Creator*, engage external defenses and destroy all foreign vessels."

Jane gasped as the Stargazer on the screen exploded, ripped to shreds by the *Pride*'s cannons.

Marcus curled his lip into a sneer. "Well, Pony, looks like you're here to stay."

CHAPTER 24

NEVER AS PLANNED

ADESINA KEPT HER GAZE ON the transparent window of her veiled Angler. The viewscreen lied, showing her empty space ahead, while she saw a large, dark blue Moray with her eyes.

She brought the veiled Angler to a halt. If she could see them, they could probably see her, although the fact that her ship was a fraction of the Moray's size gave her an advantage. In addition, her black ship, cloaked in the darkness of space, would be nearly impossible to spot without the aid of computer equipment, and her sophisticated veiling system would take care of those.

Not far ahead, a triangular Barracuda, barely visible against the blackness of space, and a sleek Silverside approached the *Pride*: Devin and the Tenebrarum woman informally known as Silver. Wouldn't be long before they got Adesina the proof she needed to arrest Streger.

It's about damn time. Adesina swiped the control screen and replaced the viewscreen's useless display with a video feed from Devin. Her cutting into his head to access the communication chip's portal hadn't been a pleasant experience for either of them, but it was the only way to watch him. Streger would detect any devices

Devin carried on his person. Fortunately, it hadn't been Adesina's first time performing such an operation. Under normal circumstances, if Adesina had wanted to modify a chip to record what the user saw, she could have done so remotely. However, given that a dead zone was the only place where she could safely communicate with her operative, she'd had no choice but to connect a slate to the portal via wire. Thanks to her steady hands and precise laser scalpel, she'd hardly left any trace of the operation. Devin's thick hair, which was on the longer side, concealed what little of a scar there was.

Devin docked his ship near the middle of the Moray's front starcar. Adesina wished she could board with him and take down Streger herself. She longed to fire up her Angler's cannons and blast the *Pride* to pieces. Streger didn't deserve due process.

Order separates us from the criminals, Adesina reminded herself sternly. As soon as Devin witnessed an incriminating statement from Streger, she would have the evidence she needed to board the ship, flash her credentials, and haul the bastard back to Kydera. Of course, there would probably be lots of drama and maybe some shooting before she could cuff him, but she was prepared for that, and so were her two cohorts.

On the viewscreen, Devin entered a grayish corridor on board the *Pride.* Its blank walls, lined with lights and internal defense guns, looked like those of any other Moray. He stopped at a four-way intersection.

About a minute later, Silver approached from the opposite corridor. She crossed her arms. With the way she popped out her hip and curled the corner of her mouth, she appeared almost flirtatious.

Must be part of her act, using her feminine wiles. She'd better be as trustworthy as Devin claims.

"So where's our secretive vendor?" Silver spoke with disdain.

A large gray robot—*security bot, by the looks of it*—with a metal mound for a head and a line of blue lights across its "face" came into view.

"Follow me. I will take you to Mr. Streger." The robot spoke with mechanical crispness.

The view shifted as Devin followed the robot down the corridor. Viewing the ship through his eyes, Adesina didn't find anything remarkable about its plain walls. Silver walked beside him, her footsteps so soft, Adesina could hardly hear them.

Adesina leaned back. A three-starcar Moray could take a while to walk through.

It should also have housed at least a few dozen crewmembers. A security guard standing by a door, perhaps, or a mechanic in search of a stimulant drink. Adesina found it strange that Devin didn't glimpse a single human being on that ship. Only more security bots and Silver.

Actually, a lot of Silver. Adesina shook her head. *I get it, kid. She's a first-class merc with a face to remember. That better not be the reason you put your trust in her.*

The thought dug up the nagging question Adesina had about why she'd put her trust in *him,* an untrained young man known to be a loose cannon. *He hasn't let me down yet.*

The minutes ticked by. Adesina wished she'd chosen a Silverside like the Tenebrarum woman's instead of an Angler. A Silverside didn't have to look for a door with a docking mechanism. If she'd wanted, Silver could have rammed her ship's sharp end into the Moray's hull, opened up the nose of her vessel, and entered wherever she pleased. Adesina longed to do just that: jump out of her ship, land in front of Marcus fucking Streger, and aim her gun in his face while she told him he was under arrest.

Won't be long now.

<hr>

A bright red icon popped onto the monitor and caught Marcus's attention. Concerned, he pressed it. A chart depicting the empty space outside the *Pride* filled a window. Or rather, what should have been empty space. The outline of a disc-shaped starship flickered. Across the bottom of the window flashed the words: "Possible threat detected."

Shit! There's a veiled starship outside!

Marcus had expected Colt to try something stupid, but he hadn't realized the idiot would bring backup.

Who could it be? How could he have planned anything?

He mentally listed all the people Colt could have gone to, and one name jumped out at him: Agent Adesina. It had to be her. She was the only one who would be bold enough—and reckless enough—to conspire against an ISARK leader. The number of times Colt had been in dead zones ran through Marcus's mind, and he realized Colt must have used the cover to plot against him.

Fuck! Marcus wasn't sure who to curse the most—Colt and Adesina for their scheming, the sonuvabitch who had invented the signal-stopping walls of dead zones, or Corporate and the AI for distracting him, thereby preventing him from watching Sector 1708 as closely as he should have. *Either way, they won't be a problem much longer.*

<hr>

A movement caught Adesina's attention. She glimpsed something bright out the window and maneuvered her ship.

Boom.

An alarm blared as the torpedo impacted, and a warning flashed across the viewscreen. *Fucking hell!*

Emergency protocols engaged to seal off the hull breach. Adesina activated her own cannons. She aimed at the *Pride*'s engines—or what she thought were the *Pride*'s engines. It was difficult to tell using just her eyes. *Streger must have a helluva computer if he can breach ISARK veiling.* Unfortunately, hers didn't seem able to breach the *Pride*'s.

A bright explosion flared: a burst of white against the distant blue vessel.

"Devin!" Adesina called, knowing her voice would be heard through Devin's modified implant. "Abort mission! Get outta there!"

Streger must have known that Devin had been followed. The attack on Adesina's ship told her two things: that Streger knew Devin's deal was a trap, and that she could get away with anything in the name of self-defense.

"I repeat: Get *out*." Adesina veered her ship to avoid a second blast. She switched her viewscreen to a forward view, looked through the window, and fired again. Before that missile impacted, she shifted her cannons slightly and fired again. After shifting and firing two more times in rapid succession, she glanced back at the viewscreen. Where the explosions landed gave her a sense of her target's shape. Devin and Silver would be all right for the time being—a Moray's hull could withstand a few warning shots.

"Send distress signal!" she ordered.

The computer buzzed to confirm that the communication had been sent. The pre-recorded message, bearing ISARK's credentials, would tell the nearest IC ship that one of the confederation's member planets had an official vessel in danger. She was actually glad Streger had fired on her.

No need for that confession now. Firing on me automatically gets you arrested, you bastard.

Adesina didn't have time to switch her viewscreen and check on Devin, but she knew her small, one-person fighter wouldn't cause the large Moray any real damage. Her Angler lurched as she avoided the *Pride*'s next few shots. She rapidly returned fire.

The blue outline of the Moray flashed on her viewscreen. Seconds later, the ship appeared. Two thirds of it, at least. Adesina must have hit something that disabled two of the starcars' veiling devices.

Not a total victory, but I'll take it!

If the *Pride* was visible, then even if Streger tried to escape, Adesina could trace him. With her goal partially accomplished, she could have run to a safer distance while waiting. But running wasn't her style. Besides, her operative, his partner, and Jane Colt, a Kyderan civilian, were still on board that ship.

She glanced at the Barracuda still docked on the Moray's side and cursed. *Devin, after you find your sister, you'd better not dally on that ship because of the AI.*

While she understood why Devin would be reluctant to view Adam as a robot, she didn't approve of his perspective. A machine was a machine, and that particular AI had been responsible for dozens of human deaths. Devin may have been willing to chalk it up to an unintentional malfunction and overlook the horror, but Adesina wasn't. She knew he was hoping to get the AI out of sight before ISARK could take it into custody. That was something she couldn't allow. She wasn't looking forward to the part where he confronted her, and she had to clear his head of whatever sentimental delusions blinded him to the facts.

The *Pride* fired another torpedo. Adesina twisted her ship to avoid it. Morays weren't meant to be armed, and since those cannons were not part of the *Pride*'s main design, they were slow compared to her Angler. As long as she could stall Streger, she would.

A second alarm blared. Annoyed by the cacophony, she flipped a switch to disable all alarms. *Beep.*

What now? Adesina briefly turned away from her target. A red communication light flashed, and a line of text across the bottom indicated that the caller was an official Kyderan vessel. Her distress signal must have reached someone. "Put it through!"

A communication window opened in the upper corner of the viewscreen. A dark-skinned woman with black hair and a no-nonsense expression appeared. "This is Commander Jihan Vega of the *RKSS Granite Flame*, responding to the distress call of—"

"No time for niceties, Commander!" Adesina fired, intercepting the *Pride*'s torpedo midflight. "I'm being fired upon by a hostile. How far are you?"

"Approximately thirty light-minutes. We will be there as quickly as possible."

"Good!" Thirty minutes sounded awfully long, but it couldn't be helped. Adesina was grateful an IC ship had happened to be so close to an uninhabited region in the first place; the *Granite Flame* was probably part of the Fringe patrol. "If you see a two-starcar Moray with an invisible third section trying to escape, do me a favor and stop them."

Adesina ended the transmission. Thirty minutes—she could delay Streger for that long. She'd have to take out his engines so he wouldn't be able to run away at the sight of the Mega. *Too bad the IC accords forbid warships from having veiling devices.*

She veered her ship and fired again.

⸻ ◦❖◦ ⸻

Fuck, fuck, fuck! Marcus didn't have a curse strong enough to express his panic. The *Granite Flame*—a fucking Kyderan *warship*—was on its way. Even if his external defenses took out Adesina, he'd lost the veiling devices on his two front starcars, and the Angler's blasts had compromised his engines.

At least the third starcar, the only one that *really* mattered, remained invisible and largely undamaged. It housed his most important research, equipment, and specimens, including the AI. Thanks to Acuitas and his Sector 1708 operations, he had enough thrones tucked away in hidden accounts to start over.

Time to cut and run. Marcus gave the *Pride*'s central computer a few last commands: to destroy Adesina's Angler and to kill Colt and the Tenebrarum woman. Although the commands were superfluous at that point, he couldn't take any chances.

He had one more command to give, one that filled him with regret. Once he gave it, he would lose everything he'd worked for. He'd already lost Acuitas, his brainchild. And Sector 1708, into which he'd invested so much effort. He'd spent years monitoring Rourke through his Net movements, using the information Acuitas gathered to piece together what he needed to know to infiltrate the Sector 1708 director's home security system. Rourke had been careful, but even the most cautious couldn't escape the reaches of Acuitas. Marcus recalled the triumph he'd felt when the bots he'd sent to knock out Rourke and bring the unconscious man to the *Pride* had succeeded. Marcus had been positively giddy when Rourke's brain implant had given him full control over such a strong-willed person. At the time, he'd believed that his efforts had bought him a lifetime of access to a top-secret government facility.

But no, a few months was all I got, he thought bitterly.

How did it all go to hell? Adam Palmer had fucked things up royally, but Marcus could have recovered. He could have eliminated Colt, the Tenebrarum woman, and anyone else who knew about him, then retreated into the blackness of space. With Rourke under his command, he could have carried on with his Sector 1708 operations.

Jane Colt.

Jane was supposed to come running to the *Pride* in a helplessly noble attempt to save Adam. Instead of just searching for Adam the way she was supposed to, the little bitch had decided to play spy. If she hadn't enticed Marcus with her infuriating yet intoxicating rebelliousness, he would never have lured her to the *Pride* in the first place.

All right, Pony, you win this round. But now, you'll burn.

"Activate self-destruct sequence." In a matter of minutes, the first two starcars would go up in flames—Marcus had already disconnected the third from the central computer. In his invisible, untraceable vessel, he would vanish, and anything that could be used to track him would be incinerated along with the ship.

He would need a few minutes to reach the third starcar from his location near the front of the first, especially since the attack he'd ordered on Colt and the Tenebrarum woman would force him to take a roundabout route. But the sooner the ship blew, the more likely it would be to take out those two even if they evaded the automated defenses. It might even catch Adesina in the blast. If he needed more than the automatic fifteen minutes given, he could always command the ship to delay. He pressed his palm against the monitor to confirm the command.

"Self-destruct sequence activated." The *Pride*'s central computer sounded unconcerned with its impending death. "Fifteen minutes to self-destruct."

⋯◆⋯

Ines dropped to the floor as another bot fired. She fired back, but her lasers did little more than dent the machine's metal shell. She rolled to dodge another blast, then sprang up and blasted the bot's weapon. The weapon, too, was evidently blast-resistant.

She dodged to avoid more blasts. "A simple job, you said." A shot from the internal defenses hit the wall behind her. She aimed and pulled the trigger three times, destroying the infernal thing. "How'd you manage to fuck things up so bad?"

"C'mon, Silver. You're not really worried, are you?" Pretender ducked under a guard bot's arm as it fired, then swerved around behind it. He pressed his gun's barrel into the joint connecting the bot's arm to its body and blasted it. The arm went limp. "It's only a few machines."

The look he gave Ines sparked her annoyance. *Is he mocking me?*

"Machines are nothing." Ines fired at the joint between a bot's head and its torso. The bot's head flew back, dangling off its body by a wire, and the metal monstrosity crumpled to the ground. "But I was only supposed to elicit a confession." She glimpsed a movement on the wall and twisted to avoid a blast from the internal defenses. "Getting shot at was not part of the deal." She'd known she'd probably have to do some shooting, since in her experience, nothing ever went as expected, but she didn't mind unleashing her irritation on Pretender.

Pretender blasted the guns that had fired at her. "Is this your way of asking for a bonus?"

His nonchalance ticked Ines off further, especially since he acted as though money was all that mattered to her. *Which it* does. *By definition, I'm all about the money.*

She glimpsed a movement and arched her back in time to avoid a shot. Her weapon flung out of her hand. Because of her momentary distraction, she'd failed to notice the other guard bot firing in her direction.

She straightened. *Enough of this.*

Instead of pulling out one of her spare guns, she grabbed the two black rods attached to her belt, the ones she'd carried on her hips since she was thirteen. It was time to show Pretender—and those fucking machines— just whom they were dealing with.

With one rod in each hand, she pressed her thumbs against their circular bases. A pair of long, thin wires shot out of the ends, glowing with fiery yellow lasers, which seemed ready to break free from the force fields confining them to the wires' movements. She spun on one foot, whipping her laser ribbons around her. Metal clunked as severed bot limbs fell to the floor. She drew a circle over her head. Sparks spewed as internal defense guns fell from their ceiling perches.

The lasers felt light in her hands, as natural as extensions of her own arms. She bent backward as a laser flew past her face and simultaneously slashed the machine responsible across its mechanical head. Twisting, ducking, and leaping, all the while retaining control over the deadly ribbons—it was an all-too-familiar dance. The smallest glimpse of a target was all she needed.

The more targets Ines hit, the faster her arms moved. She didn't think; her body knew what to do. She swept her arms in a crossing motion, taking down two bots at once. She uncrossed them, taking down two more. Another leap—she brought herself into the midst of three new bots. A spin—she swiftly took them out. She snapped her lasers toward the ceiling and destroyed a few more internal defense guns.

Her limbs moved to a deadly rhythm as she brought destruction upon her enemies. No consideration, no quarter—they would all be destroyed. Her foes were not lives created by God, but unnatural abominations.

By the time her eyes caught no more glimpses of hostile machines, she was disappointed. That dance had been the most fun she'd had in years. Weariness descended, and she breathed heavily. Heat radiated from her skin, but she didn't care. It was a sweet kind of heat, a well-earned heat.

Mechanical parts scattered down the corridor, which bore several long, thin scars from where her ribbons had sliced the walls, floor, and ceiling. Severed robot limbs, torn mechanical torsos, and broken metal heads surrounded her. Had they been human, she might have wept at the carnage. But they weren't, and her heart swelled in pure triumph.

Pretender stood against the wall, staring in disbelief. Always so cool and collected, he finally seemed to have been surprised.

Ines smirked. "It was only a few machines." She pressed the ends of her rods to disengage the lasers and retract the wires.

Pretender lifted his mouth into a slight smile. "So it was."

"Thirteen minutes to self-destruct." The ship's automated voice sounded calm.

Fuck. Ines sprinted down the corridor.

No footsteps followed her. She glanced back. Pretender headed in the opposite direction. *Idiot.* "Where are you going?"

Pretender stopped in front of a door and blasted its edges. "Go ahead. Your work here's done."

That's not what I asked. "Answer the question, Pretender."

Pretender kicked the door. The metal slab fell, and he entered the room. "Jane's on this ship. So's Adam." He emerged. "I'm not leaving without them." He approached the next door and blasted its edges.

Ines strode toward him. "Are you suicidal? This ship's about to blow!"

Pretender finished blasting. "Death catches up to us all sooner or later." He kicked down the door.

Ines stopped. The idiot would get himself killed trying to do the noble thing. It would take more than the time they had left for him to go through every room. Even if he found his sister and the kid, the chances of his escaping in time were minimal.

A part of her pushed her to continue toward him. He needed her help if he was to stand a chance.

And I have to go if I *want to escape.* She'd done what she'd been hired for. In fact, by taking out those guard bots, she'd done more. It wasn't her problem that the job had gone to hell.

Ines watched Pretender for a moment, then forced herself to turn away. There was no way she'd let herself get caught in an explosion because of that erratic sonuvabitch. Something within her—that same something that hounded her about everything involving him—cried out for her to go back.

She silenced the voice with a reminder that everything she felt was based on a fantasy, and she sprinted toward her Silverside.

CHapTeR 25

OVER

"TWELVE MINUTES TO SELF-DESTRUCT."

Devin cursed. Another intersection lay ahead. Each corridor contained at least five doors. He would have to check them all. Three starcars, each with three levels. Jane could be anywhere. Even if he found her in time, how could he convince her to take the Barracuda and run while he searched for Adam? After she left, would the *Pride* even have any escape vessels he could take once he found the kid?

He kicked down another door. Again, the room was empty. Streger had to have been the only person on board the *Pride*. Otherwise, Devin should have run into someone else.

"Devin, did you hear me?" Adesina yelled through his communication implant.

Devin ignored her. The next door lay open at the other end of the corridor. He ran toward it. Jane probably wouldn't be inside, but he couldn't take any chances. As he neared, he noticed the Acuitas logo painted on the wall.

He entered the room. *No one.*

A solitary desk stood at the center. Visible by the large chair was the end of the crescent-shaped monitor. Images flashed across the screen.

This could be Streger's office.

If the computer was still active, it might tell him where Jane was. Devin rushed to the monitor and swiped it. It didn't react—Streger must have locked it. But he'd left his applications open, including one that appeared to be a security feed. A window occupying the left side of the monitor flashed a series of videos, displaying various views of corridors.

It appeared to be a sequential feed, showing the views from numerous cameras one by one. Each video displayed its location across the bottom.

Jane's image could appear any moment, but the *Pride* had to have hundreds of cameras. The ship could blow before the app cycled through them all. Each second Devin stood in front of the monitor could have been another second spent searching. Each glance away from the screen could have been an opportunity lost. The opposing forces paralyzed him.

Empty corridor after empty corridor. The images switched so slowly. The duel in Devin's head grew fiercer. Stay, and he could fritter away minutes he didn't have. Leave, and he could lose the chance to find Jane at all.

Behind the duel, accusations hissed in his mind. His actions, his fault. Two innocent lives could end because of his folly. Each attempt at escape had buried him deeper into the pit. Mistake after mistake, all his doing.

His one solace was the thought that he wouldn't have to linger knowing that his sister had died because of him. If it all ended there, he'd gladly accept his fate. If there was an afterlife, he wouldn't deserve absolution.

"Eleven minutes to self-destruct."

Image after image, all useless, each a promise for the next and a broken promise from the previous.

I should go. She could be in the next room.

And if she wasn't? If she was in the distant corner of another starcar?

The image flicked. A man sprinted down a corridor: Streger, no doubt making his getaway. Devin glimpsed the location. Streger ran through the lowest level of the front starcar, heading toward the back. *Where's he going?*

"Get the fuck *out!*" Adesina's voice rang through his head.

Devin had been too distracted to notice her previous words. He must have subconsciously absorbed them, for he suddenly remembered her saying, "The *Pride*'s front two starcars have been unveiled."

The image changed. The present camera displayed a room with several tables. In the center, Adam sat bound to a high-backed chair, his head bent over his chest. Exposed metal gleamed under the lights. Despite the blaring alarms, he remained limp.

Devin couldn't find it in himself to ask for forgiveness.

The image changed again. More emptiness. A realization hit him. Streger planned to detach the third, invisible starcar and disappear. He had Adam. He would continue his perverse project. Did he have Jane as well?

That's it. Devin's agitation won, and he felt himself bolt out the door before his mind could catch up. If Jane was on the third starcar, she would survive the self-destruct. The security feed rotated through each camera in a certain order. Adam's image had been among the first to appear from the third starcar. It would take too long to wait for the feed to cycle through and start from the first.

More blasting, more kicking, more empty rooms. Each presented Devin with a combination of disappointment and relief. Disappointment that he hadn't found his sister, relief that each failure meant she could be in the safe zone.

A security bot approached. Devin ducked as it raised its weapon. Then he fired back, aiming for its joints. *Damn. I thought Silver got them all.*

He dodged behind the bot, jammed the barrel of his gun into the joint between its head and body, and fired. The bot went limp. *At least the internal defenses aren't firing. Streger probably thinks I'm dead.*

An open staircase lay to Devin's right. Nothing in front, nothing to the left. He ran up. A sharp stinging flared down his back from his shoulder. A laser must have grazed him. He turned into the corridor the next level up.

"Ten minutes to self-destruct."

Time remained, but was it enough to find Jane? Had he wasted too much time in Streger's office? Devin flung the question away. He couldn't afford to panic. Never mind that each empty room brought him closer to the outcome he dreaded.

Absolute One, God, whoever you are—if I can't save Jane, then please, don't save me.

A high scream, distant but piercing, cut through the alarms and the blasting. "Let me out! Please! Somebody!"

It's Jane.

Devin sprinted toward the sound, pushing himself to move faster than he ever had before. If his heart burst from his chest, if his lungs ran out of air—*let them.*

⋯⟡⋯

Jane banged her fists against the transparent wall. "Anybody! Please! Let me out!"

Tears of panic flowed down her face. She couldn't die. She had too many unfinished melodies in her soul, clawing at her heart for a chance to be heard. More importantly, she hadn't had a chance to tell Adam that he meant more to her than any of those songs. It could all end that night, and only a spattering of ash, drifting through the silent abyss of space, would remain of her. Her rage, her joy, her strife, her love—all had been in vain, and the only thing anyone would remember of her was that Victor Colt's crazy daughter, who'd once dreamed of music, had died in an explosion.

No. That won't be my requiem. I'll write my own damn requiem!

She backed up. She'd tried kicking the transparent wall down previously, only to land painfully on her back. She had to try again. What had all that training been for if she couldn't kick down a pathetic little piece of glass?

She turned to the side, then crossed one leg behind the other as she launched herself sideways toward the door. The force was strongest when kicking from behind. Though the sound of her heel against the cell's wall split the air, her leg wasn't strong enough.

She fell onto her stomach. The impact knocked the breath from her body. She forced herself to stand and let loose another scream. "Help! Somebody!"

Her ears buzzed from the loudness. If there were anyone left on the ship, they would have heard her. That not a single person had even peeked inside the room holding her left her with a growing sense of despair.

She refused to acknowledge it. Every time she'd been in a hopeless situation, she'd managed to come out all right. Her current predicament was no different. Until she was actually dead, she would believe in her ability to survive. *I'm gonna make it.*

Pain scratched her throat from all the screaming, but she ignored it. Until her vocal chords snapped, she would keep screaming. Until her hands broke, she would keep pounding at the door. Someone would answer. She wasn't supposed to die just yet.

But if I do... Hey, Absolute? Can You do me a favor? Tell Adam that I love him in more ways than I could ever express. And tell Devin that I forgive him, and that there's nothing he can do to make me turn against him. So be it, truly.

She closed her eyes and took a moment to remind herself that she'd had a decent run at life. In her twenty-three short years, she'd done and discovered more things than most could dream of doing in a lifetime. How others, hearing of her story, would judge her was beyond her control, and looking back, the only thing she truly regretted was letting Adam go so easily.

I hope you'll have more time in this world than I did, Adam. I hope you escape that sonuvabitch Streger and find everything you're looking for. If this is my swan song, well, I guess I'll see you in the beyond.

"Nine minutes to self-destruct."

She opened her eyes, inhaled, and let out another cry for help in case anyone remained on board the doomed Moray. After a few seconds, she backed up, aiming to kick the wall again.

Blasts, startling in their brightness, pierced the door outside the cell, the one leading out of the lab. *What's happening?*

The lab's door fell, pushed down by something black. Jane blinked in shock. Then, she felt a relieved smile spread across her face as she recognized the figure that came rushing in.

Devin! Her mouth couldn't form his name. So much brightness poured into her mind, she could hardly handle it. Of course her brother would have been the one to rescue her. Why should she have been surprised? He had always been there for her. Since he was there, everything was sure to turn out all right. Relief and joy and a million other things flooded her, leaving her unable to speak.

"Get back." Devin aimed the gun at the edge of her cell.

Jane pressed herself into the corner. After a few blasts along the sides, Devin instructed her to kick the wall down. Jane complied. The transparent wall fell.

She rushed out and threw her arms around him. She felt her brother's close embrace, and his head against the top of hers.

He let go. "*Run.*"

Jane rushed out of the room, and Devin ran beside her.

Despite the danger, she had to ask: "What happened?"

Devin seemed to hear all the unspoken questions swirling behind those two words. "Rourke—Streger—was holding you hostage." His words came quickly between breaths as he ran. "I found out he was selling ISARK secrets. He knew I knew, and he had his mind-controlled snipers follow you. Riley and Adam, too."

Devin paused abruptly and held out a hand to stop her. He peered around the corner, then continued forward. Jane followed him down the tunnel leading to the second starcar, listening as he gave her a condensed version of past events.

"Eight minutes to self-destruct."

Jane barely heard the ship's voice through her brother's explanation. The truth coalesced in her mind, and everything that had made no sense was explained. Devin had only revealed Adam to keep Rourke—Streger— from giving a kill order. Riley had been shot by ISARK's forces. The same or worse would have happened to Jane if Devin had disobeyed. Shock spun through her mind at the sudden influx of information, but gladness outshone it.

Of course her brother had been forced by circumstances beyond his control. Of course he'd been manipulated by a powerful evil, doing what he could to keep her safe. Any resentment she'd held against him dissipated—except one.

"Why didn't you tell me?" Jane released the question between jagged inhalations. A confession would have spared her so much anguish. Her anger sparked anew. He *should* have told her—he'd *owed* her the truth.

Before she could say anything, Devin shoved her. Blasts spewed toward her. Jane crashed into a wall. She whirled in time to see Devin's shots rip through a security bot's head. The bot crashed onto the ground.

Devin winced as he approached her. His black body armor appeared torn at the left side, near his stomach. He must have noticed her alarmed expression, for he said, "Just a graze." He glanced around, worry clouding his eyes. He firmed his expression as he stopped before her. "Adam's in the third starcar. Streger plans to detach and run."

His words made sense, but Jane didn't understand what he wanted. She gave him an inquisitive look.

Devin grabbed her hand and pressed his gun into her palm. "*Go!*"

Jane automatically wrapped her fingers around the weapon's handle. "What?"

"Streger's close to reaching the third starcar by now, if he hasn't already. I'll go to this one's control room and keep him from escaping until you get there."

Jane stared. Bit by bit, his words came together. He wanted her to leave him behind and find Adam on her own. Time was short. A manual override would keep Devin from leaving the *Pride* until she'd made it onto the third starcar. By then, he might not have time to escape the self-destruct.

"*Like hell!*" She grabbed his arm. "We've gotta go!"

Devin yanked himself out her grasp. "Jane, *listen!* Streger could detach any second!"

"Let him! We'll take your ship and chase him down!"

"He'll disappear." Devin's expression was grim.

Jane struggled to breathe. If she listened, she would find Adam, but her brother might not survive. If she insisted that they escape to Devin's ship, she might never find Adam. Even if she tracked Streger down, the bastard could have killed Adam by then.

Her brother or the one she loved. She couldn't choose. She *couldn't*.

Devin grabbed her shoulders. "For *fuck's* sake, Jane, go to Adam." The intensity of his expression startled her. "I'll make it out."

The seconds ticked away. Unable to choose for herself, she clenched her jaw and acquiesced to the authority in his voice. "You'd better. Because if you don't—"

"I know." Devin released her with a slight smile. "You'll kill me." His expression turned serious. "*Go.*"

Jane instinctively obeyed. Her legs carried her faster than she'd thought possible. Never mind the burning in her lungs. The sooner she made it to the third starcar, the sooner her brother could escape. Several minutes remained in the countdown—he had time.

She glanced over her shoulder. Devin was nowhere in sight. His gun felt heavy in her hand, and it hit her that she'd have to face Streger alone.

Drawing a breath, she tightened her grip on the weapon and sprinted forward.

⎯⎯◈⎯⎯

"Seven minutes to self-destruct."

Devin raced up the stairs. The control room couldn't be far. He swung around a corner. The double doors he sought lay before him. He reached into his belt for his second weapon. A sharp spasm pierced his side, overwhelming him. He stumbled against the wall, grabbing the injury.

Wetness seeped through his fingers. He straightened. *Not yet.*

He grabbed his gun and headed to the double doors. Three blasts down the crack between them, followed by two more on either side of the center blast. The mechanism was the same on most large spacecraft.

As expected, Devin was able to pry the doors open. Pain stabbed his side. The wetness spread. It didn't matter.

What mattered was the emergency button beneath the control panel. As long as he held it down, no starcar could detach. It seemed simplistic, but it was designed precisely for that reason—so that any crewmember could prevent a hijacking. Devin felt the button's round form and pressed it.

The large screen before him displayed the same security feed as in Streger's office. One by one, various views of the *Pride* paraded across the monitor. Devin wondered how long he would need to hold down the button. Too long, and the third starcar could be caught in the explosion. Not long enough, and Jane might not make it in time.

"Six minutes to self-destruct."

Considering that Streger hadn't detached in the time that had passed since the countdown had begun, Devin knew Jane would need at least a few more minutes. Time seemed to slow as Devin waited, but he could do nothing but hold the button. With his other hand, he clutched his wound, trying to slow the bleeding.

"Five minutes to self-destruct."

Devin kept his eyes fixed on the viewscreen, hoping luck would be kinder than it had been previously. The screen displayed views of the second starcar at present. Jane could turn up on one of them. He watched the sequence of feeds, ignoring the throbbing in his side. He suddenly realized how cold he was, and his vision swam.

A flash of motion on the viewscreen: Jane zooming toward the tunnel between the second and third starcars.

Devin collapsed forward in relief. Or was it weakness? His left elbow banged into the control panel as he caught himself. He kept his right hand on the button.

Seconds later, Jane disappeared from view. Devin's strength disappeared as well. Darkness clouded his vision, and his head fell forward. His sister would need a few more moments before she reached safety. Though his legs wanted to melt from weariness, he remained upright, hand pressed against the button.

"Four minutes to self-destruct."

She must be on board by now. Unable to support himself any longer, Devin sank to the ground. Barely a second after his hand left the button, he glimpsed a message on the screen saying that the third starcar had detached.

Time to go. He tried to stand. Blackness invaded his vision, and coldness overwhelmed him. He made it forward a few steps, then collapsed again. The blood continued spreading. He felt his heartbeat in its unrelenting rhythm.

Well, Death, looks like you've caught up. Devin let his head sink into the ground. On the screen, he glimpsed his sister running down the third starcar's corridor, her eyes snapping with energy.

A smile crept onto his lips. *Give him hell, Pony.*

CHAPTER 26

TAKE IT

JANE AIMED HER GUN AT the crack between the control room's doors. That bastard Streger lay behind them. She sprayed the crack with lasers, determined to make him face her.

Beneath the blasting, she heard a man's cry. "Colt! Colt, stop! I'll open it!"

Jane briefly gave the trigger a rest, then continued blasting. Streger could take the opportunity to activate his internal defenses or security bots. *Better keep him scared.*

The viewscreen became visible through the holes she'd created. Figuring she'd done enough damage to be able to push the door open, she approached. One good shove was all it took to send the right door sliding into the wall.

Streger, who stood against the controls, stared at her in shock. "You!"

Jane strode up to him. "What's the matter? Not the Colt you were expecting? You know, my brother may be dangerous, but *I'm* the one you should really be afraid of." She pressed the barrel of her weapon into his chest. "Take me to Adam."

Streger's eyes burned with hatred. Jane returned his glare, longing to pull the trigger. With him out of her way, she could take her sweet time searching the starcar. If anyone deserved to die, it was the bastard before her. The list of reasons could have stretched from there to Kydera.

Only the thought of Adam kept her hand still. People weren't supposed to kill other people, especially unarmed ones they'd cornered. Life was sacred, even an evil life. At least, that was what Adam would have told her. She wasn't sure if she believed the same, but she chose to listen.

Streger's gaze shifted.

What's he doing? With a flick of her wrist, Jane blasted the wall beside him as a warning. "If you try anything, I'll end you. Understand? Now, let's go."

Streger twisted his face into a dark scowl. He walked to the door. "Fine. You can have your precious robot, *Pony*." He spat the nickname with disgust.

Jane fired at the ground by his feet. Streger froze.

"Only Devin gets to call me that." She shoved him with the barrel of her weapon. "Move."

Streger exited the control room, walking at what seemed to be a glacial pace. "Where is your precious brother?" His tone mocked her. "You left him behind to get blown up, didn't you?"

Jane clenched her jaw. *No, I didn't. He told me to go, and he's gotta be on his way out by now.* "Walk faster."

"I wonder how long he has to live." Streger, still taking slow, indolent steps, glanced over his shoulder at her. "Two minutes? Three at most?"

He had to be mocking her—both with his words and with his dawdling—for a reason, probably to distract her so he could escape. She wouldn't let him. *Don't listen.*

"You're quieter than usual," Streger said. "Don't you want to know why I did what I did?"

Jane did crave answers, and she started to speak, then pressed her mouth shut. *If I talk to him, I'll give him an opening. I can worry about getting answers after he's arrested.*

Streger entered a stairwell and walked up. "I must admit—you're a lot calmer than I would have expected. You've never kept your temper in check before." He let out a quick laugh. "I loved it when you clocked your brother!"

Jane suppressed a shudder. She didn't want to think about how long Streger had watched her. He'd been at her father's funeral and backstage at her concert. He'd been in her brother's head. Every moment she'd thought her own had been a show for the creep. *I'll bet he even watched me sleep.*

She followed him up the stairs, clenching her teeth.

"Life is a game we can't win." Streger's voice was low. "I decided I might as well partake in the fun."

"Fun?" Jane couldn't contain herself any longer. "What the hell's wrong with you?"

Streger spun around, mouth twisted in an ugly grin. "Finally, she responds!"

Jane recoiled. "Stay back!"

"Life likes to throw things at us." Streger continued up the stairs, moving in plodding steps. "It screws with us, then sits back and watches us flounder." He stopped at the top of the staircase. "All I've done is imitate life's cruel sense of humor. It jerks us around to see what we'll do, and I joined in when I entered the game."

"Enough talking." Jane took a step up. "Keep walking, or—"

"Or *what*?" Marcus whirled to face her. His eyes bore into hers with a kind of hunger. "What would you do?"

He grabbed her wrist with both hands. Jane automatically pulled the trigger. Her shot missed. He pulled her toward him. She tripped on the steps. With a shove, he let go of her arm. She fell backward down the stairs and crashed into the wall below. Her body ached from the impact, and her head spun.

She hurriedly stood. Streger was right in front of her. Before she could react, he tore the gun from her grasp.

He fired, and she ducked. His blast hit the wall by her head. *Shit!*

She stared in terror as he approached, gun aimed at her. She backed away, inching closer to the doorway. If she could make it into the corridor, she stood a chance of escaping.

"Things turn quickly, don't they?" Streger's hungry eyes seemed ready to consume her. "I don't know if I want to kill you or keep you."

Keep me? A shiver shot up Jane's spine at the thought of what he could mean by that.

Streger shook his head. "If you hadn't gone running to Adam each time I prodded you, you could've had it all."

"What do you mean?" Jane asked.

"I wanted to see how far you'd go for your dearly beloved, so I sent your brother after him and let your little demon friend know what was about to go down. I never thought you'd take it as far as you did!" He let out a cynical laugh, and his eyes tilted in an expression of bewilderment. "Why would you risk everything for some AI?"

Jane took another step toward the doorway. She kept her eyes on him so they wouldn't betray her intent. *My turn to stall.* "I don't see him as an AI. I've gone through the rational stuff before: he'll bring me trouble, everything would be easier without him, and all that. But it never sticks because in the end, the thing about Adam is... I love him."

The distraction seemed to work. Streger's face twisted into something hideous, wrathful, and he moved toward her. Jane sidestepped. The doorway had to be right behind her. But she couldn't just turn and run. The gun was aimed right at her, and Streger didn't seem as if he'd hesitate to shoot her in the back.

"*Why* do you love him?" Streger's voice rose with what sounded like desperation. "Do you know *what* he is?"

Unable to help herself, Jane said, "Do you know what *you* are?"

Streger's eyes seemed ready to burst with mad rage. With his empty hand, he grabbed at her. Jane jumped back. He'd attacked her once before, and there was no telling what he'd do since he was armed.

She lunged at him and grabbed the wrist of his gun hand. The weapon's barrel stared at her. To get out of its line of fire, she pivoted so that Streger was behind her. She dug her fingers into his wrist as he tried to yank it out of her grasp. She felt his breath on the back of her neck. Disgusted, she instinctively threw her left elbow back.

The impact rippled through her bones. Streger's cry buzzed in her ear. She saw his grip slacken and threw her elbow back again. As he staggered back, she grabbed the thumb of his gun hand and peeled it back. She released his wrist and slammed her forearm into the barrel.

The gun landed on the floor with a clatter. Knowing she had to get Streger away from it, Jane kicked her heel into his stomach. As he flew back, she rushed to grab the gun.

She spun to face him. He came at her—

Bang. Bang. Bang.

Jane's eyes told her she was the one who'd pulled the trigger, but she felt nothing in her hand.

Streger sprawled on the ground. Three charred holes dotted his body. Blood seeped from each. His brown eyes stared at her. Jane expected him to blink. She kept the gun aimed at him. Any moment, he could spring up and attack her again.

Streger remained motionless. On the floor, a pool of red crept toward her. Jane watched in fascination, keeping her eyes on him. The moment she looked away, he could make his move.

Coldness enveloped her. *He won't.*

The last words she'd spoken to him echoed in her mind: *Do you know what* you *are?*

"You're dead, asshole." For some reason, she wanted to laugh.

More disturbing than the body before her was the hollowness in her heart. She should have been scared. Or sad. Or *something.*

I killed him. The words carried no impact. Streger was dead, and she wasn't sorry. In fact, she was glad.

There lay the man who had killed her father, who had shot Riley, who had tortured Adam. The man who had set her at her brother's throat just to see what would happen. Who had enslaved the minds of others, taking from each the one thing that should have been entirely theirs: their own selves.

He's evil. Why should I be sorry that I killed him? The coldness tightened its grip around her. *Does thinking that make me evil, too?*

The ship trembled, forcing Jane out of her trance. Confused, she turned around. Outside the window in the corridor, a bright explosion flared toward her, bursting from the end of the second starcar. A second explosion lit the blackness from another section of the Moray. The self-destruct sequence had started.

Devin's not in there.

A third explosion illuminated a small, triangular ship docked at the Moray's side. A Barracuda—likely Devin's.

No. I'm not buying it. He found a way out.

The universe had lied to her too many times. She wouldn't believe a thing it told her, no matter how apparent it seemed.

The explosions grew larger. Fear rose within Jane. She pushed it back down. Devin couldn't be on board. "I'm not buying it, you jerk! You don't get to go down in some glorious blaze of self-sacrifice! You're gonna die old and decrepit like everyone else!"

Parts of the ship looked undamaged. Since Streger was gone, she could take command of the vessel, go back, make sure Devin wasn't there...

But the end of the second starcar had already been obliterated by the explosions. Even if she wanted to go through with her insane idea, she couldn't. There was no place to dock.

She turned away, unable to watch any longer. Her gaze fell on Streger's body, which remained where he'd fallen. *What was I expecting? That he'd disappear?*

She closed her eyes and reminded herself why she was there in the first place. *Adam's been locked up long enough.*

She inhaled, then marched into the stairwell. Her stomach turned as she stepped over Streger. His lifeless eyes seemed to follow her.

You'd better have been leading me in the right direction.

It didn't really matter. The starcar was as good as hers, and she could search every room at her own pace. As she would have been able to if she'd just shot him in the first place. *Would've spared me a lot of trouble.*

She refused to feel anything for the sonuvabitch. After all, she'd lectured both Devin and Adam countless times for being perpetually guilt-ridden over deaths that hadn't really been their faults. When it came to Streger, she'd had no choice, either. If she hadn't pulled the trigger, she would have been the one lying at the bottom of the steps.

She stopped at the top of the stairs and considered the next flight, wondering whether Streger had been heading for the second or third level. She looked out into the door-lined corridor. *I guess I have to start somewhere.*

Intending to blast down the nearest door, she raised her gun. A flash of green caught her eye. The square security scanner by the door blinked at her. Jane tentatively pressed her hand against it. To her surprise, the door slid open.

Streger must not have locked this starcar. I guess he didn't need to, since he wasn't expecting anyone else.

The asshole had probably thought he could disappear and carry on with his life, never facing justice for his deeds. His lifeless eyes burned in her mind. Jane tried to banish the image.

She entered the room. Nothing but empty lab tables and empty cells, like the one she'd been locked in. *Twisted sonuvabitch.*

She left and moved on to the next room. Then the next. And the next.

She reached the door at the end of the corridor. Its security scanner, like the others, glowed green. She pressed it.

The door slid open. Adam, unconscious and bound to a metal chair, came into view. The gun fell from Jane's hand. A mixture of surprise and relief flooded her.

She rushed to him. "*Adam!*"

His head hung limply over his chest. She put her hands on his shoulders and peered into his face.

"Adam, it's me!"

A crescent gleamed on his face: the metal that lay beneath his synthetic skin. A small hole, tiny in circumference but apparently fairly deep, pierced his forehead. Thin scratches streaked his right hand, and holes with blackened edges covered his shirt—something had burned him in several places, scorching away parts of his skin. A gaping injury in the side of his neck revealed the machinery underneath, and it looked as if something had been ripped out.

All Jane saw were signs of Streger's cruelty. *That bastard.*

She put her hand on Adam's face and leaned toward him. "C'mon, Adam, wake up! It's over now."

He didn't react, remaining completely motionless—no breath, nothing.

Am I too late?

No, Streger wanted Adam alive. With Adam trapped and no longer a threat, Streger had no reason to kill him. But perhaps Streger feared what Adam was capable of. An electromagnetic pulse had knocked Adam out in the past. Perhaps something like that kept him unconscious at present.

The line of green lights along the edges of the chair called Jane's attention. *That's it. Something's activated here... I just have to turn it off.*

She stood and looked around. A touchscreen glowed on the wall. She approached, hoping it had been left unlocked as well. To her relief, it reacted to her touch.

A list of icons lined the left edge. One of them was labeled "lights." Figuring the rest had to control various devices in the lab, Jane quickly went down the list and deactivated them all. Machines whirred and beeped as they powered down. Too impatient to check what was what, she didn't turn around until she'd finished.

The lights on Adam's chair were dark, and the restraints around his wrists and ankles lay open, like unclasped claws.

Jane darted to his side. "Adam, wake up!"

Adam stirred.

Jane let out a breath. She put a hand on his shoulder and shook him. "Adam!"

Adam opened his eyes. His peridot eyes met hers, and he blinked in shock. His lips parted, but he seemed incapable of words.

Jane smiled. "Yes, it's really me."

"Jane?" As though hit by reality, he bolted forward. "You have to get out of here. If—"

"Streger's gone."

"What?" Adam furrowed his brow in confusion. "How are you here?"

The question sparked Jane's fury. "What do you mean, how am I here? Did you think you could disappear on me and that I'd never find out?"

"I... I didn't want—"

"*You* didn't want? What if this is what *I* want to do? What if this is where *I* want to be?" Tears filled her eyes.

"Adam, what did you think would happen? Did you really think I'd just forget you? That I'd never try to find you?" Her voice rose to practically a scream, but she didn't care. "You could have died before I had a chance to save you! And then what? *What* did you think would happen?"

"I-I'm so sorry." His voice trembled. He seemed as though he wanted to say more, but couldn't.

Jane's anger faded. "Don't cut me out ever again, okay?" She put a hand on his face. "It's over. You're safe with me."

Adam looked up. His expression held so much—shock, relief, joy, awe. He seemed too overwhelmed to speak. His eyes shone with a kind of love too deep for words, as though she were the only light in the universe. In spite of herself, Jane smiled. For that look, she would have fought Streger all over again.

She took his hand and gave it a gentle tug. "Let's get out of here."

Adam stood slowly, as though uncertain if he remembered how. Jane bit her lip. He'd been trapped in that chair for weeks. She couldn't imagine the pain he must have endured.

No one will ever hurt you again.

Jane kept his hand in hers in case he needed help. When Adam finally straightened, it hit her that he was truly safe and by her side. Flooded by a rush of longing, she leaned toward him.

The ground lurched. Remembering where she was, Jane reluctantly drew back.

Adam looked past her. "What was that?"

"Not sure." Jane wondered if it was another impact from the nearby explosion. In any case, she had to get to the control room and take command of the vessel. "C'mon."

She walked out of the lab. Seeing the entrance to the stairwell ahead, she tensed. Streger still lay there.

Knowing she'd have to come clean sooner or later, she admitted, "I killed Streger." She turned to Adam, wondering how he'd react.

Adam blinked in surprise, then put his hands on her shoulders. "Are you okay?" No horror, no judgment—his eyes held only sympathy, telling her that he was certain she'd been justified in her actions.

Unexpected relief released Jane's tension. He clearly trusted that she hadn't had a choice.

So why couldn't she trust herself? Why did Streger's eyes still burn in her mind?

"I killed him," she repeated. "I killed him..." Her breaths shortened. Each gasp failed, stopping in her throat.

Adam embraced her.

Jane buried her face in his shoulder, battling the urge to scream. "He deserved it."

She looked up. Adam's metal scar glinted beneath the light. She recalled the video of him screaming in anguish. The pain in Riley's eyes as he tried to stand. Her father's face, once so powerful and commanding, robbed of all he'd worked for.

And Devin—what kind of hell had he gone through? It occurred to her that she'd never told him that she forgave him. Why hadn't she told him? What if—

What if nothing. He made it out before the ship blew.

Her breath steadied.

Another lurch. She didn't have time to stand there.

"Streger's body's in the stairwell." Jane turned and marched forward. "Just thought I'd warn you."

Not wanting to see those eyes again, she rushed down the stairs, keeping her gaze ahead. She heard Adam's footsteps behind her.

She ran into the control room, took the pilot's seat, and grabbed the controls. Streger had left the vessel drifting through space. On the viewscreen, the detonations continued.

Jane steered the starcar away. If the explosions got any bigger, they could hit her vessel, and she hadn't come that far just to end up caught in a blast.

She felt Adam's hand on her shoulder. He must have sensed that something troubled her. She met his questioning gaze and put her hand on his. "I'll explain later." Though she knew that had she been in his place, she'd want the explanation immediately, she couldn't bring herself to relive what she'd been through in words. She nodded at the copilot's seat beside her. "Buckle up."

Adam complied.

The communications light flashed. Wondering who it could be, Jane pressed the icon to put it through.

A regal face appeared on the screen: Commander Vega, the woman who had once helped prove Devin's innocence.

"Marcus Streger." Her voice was menacing. "This is Commander Jihan Vega of the Megatooth warship *RKSS Granite Flame*. My vessel carries enough firepower to take out a fleet. If you do not reveal your location immediately, I will unleash my silo in every direction. One of the missiles will certainly hit you. You may not survive."

Jane scrambled to press the "respond" icon. "Don't fire! It's me, Jane Colt!"

Commander Vega blinked as though startled. "What are you doing here?"

"I was Streger's prisoner. I've taken control of his ship. And... he's dead. It was self-defense, I swear."

Commander Vega nodded grimly. "Very well." She snapped her face to the left. "Weapons officer, stand down." She turned back to Jane. "Unveil the vessel."

"Okay. I mean... Yes, Commander." Jane swiped through the control panel, looking for the command that would allow her to do so. She found the icon and swiped it. "Did that work?"

Commander Vega turned to her right and raised her eyebrows.

"Affirmative," said a female voice.

Commander Vega shifted her gaze. "Take us to the vessel's location." She looked back at Jane. "Stop your vessel and remain where you are."

Jane brought the ship to a halt. "Yes, Commander."

On the viewscreen, the enormous red warship came into sight. Commander Vega glanced to her left. "Activate the tractor beam."

A distant male voice responded, "Yes, Commander."

The starcar pitched. According to the navigation chart, it drew closer to the advancing warship.

Jane turned to Adam, who gazed musingly at the viewscreen. The exposed metal on his face reflected the *Granite Flame*'s image.

Jane bolted forward. *What the hell was I thinking?*

She'd instinctively responded to Commander Vega's authority, but what would happen once the starcar and the warship met? The commander would surely have her troops board.

I've gotta hide him somewhere. No—I just have to hide his injuries. A few bandages and a jacket or something should do it. I'm sure Streger has a med kit and some kind of wardrobe around here...

She started to get up.

"Remain where you are." Commander Vega's voice was stern. She looked past Jane. "Are you alone?"

Jane looked up innocently. "Yes." She wasn't sure why she'd lied, but a tight feeling in her stomach told her she couldn't let the commander know Adam was there with her.

"Are you armed?"

Jane shook her head.

"My troops will board in a few minutes. Until then, remain vigilant." Commander Vega sounded concerned.

What does that mean? "Why?"

"Agent Adesina of ISARK informed me that Streger was conducting experiments on an artificial being. The machine could be on board the starcar. Do not be afraid; it is likely confined. But for your own safety, stay in the control room and, if you haven't already, lock the door."

Jane's heart pounded. Agent Adesina had to know about Adam. Streger was gone, but ISARK still wanted him.

She turned and caught Adam's eye, then quickly ended the transmission.

The warship drew closer. Once Commander Vega's troops boarded, Jane would have no way of saving Adam. After *everything* she'd been through, she'd lose him all the same.

The cannons' controls lay before her. She could fight. But if she attacked a Kyderan military vessel, she'd be branded an enemy of the nation, a terrorist. They'd probably convict her in absentia, and the warrant for her arrest would give permission to use deadly force.

She could never go home.

Adam gave her a sad smile. "You stopped Streger. Thanks to you, he'll never hurt anyone again."

Jane couldn't speak. Didn't he care that he was about to be condemned all over again? No, of course not. He only cared that she was all right. He'd probably tell her to forget him—again.

The cannons' controls called to her. She could hear the universe's ultimatum. By her side was Adam, the one who had always been there for her, even when she'd thought she didn't need him. The one who seemed to glow with an angelic light, who loved her in spite of her craziness. As far as she knew, nothing was absolute except his love for her, a love she fiercely returned.

She could have him, the universe said. But if she wanted to keep him, she'd have to leave behind everything she knew, everything she'd worked for, with no chance of returning.

Adam leaned toward her. "It's okay, Jane."

"*What's* okay?" Rage flared through her head. "What am I supposed to do? Watch them take you away again? Spend the rest of my life wondering how long they tortured you before they let you die?" She turned to the controls. *To hell with that.*

The universe, or the Absolute, or God, or Fate—*whoever*—demanded the life she'd known in exchange for Adam.

Take it. She swiped the icon to veil the ship, then activated the cannons.

"What are you doing?" Adam sounded panicked.

"Adam, I lost you once, and it killed me." Jane aimed the cannons. "I tried letting you go, and it left me hollow." The communications light blinked frantically. She ignored it. "I can't lose you again."

She unleashed the starcar's silo at *Granite Flame*. It was a Megatooth warship—it would survive the bombardment. But she wouldn't survive the return fire.

She veered the ship and engaged lightspeed, not caring which direction she headed in. An alarm flashed as a missile flew toward her. The ship lurched.

The navigation screen told her that more missiles were on their way. But nothing could outpace lightspeed, and she was invisible. Commander Vega could fire shots in the dark all she wanted. Her previous threat must have been an intimidation tactic, and Jane wouldn't fall for it again.

"Jane!" Adam had been calling her name, and she'd ignored him.

She checked the navigation chart. Empty space stretched ahead for at least a few light-hours. Certain that her pursuer wouldn't catch her, she let go of the controls and turned to him. "I know. That was stupid. I'm a fugitive for life, now—like you."

"No." Adam shook his head. "Stop the ship. Send Commander Vega a message telling her that I did it." He unbuckled his safety belt and stood. "I attacked you, and—"

"*Adam*!" Jane smiled incredulously at his last-ditch attempt to save her from a life as a fugitive. "It's done. We'll run so far, they'll never find us."

Adam stared in disbelief. There it was again—the look that told her only she mattered to him. She wouldn't regret her choice.

She got up from the pilot's seat and walked to him. "I tried to warn you. So did Pandora. 'Stay away from Jane Colt,' we said. But now, it's too late." She took his hand. "You're stuck with me." *Forever.* She angled her mouth as a thought occurred to her. *Why not?* "Marry me, Adam. I mean it this time."

Adam tightened his hand around hers, gazing at her as though too stunned to speak.

She threw her arms around him and kissed him. Adam's arm wrapped around her waist, pulling her close. In that moment, nothing else existed. Security? Wealth? Success? The universe could have them. She'd received the better end of the bargain.

She felt herself melt into Adam's presence and wished she could remain in his embrace until the last star flamed out.

EPILOGUE

INES ENTERED MEK'S BAR, UNSURE of what she sought there. Not another job—she had more than enough money from her last mission. Considering how it had turned out, she was in no mood to get involved in anything else. She glanced at the ceiling, wondering what Mek had named his bar that night.

She blinked, startled by the word: *Winterreise.*

Must be a coincidence. She walked to the bar. Looking up, she saw that Mek had tuned the screen behind the bar to a news channel. A video of Marcus Streger at a corporate-looking event splashed across it, and the headline along the bottom stated: "Chief Architect of Acuitas dies in tragic accident."

So that's the story they're going with. Ines found it somewhat amusing how little the rest of the galaxy knew. In all likelihood, few people would ever know the truth about what had happened with Streger, Rourke, and Sector 1708. The death of someone as famous as Streger was big news, and people would undoubtedly research his life in order to write books and stage holodramas, but they would never know just how fucked up he'd been.

The bartender bot approached Ines. She glanced at it. "Flamethower, straight."

The bot beeped and floated off.

"Flamethrower, eh?" Mek approached. "You must've had a rough day."

"Every day's a rough day." Ines leaned her elbows on the bar. "What're you doing out here anyway? Someone request a room?"

"Nah, came to see my new act's first performance." He jerked his head at the stage. "She'll be going on in five."

Ines turned. *What the hell?*

Sitting at a table by the stage was none other than Jane Colt, all dolled up in a sparkling violet dress. Her copious hair, appearing almost black in the dim light, framed her face.

In the chair beside her, Adam Palmer handed her a blinking slate. A metal mask covered almost half his face, stretching across his forehead and down his cheek. A metal crown around his head secured the mask in place. Ines recognized the mask as the type usually used by those disfigured by scars or burns. A white bandage covered the side of his neck.

What happened to him? Ines regarded Adam, the first lifelike AI she'd ever seen. She supposed she should have marveled at the technological wonder or recoiled at the thought of artificial life, but she found herself unable to care. He seemed like any other kid, unremarkable and quite ordinary. Her only conclusion was that he and Jane must have pissed off someone powerful, since they'd ended up on Asylum.

Hoping to catch some hint of the reason behind their presence on the Rogue Planet, Ines kept her gaze in their direction as Jane swiped the slate on the table in front of her. In case they glimpsed her, Ines kept her eyes unfocused.

"Riley!" Jane sounded excited. "Did you find him?"

A boyish voice responded from the slate, "You bet I did!"

Jane pulled the slate close, as if anxious. "Where is he?"

"Yo, chill. He's in a hospital on Caoine."

Jane relaxed visibly. Adam did as well. Ines had a feeling she knew whom they were concerned with. She turned away as the bartender bot returned with her drink.

"Why's he at the hospital?" Jane's voice rose with worry.

"Uh... He's pretty banged up." Riley sounded nervous. "Been out since he arrived. I can send you his medical report, but basically, he got shot really bad and lost a ton of blood."

"He's been unconscious this whole time? How'd he get to the hospital?"

"No idea. From what I found, he showed up randomly in the emergency room."

Ines took a swig of her drink, wishing she could block her ears. She'd come to Mek's bar for an escape, not a reminder. She noticed Mek watching her and threw him a cross look. "What?"

"Something's troubling you." Mek peered into her eyes. He was trying to read her—he'd always seemed overly concerned with her.

"None of your fucking business."

"I get it. You want to be alone." Mek sighed. "Just consider this, Dancer: What if you're not alone?"

Ines looked up with a scowl. "What's that supposed to mean?"

"I mean you still have time to prevent tomorrow's regrets." Mek ran his fingers through his white hair. "What I wouldn't give for your youth!"

The old man's waxing philosophical. Ines turned her attention to her drink to avoid his gaze. He may have envied her youth, but she envied his certainty. He'd found his place in life and settled down somewhere he belonged. As for her—the future held more what-ifs than she cared to handle. Mek would probably tell her that it was better to have what-ifs lying ahead than haunting the past, but Ines found it easier to accept the unchangeable past than deal with the pressures of the ever-moving future.

She glanced up and saw that Mek had walked away.

"Thanks, Riley." Jane sounded relieved. Ines realized she'd missed part of the conversation, but she didn't care. From the topic, nothing Jane said would tell Ines how she'd ended up a fugitive. "Take care of him, will you?" Jane's voice was soft. "I don't know if I'll ever... I mean... Just keep an eye on him for me, okay?"

"Sure thing." Riley's voice carried a hint of pride. "I'll keep you updated."

Ines downed the rest of her drink, hoping it would silence the irksome part of her that itched to tell Jane what had happened. *What good would that do?* She slammed the glass onto the bar.

She'd jumped into her Silverside and sped away from the *Pride*. She'd done her job, and what happened next, as she'd reminded herself repeatedly, *wasn't her fucking problem.* Pretender had created the mess, and she shouldn't have given a fuck about whatever became of him.

Except she did. As she flew from the condemned Moray, she felt a tugging in her chest, as though she'd left part of herself behind. With each additional light-second, the tugging grew stronger, until she couldn't bear it anymore.

Fuck.

She'd flipped the Silverside and flown back to the *Pride*. It was God's will, she'd told herself. It had to be—why else would she care? After all the lives she'd taken, He demanded that she save just one. After all, her duty was to protect the innocents, and while Pretender didn't exactly fall into that category, he wasn't among the wicked, either. Abandoning him would have been the same as killing him, and God wouldn't allow it.

As she neared, she glanced at the place where Pretender had docked, hoping his ship would be gone. It was still latched onto the Moray's side, which meant he was on board. She swore. Not much time remained before the self-destruct sequence began. Pretender could be anywhere on the Moray. If she entered the ship and didn't find him, all she would do was get herself blown up. She tried telling herself that was a good reason to turn away, but the need to continue overpowered her.

I'm fast. I'll get out in time.

Through her window, she noticed the end of the Moray's second starcar. From the positions of the mechanisms, the third starcar of the Moray had detached; the cowardly Streger must have run away. Ines steered her Silverside toward the front of the first starcar, figuring that way, she'd run into Pretender if he headed back to his ship. "Activate invasion protocol."

"Invasion protocol activated," the computer responded.

A red circle with crosshairs appeared on the viewscreen. Ines angled her ship so that they fell on a wide, flat area. She accelerated.

The sharp front of her Silverside crashed into the Moray's hull, piercing it. Ines lurched forward from the impact, and the straps of her safety belt cut into her torso. No matter how many times she pulled that move, it was never pleasant. A flashing red circle appeared across the viewscreen. The ship hummed as it locked against the *Pride* and sealed off any breaches.

Ines unbuckled herself and stood. She pushed a lever on the controls. Beeping alarms told her it wasn't safe to exit yet, but she ignored them. The countdown wouldn't wait for the magnetic seals to find every crack she'd created in the Moray's hull and close them off, making the tunnel airtight. According the control screen, the remaining breaches were small. She'd be all right.

A hatch beneath her slid open, leading to a short tunnel. She crawled out, entering a room on the *Pride*, and straightened. Pretender had evidently been that way, since the room's door lay flat on the ground, its edges charred by laser blasts. She sprinted out the doorway.

"Pretender!"

No response. She raced down the corridor, following the blasted doors and calling for Pretender.

"Three minutes to self-destruct."

Good, I have some time. Ines continued running, not bothering to look inside the rooms unless the doors were open. Pretender would have no reason to enter a room and close the door behind him.

Maybe he was on the third starcar when it detached. That was a logical possibility, but some instinct within her refused to believe it. Every fiber of her being pressed her to keep going. But she didn't have time to cover the entire top level.

She stopped by the doorway to a stairwell. "Pretender!"

Again, no response.

"Two minutes to self-destruct."

Figuring he would have responded if he were nearby, she ran down a flight of stairs and searched the starcar's second level. Each time her shouts were met with silence, part of her wanted to believe that he'd left already, but each time, a fierce drive within pushed her to continue.

Another stairwell greeted her ahead. Though she'd only covered a fraction of the level she was on, she should have heard some sign of him if he were there. She dashed down to the lowest level.

"One minute to self-destruct."

I've been in more dire situations. Once again, she found herself racing through empty corridors and shouting at the top of her lungs. She cursed the Moray for being so large. After calling for Pretender one more time, she decided he couldn't be on the first starcar. *If he were, I would have encountered him or heard him by now.*

She crossed the tunnel between starcars and entered the second. "Pretender!"

The sonuvabitch *still* didn't respond. With time so short, he should have been heading for his Barracuda to flee, which meant he should have crossed her path. *He must have been on that third starcar when it detached. Ten more seconds of this, then I'm getting out.*

She swung around a corner, her lungs burning from the effort of running so quickly. A wide open door lay ahead, leading to a room with curved walls. She recognized it as a Moray's crew lounge, which meant the open door on the other side of it led to the control room. *No reason for him to be in there. If he were, he would have responded when I called.*

She started to turn away. A splotch of dark liquid on the ground caught her eye. She froze, staring at it. The pool seemed to grow. *Blood.*

Her heart jumped. *"Devin!"* The name spilled out of her mouth.

She bolted into the room. He lay face down on the ground, his eyes closed. The blood flowed from his side, spreading toward her. A silent scream filled her head. Unable to see any injuries on his back, she dropped down beside him, grabbed his shoulders, and turned him over. Slipping her hands onto the torn part of his body armor, she felt a gaping wound and pressed her hands into it.

There was so much blood—her efforts were likely futile. She leaned forward and pressed her ear against his chest. A heartbeat. A soft breath rustled her hair.

He's alive.

He didn't have long. Neither did she. Seconds remained before the self-destruct sequence began. Dragging him back to the Silverside would take too long.

She took her hands off the wound to pull out her slate. Devin's blood smeared the touchscreen as she swiped the emergency invasion icon, which would command her Silverside to disengage from wherever it was and ram into the slate's location.

She flung the slate into the crew lounge to give the Silverside some space, then pressed her hands into Devin's wound again.

"Self-destruct sequence initiated."

A distant explosion. Ines closed her eyes. *God, if I've done anything good in my life, hear me now. Let me fulfill Your command to save him.*

Another explosion, close enough that heat scorched Ines's skin. Her conscience scratched at her heart. She could lie to herself, but not to God. Though she tried to deny it, she knew the true reason she'd come back. *Forgive me. I confess: I want to save him. God, please let me save him. So be it, truly.*

A noise boomed through the air—not an explosion. The ground shook. The *whoosh* of escaping air filled her ears.

Ines opened her eyes. Wind swirled around her as air rushed from the breach created by the Silverside. The metal point of her ship protruded from the floor. The square entrance slid open. *Thank You.*

She'd managed to drag Devin onto the ship. Each second she'd spent at the controls had felt too long. After steering the Silverside away from the Moray, she'd set the autopilot and rushed to grab her medical kit. Sophisticated as her equipment was, she couldn't count on her healing skills.

It had taken hours to reach the nearest IC system. She'd remained by Devin's side the entire time, held there by the fear that if she left, he'd slip away. At the same time, she'd avoided looking at his face, for each time she did, her heart stirred in a way she wished it wouldn't, and she didn't dare un-cage those feelings. She'd followed them in the past, and they'd led her to nothing but misery.

The bartender bot collected Ines's empty glass and asked if she wanted another.

"Yes. Same." Ines stared blankly at the metal bar.

Caring was a liability. Yet she'd cared—enough to make a miserable attempt at doing something good. And enough to call Devin by his name. Since she had, she couldn't go back to knowing him as Pretender. Names were more powerful than most realized. They were a piece of a person, an unshakable part of who they were. She'd denied his real name for a reason. Pretender was a fake merc with ISARK troubles and a willingness to pay. He was just a figure passing through her life. But Devin Colt was a person, a person she couldn't get out of her head.

What a joke. He's just a projection of a fantasy.

She would never see him again. Even if he ventured into the Fringe, she'd make sure their paths never crossed.

A girl's voice wafted through the air, shimmering above the noise of the bar. Mek's new act had taken to the stage.

Trusting still, though I'm deceived,
For all that's real is what's believed,
The rest, illusions...

Figuring she couldn't avoid seeing Devin's sister forever, Ines turned around. Jane stood alone center stage, singing to a crowd of marginally interested bar patrons. At the table in the front, Adam watched her. From the look on his face, he might have laid eyes on Heaven itself. Jane glanced down at him, and her lips lifted into a glowing smile. Ines could almost see the connection between them, a kind of bond meant for the innocent and hopeful, the kind she'd once yearned for but knew she could never have.

Unable to stand the sight, Ines turned back to the bar. The bot placed her second drink before her. She grabbed it, staring at her image in the bar's reflective surface.

Ines Valentin stared back. Not Flame Dancer, not the Tenebrarum Woman, not the Lady Merc with Silver Armbands. Ines Valentin, whose shields had failed her, and who had emerged from her cell to save a life that shouldn't have mattered.

OTHER BOOKS BY MARY FAN

Artificial Absolutes

acknowledgments

Special thanks to Elizabeth Corrigan for beta reading this book and offering her valuable input. And thanks to my roommate, Joanna Schnurman, for supporting me through my writing ventures and putting up with my rants.

Thanks to my fantastic editors at Red Adept Publishing, Karen Allen and Misti Wolanski, for whipping my book into shape.

And, of course, thanks to Lynn McNamee, captain of the starship Red Adept.

ABOUT THE AUTHOR

Mary Fan lives in New Jersey, where she is currently working in financial marketing. She has also resided in North Carolina, Hong Kong, and Beijing, China. She has been an avid reader for as long as she can remember and especially enjoys the infinite possibilities and out-of-this-world experiences of science fiction and fantasy.

Mary has a B.A. in Music, specializing in composition, from Princeton University and enjoys writing songs as much as writing stories. She also enjoys kickboxing, opera singing, and exploring new things—she'll try almost anything once.